THIS IS THE DAY THEY DREAM OF

Robert Goddard

PENGUIN BOOKS

TRANSWORLD PUBLISHERS

UK | USA | Canada | Ireland | Australia
India | New Zealand | South Africa

Transworld is part of the Penguin Random House group of companies whose addresses can be found at global.penguinrandomhouse.com.

Penguin Random House UK, One Embassy Gardens,
8 Viaduct Gardens, London SW11 7BW

penguin.co.uk

First published in Great Britain in 2025 by Bantam
an imprint of Transworld Publishers
Penguin paperback edition published 2026

001

Copyright © Robert Goddard and Vaunda Goddard 2025

The moral right of the author has been asserted

This book is a work of fiction and, except in the case of historical fact, any resemblance to actual persons, living or dead, is purely coincidental.

Every effort has been made to obtain the necessary permissions with reference to copyright material, both illustrative and quoted. We apologize for any omissions in this respect and will be pleased to make the appropriate acknowledgements in any future edition.

No part of this book may be used or reproduced in any manner for the purpose of training artificial intelligence technologies or systems. In accordance with Article 4(3) of the DSM Directive 2019/790, Penguin Random House expressly reserves this work from the text and data mining exception.

Typeset in 9.9/13.95 pt Times NR MT Pro by Six Red Marbles UK, Thetford, Norfolk
Printed and bound in Great Britain by Clays Ltd, Elcograf S.p.A.

The authorized representative in the EEA is Penguin Random House Ireland,
Morrison Chambers, 32 Nassau Street, Dublin D02 YH68.

A CIP catalogue record for this book is available from the British Library

ISBN
9780552178495

Penguin Random House is committed to a sustainable future for our business, our readers and our planet. This book is made from Forest Stewardship Council® certified paper.

Wenn du lange in einen Abgrund blickst, blickt der Abgrund auch in dich hinein.

(If you gaze for long into an abyss, the abyss gazes also into you.)

Friedrich Nietzsche
Jenseits von Gut und Böse

A glossary of acronyms, foreign phrases and personalities from Algerian history mentioned in this book can be found at the end.

Praise for Robert Goddard

'The world's greatest storyteller'
Guardian

'One of the finest crime writers of any generation'
Daily Mail

'Truly ingenious'
The Tablet

'Goddard sprinkles head-turning double-crossing with delightful by-play between his two leads'
The Times

'Fast-paced, beautifully crafted with some excellently drawn characters . . . engages from start to finish'
Choice Magazine

'Goddard writes amazing novels of mystery/suspense'
Stephen King

'Our finest practitioner of the double-cross plotting'
Mick Herron

www.penguin.co.uk

Also by Robert Goddard

Past Caring
In Pale Battalions
Painting the Darkness
Into the Blue
Take No Farewell
Hand in Glove
Closed Circle
Borrowed Time
Out of the Sun
Beyond Recall
Caught in the Light
Set in Stone
Sea Change
Dying to Tell
Days Without Number
Play to the End
Sight Unseen
Never Go Back
Name to a Face
Found Wanting
Long Time Coming
Blood Count
Fault Line
Panic Room
One False Move
The Fine Art of Invisible Detection
This is the Night They Come for You
The Fine Art of Uncanny Prediction

The Wide World trilogy
The Ways of the World
The Corners of the Globe
The Ends of the Earth

ONE

THE SUMMER OF 2021 WAS BRUTALLY HOT IN ALGERIA, BUT THE arrival in August of Anticyclone 'Lucifer' surpassed everything that had gone before. It was aptly named, for the Qu'ran relates that Iblis, before he became Satan, was a djinn made of fire. And fire was what came to Algeria that month. The temperature climbed through the upper forties, edging close to an unimaginable fifty degrees. Dozens died in wildfires. A suspected arsonist was lynched by a mob. In his Algiers apartment Police Superintendent Mouloud Taleb felt as if he was being baked in a kiln.

Fortunately, unlike most of his suffering fellow citizens, he had access to an air-conditioned refuge: his office at Police HQ. And there he slept through the worst of the sweltering nights.

True, the system shut down from midnight to six a.m., but Taleb could start that period at a cool twenty degrees and the temperature would still not have reached thirty by the time it ended. He affected to be routinely working late, but the night staff were well aware of what was really going on. He thought it unlikely he was the only surreptitious sleeper in the building.

At some point, normally around three a.m., he would struggle up and descend two floors to the loos. He didn't need to turn on any lights to find his way. Those in the loos came on automatically. The foray was a nightly ritual insisted upon by his prostate.

He put on all his clothes to undertake the trip in case he bumped into anyone, though he never actually did. He sometimes lingered on a landing on the way back to smoke a cigarette and gaze out at the lights of the city.

It was after such a cigarette pause that he returned one night to his office and became aware, as he approached along the corridor, that the door was wide open, whereas he generally left it ajar. This was as much as he could make out for certain amidst the shadows and yellow polygons of street-lamp glare shafting in through the windows.

He switched on the corridor lights as a precaution, the fluorescent tubes flickering into life at varying rates. Aside from the clicking of the tubes, there was no other sound. He began walking steadily towards the door of his office.

He glimpsed the shadow of a movement a fraction of a second before he heard something – cardboard, paper – falling to the floor. Then a man, dressed in black, emerged from the office.

He was tall and athletically built, with crewcut hair. Taleb noticed at once a long scar on his face, running for ten centimetres or so down over his left eyebrow and cheek – a knife-wound would have been his guess. He didn't have time to notice much else as the man advanced on him at a rapid stride.

'Stop where you are,' Taleb shouted, with little hope he'd be obeyed.

And he wasn't. The man locked eyes with Taleb as he closed on him, then shoved him aside with a powerful thrust of his right arm. Taleb cannoned against the wall and the man was past, running towards the door that led to the landing.

It took Taleb a few moments to recover his breath. He'd left his gun locked in his desk drawer and there was certainly no time to go back for it. He set off in a pursuit he knew to be futile.

Sure enough, by the time he reached the landing and looked down the stairwell, the intruder was just a shadow descending at speed and already halfway to the ground floor. Taleb hurried back along the corridor to the nearest office, grabbed the phone and dialled the number of the night security desk.

No one picked up. Answering a call of nature? Asleep? On patrol? The last was the least likely.

It hardly mattered anyway. The intruder was long gone by the time the alarm was raised. All that remained of him was a blurred rear view from a CCTV camera monitoring the side door he'd exited by. As identification it was useless, but at least it cleared Taleb of the suspicion that he'd imagined the whole thing. The senior security officer's opinion, vouchsafed the following day and laden with sarcasm, was that some desperate member of the public had sneaked their way in to benefit from the building's air-conditioning.

It wasn't as if Taleb could report anything missing – he'd seen for himself that the man had left empty-handed – or suggest a reason why his office should have been targeted. The filing cabinets and the cupboard might have been searched – it was hard to tell – but his computer terminal was offline, so nothing current could have been accessed.

The only thing Taleb could be certain had attracted the intruder's attention – because its contents were scattered across the floor of his office – was a large cardboard box that had been stored on top of the cupboard. It contained various items left behind by his former superior, Superintendent Meslem, when he'd retired. It had his name scrawled on the side in felt-tip pen. It was impossible to believe the items were actually of interest to anyone, however. Who would want a dozen or so dog-eared Maigret novels, several empty cigar boxes, a rolled-up street map of Algiers dating from the colonial era and numerous copies of a Russian chess magazine passed on to Meslem by an official at the Soviet embassy he often played chess with? (Meslem's knowledge of Russian was limited strictly to what he needed as an avid chess enthusiast to be able to follow the moves in recent tussles between the Soviet grandmasters who dominated the game.)

Fearing that pursuing the matter further might lead to an explicit ban on his use of the office as an air-conditioned bedroom, Taleb did his best to put the incident out of his mind. Meslem was long dead, after all, and he hadn't bothered to remove the items while he was alive, so they could hardly be of any value. Taleb should probably take this as a cue to throw them away.

He didn't, though, out of some professional instinct that such things, however apparently unimportant, should never be disposed of. But he did swing the box round so that Meslem's name faced the wall.

And nothing more was heard of the mystery of the nocturnal intruder, which merely accreted itself to the amorphous body of innumerable other unresolved enigmas, some trifling, some not, accumulated in the course of Taleb's long career; unresolved and unremembered – unless fate decreed otherwise.

Anticyclone 'Lucifer' eventually loosened its grip. Autumn came. And winter. 2021 ended. 2022 began. And circumstances started to conspire against Mouloud Taleb, slowly but remorselessly, without his even being aware of it.

The past – and all the grief it holds – is closing upon him. He doesn't know it yet. Soon, however, very soon, he will.

A television studio isn't natural terrain for Superintendent Taleb. But his boss, Director Bouras, insisted that the invitation for a representative of Algeria's brave and unappreciated police force to take part in a special edition of the prestigious Sunday evening current affairs programme *Microscope* couldn't be rejected. Indeed, the Ministry of the Interior had already told Bouras it couldn't be rejected some hours before he summoned Taleb to his office and informed him that so far as he could establish the only senior officer still serving who'd been on the force at inspector level or above when Algeria's dark decade of unspeakable violence – *la décennie noire* – broke out in January 1992 was none other than . . . Taleb.

'You can hardly complain,' Bouras remarked with a smile. 'It was your idea to delay your retirement.' And so it was, although Bouras had been all for Taleb staying on as well – though not, so far as Taleb could recall, with assignments such as this in mind.

Microscope proposed to use the thirtieth anniversary of the outbreak to explore the consequences of those terrible events in a mature and reflective discussion between people who'd experienced them first hand – so went the producer's pitch – and the ministry had decreed that the police point of view needed to be part of such a discussion. Just so long, that is, as the chosen officer didn't actually say anything controversial or provocative or . . . in any way interesting at all. 'We need to be seen and heard, Taleb, without drawing attention to ourselves,' the director went on. 'Don't argue with any of the other guests, don't admit or deny anything I wouldn't admit or deny, don't speculate, don't . . . don't . . .'

'Rock the boat?'

'Exactly.' Bouras gave him a long hard look for emphasis. 'Make no waves, Taleb. Not so much as a ripple.'

So, those were his instructions. Taleb kept reminding himself of them as his televised date with the traumas of three decades ago approached. But the anniversary has stirred memories for him which he is usually more adept at suppressing. Eating a frugal meal at his apartment before setting off for the studio, it was hard not to recall much tastier dishes his wife had conjured up for him. He thought at one moment he heard her footsteps in the kitchen – something he'd once imagined on a virtually daily basis, but hardly at all in recent years.

It required a conscious effort of will at that moment not to picture Serene and little Lili in his mind's eye: a quarter of a century plucked away like a curtain being opened. But he would not open it. He would not allow himself to. They were gone, like countless other victims of the dirty war between the government and the Islamists that he was supposed to sit down and discuss rationally and calmly that evening in front of the cameras and however many of his misguided fellow citizens chose to watch.

In truth, it was too much to ask of him. But it *had* been asked of him. And he was bound to do it.

The TV company had offered to send a car for him, but Taleb had decided he preferred to walk. He's not sure now why he took that decision, since the climb from his apartment to the studio provided an unwelcome reminder of the poor state of his lungs. A couple of cigarette stops on the way didn't help and the chill, damp weather soon set off his cough. Algiers on a Sunday evening in winter has little to distract the wayfarer. And nothing to lift melancholy from a man once it's settled on him.

After sitting on a wall outside for several minutes, recovering his breath and some measure of composure, Taleb enters the building. There's too much white paint and gleaming steel for his liking in the reception area. He already feels as if he's on the set of a game show. He's greeted with transparent relief, though the lateness of his arrival goes unremarked upon. Adorning the walls are framed stills from the station's assorted programmes, several featuring the presenter of this evening's debate, Malik Issam. He is the roguishly handsome, expensively suited front man for *Microscope*, with a smile more dazzling in the pictures on display than it has ever seemed on television, though Taleb suspects the fuzzy definition on his ancient Sonelec set may be responsible for that.

A young woman who introduces herself as Issam's assistant – a babe unborn, Taleb judges, when *la décennie noire* began – pilots him to the green room, where the other participants in the debate have already gathered.

Taleb knows who they are from information supplied by the TV company: a retired government minister who can be relied upon to toe the party line – he is a lifelong FLN loyalist; a professor of politics from the University of Algiers who will presumably confer academic gravitas on the proceedings; a woman famous for campaigning tirelessly on behalf of wives and mothers for information about *les disparus* who vanished in their thousands during the conflict; a veteran spokesman for one of the Islamist parties now in official existence; and a journalist who reported on many of the worst outrages of the dark decade. Plus Taleb himself, of course.

But there is a surprise. As the assistant informs Taleb even while she's offering him a choice of fruit juices, the journalist originally scheduled to appear has fallen ill and been replaced at the last moment – 'We're so fortunate he was available' – by one Rochdi Abidi.

Taleb's misgivings about the evening now acquire a concrete and baleful form. Rochdi Abidi is the last man in Algiers he would wish to share a TV screen with. Tall and once imposingly built but now running to fat, he has a full head of grey-white hair, a ruddy complexion, a wide, moist-lipped mouth and a tone of false amiability. He has worked as a reporter for several newspapers over the years and is now freelance, his byline seen less and less in print.

No one, including Taleb, could accuse Abidi of toadying to the establishment, of making the accommodations others in his profession have with *le pouvoir*, the secret power structure thought by most Algerians to be the ultimate arbiter of their country's destiny. But for all his principles Abidi has never been easy to like. His gift for gathering information has only been matched by his disloyalty to his sources. If there was ever a choice to be made between their anonymity and his reputation as a fearless campaigner for truth and justice, word was that his reputation won every time. For a public servant such as Taleb, he has always been dangerous to be seen with. In his company words have to be watched as carefully as you would guard your wallet in the presence of a practised pickpocket. Every time their paths have crossed Taleb has wished it would be the last. But somehow, so far, it never has been.

'We're old friends, the superintendent and I,' Abidi informs the assistant. 'Isn't that right, Mouloud?' Using Taleb's first name to imply an intimacy that doesn't exist, he grins teasingly across the room and pops a complimentary cashew into his mouth.

'We've met before,' Taleb reluctantly acknowledges.

'Yes, many times,' says Abidi, still grinning.

'That should make for interesting debate, then,' a voice booms from behind them. Presenter Malik Issam has entered the room, preceded by a waft of expensive cologne.

He is wearing a powder-blue suit of Parisian cut, with a sparklingly white shirt collared in the Italian style. Even his tailoring, it seems, aspires to cosmopolitanism. He bestows his camera-pleasing smile upon them, accompanied by a lordly sweep of the hand. 'It is time, my friends, to go before our public,' he declares. 'I trust you're ready?'

There are affirmative nods and murmurs from Taleb's fellow guests, but he does not join in. Then a general progress towards the broadcasting studio begins. Abidi contrives to fall in beside Taleb. 'I can't tell you how surprised I was to learn you hadn't retired yet,' he remarks. 'Have you been decreed indispensable?'

'No one is that,' Taleb responds under his breath.

'Very true. But until we are dispensed with we must do whatever we can, mustn't we, for our sadly mistreated country?'

'Is that what you're doing?'

'It is. You may not like me, Mouloud, but you have to give me this: I am a patriot.'

'I'll try to remember that.'

To Taleb's relief, a member of the studio crew pulls him aside at that moment. He is ushered into a curtained-off area, where a matronly woman with an endearing smile applies some make-up to his face. 'We don't want you looking sweaty, do we?'

Taleb isn't sure what the answer to that question is, but he lets it pass.

The delay is brief – hardly more than a couple of minutes. Then he is moving across the brightly lit *Microscope* set to join the panel.

They are seated in cream leather swivel chairs, three to Issam's right, three to his left. He presides on a slightly larger, higher-backed chair. Taleb is alongside the ex-minister and the Islamist politician. Abidi, the professor of politics and the *disparus* campaigner are opposite them.

The lights are bright and unforgiving. Taleb envies the cameramen who are busying themselves in the shadows beyond the reach of the lights. He'd like to be in the shadows himself.

'Everyone set?' asks Issam. 'Good,' he adds, when no one demurs. 'I think this is going to be one of our more memorable programmes.'

A few minutes pass, then the lights dim. Someone out of Taleb's line of sight counts down, 'Three, two, one, cue music and we're on air.'

The faintly ominous oud and zither duet that introduces every edition of *Microscope* emerges from an unseen speaker. As it fades, the lights come up again. A hush falls. And Issam begins.

'Good evening. And welcome to this *Microscope* special in which we'll be assessing the effects on individual Algerians – seeking to come to terms, if you like, with the long-term impact – of *la décennie noire*, that awful period in our nation's history which even those too young to remember it will be well aware of and which began thirty years ago this month.'

As ever, Issam sounds sincere and authentic. Taleb suspects he's neither, but he'd be hard pushed to back up his suspicion with any evidence. Resenting a man because he's handsome and stylishly dressed isn't, he's well aware, a sound basis for rational judgement.

'Some may quibble over my dating the beginning of *la décennie noire* to January 1992. It's true that the worst of the violence was still a year or more away at that stage. But by common consent the resignation of President Chadli Bendjedid and the dissolution of parliament on January eleventh, followed by the annulment of the election held the previous month, in which the Islamist FIS had won most of the seats, and the cancellation of the imminent second round of voting constitute the tipping point for the carnage that followed. Nothing was inevitable, of course, nothing was preordained, though perhaps as we look back it feels as if it was. I'll be exploring that theme and others with my guests this evening.'

He introduces the guests to their audience, thanking each with varying degrees of effusiveness for agreeing to take part. Taleb's qualifications for discoursing on the subject in hand are more lightly sketched than the others'. He senses Issam may have agreed to a police officer taking part under protest. Perhaps he thinks they are all the same: willing servants of the state, crushing protest of whatever hue, doing the bidding of *le pouvoir* without recourse to conscience. As if life as a police officer were as simple as that.

Suddenly, the professor of politics is speaking, seizing his moment to take the lead. 'You could also have mentioned in your list of significant events in January 1992 the return from long-term exile in Morocco of Chadli Bendjedid's successor as president, Mohamed Boudiaf. Many then, including me, dared to believe he would plot a peaceful course for our country.'

'Indeed so,' agrees Issam. 'But sadly that did not turn out to be the case.'

'I too put my trust in Boudiaf,' remarks the *disparus* campaigner.

'Many did,' Abidi joins in. He catches Taleb's eye. 'But not all of my fellow guests did, I imagine.'

'That's quite a . . . provocative statement,' says Issam, frowning slightly as he does so. 'Would you . . . care to expand on it?'

Would he care to expand? Who, Taleb wonders, could possibly stop him?

Taleb braces himself, not so much against the onslaught of conspiracy theories he suspects Abidi may be minded to advance as against the tide of recollections that is rushing in over him. He cannot hold them back. They have the momentum of his own lived experience. They bear him down. Into the past that discloses itself in a flood of memories, sharp as daggers, deep as ocean trenches.

It was the last Monday of June 1992. The weather was fine and warm. Serene had suggested a trip to the beach that evening as a treat. Lili loved the seaside and there, by the shores of the Mediterranean, it might be possible to forget the woes of the country as Lili shrieked in glee at the inrushing waves and the sparkling sunshine.

That prospect was at the back of Taleb's mind as he drove Superintendent Meslem in his chocolate-brown Citroën back from a meeting at the Ministry of the Interior. Meslem was a devoted and skilful detective, whose forte was interrogating a suspect and luring them into damaging admissions. About the art, as distinct from the science, of detection he had taught Taleb most of what he knew. Meetings, on the other hand, especially at the ministry, were for Meslem a form of torture. 'I don't object to wasting time in principle,' he complained as they neared Police

HQ. 'But I do object to wasting it in the company of civil servants whose only concern is covering their cowering backs.'

Superintendent Meslem, it was fair to say, wasn't in the best of humours. At such times the flesh around his mouth formed heavy pouting lines that seemed to extend the droop of his moustache. He ran his hand over his bald head and sighed wearily. 'Such people, Taleb. I do not envy our president having to rely on such people to put his policies into effect.'

This was the latest of several remarks Meslem had made that implied he, like Taleb, was pinning his hopes for the future on the septuagenarian veteran of the independence struggle called back from Morocco earlier in the year. Modest, incorruptible and undeniably a man of the people rather than a creature of *le pouvoir*, Mohamed Boudiaf had already released thousands of FIS sympathizers in an effort to stem Islamist outrage at the annulment of their electoral victory by a clique of army and intelligence officers that thought they could run the country – and might succeed if they could bring Boudiaf to heel.

But he'd shown no sign so far of being willing to serve as their stooge and was promoting a new programme for government, including the launch of his own political party that would take the country into the modern age and end the divisions of the past. Too good to be true? So Taleb thought in his gloomier moments. But maybe goodness could be true sometimes – even in Algeria.

In the clear, bright light of a summer's morning, he could almost believe that. Certainly Serene believed it. 'This is a man who can be trusted, Mouloud,' she'd said to him recently. 'He is our saviour.' And there was no doubt that a saviour was what their country needed.

Taleb comforted himself with the thought that Serene was right as he slowed for the turn into the car park behind Police HQ.

He edged towards the entrance gate, waiting for it to open.

A guard nodded to him from the control kiosk and pushed a button. The gates began to swing apart.

At that moment a man walked out in front of the car, looked round at Taleb and suddenly seemed to lose his balance. He tottered and bent over, resting his hands on the bonnet to steady himself. He shook his head, as if confused or uncertain about something. He was thirty or so, respectably dressed in a dark if rumpled suit. He was clean-shaven, with neatly cut hair. There was nothing in any way suspicious about his appearance. Only his disorientated behaviour was hard to account for. Taleb waved for him to move on, but he stayed where he was.

'What's wrong with him?' said Meslem.

'I'll go and see, chief,' Taleb responded, opening the door.

'Be careful.'

'I think he must be ill.'

'Then tell him to call a doctor.'

There would come a time – and it would come soon – when Taleb would suspect such behaviour was a trap and react accordingly. But the world he existed in had not yet shifted on its axis. The days of madness had not yet dawned. So he climbed out of the car, gestured for the guard to stay in his kiosk and walked slowly round to where the man was still leaning on the bonnet.

'You need to get out of our way, friend. What's the problem?'

'What's the problem?'

'Yes. What is the problem?'

'You ask me that?' The man gaped at Taleb in disbelief. 'Haven't you heard?'

'Heard what?'

The man looked round at the building behind them, as if registering where he was. Then he squinted at Taleb. 'You're a policeman, right?'

'Yes. I am.'

'Then you must know. Don't you people hear the bad news

before it's announced? Or maybe you don't think it's bad news. You're all in league with the DRS, I suppose.' The suggestion that the police did whatever the DRS – the dreaded secret service – told them to do was widespread. Up to a point, it was even true, much as Taleb would have hated to admit it. 'They're behind this, aren't they? They must be. They're *le pouvoir*'s enforcers.'

'I don't know what you're talking about. You need to move.'

The man grasped Taleb's arm. 'You *really* don't know?'

'What is it I don't know?'

'They've killed the President.'

'*What?*'

'Boudiaf. Assassinated.'

'That can't be true.'

'But it is. Things that can't be true *are* true in this country. They got him. Just like they were always going to.'

A few seconds passed in a daze for Taleb. Boudiaf dead? How could that have happened – and this man come to know – in the short time it had taken them to drive from the Ministry of the Interior? They'd stopped briefly to buy ice creams, it was true – the route had taken them past Meslem's favourite ice cream parlour – but even so—

'What's he saying?' Meslem's voice carried from the open passenger window of the car. Taleb looked round. The man was moving away from him, weaving from side to side and raising his hand to his head – still confused, still confounded. 'What's wrong, Taleb?' Meslem shouted. The noise of passing traffic must have meant he hadn't heard what was said. He hadn't heard the news. Yet.

Taleb stumbled round to the open window. 'The President's been assassinated,' he said in as steady a voice as he could muster.

Meslem stared at him in astonishment for a moment. 'Assassinated?'

Taleb nodded. 'So that man said. And I don't think he was making it up.'

For an overweight man, Meslem could move surprisingly quickly when he needed to. He waved for Taleb to step back, flung the door open and hoisted himself out of the car. He'd absorbed his astonishment and had switched to reactive mode. 'Join me upstairs,' he growled. 'This is a disaster. And there'll be consequences we have to deal with.'

With that he headed for the front entrance of the building, leaving Taleb to walk round the car towards the driver's door.

By then the guard had ventured out of his kiosk, worried perhaps by how long the gate was being held open. 'Everything all right, Inspector?'

Taleb looked round at him. 'The President's been assassinated,' he said bleakly.

The guard closed his eyes for a moment. He said nothing. He could find no words.

Taleb had little recollection of driving the Citroën into the car park and finding a space. He must have lit a cigarette at some point, however, because he was smoking one when he reached the operations floor and entered what he would have expected to be a place of shock and mourning.

But the atmosphere was not that. There was seriousness and bustle, but no dismay. It could almost have been business as usual.

A sightline opened up along the corridor between cubicles to Meslem's office. The door was open, with a couple of trailing electric cables snaking through it from the adjoining cubicle of his secretary. Taleb could see Meslem sitting behind his desk, looking surprisingly unperturbed. He spotted Taleb in that instant and beckoned him in.

Entering the office, Taleb saw Lieutenant Dif propped on the edge of a table otherwise occupied by files. A television set, to which the trailing wires were attached, was in the corner, the sound turned down low. Dif and Meslem were both looking at the screen. Through a fog of bewilderment, Taleb recognized President Boudiaf's voice. And when he looked at the television there was Boudiaf's face. He was seated somewhere, grey-suited and solemn as ever, perorating about the political situation.

'Is this some kind of tribute?' Taleb asked weakly.

'No, Taleb,' Meslem said, with a baffling smile. 'It is a live broadcast of a speech being delivered by our president in . . . Annaba, is it, Dif?'

Dif nodded so enthusiastically a lock of hair bounced over his forehead. 'Maison de la Culture, Annaba, Super. Capacity audience by the look of it.'

Taleb glanced at the screen. The camera had cut away to show the audience. Every seat appeared to be taken. The faces were rapt and smiling. Laughter broke out at some remark by Boudiaf, the humour of which was lost on Taleb. The camera switched back to the President, who continued speaking, confidently and briskly.

'It appears we were the victims of a hoax, Taleb,' said Meslem, taking a relieved draw on his cigarette. 'There's been no assassination.'

'Why would anyone . . .' Taleb began his question, but did not finish it.

'A pity you didn't take his name and address. We could have prosecuted him for spreading false rumours and wasting police time.'

'He seemed to believe what he was saying.'

'Probably a nutcase,' said Dif. 'There are a lot of them about. The asylums must be running out of space.'

'Well, I'm just glad he was wrong,' murmured Taleb.

'Perhaps we can turn this off now,' said Meslem. 'We'll hear the gist of what he's saying later.'

'Sure, Super.' Dif hopped off the table-edge and moved towards the television.

Boudiaf was in the middle of some remark about scientific innovation when a noise off to his left caused him to turn his head.

Then there was a much louder noise – an explosion. The picture cut out momentarily, then resumed, showing rows of empty seats in the audience. Another explosion and a rattle of gunfire. Taleb realized the occupants of the seats had dropped to the floor. The camera swung crazily. The ceiling appeared through a haze of smoke. Then the podium. Boudiaf wasn't there any more, only an aide, with his head in his hands. A melee of figures came next. And a glimpse of Boudiaf, lying on the floor, with someone's jacket draped over him. Then the picture cut out again.

Abidi has laid out his fundamental allegation. That Boumaarafi, the disgruntled member of Boudiaf's security team convicted of assassinating him, was simply the front man for a conspiracy by *les décideurs* – the decision-makers at the heart of *le pouvoir* – to eliminate a leader they couldn't suborn or corrupt. Issam, the presenter, grows a little nervous, it seems to Taleb. He cuts Abidi off and tries to draw in the other guests, hoping they will divert discussion onto less inflammatory territory. He doesn't ask Taleb for his personal recollections of the assassination, though Taleb suspects Abidi eventually will. What should he say then? What *can* he say? That the best evidence of a conspiracy is that someone knew Boudiaf was dead – before he actually was?

Many hours passed before Boudiaf was officially declared dead. He was flown to the Aïn Naâdja military hospital in Algiers, where the announcement was made. Back in Annaba, Boumaarafi was under arrest. There didn't seem to be any doubt he'd carried out the act, though at Police HQ no one would have jumped to the conclusion that he'd acted on his own initiative even without the eerie foretelling of the President's death by the man Taleb had spoken to. The involvement at some level of *le pouvoir* was an automatic working assumption – so much so that it was never actually put into words. It didn't need to be.

Many of the staff were in shock. Taleb realized he wasn't the only one pinning his hopes for Algeria's future on Boudiaf. Now he'd been struck down, darkness was all that seemed to lie ahead.

Meslem's secretary was so distressed he sent her home. The superintendent himself remained as impassive as ever, though the depth of the frown lines on his forehead hinted at the intensity of his feelings. He closeted himself in his office with Taleb.

'Only a handful of people know about our strangely prescient lunatic,' he said sombrely. 'Keep it that way. Word of it mustn't reach the DRS if at all possible.'

'What about the director, chief?'

'I'll tell him if and when I judge it necessary.' That was no doubt wise. Director Lamri was notoriously prone to panic.

'Are we going to try and forget it ever happened?'

'No. We are not. In fact, I want you to relate to me everything he said to you – word for word, preferably.'

'But if he is a lunatic . . .'

'Then his ramblings meant nothing. And the timing was merely a grisly coincidence.'

'And if not?'

'Then we will need to consider – very carefully – what significance the encounter had. So, while it is still fresh in your mind . . . reconstruct the conversation for me.' Meslem smiled. 'As accurately as you can.'

In the studio, the ex-minister has sounded calm and reasonable for the benefit of the television audience, sitting back in his chair and lamenting the travails of the past before praising the policies of the present government and emphasizing how fortunate Algeria has been to escape the fate of other states caught up in the turmoil of the Arab Spring. The Islamist politician has taken issue with him and the *disparus* campaigner has contended that the price her generation of wives and mothers paid for this supposed good fortune was far too high. Taleb has tried to concentrate on their words in order to shut out the memories that have assailed him. But in this he's only been partially successful. And every time he's caught Abidi's eye he's sensed that trouble is brewing. The past isn't going to leave him alone. Abidi isn't going to let it.

The news of Boudiaf's assassination had hit Serene hard. When Taleb arrived home, it was obvious to him she'd been crying. Lili was also upset. Why was her mother so unhappy and why had the trip to the beach been cancelled? She was too young to understand what had happened beyond the fact that it was very bad.

Lili was having a bath before bedtime when the telephone rang. Serene's mother had already called and surely couldn't be calling again. Taleb sensed in fact that the call was for him. And so it proved.

'I hope I'm not disturbing you, Taleb,' said Meslem.

'It's been a disturbed evening all round, chief.'

'I know. The army have been patrolling the streets. How is your wife?'

'She is sad for our country.'

'As well she might be. This is an evil turn in our nation's affairs. I have given it much thought.'

'Me too.'

'What are your plans for tomorrow?'

The director had authorized personnel to report late for duty in order to allow them to visit the mosque if they felt the need. Taleb didn't know whether he'd feel the need or not. 'I'm not sure, chief.'

'Well, I want you to come into the office early. Can you be there at six?'

Six *was* early. 'Yes. If it's, er . . .'

'Important? Oh yes, Taleb, I think it's very important.'

'Has this to do with—'

'We will not discuss the matter on the telephone.' So, Meslem was already taking precautions. That told Taleb all he really needed to know. 'I will see you tomorrow.'

One of the speakers has mentioned the DRS. Taleb can't be sure which one it was. He is dismayed to realize that in his mind for some minutes past he's been cradling Serene in his arms as they lie in bed, sleepless for much of the warm June night, each contemplating the turmoil into which the assassination of President Boudiaf is likely to plunge their country. He has been with the woman he loves but can never see or speak to or touch again.

The present, *his* present – the *Microscope* TV studio – demands his attention and he struggles to confer it. The professor – yes, he thinks it was the professor – has suggested that if the DRS had still existed at the time, the *Hirak* protest movement that brought an end to Bouteflika's long presidency in 2019 would have been ruthlessly crushed. That it was not he sees as proof of progress.

Up to a point, Taleb reflects, he is surely right. The DRS was feared by all until its dissolution in 2016. It was renamed the DSS and remodelled as a supposedly more restrained organization fully answerable to the government. Taleb cannot imagine Agent Souad Hidouchi of the DSS, with whom he has a close if largely clandestine working relationship, prospering – or even surviving – under the previous regime.

'All well and good,' cuts in Abidi, 'but what have we seen since Bouteflika resigned? *Hirak* has essentially failed. *Le pouvoir* still runs this country.'

'That is a gross exaggeration,' retorts the ex-minister. '*Le pouvoir* only exists in the inflamed imaginations of people such as you.'

'Oh really? Tell that to the thousands of relatives of those murdered during *la décennie noire*. Do you seriously think they believe *le pouvoir* bears no responsibility for the horrors of those years? Do you genuinely suppose they doubt the DRS played some part in the assassination of President Boudiaf?'

'That is an outrageous suggestion. The assassination of President Boudiaf was the work of one man, who was swiftly apprehended and remains in prison to this day.'

'One man?' Abidi rolls his eyes. 'Nothing in this country is the work of one man. As I'm sure Superintendent Taleb would agree.'

Taleb senses rather than sees the camera swing towards him. Issam sits forward in his chair. He has a defeated look about him, as if he's abandoned his attempts to deflect Abidi and decided to let him have his head, whatever comes of it. He gazes intently at Taleb. 'Would you care to comment, Superintendent?'

Would he care to? No. A thousand times no. But the silence is expectant. It seems he is going to have to comment. He is going to have to say *something*.

Police HQ was quiet and largely empty early that Tuesday morning, the last day of June 1992. Taleb rode the lift alone, hearing the cables creak above him. There were no typewriters clacking or voices barking on telephones as he stepped out onto the operations floor. Motes of dust floated in slanting rays of sunlight. Doors stood open on unoccupied offices.

But one room was not unoccupied. He saw a shadow move through the glazed portion of the door of Meslem's office. And even at this range he could smell Meslem's cigarette. They smoked different brands, Meslem favouring more expensive imported French Camels to Taleb's humdrum Nassims.

He advanced along the corridor to the half-open door and stepped into the room.

Meslem was seated behind his desk, studying a copy of that morning's *El Watan*, on the front page of which was a large photograph of the late president. *A country in mourning*, read the headline above the photograph.

'Sit down, Taleb,' said Meslem, looking up from the newspaper.

Taleb sat. The sky, visible through the slats of the Venetian blinds at the windows, was duck-egg blue, clear and perversely untroubled.

Meslem took a long, slow draw on his cigarette. 'Suppose, Taleb,' he began, 'for the sake of argument, that the man you spoke to yesterday at the entrance to our car park was not in fact a lunatic, but entirely sane and was behaving, as he saw it, quite rationally. What, then, might he have been seeking to achieve?'

'I'm not sure I understand, chief. If he was behaving rationally, then he must have known – for a certainty – that the President was about to be assassinated. Though even then . . .'

'Yes?' Meslem cocked his head.

'Well, if he knew that, why didn't he warn us far enough in advance for us to do something about it?'

'We would have acted on such a warning, would we, from a stranger in the street?'

'Well, obviously we'd have insisted he identify himself before—' Meslem's point began to dawn on Taleb. 'He couldn't warn us without revealing who he was. And if he was betraying a plot hatched at a high level within *le pouvoir* . . .'

'He'd have been signing his own death warrant. Sooner or later, his identity would have become known to the plotters, at which point . . .' Meslem stubbed out his cigarette and lit another. 'He accused us of being in league with the DRS, didn't he?'

'Yes.'

'Why? Why say such a thing? He had nothing to gain by provoking us. Some police officers would have responded rather less tolerantly than you did to such a suggestion.'

Taleb thought for a moment, then said, 'Was he . . . using the jibe to . . . make us aware that the DRS were behind what was about to happen?'

Meslem nodded. 'I think he was. Which raises the question: how would he know they were behind it?'

'He would know because . . .' The answer came simply when it did. 'He would know because he's DRS himself.'

'Exactly, Taleb. Exactly so.'

'But . . . he didn't stop the assassination happening, so . . . why do anything?'

'Because he wanted us to know who was responsible. He didn't act in time to save Boudiaf's life, either because he was too worried about his own safety or because he reckoned the plotters would cover their tracks and try again later, so there was no point in taking the risk. But he has a conscience, coward though he may be. He wanted us to know.'

'But if he thinks we're all in league with his own paymasters . . .'

'Not all of us, Taleb.' Meslem leant forward and fixed Taleb with his gaze. 'I think he may have chosen us – you and me. I think he may have been waiting for us. I think he's gambling that we won't let the matter rest.'

There was a lengthy silence. Both men drew on their cigarettes, Taleb rather more anxiously than Meslem. 'What can we do, chief? We don't know much more than the average cynical citizen who sees the hand of the DRS in every bad thing that happens.'

'We can find our informant – and pressurize him into naming names.'

'How can we do that? There was nothing distinctive about his appearance. I could walk past him in the street tomorrow and not recognize him.'

'Perhaps not. But there *is* something distinctive about him. Unique, in fact. You just mentioned the hand of the DRS. Well, what if we had this man's fingerprints? As a state employee in a sensitive department, his fingerprints would be on file. And we have access to such records. Which means we could identify him.'

'But we don't have this man's fingerprints, chief.'

'Ah, but we do.' Meslem smiled. 'Remember how he leant on the bonnet of my car? I don't have the vehicle washed anything like as often as I should. The bodywork's covered in a layer of dust, oil and city grime that turns out to be an excellent medium for fingerprint preservation. Nachef lifted virtually a full set of prints last night.' Nachef was one of the more reliable members of the forensics team. His expertise counted for a lot.

'Where are the prints now?'

'He scanned them and is running a comparison with the criminal database on our wonderful computers, the workings of which I probably know even less about than you do.'

'Not sure that would be possible, chief.'

'Just as well Nachef is doing the work for us, then. I told him to extend the search to the administrative database as well. He looked surprised, but he didn't argue. I also swore him to secrecy, which I think we can rely on. His father and I served together.' This was a rare reference to Meslem's teenage years in the liberation army fighting the French, his reticence about which Taleb had always respected. 'In general, though, we're going to have to keep to an absolute minimum the number of people who know what we're doing.'

'Understood. When will we know the results?'

'He said he'd come up from the lab as soon as he had something. I gather we're to expect a list of names in order of the closeness of—' Meslem broke off. 'Hear that?'

Taleb strained his ears – and heard the distant creak of the lift cables.

'I think he may be on his way.'

'It's only fair to point out,' Taleb begins guardedly, having been left with no choice but to speak, 'that the High State Council concluded in its report on the assassination of President Boudiaf that it was in all likelihood the result of a plot, despite Boumaarafi insisting he acted alone.'

'But they didn't identify the plotters,' Abidi objects.

'No, they didn't. But they did suggest the FIS benefited more than anyone from the event.'

'Come, come, Superintendent. It's common knowledge Boudiaf was set on rooting out the corruption on which *le pouvoir* thrives. He sent an aide, General Mourad, to Paris to investigate the diversion of state funds into private bank accounts held in France and Switzerland. Mourad was murdered shortly after returning from that mission, the DRS having doubtless been tipped off about his activities by the DGSE.'

'You're suggesting the DRS acted in league with the French secret service?' the ex-minister cuts in. 'That is a gross slander.'

'Your fulminations won't *un*murder General Mourad,' Abidi retorts. 'Or *un*assassinate President Boudiaf. He couldn't be allowed to pursue his agenda. It threatened too many powerful people who'd helped themselves to our country's wealth. He had to be stopped. And he was. Superintendent Taleb knows I'm speaking the truth. He even knows the name of the senior DRS officer who was entrusted with organizing Boudiaf's elimination.'

'Do you?' asks Issam, looking at Taleb with genuine curiosity as well as surprise.

'Go on, Superintendent,' Abidi says with a glutinous smile. 'Unburden yourself. It's been thirty years. You may as well speak the name of the guilty man.'

'Our investigations at the time did not progress to the point where we were able to be certain who – if anyone – acted behind the scenes to facilitate the assassination,' Taleb responds, choosing his words with the delicacy of a diner picking the bones from a fish. 'Superintendent Meslem, who I worked under then as an inspector, was a fine and dedicated officer. If there had been sufficient evidence to justify charging any individual in connection with the assassination, he would have done everything he could to ensure that such a charge was brought. But it never was.'

'There you have it,' says the ex-minister. 'I for one have full confidence in the professionalism and integrity of our police force, then and now. I can see no point in pursuing this subject any further.'

'Indeed,' says Issam. 'Perhaps we should move on.'

'We're not moving on,' says Abidi, 'until Superintendent Taleb tells us what he knows . . . about Youcef Ghezala.' And as he speaks the name he holds Taleb with his gaze.

'Youcef Ghezala is the first name on the list,' reported Nachef with breathless eagerness.

'And therefore overwhelmingly likely to be our suspect?' Meslem enquired.

'I wouldn't say overwhelmingly. The condition of the prints I obtained introduces a small element of uncertainty, although they're of a relatively unusual compound nature, which significantly reduces the range of possible matches. Besides, the second name on the list is that of a known criminal, whereas the first . . .'

Meslem put on his glasses and peered at the list. 'Is DRS.'

'Yes, chief, but on an administrative grade.'

'A pen-pusher?'

'I don't know. He's middle grade, as you can see.'

'But the computer ranks him as favourite?'

'Well, the computer just . . . does what it's programmed to do.'

'Leaving us to do the rest?'

'Er . . . yes.'

'You've been invaluable, as ever.' Meslem beamed at Nachef. 'We'll take it from here.'

'Right. Shall I . . .'

'Yes. You can go. Thank you, Nachef.'

'OK. Glad to have helped.' Nachef appeared relieved to have

been given his marching orders. He nodded to Taleb and turned towards the door.

'Oh, Nachef,' said Meslem.

'Yes, chief?'

Meslem looked up at him over his glasses. 'The DRS connection makes this a rather . . . sensitive matter. It would be best if you mentioned it to no one.'

'You wouldn't want them getting to hear you'd pointed the finger of suspicion at one of their own, would you?' added Taleb.

Nachef grimaced. 'No.' That was clearly an understatement.

'So . . .' Taleb pulled an imaginary zip across his mouth.

Nachef nodded. 'Not a word.'

'Splendid,' said Meslem with a smile. 'Let us worry about this from now on.'

'Right, chief.'

With that Nachef left, at a smart clip.

Meslem passed the list to Taleb. They both lit cigarettes. Neither man spoke until the lift had reached their floor and then set off again, with Nachef on board. Taleb rose and closed the door, then sat down again.

'Youcef Ghezala, administrative officer middle grade, born 1960.' Meslem gazed across his desk at Taleb through a haze of smoke. 'Sound about the right age to you?'

'He does.'

'And DRS with it. The very body he accused of being responsible for the assassination . . . before it had even happened.'

'That he did.'

'Well, his home address is listed.' Meslem glanced at his watch. 'He's likely to be there at this hour. I think we should pay him a call, don't you? Or rather I think *you* should pay him a call.'

'You're not coming with me, chief?'

'You spoke to him. He might trust you, whereas two of us . . .'

'I'll see what I can get out of him.'

Meslem raised a cautionary finger. 'Tread carefully, Taleb. It is vital the DRS does not learn of this.'

'I'll be careful, chief.'

'Then go. Don't phone with news. Simply report back here. We discuss this face to face only. You understand?'

Taleb nodded. He understood all too well.

'Youcef Ghezala?' Taleb frowns for the benefit of the camera. 'I'm not sure I recall the name.'

'There's nothing wrong with your memory.' Abidi almost spits out the words. 'It's your conscience that's degraded. What about General Mokrani of the DRS? That name mean anything to you?'

'He's a senior DRS officer, now retired. I know his name, yes. As I know the name of many in government service, past and present.'

'Ever met him?'

'I may have.'

'Ghezala worked for him, didn't he?'

'Did he?'

'Are you really going to sit there and pretend you don't know what the connection was between Mokrani and Ghezala . . . and you?'

'This is a group discussion,' Issam intervenes. 'I don't think it's appropriate for you to seek to interrogate—'

'Not *appropriate*?' Abidi shouts. 'Let *Superintendent* Taleb' – he points an accusing finger at Taleb – 'tell me – tell us and everyone watching – that he genuinely and truly doesn't know what I'm talking about. Then we can all be the judge of . . . the *appropriateness* of my questions.'

A brief, expectant silence falls. Prevarication has aided Taleb little. He is going to have to choose, as Abidi clearly means to force him to, between the truth . . . and a lie.

*

The air was sweet at that hour of a June morning. The city through which Taleb drove was quieter than it would normally be on a Tuesday. The knowledge of Boudiaf's assassination cast its invisible shadow over the sloping streets and sun-struck roofs. What a man saw could not be separated from what he felt. Foreboding carried winter into the heart of summer.

It didn't surprise Taleb that the apartment block Youcef Ghezala lived in was smarter and more salubriously located than his. The chagrin he felt was entirely predictable. The DRS offered its staff higher salaries and better prospects than the police. As long as you were willing to overlook the department's grisly reputation and its contemptuous attitude to civil rights, progression within its ranks could be rapid *and* remunerative. As no doubt it had been for Ghezala. Until his conscience had begun to trouble him.

The fully functioning lift – another contrast with Taleb's domestic existence – bore him to the sixth floor, where he made his way along a blandly decorated but spotlessly clean corridor to the door of Ghezala's apartment. It was only just gone seven fifteen and he shared Meslem's hope that Ghezala would still be at home. If not, Taleb would have to try to contact him via the DRS switchboard, which he much preferred to avoid.

He pressed the doorbell and was relieved to hear a sound of approaching footsteps from within.

But the door wasn't opened by Youcef Ghezala. Instead a tall, good-looking man in a dove-grey suit and white shirt looked him in the eye with a directness that bordered on hostility and asked, 'What do you want?'

In the second before answering Taleb took the measure of the man. The upper arms of his suit jacket strained round his muscular biceps. He was chewing gum and had a cocksure air of restrained arrogance about him. That probably explained why he'd chosen a suit that didn't fit loosely enough to conceal the bulge of a shoulder-holstered gun beneath his left arm. He might as well have had DRS tattooed on his forehead.

'I'd like to speak to Youcef Ghezala,' said Taleb. 'If that's possible.'

'Come in.' The man stood back, allowing Taleb to enter.

They were in a short passage leading towards the kitchen on one side and a lounge on the other. Taleb's immediate impression was of neat, solitary living. Youcef Ghezala wasn't a family man.

'What's your business with Ghezala?' the man asked as he closed the door.

'Is he here?' Taleb asked coolly.

'No. He isn't.'

'Then . . .'

The man reached into an inner pocket of his jacket and took out an ID card. DRS, as Taleb had guessed. His name was Khaled Zoubiri. 'State your business here.' His tone had already hardened.

'Police business.' Taleb flourished his own ID card.

Zoubiri squinted at it suspiciously. 'Police? OK. What's Ghezala done? Parked illegally?'

'I'm not in the traffic division.'

'No? Well, be careful you don't get transferred there for obstructing a DRS operation.'

'Is that what this is?'

'You know Ghezala's one of us, right?'

'Yes,' Taleb replied, with a cautious elongation of the word.

'So, what do you want with him . . . Inspector Taleb?'

'He, er . . . called our office yesterday.' Taleb was improvising frantically while trying to sound merely hazy about details. 'He said he wanted to report something . . . important.'

'Which was?'

'He never actually said. The office was very busy yesterday, as you can imagine, following the, er . . .'

'Assassination?'

'Yes.' Taleb meets Zoubiri's gaze. 'The assassination.'

'Did you speak to Ghezala?'

'Not personally. But he sounded . . . anxious, according to the person who did. When he was informed he couldn't be put through to anyone senior, he . . . rang off.'

'You actually follow up calls like that?'

'We try to.'

'Even when you're very busy?'

'Even then.'

'He gave you his address, did he?'

'No.' Taleb had noted the wall-hung phone in the hall as he entered. He calculated that made his next piece of improvisation safe enough. 'We traced this address from the phone number he supplied.'

'Why not just call him back?'

'I did, but he didn't pick up. Maybe because . . . he wasn't here. Can I ask . . .'

'Colleagues reported Ghezala had been behaving strangely in recent weeks. There were signs of . . . mental instability. They said they thought he was becoming . . . paranoid. I guess that tallies with the call he made to you people.' Zoubiri gave Taleb a superior smile. 'I came round to check on his . . . welfare.'

'But he wasn't here . . . to let you in?'

Zoubiri held his smile. 'No. But he leaves a key with a neighbour.'

Taleb nodded. 'Right.'

'His bed's not been slept in. So, he must have spent the night somewhere else. Maybe he slept on the beach. Who knows? The poor guy obviously needs help. Which we'll make sure he gets, just as soon as we track him down. You can leave that to us.'

'There's the question of . . . what he wanted to report . . . to someone senior.'

'Like I told you, Taleb, Ghezala has been losing it.' Zoubiri tapped his forehead. 'Screw loose, you know? He had nothing to report.'

'How can you be so sure?'

Zoubiri took a half-step towards Taleb and narrowed his gaze. 'He's our problem, not yours. Is that clear?'

'Well . . .'

'Only if it isn't clear then you *will* have a problem. The sort of problem you really don't want. My advice? Leave this to us. Forget Ghezala. OK?'

'OK.' There was little else Taleb could say. Refusing to heed advice from the DRS wasn't a recipe for good health.

'Off you go, then. I'll sort things out here.'

Taleb was tempted to ask several more questions, but he knew he wouldn't get satisfactory answers and antagonizing Zoubiri would accomplish nothing – apart from drawing more attention to himself than was remotely wise. There was a time to resist and a time to give way. And this was abundantly the latter.

'I'd have thought you people would be concentrating on ensuring the President's funeral goes off peacefully,' said Zoubiri as Taleb turned towards the door.

'Crowd control isn't my area of responsibility,' Taleb remarked mildly.

'No? Well, make sure I don't have to find out what *is* your area of responsibility.'

Taleb glanced back at Zoubiri as he opened the door. A riposte hovered on his lips. But he didn't utter it. He simply nodded and made as dignified an exit as he could contrive.

The grisly cavalcade of events that followed Boudiaf's assassination bathed the rest of the 1990s in blood, mostly the blood of innocents, including Taleb's wife and daughter. Their faces – Serene's and Lili's, forever smiling in his memory – hover before his mind's eye as he looks across the starkly lit TV studio at Rochdi Abidi, whose features are distorted by something between a scowl and a leer. It's unclear to Taleb whether Abidi would prefer him to persist in lying or tell the truth – the whole grim unvarnished truth – about Ghezala and Mokrani and Zoubiri and come to that Abidi himself.

The simple truth at this moment is that he can't bring himself to lie any longer. It's not a conscious decision as such. It's more akin to a physical reaction. And so the words spill from his mouth even though he knows he should hold them in. He knows – but he speaks them anyway.

'Youcef Ghezala was a DRS official who worked under General Mokrani at the time of the assassination. At Superintendent Meslem's direction, I followed up some evidence pointing to Ghezala's . . . and therefore General Mokrani's . . . apparent . . . foreknowledge of the event.'

'Foreknowledge?' Issam can't help looking intrigued by the remark.

'We established that General Mokrani's area of responsibility within the DRS at that time was . . . pre-emptive operations.'

'Excuse me,' says the Islamist politician, frowning at Taleb. 'Let me understand. The DGSN' – he employs the initials by which the national police force is formally known – 'had evidence in their possession that a senior figure in the DRS – this General Mokrani – knew President Boudiaf was going to be assassinated?'

'Evidence, yes. But not proof.' No. Not proof. Though perhaps Ghezala could have delivered proof. Perhaps he would have lived to deliver it – if Taleb hadn't allowed himself to be warned off by Zoubiri that morning at Ghezala's apartment. He couldn't escape some degree of responsibility for what had happened.

'If the DRS knew of the plot,' asks the *disparus* campaigner with genuine bafflement, 'why didn't they do something about it?'

'Because it was their plot,' says Abidi. He smiles pityingly at her. 'Don't you see? *They* killed Boudiaf.'

'Is that true?' The woman stares across at Taleb. She will have heard such things suggested before, of course. No Algerian could grow to adulthood without being exposed to the rumours of dark and devious conspiracies that feed the public image of *le pouvoir*. But still she has difficulty believing it. Still she does not really *want* to believe it.

'Police officers can't afford to reach hard and fast conclusions about what's true and what isn't,' says Taleb, some of his former defensiveness reasserting itself. He knows he's already gone too far. And he knows he definitely shouldn't go any further. 'We deal in evidence.'

'But the evidence pointed to Mokrani, didn't it?' presses Abidi.

'Well . . .'

'Did it or didn't it?'

'It pointed . . . in his direction.' Taleb actually feels relieved now he's said it. His relief won't last long, of course. It'll soon be replaced by regret that he's been so indiscreet. But in this moment he can't think of that. He's been cautious all his life. Throwing that caution aside is like taking a deep breath of cool fresh air. 'It certainly pointed in his direction.'

TWO

IT TAKES TALEB NO MORE THAN A FEW SECONDS WHEN HE WAKES UP the following morning to recall with horror the things he said last night on national television. *On national television.* Sweat starts out on his face. How could he have been so stupid? How could he have forgotten the rules he has followed for so many years? Think what you like. *Say* what you like, to those you trust. But don't speak out in public. Don't stand up to be counted. Because you will be counted. You will be counted out.

Assuring himself that the DRS is no more, its power and influence swept away, that Algeria post-Bouteflika, post-*Hirak*, is a different country from the one in which every word had to be weighed by someone such as him, does no good. Because he believes it only on a superficial level. Deep down he knows – he fears – that though the names and the initials and the faces may change, nothing *really* changes. The future is still firmly gripped by the past.

He showers, shaves and dresses, mechanically following the routines he lives by. He has no stomach for breakfast beyond a cup of coffee, which he drinks standing in the kitchen, looking out at the dawn stealing across the city. He keeps glancing at the telephone on the wall, expecting it to ring at any moment. But it does not ring. He hasn't turned on his mobile yet, dreading the messages that may be waiting for him. Until he reads them it's possible to imagine they don't exist. It's possible to imagine this is the start of a perfectly normal Monday.

And maybe it is. Who watches *Microscope* anyway? Who cares what some talking head may have said about the role a retired DRS officer *may* have played in the assassination of a president most of the population is too young to remember anyway? Thirty years buy a lot of forgetting.

Just not enough forgetting, he strongly suspects. Not enough by a long way. And he has little doubt that Agent Hidouchi, his DSS partner in setting right some of the wrongs of the past, will have paid close attention to what he said and regarded it as completely crazy, not to mention professionally embarrassing for her. The wrath of Souad Hidouchi is a terrible thing to contemplate.

He leaves the apartment block and heads for the nearby garage where he stows his car. It was an arrangement he first entered into during *la décennie noire*, when it became too dangerous for a police officer to park his car on the street. It might have made sense to revert to street-parking in the more peaceful years since, but Taleb has never quite trusted those times to last. And so he still retains his spot in the gated half-roofed courtyard.

Akram, one of the two brothers who run the garage and whose shifts tend to coincide with Taleb's comings and goings, greets him rather more animatedly than usual from his shadowy cubbyhole just inside the gate. 'It is good to see you, Inspector. Or should I say Superintendent?' He emerges into the dust-filtered light as a pigeon takes off explosively from a nearby rafter. 'When were you promoted?' he asks with an inquisitive tilt to his head.

'Fourteen years ago.'

'You should have mentioned it.'

'Would it have got me better service?'

'Absolutely not.' Akram's smile reveals an uneven rank of tobacco-stained teeth. 'This is an egalitarian garage.'

'I'm glad to hear it. Anyway, you can carry on calling me Inspector if you like. Changing how you address me after all these years really isn't necessary.'

'Is that your way of telling me you anticipate a demotion after your . . . performance last night?'

'I didn't have you down as an example of *Microscope*'s target audience.'

'The batteries died in the remote and I was out of spares, so I couldn't change channels.'

'That must have been a blow.'

'On the contrary. It was more exciting than the football I was planning to watch. That ended nil-nil. But we certainly saw some goals scored on *Microscope*, didn't we? Maybe an own goal in your case. Honestly . . . Inspector . . . what got into you? You've always struck me as a cautious man.'

'I've always struck myself as that too.'

'So . . . what happened?'

'I think caution is like those batteries of yours, Akram. One day, just when it's least convenient, it dies.'

Akram nods. It seems he understands. 'Maybe you should have retired before it came to this.'

'You could be right. Maybe I'll have to now.'

'Maybe.' Akram nods again and looks at Taleb as if weighing his chances. 'If you're lucky.'

With his mobile still determinedly turned off, Taleb drives slowly towards Police HQ, chain-smoking and grappling with the recalcitrant gearstick of his aged Renault as he goes. The police radio crackles out run-of-the-mill incident reports and squad car directions. No murders, no bombs, no riots, not even a classy hold-up. Nothing, in other words, to distract Bouras from the question of how best to deal with the idiot superintendent who shot his mouth off on national television last night. This isn't going to be a pleasant day.

He enters by the back door from the car park and takes the stairs to his office, unable to face the lottery of which sarcastic colleague he may have to share the lift with. It's a slow climb, thanks to the poor state of his lungs. He arrives breathless and bedraggled. And never makes it to his desk.

'The director wants to see you,' says Lieutenant Lahmar, without looking up from his computer screen.

'Thank you.'

'Said you should go straight up as soon as you got here.'

'Yes. *Thank you*.'

'No problem.'

Bouras's secretary sends him through the outer office with a stern look and a twitch of the head. Taleb taps the door of the inner office with his knuckle and enters, taking a deep breath as he does so, which sets off a cough he does not entirely succeed in stifling.

Director Farid Bouras, smartly suited and immaculately groomed, normally bears an expression of mild self-satisfaction, as befits a man who has progressed to such a senior position without sacrificing every one of his principles whilst escaping the snares of career-stunting miscalculations.

He appears far from self-satisfied this morning, however. He looks steadily across the room at Taleb without speaking and, more worryingly still, without inviting him to take a seat. He flicks shut a folder that lies before him on his desk, reaches out and lifts from the groove in the rim of his marble ashtray a thin cigar. He draws on it thoughtfully.

'Director . . .' Taleb hesitantly begins.

'Don't speak, Taleb,' says Bouras. 'You have spoken quite enough, I think. And to a large audience. Yes, a *very* large audience. They have had the benefit of your opinion about possible DRS involvement in the assassination of President Boudiaf. Indeed we have all now had the benefit of that. Except, of course, that it is not a benefit. Not to me, certainly. And not to the Interior Ministry, as they have already told me at some length. Nor to the DSS in its attempt to turn the page on its DRS days. For all of those groups and individuals your . . . *opinion* . . . is as unwelcome as it was unsought. I instructed you, quite specifically as I recall, to say nothing controversial during the *Microscope* broadcast. Nothing *remotely* controversial. But I believe you'll agree that what you actually said could hardly have been more so.'

Bouras rises from his chair and moves to a position by the window, which commands a wide view of the port and the broad blue bay beyond. He gazes out, his back turned on Taleb, who imagines such a vista, contrasting starkly as it does with the phalanx of dilapidated city roofs visible from his own office, must have a soothing effect. There is certainly a lot of clean clear Mediterranean to be drunk in from here. And Bouras is definitely in need of soothing. Taleb holds his silence.

'You allowed yourself to be provoked by the journalist Abidi,' Bouras continues after a moment. 'I would have expected an officer of your seniority and experience to be able to deal with the likes of Abidi. Was that an unreasonable expectation?' He turns round and looks at Taleb. 'You may speak now.'

'No, Director. It was not unreasonable.'

'Why did you let me down? Why did you let *yourself* down?'

'It is hard to explain.'

'Nevertheless, I would like you to.'

'I believe Youcef Ghezala was trying to tell us that the DRS planned the Boudiaf assassination, probably for the reason Abidi put forward: the President's anti-corruption drive. And Ghezala's boss, General Mokrani, was responsible for what the DRS called "pre-emptive operations", so he'd be the obvious candidate for the role of setting up the hit. Superintendent Meslem hoped we could extract clinching evidence from Ghezala, but I let slip just about the only chance we had of obtaining some by allowing a DRS officer to turn me away from Ghezala's apartment the morning after the assassination. And within days . . . Ghezala was dead.'

'Am I to take it your accusations against Mokrani were motivated by . . . regret . . . for not going after him more energetically thirty years ago?'

'I regret it a great deal.' Taleb can see nothing for it now but to be completely frank. 'The truth is that I've often asked myself whether all those other . . . pre-emptive operations . . . I suspect Mokrani launched during *la décennie noire* would have happened if we'd been able to stop him in his tracks in 1992.'

'Including the supposed GIA raid in which your wife and daughter were killed?'

Taleb nods. 'Including that. Information I obtained afterwards suggested it was a false flag operation.'

'Ordered by Mokrani?'

'Maybe. Directly or indirectly.'

'So, Abidi hit a raw spot when he mentioned Ghezala.'

'He did. But it's no excuse. I should have bitten my tongue. Besides, I don't think we can ever hope to know for sure which outrages were committed during those years by Islamist forces or by DRS-backed forces posing as Islamists in order to discredit them – or some other lawless mob taking advantage of the situation to settle old scores. In the end, it probably doesn't matter. Those who died died, whichever group actually killed them.'

'Remind me why your wife and daughter were in the village where the raid took place.'

'I sent them to stay with my wife's parents because I thought my position as a police officer made it too dangerous for them to remain in Algiers.'

'But, as it turned out . . .'

'They would have been safer – and probably alive to this day – if they hadn't left.'

Bouras replaces his cigar carefully on the rim of the ashtray and walks slowly across the room to where Taleb is standing. He lays a hand on his shoulder. 'You should not suppose that because I am angry – *very* angry – about the difficulties you have caused me I am not also sympathetic to your situation.'

'Thank you, Director.'

Bouras removes his hand. 'Nor am I unaware of the good work you have been able to do in conjunction with DSS agent Hidouchi since we agreed eighteen months ago to postpone your retirement.'

'We have brought a few malefactors to justice, it is true.'

'But they do not include – nor are they likely to include – retired DRS officer General Hamza Mokrani.'

'No. They do not include him. He is too close to *le pouvoir* to be touched by the likes of me.'

'Whatever you may blurt out in a television studio.'

'Whatever.'

'So, you would agree your . . . performance . . . last night was entirely counter-productive?'

'Yes, Director. Entirely.'

'And you would also agree antagonizing a man such as General Mokrani is deeply unwise.'

'Yes.'

'If he feels you have damaged his reputation . . .'

'He may make some move against me or Abidi, I suppose. Although that would only strengthen the suspicion that he really was implicated in the Boudiaf assassination. I think he'll prefer to play the role of the wronged innocent.'

'Let us hope you are right.' Bouras sighs. 'We will be issuing a press release making it crystal clear – even if, strictly speaking, it is not – that we have never been in possession of any evidence linking Mokrani to the Boudiaf assassination and that your on-air comments carry no official weight whatsoever. As to your own situation, the Interior Ministry, having inquired into the matter and expended their mighty resources to the extent of discovering your date of birth, initially proposed you be retired with immediate effect. They only hesitated because that would be an out-and-out surrender to the DSS. It transpires the DSS's complaint to our ministerial superiors was not on behalf of General Hamza Mokrani, who is regarded by them as a relic of the bad old DRS days, but of his son, Karim Mokrani, a serving DSS officer whose position might be compromised by the circulation of such allegations as you made against his father.'

'I didn't realize Mokrani had a son in the DSS.'

'Well, he does. And Karim Mokrani is well thought of, apparently. Be that as it may, however, since the DSS is overseen by the Defence Ministry, the Interior Ministry does not wish to lose face in this matter. Which is why they were receptive to the compromise I suggested.'

'Compromise?' Never has the word sounded sweeter to Taleb.

'You have been working under a lot of pressure on unspecified tasks of a demanding nature. It appears we may have asked too much of a dedicated officer. Your behaviour on *Microscope* was the most dramatic of several indications that the strain has told on you. You are therefore taking an open-ended period of sick leave.'

'I am?'

'Yes. Starting today. In fact, starting as soon as you leave my office.'

'But . . .'

'I strongly advise you not to argue with me, Taleb. It is

necessary for you to go to ground for a while. To have no contact with journalists, especially not Rochdi Abidi. To say nothing to anyone about General Mokrani. To give him no reason to think you will say anything more on the subject of the Boudiaf assassination. For the next few weeks you should practise silence and invisibility. Then, when interest in this matter has subsided and the ministry is no longer looking over my shoulder . . .'

'I can resume work?'

'If all goes well. If all goes *quietly*. To which end . . . I have a cousin in Oran – a lawyer, actually – who owns a small house in Beni Saf, a charming fishing village where he and his family spend weekends and summer holidays. I have a standing offer of the use of the property. I know he would have no objection to someone I can personally vouch for staying there for a while.'

'Beni Saf? That's . . . most of the way to Morocco.'

'It is undeniably a long way from Algiers. Which is its principal advantage from our point of view. There is no danger of you bumping into journalists in Beni Saf. In fact, at this time of the year, there is very little danger of you bumping into anyone. I've only been there in the summer, when it's overrun by holidaymakers. But right now it should be beautifully peaceful. You can relax, get some fresh air into your lungs, maybe walk a little. It'll do you good, Taleb. It'll be just the break you need.'

Taleb does not feel in need of a break. He has no desire to sample the charms of a distant fishing village in January. He has no idea – absolutely none – what he could find to do there.

But that is not the point, as he is well aware. Bouras has secured him a lifeline. And he must grasp it.

'I could set off tomorrow morning.'

Bouras looks meaningfully at him.

'*First thing* tomorrow morning.'

And at that Bouras nods approvingly.

*

Lieutenant Lahmar appears monumentally unsurprised by the news that Taleb is departing on immediate sick leave. He makes a few clumsy remarks about the unreasonable demands of the service. These Taleb greets with what he considers to be remarkable forbearance, since he strongly suspects Lahmar has already concluded his boss will not be returning and is busily calculating whether this will mean a leg-up in the hierarchy for himself. There will be some satisfaction to be derived from disappointing him on that score.

After issuing a cursory briefing on the current state of several ongoing investigations, Taleb shrugs on his raincoat, grasps his briefcase and leaves, uttering a silent prayer as he goes that this really won't be his final exit from Police HQ.

With the rest of the day suddenly stretching emptily before him, he decides he will drive down to Promenade des Sablettes. The bayside park should be thinly populated at this hour and he hopes the sea air will help him take stock of his situation. He also hopes he'll be able to summon up the courage to turn on his mobile and discover what kind of message – or messages – Agent Hidouchi may have sent him.

As it turns out, however, he won't need to turn on his mobile in order to hear from Hidouchi. As he pulls out of Police HQ's car park and heads south, he notices a motorcyclist tagging along behind him. The machine is powerful – he can hear the pantherlike growl of its engine through the half-open window of his car – but the black-leather-clad rider makes no move to overtake, despite his sedate pace. Hidouchi clearly doesn't intend to wait patiently for Taleb to call her. He is going to have to explain himself to her face to face.

At the weekend, even at this time of the year, Promenade des Sablettes would be thronged with joggers, cyclists, frolicking family groups and bashful couples. Mid-morning on a Monday finds it thinly populated, the Ferris wheel out of action and most of the concession stalls closed. On the parkside road Taleb gets out of the car and lights a cigarette. Hidouchi pulls in behind him. There's no running from this encounter.

Hidouchi props her bike, removes her crash helmet and stows it on the handlebars. She shakes out her long dark hair as she strides towards him, carrying herself, as ever, with confidence. She looks what she is: a proud and strikingly attractive modern Algerian woman. She is the future, whereas Taleb could hardly deny that he embodies the past. They have virtually nothing in common except a determination to do what they can to rid their country of corruption.

That plus the small matter of trust. Having worked together during the Zarbi-Laloul investigation in the summer of 2020 and survived its many hazards thanks largely to relying on each other because there was no one else they *could* rely on, they are bound by the trust that has been forged between them. However roundly Hidouchi is planning to condemn Taleb's conduct, he knows she is never going to accuse him of betraying her – because she will never have reason to. As she also knows.

She looks at him with a mixture of exasperation and incomprehension. Her gaze narrows. 'How are you feeling?' she asks with an acid edge to her voice.

'Ashamed of myself, since you ask.'

'Does that mean you weren't engaged in some devious ploy when you said what you did on television last night – that it really was just as . . . stupid . . . as it seemed to be?'

Taleb nods. 'That's what it means.'

She shakes her head. 'Have they fired you?'

'Surprisingly, no. Bouras negotiated a compromise. I've been put on sick leave.'

'What's the illness?'

'Stress, apparently.'

'Whose? Yours or Bouras's?'

Taleb winces and takes a long draw on his cigarette. 'Would it help if I apologized?'

'Not in the slightest.'

'I *am* sorry, even so.'

'We were doing good work, Taleb, you and I. We've put several key *hizb fransa* operatives out of action since we started. We've made it harder for the DGSE to interfere in this country's affairs.'

Hizb fransa is a catch-all phrase describing the agents and sub-agents deployed by the French external intelligence service, the DGSE, to manipulate events in Algeria to France's advantage – the former colonial masters' way of never letting go. Corruption of every kind is their currency. Their defeat is obviously unattainable for one police officer and one DSS agent. But Taleb and Hidouchi have succeeded in impeding their activities. Which will be much more difficult now Taleb has put himself out of action.

'How long are you likely to be sick?'

'A few weeks. Maybe longer. It depends.'

'On how soon the storm you whipped up blows over?'

'Are your DSS colleagues making a lot of it?'

'What do you think?'

'Can I buy you an ice cream?'

'*What?*'

'There's a kiosk near the Ferris wheel that's always open. And now I'm on sick leave I suppose I should try to enjoy a few modest pleasures. So, salted caramel for you?'

They find the ice cream kiosk is indeed open, though doing little business. Taleb buys apricot for himself, prompted by the recollection that Superintendent Meslem adored ice cream and apricot was his favourite flavour. He doesn't mention the association as they walk slowly away from the Ferris wheel, the sea lapping gently on the narrow beach below the promenade. The sky is grey, the bay placid, the weather still.

'Why have you never told me about the Ghezala case?' Hidouchi asks.

'Because it led nowhere. Because my part in it was so ... discreditable. Besides, you don't need me to tell you the sort of things the DRS got up to in the nineties. Abidi wasn't saying anything about the Boudiaf assassination a lot of people didn't already suspect.'

'But they wouldn't have expected a senior police officer to reinforce their suspicions on live television, would they?'

'I let him get under my skin. It was stupid of me. As you kindly pointed out.'

'He got under your skin because you blame General Mokrani's pre-emptive operations outfit for the deaths of your wife and daughter. That's it, isn't it?'

Taleb confronts his ice cream. Lili's favourite flavour was chocolate. He can still hear her laugh and see her smile. 'I have no secrets from you, Souad,' he says softly.

'Are you aware Mokrani's son is a DSS agent?'

'I am now. Bouras told me. He won't welcome his father's past being dragged up by me.'

'He certainly won't. Though the word is there's no love lost between them. So, he's not likely to come after you. Besides, I'm told he's out of the country. And probably too busy to bother about your *Microscope* comments. They aren't going to make it to CNN, after all.'

'That's reassuring.'

'Abidi might not want to let matters rest, though. What's his game, do you think?'

'No idea.'

'That's a pity, since you ended up playing it. Abidi introduced Mokrani's name into the debate. Watching him, I had the sense it was part of a carefully planned strategy. He knew what he was doing, even if you didn't.'

'Well, I won't be asking him to explain himself. Bouras was emphatic I was to have no contact with him – or any other journalists.'

'Maybe I'll have a quiet word with Abidi.'

'I'd rather you didn't. I'd rather you forgot everything I said last night.'

'If I'm to do that, I'll need to know what I'm being asked to forget. I'll need to know all about the Ghezala case. Talk me through it, Taleb. Tell me exactly what happened.'

'Don't you have other duties to attend to?'

'Yes. So, the sooner you start the sooner I can get back to them.' She looks round at him, her eyebrows arched expectantly. 'I'm listening.'

Taleb recounts the events of June 1992 as dispassionately but as fully as he can. If anyone has a right to know how the Ghezala case progressed to its dismal conclusion it is Souad Hidouchi. At times such as this Taleb is reminded, to his astonishment, that this woman, who is more than thirty years his junior and entirely out of sympathy with his generation's view of the world, has become his friend and confidante. But so it is.

From his first – and as it turned out last – encounter with Youcef Ghezala outside Police HQ on the day of Boudiaf's assassination, he takes the story forward through the fingerprints lifted from the bonnet of Meslem's car to his crossing of paths with DRS agent Zoubiri at Ghezala's apartment the following morning.

Meslem interpreted Zoubiri's presence there as confirmation that General Mokrani was in some way involved in the assassination, but gloomily acknowledged that it would now be formidably difficult to make any progress with their investigations. Certainly he could not do much more without notifying Director Lamri, who would surely veto any action likely to incur the wrath of the DRS.

Meslem's most optimistic conclusion was that Ghezala had gone into hiding, his whereabouts unknown to the DRS. If so, the challenge was to find him before the DRS did. Then, if he offered to supply hard evidence against Mokrani, Lamri *might* be shamed into letting them take the matter further. But how to find him?

Taleb headed back to Ghezala's apartment block that evening, calculating that Zoubiri would no longer be there, though he might well have left a surveillance team on site in case Ghezala showed up. With that in mind, he left his car some distance away, approached on foot and made his entrance via the service alley at the back of the building.

He followed a shadowy corridor in from there, hoping it would lead to the lift. His plan was to tap Ghezala's immediate neighbours for clues as to where he might be. But the corridor took him past a small and even shadowier room from which a short, wiry, boiler-suited figure wearing what looked like an original FLN forage cap emerged into his path with the speed of a striking viper. The caretaker, Taleb assumed. And he seemed to have a highly developed territorial instinct.

'Who are you?' he demanded at once.

'Police.' Taleb produced his identity card. The caretaker squinted at it suspiciously.

'Not DRS?'

'Not DRS.'

'That's something.' The caretaker leant back through the doorway of the room he'd come out of and spat into something metallic. He clearly had no fondness for the DRS, which might prove to be good news.

'I'm making inquiries about one of your residents – Youcef Ghezala.'

The caretaker grinned toothlessly. 'Of course you are.'

'Know him, do you?'

'I know all the residents. Like I told the DRS goon.'

'What else did you tell him?'

'Nothing.'

'Was that because there was nothing you *could* tell him?'

Another grin. 'He didn't ask nicely.' The caretaker was clearly enjoying himself. He and Taleb shared a distaste for the secret organs of *le pouvoir*. The police occupied a middle ground where the normal give and take of human relations could function. It was a small but significant advantage.

'I'm asking nicely.'

'Ghezala's a loner. Keeps himself to himself. He's never caused me any problems. He's very polite, which not all of them are. I like that.'

'Any idea where I could find him?'

'No. Gone to ground somewhere, I'd guess. But he'll be back sooner or later.'

'How can you be so sure?'

The caretaker shrugged. 'Just a feeling.'

'If I find him before the DRS does, it'll go better for him. Much better.'

'I don't doubt it.'

'So . . .'

'What's he done? The DRS goon wouldn't say. Just gave me some camel shit about a psychiatric disorder.'

'It concerns yesterday's assassination.'

The caretaker's eyes widened. He wasn't expecting anything so sensational. 'Ghezala was mixed up with that?'

'It's more that he may be able to identify those who were.'

The caretaker plucked a pack of cigarettes – Nassims, Taleb noticed – out of his boiler suit pocket. He pulled one from the pack with his mouth and lit it, then gave Taleb a long up-and-down look. 'You sure you're not out of your depth, Inspector?'

'Not sure at all.'

'I liked Boudiaf.'

'So did I.'

'I doubt I'll like whoever they replace him with.'

'I think you're right to be doubtful.'

Taleb waited through a couple of thoughtful draws on the cigarette. Then the caretaker said, 'Thing is . . .' Taleb waited a little longer, then: 'Ghezala doesn't know I know where he's hidden his . . . box of secrets. If that's what it is.'

'Where has he hidden it?'

'I caught him coming down from the roof a couple of times. He said he liked the view. I never swallowed that. Then one time I noticed the door of the water tank shed up there wasn't closed the way I close it. I took a careful look inside. Found this . . . box shoved round behind the tank.'

'Did you open it?'

'No. He'd tied it closed with string. And he's the type who'd notice if someone else had tied the knot.'

'So, it's as he left it?'

'I guess so. The DRS goon never went up there.'

'Because you didn't tell him about the box?'

'Well, the way I see it he's probably one of the people Ghezala's hiding the box *from*. And the residents have a right to expect I'll . . . take care who I discuss their affairs with. But catching Boudiaf's killers – whoever they really are – trumps that, doesn't it?'

Taleb nods. 'It does. So . . . how do I get to the roof?'

Taleb took the cramped service lift to the top floor, then climbed narrow ill-lit stairs from there to the roof. He emerged into a wide panorama of the city suffused by summer dusk: *Alger la blanche* become *Alger la rose*. Its beauty seemed indecent for the eve of a president's funeral.

The water tank shed was more or less in the centre of the roof. Taleb hurried across to it and pulled the double doors open. There wasn't much of a gap between the tank and the wall of the shed and Taleb wasn't as thin as the caretaker, but he managed to squirm his way in. Reaching behind the tank, he found the box, wedged behind the wooden plinth on which the tank stood. He pulled it free.

It was wrapped in black plastic, fastened with string. He knelt in the shed doorway, untied the string and removed the plastic, revealing a cardboard box bearing faded lettering that proclaimed its original contents had been a French encyclopaedia.

He lifted the lid. Inside the box was a sheaf of papers – photocopies of documents, by the look of them, many bearing DRS headings. He spotted Mokrani's name at the top of several circulation lists.

But he never had the chance to examine the documents. A shadow fell across him and, turning, he saw Zoubiri standing behind him. He was holding a gun. Another man was standing by the door from the stairs, also with gun in hand.

'Put the lid back on, Taleb, and set the box down,' said Zoubiri levelly.

Taleb obeyed.

'Now stand up.'

Taleb rose cautiously to his feet.

'I think you must have underestimated our surveillance capability,' said Zoubiri with a smile. 'I had an idea you'd be back – and that you'd have more luck with the caretaker than I did. So I bugged his office.'

There was plenty Taleb was tempted to say at that moment, but he reckoned all of it was less wise than saying nothing at all.

'Those are secret and confidential DRS documents,' said Zoubiri. 'Removed from our offices by Ghezala without permission. You'll agree, won't you, *Inspector* Taleb, that you have no legitimate interest in them?'

'Does it matter whether I agree or not?'

'Not to me. But you should agree, even so. Then we'll just let you go – and forget you were ever here. If not . . .' Zoubiri shrugged. 'Your choice.'

'Do you know where Ghezala is?'

'I'm sure he'll . . . come to light. Before long.'

That sounded bad for Ghezala. And it could be bad for Taleb as well. Unless he did as he was told. That was how it was with the DRS. Ground was either given – or taken. It was time to give.

'Are you going to leave now of your own accord?' Zoubiri asked. 'Only I should warn you that your opportunity to do so won't last much longer.'

'What about the caretaker?'

'He'll come to no harm. *If* you leave now.' Zoubiri gestured towards the man standing by the door that led to the stairs. 'My friend will see you off the premises.' He smiled. 'I wish you a good evening.'

'So, there you have it,' Taleb says, contemplating the empty end of his ice cream cone. 'I crept away with my tail between my legs.'

'What happened to Ghezala?' Hidouchi asks.

'As Zoubiri predicted, he came to light. A couple making out in the Forêt de Bainem two evenings later found him hanging from a tree. The pathologist reckoned he'd been there at least twenty-four hours. He probably breathed his last around the same time Boudiaf was being laid in the ground.'

'Suicide?'

'Officially.'

'Ever hear from Agent Zoubiri again?'

'No. I'm glad to say I never did.'

'I don't recognize the name.'

'He was about my age, so he was probably pensioned off when the DRS was folded up.'

'I'll check.'

'It'd be safer not to. This isn't going anywhere, Souad. I should have left it where it was.'

'You should have, I agree. But you didn't.'

'And a spell of compulsory sick leave is my reward. So, I'll take my medicine, as I have to. It won't be so bad really. Bouras has kindly arranged to get me out of the way by sending me to stay in the holiday home of a cousin of his at Beni Saf.'

'I know Beni Saf. It's a lovely place.' Hidouchi smiles. 'You'll hate it.'

'Why?'

'You don't swim, you don't sail, you don't hike and you're hopeless at just lazing around. You'll go mad.'

'You think so?'

'I do.'

Taleb summons a rueful grin. 'Well, in that case, I suppose I really will be on sick leave.'

THREE

ACCORDING TO THE OCCUPANTS OF THE PATROL CAR PARKED outside Taleb's apartment block, they'd been sent there by Director Bouras for his protection and would be staying all night. Taleb didn't believe he needed protection and harboured a suspicion that Bouras actually wanted to ensure he left for his enforced holiday promptly the following morning.

If that was Bouras's concern, he had no need to worry. Taleb knew he had to toe the line if he was to be reinstated as fit for service. The holiday he didn't want was going to have to be endured. And the numerous messages left on his phone by journalists were going to have to be ignored.

Setting off alone, with only the road for company, Taleb finds it hard not to dwell on his recent missteps and misjudgements. And not only his recent ones. He still feels – as he knows Meslem felt until the day he died – that they should have done more to probe Mokrani's connection with Boudiaf's assassination.

He recalls the resignation – or realism, as some would call it – he surrendered to after handing over Ghezala's cache of documents to Zoubiri. It had still held him in its grip when he accompanied Ghezala's father – a frail old man crushed by grief – to the mortuary at Mustapha Bacha Hospital two days later to identify the body cut down from a tree in the Forêt de Bainem.

As they emerged into the open air, Taleb lit a cigarette to clear the lingering taint of formaldehyde from his nostrils and tongue. He offered one to Ghezala senior, who declined with a shake of the head. Maybe the old man didn't want to forget so quickly the atmosphere in which he had viewed his son's corpse.

Then, suddenly, Rochdi Abidi – notorious scandal-mongering journalist – was standing in front of them. What was he doing there? Whatever questions he might have, Taleb certainly had no wish to answer them.

'Inspector Taleb?' Rot the man: he was well informed. 'I'd like some information about the death of Youcef Ghezala.'

'This isn't the time or place. I'm with his father.'

'To whom I extend my sincere condolences.'

Ghezala senior looked blankly at Abidi, then wandered aimlessly past him.

'Get lost, Abidi,' Taleb said. 'It was a straightforward suicide. There's nothing for you here.'

'Nothing? What about the box Ghezala hid on the roof of his apartment block?'

He'd obviously been talking to the caretaker. But why? What had put him on Ghezala's trail in the first place? Taleb would have liked to know, but couldn't afford to feed Abidi's hunger for a story. 'I don't know what you're talking about.'

'What was in the box?'

'What box?'

'Come on, Inspector. If it was just a straightforward suicide, you wouldn't be here. Ghezala was DRS. And he was that rare thing: DRS with a conscience. There's a tie-in with the President's assassination, isn't there? Ghezala knew something. And he kept evidence of what he knew. Did you find it?'

'Ghezala was depressed; psychologically troubled. He took his own life while the balance of his mind was disturbed.'

'He worked under General Mokrani, didn't he?'

'I don't know who he worked under. My understanding is that he was a relatively low-level officer. A clerk, basically.'

'You handed the documents over to the DRS. That's it, isn't it? You're their stooge.'

'I'm no one's stooge.'

'They buried a lot of hopes for the betterment of this nation with Boudiaf. Doesn't that bother you – even slightly?'

'The assassin is already under arrest.'

'Maybe. But who set him up to do it? Who *enabled* him to do it? Ghezala's boss is my guess: Mokrani, acting on orders from the top.'

'I know peddling conspiracy theories is how you make a living, Abidi, but I'm a policeman. We deal in evidence. And there's no evidence of any connection between Ghezala – or General Mokrani – and the tragic event in Annaba.'

'What was in the box?'

'There was no box.' Taleb brushed past Abidi. 'I have to go.'

'This is on your conscience now, Inspector,' Abidi called after him. 'And it's going to stay there. One day you'll wish you'd defied the DRS and followed where the evidence led.'

Taleb didn't reply. There was nothing he could say. And nothing he could do. As Meslem had already acknowledged, they would never have been allowed to pursue a case against Mokrani, whatever the documents Ghezala had copied might reveal. There was a limit to what they could accomplish. To safeguard themselves and their families, they had to accept the reality of their situation. In Algeria, survival was the only victory anyone could hope for.

*

Taleb's despondency abates slowly as his journey continues. It's almost a pleasure to drive west for so long and so far. The A1 autoroute sweeps through the foothills of the Ouarsenis massif above the Chéliff valley on a day of quiet winter sunshine. He begins little by little to relax. He starts telling himself he should stop agonizing about the many mistakes he's made, in the past as well as the present. Maybe, he reflects, what's happened is for the best. Maybe this really will be a beneficial break from routine. Maybe he'll even confound Hidouchi's prediction and enjoy himself in Beni Saf.

Or maybe not. Beni Saf sits picturesquely on a promontory above the Mediterranean. A huddle of colourful roofs overlooks a beach that stands largely empty. The town is quiet and slow-moving on an out-of-season afternoon. Taleb follows the directions he has been given to the home of the woman who takes care of Bouras's cousin's seaside retreat. She is polite but wary. Maybe she knows Taleb is a policeman. Maybe she recognizes him from the television. If so, she hides it well. She gives him the key to the house and reels off instructions about how to manage the door lock, when to put out refuse and where to shop for essentials.

Absorbing about half of what she tells him, Taleb transfers to the house. It is clean and attractively furnished in a modern stripped-back style. It has a fine view of the harbour, where fishing boats and yachts are bobbing at anchor. The sun is going down and there is much to admire in the scene below him.

Gazing at it, Taleb confronts the reality of his own nature. He is not a man of leisure. He has no hobbies. He does not read for pleasure. He is entirely unsuited to lazing around. He will have to do some shopping, of course. After that . . . there will be no calls on his time. His days in Beni Saf hold nothing, either to dread or to look forward to. He will be his own master. But he will have no purpose.

The prospects are grim.

*

In Algiers, the late afternoon finds Souad Hidouchi walking purposefully towards the Café Pamplemousse off rue Larbi Ben M'hidi. Glancing around at the other pedestrians, she feels little affinity with them. She is a servant of the state who is not convinced the state is deserving of her dedication. Her solution to this problem is to do whatever she can to improve it, thankless though the task is. She once believed that the DSS, where she is an agent with a hard-won reputation for bravery and commitment to any mission assigned to her, had decisively put behind it the excesses of its predecessor body, the dreaded DRS. For some time now she has not been so sure. Corruption, much of it bequeathed by the French, runs deep in the country. *Le pouvoir*, of which the DSS is ultimately a servant, is concerned only with the maintenance of its privileges. Its settled will is that the future of Algeria should be as much like its past as possible. Change is its enemy. Reform is to be spoken of approvingly but never actually implemented. And therefore the kind of country Hidouchi believes Algeria should become can never be permitted to exist.

To some extent this is only what her father warned her against. 'You cannot alter the rules by which we live, Souad,' he told her when he realized how determined she was to join the DSS and become one of its few female agents. 'You should not pursue this course.' Marriage to a well-connected husband was the course he would actually have advocated for her, followed by motherhood and the provision of grandchildren to brighten his old age. Instead she is unmarried, childless and over thirty, a state of affairs that is the despair of her mother and, come to that, her sisters.

Having patience neither for the repressive negativity of *le pouvoir* nor the naive libertarianism of the *Hirak* protestors, Hidouchi knows her aspirations for her country are essentially unattainable. But that knowledge does not deflect her. She will do whatever she can to make the future a better place.

In this she has only one true ally: a police superintendent a few years older than her father – Mouloud Taleb, overdue for retirement, addicted to a noxious brand of cigarette and entirely cynical about the state of the nation. Thrown together by the Zarbi-Laloul case in 2020, their bond was forged by the hazards of the confrontation it drew them into with the sinister intertwining of *le pouvoir* and French intelligence. To survive they had to trust each other. And that trust endures.

But now Taleb has endangered her as well as himself by shooting his mouth off on national television about the possible involvement of a former senior DRS officer, General Hamza Mokrani, in the assassination of President Boudiaf in June 1992. She has made her exasperation with him for behaving so stupidly abundantly clear and he has retired sheepishly to the distant seaside resort of Beni Saf on an enforced holiday, hoping the dust will settle in his absence.

As it probably will. The media will presumably lose interest now the DGSN have formally disowned Taleb's remarks and emphasized there is no – absolutely no – evidence of Mokrani's complicity in the assassination. Meanwhile the DSS does not wish to align itself too closely with a dinosaur of the bad old DRS days such as Mokrani. It is in everyone's best interests to let the matter drift out of public consciousness.

But Hidouchi is not certain this will be so simple. Nothing is ever what it seems in Algeria, as Taleb has often reminded her. The motivations of the journalist Rochdi Abidi are unclear. If he was manipulating Taleb, it is equally possible some unknown third party was manipulating *him*. But why? What purpose is served by reviving conspiracy theories about an assassination thirty years in the past? Is Mokrani the target? Or is he the one taking aim? Hidouchi does not feel comfortable knowing the answers to none of these questions.

That is why she has arranged to meet Fatima Remichi, a former administrative officer at the DRS and later the DSS, for coffee and cake at the Café Pamplemousse. Fatima gave Hidouchi a lot of help and advice when she started out at the DSS and they have stayed in touch since her retirement, though she knows nothing of Hidouchi's off-the-books cooperation with Taleb. Fatima is a tough-minded woman who devotes much of her spare time to an association for the support of those – like herself – who have lost a child to leukaemia. Hidouchi likes and respects her – and believes she may be a source of valuable information about former DRS agent Zoubiri as well as the infamous General Mokrani.

Fatima is waiting for Hidouchi at one of the tables with a view of the inner courtyard, where the café's eponymous grapefruit tree grows. She looks well and contented – noticeably more contented than when she had to dance to the tune of various overbearing superiors at the DSS. 'I always forget how tall you are, Souad,' she says, smiling up at her as she approaches. 'It is good to see you.'

'Likewise.' Hidouchi sits down. 'Retirement clearly agrees with you.'

'I am gladder every day to have left all of it behind. Life holds more than filing intelligence reports.'

'Your work held more, as I recall.'

'Maybe. But let's not talk about that.' She catches something in Hidouchi's expression. 'Ah. I see.'

'What do you see?'

'That you have not made time to see me in the middle of the working week merely for the pleasure of my company.'

'Well . . .'

'Don't worry. I'm not offended. I know how busy you must be. Are you here to tap my memory?'

'Yes, Fatima. I confess I am.'

'Then I will need an extra large slice of the lime and pomegranate cake. Once I have eaten a few forkfuls of that . . . you can ask me whatever you like.'

*

Cake is duly ordered – and delivered, along with mint tea for Fatima and black coffee for Hidouchi. The Pamplemousse is free of the masculinity of some cafés. There are no shisha pipes in use, no knots of domino players. Two women may meet here and speak freely, though in their case Hidouchi and Fatima proceed in a guarded *sotto voce*. The intelligence world is governed by caution at all times and places. And it is not a world from which complete retirement is possible.

As it turns out, Fatima mentions Mokrani before Hidouchi even asks her about him. 'I didn't see *Microscope* on Sunday evening – current affairs programmes depress me – but I gather a DGSN officer made some highly injudicious remarks on air suggesting General Mokrani was implicated in the Boudiaf assassination. Would that happen to be connected in any way' – she eyes Hidouchi over the rim of her tea glass – 'with the questions you have for me?'

'It would,' Hidouchi concedes.

'But the DGSN have subsequently exonerated Mokrani and he's *persona non grata* with the DSS, so . . .'

'I can't go into details, Fatima. As you know, his son is a serving DSS agent. It would be . . . problematic . . . if he were compromised by revelations about his father's past activities.'

'Well, if you're asking me whether there was any substance to what the policeman said on television, once upon a time I'd have ridiculed the idea. But now I think . . . anything's possible. If not probable. I didn't realize what a sinister organization I was actually part of. Things improved after the DSS came into being, but during *la décennie noire* . . .' Fatima shrugs. 'I'm sure you don't think the DGSN statement clearing Mokrani of suspicion means anything one way or the other.'

'No. I don't.'

'There's really not much I can tell you about Mokrani. He was typical of his kind. Arrogant, demanding, short-tempered. The sort of man a young woman was wise to avoid finding herself alone with. Probably not the most unpleasant of the people I ever worked for, but close. And in charge of pre-emptive operations. Which could mean . . . whatever he and his kind wanted it to mean. The DRS made its own rules in his day.'

'So I understand.'

'Maybe I could be more helpful if you told me exactly what you're trying to find out.'

The time has come to be more specific. Hidouchi leans forward, lowering her voice still further. 'Did you know an agent called Khaled Zoubiri?'

'Yes. He worked for Mokrani. His right-hand man, you could say.'

'When did he leave the service?'

'At the same time as Mokrani. *Exactly* the same time, as I recall.'

'He retired as well?'

'No. He was some way short of retirement age. He just quit. Went to work privately for Mokrani, so the story went.'

'Work for him as what?'

'Bodyguard, general assistant, fixer. That kind of thing.'

'So, he and Mokrani were always close?'

'Yes. But why are you interested in Zoubiri?'

'Oh . . .' As much for Fatima's sake as her own, Hidouchi cannot answer the question. All she can say is: 'Something's come up . . . in which he may be involved.'

A narrowing of Fatima's gaze suggests the ambiguity of Hidouchi's reply is not lost on her. 'Tell me, Souad, are you acting . . . on your own initiative?'

'What if I were?'

'I'd advise against it. People like Mokrani and Zoubiri . . . aren't people you should mess with.' Fatima sips her tea and cocks her head slightly as she looks at Hidouchi. 'But you already know that, of course. And my advice is entirely futile, isn't it?

You're going to do whatever it is you've decided to do. You're that sort of person. It's in your nature.'

'I guess it is.'

'Did you know I own a share in a property in the Casbah?'

'No.' Hidouchi isn't sure Fatima is to be envied on that account, despite the Casbah's historical significance as the heart of the pre-colonial city, redolent of a bygone age with its tangled alleyways and crumbling steps and secluded courtyards. Decades of neglect have brought dereliction and disintegration to many of its buildings. 'Did you inherit it?'

'Yes. From a great-uncle. It's uninhabitable now. Falling apart, in fact. It's propped up with joists. My brothers and sisters would like to sell it. So would I. For whatever it would fetch, however little. It's no use to us.'

'So, is there a problem about selling?'

'We can't trace all the owners of a share. There are countless cousins we've lost touch with who would also have to agree. Legally, it's a nightmare. And so . . . it just stands there, mouldering.'

'That's a pity.'

'Yes. It is. But my point, Souad, is that's how this country is. Full of tangled relationships and intractable problems. Don't make the mistake of thinking you can actually resolve any of it. It's impossible. You can only be happy if you understand and accept that.' Fatima frowns. 'I'm wasting my breath, aren't I?'

Hidouchi responds with a smile. And says nothing.

Wednesday and Thursday pass slowly and uneventfully in Beni Saf. The fishing boats come and go. The sun rises and sets. Taleb cooks modest meals for himself, wanders the streets and sits on benches in sheltered spots smoking – the housekeeper having told him smoking in the holiday home of her employer will not be tolerated.

Trawls on his laptop of assorted Algerian and French newspapers reveal that the story of his outburst on television has rapidly faded from the attention of the media; it appears Bouras's strategy of denying Mokrani ever came under official suspicion for involvement in the Boudiaf assassination and despatching Taleb on indefinite sick leave has paid off.

Taleb double-checks by buying a selection of daily papers from a small *magasin de journaux* down by the harbour. *Le Monde* and *Figaro* are both stocked there. They have made rather more of Abidi's allegation of French complicity in the assassination than Mokrani's role and have managed to misrender Taleb's name as Tabel – a typographical error for which he decides he should be grateful. *El Watan*, meanwhile, helpfully dismisses the matter as '*une tempête dans un verre d'eau*'.

Taleb assumes the looming weekend will attract visitors to Beni Saf, even at this time of the year, and mentally prepares himself to lie low for the duration. He is feeling relatively optimistic about being recalled to Algiers and active service before too long and tries, with some success, to brighten his Thursday evening by preparing a sardine supper according to a mildly ambitious recipe he finds in the kitchen of his home from home.

This goes surprisingly well and he is relaxing afterwards by watching a roustabout Gérard Depardieu film on the television, the multiplicity of available channels having come as a revelation to him, when his telephone rings.

He has not answered most of the calls he has received since arriving in Beni Saf, but, checking the caller's number in this case, he answers instantly. Unfortunately, his simultaneous attempt to lower the volume on the television achieves the opposite result and only after conclusively silencing Depardieu by turning the set off is he able to make himself heard.

'Director?'

'You have company, Taleb?'

'No, Director. I'm alone. I'm sorry. I pressed the wrong arrow on the remote. I was, er, watching a film.'

'Really? Well, I hope you weren't enjoying it. Because you won't be seeing the end.'

'I won't?'

'Your holiday is over, Taleb. I want you back here. Immediately.'

'Has . . . something happened?'

'It has. But I can't discuss it with you over the phone. Suffice to say we are dealing with an urgent problem. I will need you here tomorrow morning.'

Since tomorrow is Friday, the urgency is apparent. 'Can I ask—'

'No,' Bouras interrupts. 'You cannot ask. I will meet you in the car park at Ben Aknoun Zoo at nine o'clock.'

'But . . . I will have to drive through the night.'

'I'm afraid you will, yes. I'm sorry, Taleb, but you have helped to create this situation. We must all accept the resulting inconvenience. I had other plans for tomorrow myself.'

'Is there . . . some reason . . . why we aren't meeting at HQ?'

'Yes, Taleb. There is some reason. Which I will explain to you. Tomorrow morning. Now, I suggest you start packing.'

Pressure of work – *official* work – has prevented Hidouchi from doing much digging into the affairs of General Hamza Mokrani. She has established the location of his villa, a sprawling residence in Hydra with walls high enough to guarantee almost total privacy. She has managed a few hours of nocturnal surveillance, during which she observed the departure of the general – a jowly, muffled figure – in a black limousine driven, she is more or less certain, by Khaled Zoubiri. But this amounts to very little in the way of hard information.

The same could be said for her accumulation of intelligence on Rochdi Abidi. He has a comfortable apartment in Telemly, but his comings and goings are difficult to track. All she has managed to do so far is follow him one evening to an expensive restaurant, where he dined on apparently jovial terms with a man she sneaked a picture of on her phone, later running the image through the DSS's facial recognition system – with no result.

She wonders if she should heed Fatima's advice and leave well alone. But even as she wonders she knows she isn't going to do that.

Not yet, anyway.

FOUR

THE LONG DRIVE BACK TO ALGIERS THROUGH THE DAMP JANUARY night is an ordeal; Taleb's eyesight isn't, he realizes, what it used to be. Nor is his stamina. He's soon too exhausted to feel apprehensive about why Bouras has recalled him from exile. The facts will be made known to him when the time comes.

He is at least early for his appointment with Bouras: dawn has not yet broken. Accordingly, he stays on the autoroute to the airport, where he has a rudimentary wash and shave and some filling though tasteless breakfast. He doesn't exactly feel better, but he is at least more alert. A couple of cigarettes, standing outside in the damp twilight, apply a modest sharpening of his senses.

He heads into Algiers. The roads are largely empty at this hour on a Friday morning. No one is moving. The city stirs with leaden reluctance.

Ben Aknoun Zoo is not open yet and there is little to remind Taleb of his last visit, with Serene and Lili, close to thirty years ago. That was a summer Saturday and somewhere he has a photograph of Lili standing grinning in front of the zoo's main entrance, with three carved elephants parading over the gate above her head. He hasn't looked at it – hasn't looked *for* it – for a very long time. And he wishes he hadn't thought of it now.

He pulls into the car park. The only vehicle there is Bouras's Mercedes. The director is visible behind the steering wheel, his expression unreadable at this distance. But Taleb doubts he is smiling.

He pulls up beside the Mercedes and climbs out. He takes a deep breath, bracing himself for whatever is to come, as he walks round to the passenger side of the car. The lock stalks inside the Mercedes rise. He opens the door. Bouras's natural cast of face verges on placidity. But there is nothing placid about the frown he gives Taleb this morning. 'Get in,' is all he says.

Taleb obeys. He closes the door behind him and catches the scent of Bouras's aftershave. The director is always meticulously groomed, even in a crisis.

'Don't rock the boat,' he says quietly. 'That was my instruction to you before your television appearance, wasn't it? Make no waves.'

'It was, Director. Word for word.'

'And yet . . .'

'*El Watan* dismissed the matter as a storm in a glass of water.'

'They were wrong.'

'They were?'

'Assuredly.' Bouras sighs. 'There has been, I have to tell you . . . an escalation.'

'What, er, exactly . . .'

Bouras starts the Mercedes, reverses clear of Taleb's Renault and drives towards the exit. 'I will explain on the way. There is no time to be lost.'

'Where are we going?'

'General Mokrani's villa.'

'What . . . what has happened?'

'You will recall Mokrani's son is a serving DSS agent?'

'Yes.'

'That makes the situation difficult – for us as well as the DSS.'

'What, er . . . is the situation?'

'Karim Mokrani has been undertaking a sensitive mission in France. Somehow, a hostile group identified him as Mokrani's son. Inflamed, apparently, by the allegations you and Abidi made against the general, they kidnapped him and are now demanding a substantial ransom for his release.'

An escalation, Bouras called it. Yes, Taleb concedes to himself, it is certainly that. The storm is no longer confined, if it ever was, to a glass of water. 'The kidnappers actually referred to the *Microscope* broadcast?'

'Yes, Taleb, they did. Specifically to a *Canal Plus* report on the broadcast, which evidently gave short shrift to our denial that Mokrani had ever been a serious suspect after the Boudiaf assassination. The kidnappers call themselves *les souveniristes* and say the ransom money will be donated to surviving relatives of people killed during *la décennie noire* – killed, in their contention, by General Mokrani and his kind.'

'How much are they asking for?'

'Five million Swiss francs.'

'*Swiss francs?*'

'Yes. About half a billion dinars at the current exchange rate. Evidently they have as little faith in our currency as most investors.'

That is understandable, though to Taleb's mind a little odd. If they really intend to give the money away as they claim, they would want dinars. He decides against raising the point, however. 'How did they find Karim Mokrani?'

'Who knows? The DSS isn't eager to reveal what he was doing in France. If we knew, it might explain how he came to the attention of these people. For the moment, it hardly matters.'

They're on the autoroute now, heading back the way Taleb came from the airport. The exit for Hydra's not far ahead, which means their encounter with Karim Mokrani's anxious and outraged father doesn't lie very far in Taleb's troubled future, especially given the speed Bouras is driving at, which by Taleb's estimate is about twenty kilometres per hour above the limit. 'I'm still not sure, Director, about why we're calling on General Mokrani.'

'Are you not?'

'Does the DSS propose to pay the ransom?'

'General Mokrani will pay it. Perhaps with an unofficial contribution from DSS funds. Perhaps not. I cannot say.'

'But without negotiation? Five million Swiss francs?'

'It's a lot, I agree. But I suspect the DSS is desperate to retrieve its agent before his captors – aggrieved expatriate Algerians, it seems safe to assume – extract damaging information from him. I'm told the French authorities know nothing of the kidnapping – or of Karim Mokrani's original mission – and the DSS want to keep it that way. So, the arrangements for payment of the ransom and his release are likely to be . . . fraught with difficulties.'

'I should say they are.'

'We are meeting General Mokrani this morning in the company of DSS Deputy Director Kadri to discuss the issue.' Kadri is Hidouchi's immediate superior at the DSS and has long harboured suspicions about her dealings with Taleb. Taleb has never actually met him and has no wish to. The same goes for General Mokrani. But clearly his wishes have no bearing on the matter.

'What exactly . . . do they want to discuss?'

'They have not told me. But Kadri insisted you be present.' Bouras flicks down the indicator for the Hydra exit. 'I have pondered why that might be, of course.'

Taleb is pondering the same thing. 'General Mokrani won't simply want to berate me for endangering his son.'

'No, Taleb. He won't.'

'You think . . .'

'I think the DSS does not wish to send one of their own to deal with this for fear he or she will become a second hostage. As far as they are concerned, direct engagement with the kidnappers is not an option. To carry out this negotiation they require the services of a neutral party.'

'Such as the police officer who pointed *les souveniristes* in Mokrani's direction in the first place?'

'Who is clearly not in the DSS's pocket and has the additional advantage of knowing nothing that could be useful to *les souveniristes*.'

'Me.' Taleb states this more as a dismal fact than a question.

'Exactly so.'

They drive on in silence for a minute or so. Bouras has slowed to a respectful forty now they are cruising along the leafy villa-lined roads of Hydra. Taleb wonders if he should ask the director to stop and let him out. He cannot be forced to do the DSS's bidding. He can walk away from this if he really wants to.

'Your cooperation with the DSS will clear the air between our departments, Taleb, which would be of great assistance to me,' says Bouras. 'And it will atone for your recent lapse of judgement, facilitating your immediate return to active police service.'

'An opportunity too good to miss, then.'

Bouras chuckles mirthlessly. 'We know far too little – indeed, nothing – about what is really at stake. Everyone is likely to have a hidden agenda. If something goes wrong – which in ransom handovers and hostage releases is hardly unusual – you will be on your own and far from home. I will not be able to protect you.'

'That is understood, Director,' says Taleb bleakly.

'You'll do it, then?'

'If that's what they ask of me.'

'Well, as to that, we'll soon find out. We're here.'

Bouras slows to a crawl and turns into the gated entrance of a high-walled villa. He lowers his window and speaks into a microphone set in the wall leading to the gates. All he says is, 'Bouras and Taleb, DGSN.'

It is enough. The gates swing open. Bouras drives through.

They head along a curved and cobbled drive towards a large white-rendered villa of conventional design. It appears to Taleb's eye to be the standard high-end retreat for those who have prospered from assiduous service to *le pouvoir*: comfortable in an overdone and tasteless manner, probably with gold taps in the likeness of dolphins in the bathrooms and gilt-framed ceiling mirrors in some of the bedrooms. Not that he is likely to see anything of the bathrooms *or* the bedrooms. He and the director are here on sufferance – and on very serious business.

A figure steps out onto the drive as they near the front door and waves for them to carry on round towards the rear of the villa. It appears a formal greeting is not going to be extended to them.

They pass a swimming pool, covered for winter, on their way to a wide-porticoed area on the garden side of the villa. A man dressed in a black suit and white shirt is waiting for them beneath the portico. He signals for them to stop. Bouras pulls up beside him.

Looking at the man out of the window, Taleb is shocked to realize who he is: Khaled Zoubiri, thirty years older than when they last met, his good looks then turned to thin-haired gauntness now. But he still appears muscular – and arrogant with it.

He casts Taleb a dismissive glance as he rounds the car and opens Bouras's door. '*Sabah al-khair*,' he says expressionlessly. 'Deputy Director Kadri is already here.'

Bouras gets out of the car. 'You are with Kadri?' he asks.

'No. But Taleb knows me.'

Taleb has got out on his side of the car. When Bouras looks across at him, he nods in confirmation. 'His name is Zoubiri. He was with the DRS in 1992. Now . . . I'm not sure.'

'I assist the general,' says Zoubiri.

'Nothing's changed, then.'

'Let's go in,' says Bouras. His glance in Taleb's direction carries a warning that he has no time for snide bickering between the two men.

They follow Zoubiri into the villa and along a short hallway, then turn in to a large high-ceilinged room furnished as if for conferences, with a long central table, around which a dozen or so chairs are arranged.

Two of the chairs are already occupied. In one sits a slightly built man in a suit and tie, balding and bespectacled, with a laptop open in front of him. He barely looks up from the screen as they enter. The other man Taleb assumes to be Kadri, whom he's never met but feels as if he recognizes from Hidouchi's descriptions of him: lean, sleekly dressed, with short-cropped dark hair, a suggestion of designer stubble and a smile that verges on a sneer. He rises to greet them.

'Director Bouras, Superintendent Taleb. Thank you for coming.' Naturally, he doesn't look grateful. He nods to Zoubiri. 'Please tell General Mokrani we're ready for him.'

Zoubiri retreats, closing the door behind him. A brief silence falls, broken only by the delicate tappings of the seated man on his laptop keyboard. He looks up again and nods to Taleb and Bouras. 'Spühler,' he announces, apparently by way of introducing himself. The name and the accent sound German.

Kadri swiftly supplies clarification regarding Spühler's nationality. 'Herr Spühler has flown from Switzerland to join us. He manages General Mokrani's finances.'

Of course he does, thinks Taleb. The final mark of success in the world governed by *le pouvoir* is to store one's dubiously acquired wealth in the country devoted to the storage of dubiously acquired wealth – and to have it managed by someone like Herr Spühler. He wonders if the kidnappers knew Mokrani's money was safely hidden from prying eyes in Switzerland when they specified payment in Swiss francs. Perhaps they wanted to spare him the inconvenience of conversion into another currency.

'I hope General Mokrani understands that we are here to consider proposals for assisting in his son's release on a strictly unofficial basis,' says Bouras.

'We are all here on a strictly unofficial basis,' Kadri responds. 'This meeting is not taking place.'

'I suppose you have many meetings of that kind,' says Taleb, drawing another glance of reproof from Bouras.

Kadri seems unoffended. 'I do. But I believe you have some familiarity with our working methods, Superintendent, so you shouldn't be surprised.'

Before Taleb can fashion a response, a set of double doors on the far side of the room opens and General Hamza Mokrani arrives amongst them.

Stout and wheezing, with a loose-fleshed face, thin lacquered hair and a moustache apparently modelled on the late President Bouteflika, Mokrani is wearing a baggy black tracksuit, which despite its bagginess does not conceal his substantial paunch. The excessively large gold watch glittering at his wrist is the only sign of his wealth. Taleb takes it to be one of those impossibly expensive brands which keep perfect time under the ocean or in outer space. His inability to tell which of those brands it is says everything about his lowly place in the pecking order.

'You are the man who put my son in danger.' Mokrani points a wavering finger in Taleb's direction. 'I curse you for that.' It is not a promising start to their exchanges.

Bouras looks at Taleb, silently insisting that an apology be offered up. Taleb does his best to comply. 'I deeply regret if anything I said during the *Microscope* broadcast had that effect, General.'

'The lies you told, you mean? The foul and groundless accusations you made against me?'

'I think it was the journalist, Abidi, who made allegations against you. I merely—'

'Did your best to best to back them up with weaselly words about my supposed "foreknowledge" of the Boudiaf assassination.'

'Please, General,' interjects Bouras. 'Recriminations at this stage are pointless. Superintendent Taleb had no way of knowing your son's current duties at the DSS put him in a vulnerable position. Or that this group, *les souveniristes*, would be provoked into such extreme action by exaggerated reports of what he said.'

Mokrani plants a large hand on the table and rests his substantial weight on it. He glares at Bouras and Taleb in turn. 'Perhaps not. I assume nothing where Superintendent Taleb's loyalties are concerned. What I require is proof of his commitment to securing my son's freedom.'

'If you want me to attempt to negotiate his release, General, I will.' Taleb speaks slowly and deliberately. He assumes an unconditional offer such as this is the only kind of proof Mokrani is likely to accept.

Mokrani goes on glaring at him. 'I have only agreed to involve you because the kidnappers insist on speaking to someone not linked to the DSS.'

'And we think they will accept you as a neutral party because of your performance on television,' says Kadri. 'Director Bouras has assured us you are – *usually* – one of his most diligent and reliable officers.'

'I will do everything I can,' says Taleb.

'For your sake,' Mokrani growls menacingly, 'your *everything* had better be enough. If this goes wrong because you mishandle the situation, you will answer to me. You understand?'

'Yes.' Taleb certainly does understand. He suspects Mokrani will come for him if his son ends up dead, whether or not such an outcome is Taleb's fault. Failure simply isn't a healthy option.

'I suggest we sit down and discuss the details,' says Kadri with a sickly smile.

There is a drawing back of chairs and a settling at the table.

Spühler closes his laptop and begins to give them his attention, as if the wrangling to this point has not concerned or even interested him.

'Perhaps we should begin with the particulars of when Agent Mokrani was taken and how the kidnappers made contact,' Bouras proposes, reasonably enough.

'Agent Mokrani has been engaged for several weeks in France on a sensitive mission, the nature of which you do not need to be made aware of,' says Kadri. Taleb has his doubts about not needing to know what Karim Mokrani has been doing in France, but he's quite sure contesting the point isn't a good idea. 'He has been staying at a villa near Aix-en-Provence, to which he did not return following a drive into Aix the evening before last. His car was found abandoned on the roadside about three kilometres from the villa. Yesterday morning, the kidnappers telephoned General Mokrani – having obtained his number from Agent Mokrani, we assume – and delivered their ultimatum. They require a cash payment of five million Swiss francs – purportedly to be passed on to the families of people killed during *la décennie noire* – in return for Agent Mokrani's release. They claim he is a legitimate target because of his father's involvement in the Boudiaf assassination, a malicious fiction devised by the journalist Abidi and given regrettable credence' – Kadri looks directly at Taleb – 'by your ill-judged comments during the *Microscope* broadcast. But that is their perception and we have to work with it, since denials on our part will be treated by them as a refusal to negotiate, which is not our position.'

'Have they set a deadline for payment?' asks Taleb, instantly regretting his use of the word *deadline*.

'Not precisely,' Kadri replies. 'They said they will call again tomorrow morning to agree terms. By then they require our neutral negotiator to be on hand at the villa to arrange delivery of the money and Agent Mokrani's release.'

'Is the money, er . . . readily available?'

'It will be in place by tomorrow morning.' Spühler's words emerge from his mouth almost with an echo, as if from a place of depth and darkness.

'We have booked you on a flight to Marseille this afternoon,' Kadri announces. 'A hire car will be waiting for you at Marseille airport. Herr Spühler will be on the same flight. You will follow him to the villa. The owners have agreed to accommodate you for the duration of the negotiations.'

'Who are the owners?'

'Their name is Elasse. They are . . . assisting us in another matter, which was the reason Agent Mokrani was there. But that is not relevant to your activities and it must be understood that you will confine your activities to what is strictly necessary to securing his release.'

'He will not interfere with an ongoing DSS operation,' says Bouras. 'Will you, Taleb?'

'Absolutely not,' says Taleb solemnly, wondering as he does so whether he will be able to abide by the pledge. Every time Kadri says Karim Mokrani's mission is unconnected to his kidnapping Taleb's suspicion grows that it might be.

'Agent Irmouli is also present at the villa,' says Kadri. So, a second DSS agent is on the scene. Whatever the supposedly irrelevant matter is it can hardly be trivial. 'He will assist you as best he can, although responsibility for arrangements made and decisions taken will rest solely with you. I trust that's clear.'

The buck would start, stop and stay with Taleb. *That* was certainly clear to him. 'What can you tell us about this group – *les souveniristes*?' he asks.

'Very little,' Kadri replies airily, as if his department's lack of information about the kidnappers isn't any kind of reflection on their competence. 'They're evidently quite a new grouping. Their affiliations and purposes are . . . obscure. We believe our French counterparts may know something about them, but we don't wish to involve the DGSE in this matter for a variety of compelling reasons, so regrettably . . .'

'I'll be operating in the dark?'

Kadri looks down his nose at him. 'Any intelligence we turn up will be communicated to you as soon as possible.'

In the dark, then. There it is.

'Agent Irmouli will supply you with a gun.'

'He will?'

'Yes, since you won't be able to take your DGSN Beretta with you on the flight to Marseille. Unless you prefer to be unarmed, of course.' Kadri smiles, perhaps in recognition of the irony that in so many ways Taleb will be unarmed, with or without a gun.

'How will you put the kidnappers in touch with me?'

'When they call General Mokrani, he will give them the number of this phone.' Kadri takes a phone out of his pocket and slides it across the table towards Taleb. 'They will then call you. And you will comply with whatever arrangements they specify for the handover of the money and the release of Agent Mokrani.'

'Handover and release will have to be simultaneous. Otherwise they may get the money and we may get . . . nothing.'

'What does he mean?' Mokrani cuts in.

Kadri ignores the question, a reaction Taleb finds as interesting as it is disturbing. Evidently the general isn't calling the shots even if he thinks he is. 'Have you ever handled a kidnapping before, Superintendent?' Kadri asks.

'Yes. I have.' There is no need to relate how that turned out and Taleb senses Kadri has no intention of asking.

'Then you will be well equipped to deal with the complexities of such matters. Our priority – our absolute priority – is the release of Agent Mokrani.'

'He must be freed.' General Mokrani's voice is knotted with emotion. Whatever Taleb's opinion of the man, he is still a father, beside himself with worry about his son. Some truths transcend others.

'There is a possibility,' says Taleb, choosing his words carefully, 'that the kidnappers may demand more money once they realize we are willing to pay the ransom. Such people tend to be greedy in my experience, whatever their motivations.'

'Pay what they ask for,' says General Mokrani.

'But surely—'

'Supplementary funds can be made available,' comes a reverberating intervention from Spühler. 'If necessary.'

Taleb catches Spühler's eye. It is not apparent from his expression what ceiling there would be on any payment. But it is obvious Hamza Mokrani is an extremely wealthy man. As to the origins of his wealth, Taleb suspects he would agree with *les souveniristes* about that.

'The cooperation of your department is appreciated, Director,' Kadri says to Bouras. 'Of course, the need for such cooperation would never have arisen if Superintendent Taleb had exercised more self-control.'

'Is anything to be gained by pursuing that point?' Bouras looks sharply at Kadri. 'Superintendent Taleb can hardly do more to make up for his . . . lapse of judgement . . . than to agree to act as your negotiator in this . . . unfortunate matter.'

'You will free my son.' General Mokrani stares intently at Taleb. 'Otherwise . . .' His lip curls. He clearly wants to say more, perhaps to utter some dire threat. But in the end he says nothing.

It doesn't matter. The message is clear. *Les souveniristes* have a second hostage without knowing it: Taleb. His life is on the line along with Karim Mokrani's.

'I think everything has been said that needs to be said.' Kadri casts a cautioning glance at General Mokrani, as if to remind him that the DSS – not the DRS as it was when the general and others like him were in charge – is running this show. Though what the show actually is, Taleb is unsure. Something subtly or maybe not so subtly different from what has been presented to him. That would be his far from comforting guess. 'Let us hope all goes well.'

'The flight is at fourteen thirty hours,' intones Spühler.

'Quite so.' Kadri makes a show of consulting his watch. 'And time marches on. I suggest we terminate this meeting.'

There is no dissent on the point, although a low and indistinct rumbling emerges from Mokrani as he rises from his seat. His bloodshot eyes remain fixed on Taleb. It does not appear he is minded to wish him luck, though logically he ought to. Because Taleb suspects he is going to need all the luck that's going.

Kadri and Spühler linger as Taleb and Bouras leave the room. Perhaps there is more they need to discuss with Mokrani.

Outside, Zoubiri is loitering by Bouras's car. He eyes Taleb contemptuously, but says nothing. He moves towards the driver's door as Bouras approaches.

Suddenly, from somewhere out of sight, a stout elderly woman appears, dressed in a loose black *abaya* and a white headscarf. Her eyes are red and it's obvious she's been crying. She makes a bee-line for Taleb and clasps his hand in both of hers.

'*Salam alaykum*,' she says breathlessly, staring imploringly at him. 'You will save my son?'

'Come away,' says Zoubiri, grasping her by the arm and pulling.

'It's all right,' says Taleb. 'Let go of her.'

'She's not supposed to talk to you.'

The prohibition is puzzling. The mother of Karim Mokrani surely has as much right to be worried about him as his father.

'Take this.' The woman presses a photograph into Taleb's palm. Looking down at it, he sees a head-and-shoulders snap of a smiling, smartly suited young man, dark-haired and bright-eyed.

'There's no need for that,' snaps Zoubiri. 'It's years out of date anyway. We'll be sending you a recent picture.'

'I love him,' the woman says, still clasping Taleb's hand. 'He is my only child. I would give my life for him.'

'I know you would,' says Taleb soothingly. 'We're going to get him back for you.'

'You promise?'

'I promise to do everything in my power.'

'I pray every hour for his release.'

Zoubiri succeeds now in pulling her away, though the photograph remains with Taleb. She looks round fearfully at Zoubiri, then back at Taleb.

'They should not have taken Karim to punish us for his father's misdeeds.' So, she has no illusions about her husband's character – or what he may have done in the past. Taleb logs the thought.

'Be quiet.' Zoubiri's tone is harsh. He claps his hands on her shoulders and steers her towards the villa. 'Go inside.'

She obeys, gathering her scarf around her face as she goes. She casts one soulful glance back at Taleb before she vanishes from view. He thinks he will remember the anguish in her eyes for a long time. He has no doubt she is a suffering innocent in all of this. And he knows she is relying on him to save her son.

'Shall I take that?' Zoubiri reaches for the photograph. 'The general wouldn't want to lose it. And, like I say, we'll supply you with an up-to-date picture. Karim Mokrani doesn't look much like that any more.'

'I'll keep it.' Taleb slips the photograph into his jacket pocket. 'It would probably upset her to know I hadn't hung on to it. And I'll take good care of it.'

Zoubiri scowls. He appears tempted to take the matter further. But it's a bad idea, as he soon realizes. He steps back.

'Let's go,' says Bouras, opening the driver's door for himself and climbing into the car.

'Excuse me,' says Taleb, stepping round Zoubiri on his way to the car. 'I have a plane to catch.'

They drive away from the villa, initially in silence. Then Bouras says, 'You don't have to go, Taleb. You do know that, don't you?'

'I thought you wanted me to?'

'It's to the department's advantage for you to be seen to help the DSS out. And it redeems your tarnished reputation. But there's clearly a lot they're not telling us. Altogether too much for my liking.'

'Do I have a choice? If I change my mind and pull out, how will General Mokrani react?'

'Badly. You would probably have to remove yourself to some more distant spot than Beni Saf to escape his wrath. But in the circumstances . . . I would not blame you. Personally, that is. Obviously I *would* blame you when the ministry asked me to explain what had happened. I would have no alternative.'

'I understand, Director.'

'Yes. You understand. I sometimes think your problem, Taleb, is that you understand too much.'

'For that I can only apologize.'

'There is no need. Since I gather you do not intend to pull out.'

'I gave Karim Mokrani's mother my word.'

'Interesting. Your promise to her outweighs the undertakings you gave his father?'

'By a long way.'

'She would be glad to know that. He, on the other hand . . .' Bouras flaps a free hand expressively. 'Never mind. You're catching that flight?'

'Yes.'

'Then you should speak to Agent Hidouchi before you leave. We need – *you* need – to know what's really going on. Starting with the nature of Karim Mokrani's mission. I doubt it's as unrelated to his abduction as Kadri claimed. And then there are these . . . *souveniristes*. What's known about them? And who are the Elasses – Mokrani's French hosts? She's well placed to find the answers to those questions. And those answers may make all the difference.'

The same thought has already occurred to Taleb. The surprise is that Bouras has voiced his doubts and isn't disposed to do whatever the DSS tells him to. The director has never been the creature of the system he's widely believed to be. His true nature reveals itself at unexpected moments. And this is one of those moments.

'Call her now, Taleb. There's no time to be lost.'

Taleb phones Hidouchi's number. It rings . . . and it rings. Eventually, he has to leave a message. *'Call me as soon as you get this. It's urgent.'*

'How does Agent Hidouchi normally spend her Fridays?' Bouras asks.

'I don't know, Director. We don't live in each other's pocket. But I'm sure she'll check her phone.'

'Let's hope so.'

A movement in the wing mirror suddenly catches Taleb's attention. He bends forward and squints for a clearer view. Then he sees what it is: a motorcyclist, black-clad and tailing them at matching speed. 'She might have gone for a ride on her motorbike, of course.'

'You think so?'

'As a matter of fact, Director, I'm sure of it.'

She follows them into the still largely empty car park at Ben Aknoun Zoo and pulls up beside them. Taleb looks out of the open passenger window as she props her bike, removes her crash helmet and shakes out her hair.

'Only a very short holiday, then,' she says with a little half-smile Taleb has grown used to seeing.

'It was *cut* short.'

'So I see.'

'Did you follow us from Mokrani's villa?'

'Yes. I thought it might be worth checking if anything was happening there. I didn't expect to see my own boss going in – followed by you and Director Bouras.'

'We were never there,' says Bouras with a sigh.

'Of course not. Neither was Deputy Director Kadri. There was a meeting of people who were actually somewhere else.'

'I intend to go to the mosque as usual at noon. And to have lunch afterwards with my wife and daughters. That is the sum total of my ambitions for this particular Friday. Taleb, on the other hand . . .'

'Has lost his faith. And I am a woman. We have no commitments at noon.'

'Taleb is catching a flight to Marseille this afternoon. He has quite a wide range of commitments, as a matter of fact. I feel sure he will be happy to tell you all about them.'

'They involve Mokrani?'

'Oh yes. Father *and* son. Would you like to get out of the car, Taleb? I'm leaving.'

'Of course, Director.' Taleb clambers out.

'Keep me apprised of developments.' Taleb assumes he means by using the phone reserved for communications between the three of them they don't want others to know about: it has been a long-standing arrangement. 'And may Allah bless your endeavours.'

Taleb has never known Bouras to invoke the Almighty's name in such a way. Perhaps it is simply because today is Friday. Or perhaps he thinks divine intervention will be necessary if Taleb is to succeed. Either way, it doesn't sound like a resounding expression of confidence.

As Bouras drives away, Hidouchi gives Taleb a questioning look. 'Well?'

'I have a lot to tell you.'

'Evidently.'

Taleb glances around. There is no one anywhere close; no one, in fact, in sight at all. But still he lowers his voice. And begins.

When he's finished, he lights a cigarette and stands in a patch of weak sunshine, awaiting her verdict. It's not long in coming.

'I've never heard of *les souveniristes*, which I should have done if they're an extant terrorist group. I have no idea what Karim Mokrani's mission in France might have been. And I have no knowledge of the family he was staying with – the Elasses. The circumstances of Mokrani's abduction are suspicious on so many levels I think we can safely assume Kadri was lying to you – or at the very least giving you a lot less than all the facts.'

'You think I'm being set up?'

'I think someone is. I just don't know who. Or why.'

'Perhaps it doesn't matter. They want Karim Mokrani back. And they're happy to pay to get him. If most or all of it's his father's money, why should the DSS care?'

'You should care. You should tread warily over there.'

'I always tread warily in the land of our former colonial masters.' Not that Taleb is a frequent visitor to France. This will only be the fourth time he has been there. The first was his honeymoon, which hardly counts as it was so long ago. It was a different world in 1983. And he was a different man. 'But I have to go. And I won't have much choice about what happens when I get there.'

'Do you think Abidi is involved in this?'

'Why would he be?'

'Because he set it all in motion – with your unwitting assistance.'

'Well then . . . maybe.'

'It's time I gave Abidi some close attention.'

'Bouras would be pleased to hear that. He wants you to try and find out what's really going on.'

'While he sits safely behind his desk at Police HQ?'

'Sitting safely behind a desk goes with his job. But not with yours or mine, unfortunately.'

'You wouldn't want it any other way.'

'Sometimes I think I would, actually.' He takes a last drag on his cigarette, drops the butt at his feet and stubs it out meticulously with his shoe. 'Sometimes I think I'm too old for this kind of work.'

'Oh you are, Taleb, there's no doubt about it.' Bewilderingly, she smiles at him. 'Just as well you have me to back you up, isn't it?'

They agree to stay in contact by phone. Taleb tells Hidouchi to be careful and take no unnecessary risks. She tells him to stop talking to her like her father and to concentrate on his own safety. 'You're the one who's going to be on alien territory.'

Hidouchi is right about that. There's no doubt he'll be facing numerous hazards, most of which are all the more hazardous because he doesn't know what they'll be. For the moment, though, he's too tired from his overnight drive to think about the task that lies ahead. He drives to the parking garage, unattended at this hour on a Friday, and leaves his car by the gate, then drops the keys into the letterbox with a note asking Akram to move the car inside when he returns from the mosque.

Taleb doesn't need to return to his apartment, having all he's likely to require for travelling in the bag he took with him to Beni Saf. There's nothing to be done now but footslog his way down through largely empty streets to the railway station and catch the next shuttle train to the airport.

Once seated, he falls instantly asleep.

*

He's barely more than half awake when he navigates check-in at the airport and joins the gathering at the boarding gate for the flight to Marseille. There's no sign of Spühler until the last moment, when he appears as if by magic, presumably by some special route from the executive lounge where he's probably been nibbling cashews and sipping nectarine juice. Taleb catches his eye, but is rewarded with no more than an eyebrow-twitch of acknowledgement.

Spühler is in the small group of priority passengers boarding first and has doubtless already settled in his business class seat at the front of the plane when Taleb struggles along the aisle to his place near the rear. He's grateful to be as exhausted as he is, since he knows he'll soon be asleep again.

There's the usual chaos of luggage-stowing and settling in seats, then the standard announcements as the plane backs away from its stand and turns towards the runway. Taleb closes his eyes and lets his mind drift.

Into it, unbidden, come thoughts of the troubled history of relations between Algeria and the country he's flying to. His father was born in 1915 and often recalled playing as a child with his great-grandfather (Taleb's great-great-grandfather), who was then in his nineties and was at his birth in 1829 a citizen of the Ottoman Empire. The following year the French invaded and seized control of the country. In due course all Algerians became compulsorily French and Taleb's grandfather died fighting for France in the First World War. No one in Algeria appreciated or commemorated his sacrifice. He was simply one more casualty of historical irony.

As, it was distinctly possible, Taleb might himself become – a citizen of a free and independent Algerian republic since he was seven years old, but still held, like his forebears, in the grip of the past.

'Happy landings,' he murmurs under his breath like a prayer as the plane takes off and climbs into the sky.

FIVE

DUSK IS ALREADY ENCROACHING WHEN TALEB EMERGES INTO THE car park at Marseille airport and follows the directions given him at the Europcar hire desk to the vehicle he's been allocated: a Renault somewhat smaller and a lot newer than his own. The controls seem to have been redesigned with the bafflement of Renault drivers of a certain age as their specific objective. While Taleb's still struggling to stop the windscreen wipers, which launched into top speed mode as soon as he started the engine, Spühler cruises to a halt beside him in a beautifully restored grey Citroën that de Gaulle might have been willing to travel in and frowns impatiently at him through the open window.

'We need to go, Superintendent,' he says acidly. 'In case you hadn't noticed, it's not raining.'

'I had noticed, thank you.' The next twist of the wipers stalk mercifully does the trick and the manic squeak of dry rubber on glass ceases. 'That's got it.'

'Good. Let's go.' Spühler extends an arm through the window, offering a card to Taleb. 'Take this.'

'What is it?'

'We'll be following the D9 towards Aix and joining the

autoroute later. You'll need that to pay the toll. Unless you have the exact money in euros, of course.'

Taleb smiles tightly. 'Thank you.'

'You're most welcome.'

Welcome? In France? In Spühler's company? Assuredly, he feels neither.

Dusk is also encroaching in Algiers as Hidouchi walks towards the entrance to the colonial-era residence in Telemly that has been converted into expensive apartments, where Rochdi Abidi, veteran campaigning journalist, lives. The building and its surroundings look out of the price bracket of a mere journalist, particularly one who has often been a thorn in the flesh of *le pouvoir*. This is one more reason why Hidouchi harbours deep suspicions about his motives for staging his attention-grabbing show on national television the previous Sunday. Whatever his real motives, she feels certain they amount to rather more than exposing the truth about the Boudiaf assassination. That happened nearly thirty years ago. Something else – something in and of the present – is happening now.

She needs to speak to Abidi and she needs him to unburden himself to her. The best way to achieve that is to make him believe she has information valuable to him. So, rather than threaten him, which as a DSS agent she's well placed to do, she proposes to tempt him.

The area is reassuringly quiet and Hidouchi is discreetly dressed. She hasn't come on her motorbike. She's drawn no glances from the few passers-by she's encountered. Everything is going as she hoped.

She walks briskly but without hurrying up to the row of letterboxes serving the apartments and drops the letter she's written in a disguised hand into Abidi's box, then turns and moves calmly away.

She could have contacted Abidi by phone or email, but it's

vital there should be no trace of her approach to him. In addition to her official DSS phone she has a second unregistered one, which she tops up with cash only. It's essential for activities she wants her boss, Deputy Director Kadri, to know nothing about, which there seem to have been more and more of as her cooperation with Taleb has deepened.

She doesn't trust Kadri and it's perfectly obvious he doesn't trust her. But she can live with that. Just so long as she can operate without his oversight when she needs to.

The letter she's delivered to Abidi is intended to draw him out without giving anything away. She's confident it'll do the job. Journalists are curious by nature. They can't help following their nose. *I saw you on Microscope*, the handwritten message reads. *If you want inside information about double-dealing by the DRS in the past and the DSS in the present, call me. There are things I don't think should be kept secret any longer.* Beyond that there's just the number of the unregistered phone.

If he doesn't bite, she'll have to resort to more confrontational tactics. But she doubts it'll come to that. Abidi will call her. He won't be able to stop himself. She simply has to wait for the call to come.

Taleb drives north-east from Marseille airport, tailing Spühler's Citroën as it cruises through the gathering darkness into wooded countryside, then down into the valley where a carpet of light signals the proximity of Aix-en-Provence. They skirt the southern fringe of the city on the A8 autoroute, exiting a few kilometres to the east and heading north into the hills.

To this point Taleb has kept his bearings, despite having little to go on beyond road signs and the Renault's odometer. But now, in the deepness of the rural night, all he can do is concentrate on the rear lights of the Citroën. The going slows as the road narrows. Pebbles and dust kick up in the lead car's wake.

Then light glimmers ahead. Spühler turns in through a high-pillared gateway and Taleb glimpses in the headlights' glare a name carved into one of the pillars: *VILLA DES ORMEAUX*.

A curving tree-lined drive takes them to a gravelled area in front of the villa. Taleb can make out little of the building in the darkness. It's three-storeyed, with deep eaves and lights burning in most of the lower windows. There's a central block, with a wing attached on one diagonal. The entrance is ornately porticoed.

A couple of large SUVs are parked off to one side. A figure emerges from between the vehicles and moves forward as Taleb draws up beside the Citroën. He's tall and thin, dressed in dark clothes. There's something hawk-like about his profile. Taleb catches a reflected flash of light in his eyes that makes him look more predatory still. He opens the door of Taleb's car.

'Welcome to the Villa des Ormeaux, Superintendent. I am Agent Irmouli.'

'Pleased to meet you,' Taleb responds formulaically. He climbs out of the car. As he does so, he notices a second man, more heavily built, lingering in the shadows near the SUVs.

'Agent Jahid,' says Irmouli, reading the direction of his glance. 'Don't worry about him. Don't worry about *me*. We're here to make sure everything goes smoothly.' Irmouli smiles. 'As I hope it will.'

'Me too.'

'You should hope that. These kidnappers aren't playing games.'

'I'm here to secure Agent Mokrani's release. I'm not playing games either.'

'I am glad to hear that. Herr Spühler—' Irmouli turns towards the Citroën. Spühler gazes out dispassionately at him through the open driver's window. 'The finance will be ready?'

'Of course. I will return with the money when I hear arrangements have been made. Until then . . .' He looks at Taleb. 'The fate of my client's son is in your hands, Superintendent. I wouldn't advise you to disappoint him.' With that, he raises the window. The Citroën circles tightly, then heads back along the drive towards the gate at some speed.

'They breed them cold in Switzerland,' says Irmouli. 'But I'm told we can count on him.'

'It seems we have to – literally.'

'Quite. Let's go in.'

They take the few steps up to the portico and enter through double doors. A long, wide marble-floored hall greets them. There are doorways to either side and a grand curving staircase ahead. Beyond the staircase a ground-floor gallery leads off towards the rear of the house. A middle-aged woman dressed in black – skirt, high-necked jacket and headscarf – moves briskly towards them along the gallery. Taleb wonders if she is a member of the family that he's been told owns the villa – the Elasses – but she looks far more Algerian than French.

'This is Taleb?' she asks. There is no smile and no warmth in her tone. She carries with her an air of authority.

To which Irmouli is not immune. He almost bows to her as he says, 'Yes, this is Taleb.'

'I am Lydia Seghir,' the woman announces. 'Thank you for coming, Superintendent.'

'I'm here to help in any way I can.'

'Delivery of the ransom payment and the release of Agent Mokrani. That, I think, will be quite enough for you to accomplish.'

Taleb wonders if Lydia Seghir can really be DSS, as Irmouli's subservience to her implies. Hidouchi has never mentioned her, which he feels she would have. He begins to reach for the words that will enable him to clarify her status. 'Are you . . . that is . . .'

'I am a ministerial official, Superintendent, charged with conducting confidential business here with DSS assistance.'

'You're with the Defence Ministry?' It seems the obvious answer, since the DSS falls under Defence Ministry supervision.

'No,' says Seghir. 'Not Defence.' She doesn't appear minded to be more specific than that. And the steadiness of her gaze suggests she won't welcome further enquiries from Taleb.

'Whatever you need to facilitate your success in freeing Agent Mokrani will be supplied to you, Superintendent,' she continues. 'But I must warn you that there are discussions taking place here between influential parties into which our government has entered on condition of complete secrecy for all involved. You are not cleared to be told the nature or purpose of those discussions and you will therefore conduct yourself as inconspicuously as possible while you are here. Business has been suspended today, but will resume tomorrow, when you may see various people coming and going. It would be best if you did not make any approach to them. Generally, other than when meals are served, they will be in the conference room at the rear of the villa. You will kindly regard that as a no-go zone and confine yourself to the upper rooms which will be placed at your disposal.'

'I understand.' He does not understand, of course. Nor is he intended to. But the word *secrecy* has not eluded him. Algerian government participation in confidential discussions with unidentified parties on French soil is a big deal, potentially a *very* big deal.

'It would also be desirable for you to refrain from contacting Monsieur and Madame Elasse, our hosts here. I am sorry to put it like this, Superintendent, but the fewer people you have any dealings with during your stay the better.'

'I'll do my best to keep out of everyone's way.'

'That would be appreciated. If you need to speak to me about operational matters concerning your business here, advise Agent Irmouli and he will let me know. Is that clear to you?'

'It is.'

'Good. I'll leave you to settle in.'

She gives him a tight little smile, then turns and walks away along the gallery.

'She has an assistant with her called Touati,' says Irmouli in an undertone. 'Jahid and I are also on site. And there's back-up in reserve off site. That's what our presence amounts to. The various . . . delegates, shall we call them? . . . have security of their own. Give them a wide berth.'

'I'll do that.'

'Don't ask any questions. Don't stick your policeman's nose into anything. Concentrate on paying the kidnappers off and getting Mokrani released, alive and well. Got it?'

'I got it before I left Algeria.'

'OK. Follow me, then.'

They set off up the stairs. 'Nice house,' Taleb remarks conversationally as they go, though *nice* is a considerable understatement. Richly patterned rugs, gleaming chandeliers and heavily framed oil paintings of rustic scenes all have the unmistakable flavour of affluence.

'Fancy living somewhere like this, do you?'

'I'm not saying that. Just that it's . . .'

'French. French is what it is.'

They reach a broad circular landing, then climb a second flight of stairs to a humbler part of the house, where Irmouli opens a door that gives access to a much narrower flight of stairs. They start to climb again.

'They'd have put the children and the servants up here in the past,' Irmouli goes on. 'Now it's just used for tame Algerians like you and me.'

The ascent is taking its toll on Taleb. He pauses to catch his breath. When he looks up, he sees Irmouli is already at the top of the stairs, gazing down contemptuously at him.

'Too long out of the field, Taleb?'

'Maybe. But apparently . . . I'm the man for this job.'

'So I'm told.'

Taleb makes it up to the attic landing, where the ceilings are significantly lower. Irmouli leads the way along a narrow passage, then turns in through an open low-lintelled doorway.

Taleb follows him into a small dormer-windowed bedroom. It's clear he isn't going to be luxuriously accommodated. The furniture comprises a narrow bed, a wardrobe and a dressing-table.

'You can use the room next door as well,' says Irmouli. 'There's a desk and chair in there. And a telecoms socket I've confirmed is functioning. You should keep the phone they're going to call you on fully charged.'

'You think so?'

Irmouli acknowledges the sarcasm with a slight tilt of the head. 'I'm just reminding you to concentrate on the task you've been set.'

'You don't need to.'

'I've been told to give you this.' From inside his coat Irmouli takes a gun – a Beretta, like the one Taleb normally carries. He hands it over. 'Let's hope you don't need to use it. But just in case . . .' He adds a box of bullets.

'Thank you.'

'You'll be careful not to shoot anyone you shouldn't, won't you?'

'I'm always careful.'

'That's good to know.'

'What about Mokrani? Was he careful? How did he manage to get himself kidnapped – considering all his training and experience?'

'He was fast-tracked for promotion. I reckon it went to his head and made him sloppy.'

It didn't sound as if Irmouli was either a friend or an admirer of Karim Mokrani. 'I was surprised to hear the DSS knows nothing of the kidnappers – these *souveniristes* as I gather they call themselves.'

'It's been a nasty surprise for all of us.'

'Especially Agent Mokrani.'

'Yes. Especially him.'

'Do you think they've been keeping the villa under surveillance?'

'If they were, they aren't any longer. We've combed the surroundings and all possible observation positions.'

'And the ... discussions ... you're staging here? They go on regardless?'

'They do.'

'Aren't any of the ... influential parties ... concerned there might be a threat to their security?'

'They're happy to continue.'

'So, they're not concerned?'

'You're in danger of straying beyond your remit, Taleb.'

'They do know about the kidnap, don't they?'

'I don't communicate directly with the participants. That is a matter for Seghir.'

'Are you saying they haven't been told?'

'I'm saying you have a job to do here and I recommend you focus on doing it. There's a bathroom at the end of the passage. And if you want anything to eat you can go down to the kitchen. The cook's Algerian. Her name's Noussa. She'll keep you well fed. For the rest ... stay out of it. Stay *well* out of it.'

Taleb registers the warning, but is already more or less certain it won't be possible to ignore what's going on at the villa. He's only been given half a story and there are plenty of inconsistencies in it, most of which he strongly suspects have some bearing on the kidnap. For the present, though, he'll play along obligingly. He has to.

Unpacking takes all of about five minutes. Then, with Irmouli off the scene, Taleb descends to the kitchen. During the last flight of stairs down into the basement he's lured on by an appetising aroma and soon he encounters Noussa the cook, an encouragingly rotund woman of sixty or so, with a beaming smile and a halo of grey hair. She's clearly been told to expect him.

'I hope you like tajine,' she says, turning from the range to greet him, wooden spoon in hand.

'I'm Algerian,' he responds, grinning in eager anticipation.

'It's mutton.'

'My favourite.'

'Sit down, then. It'll be ready soon.'

Taleb takes a seat at a large old table. 'My name is Taleb,' he says. 'Police Superintendent Mouloud Taleb.'

'Agent Irmouli told me. I am Noussa Rezig. My husband is the gardener and handyman. I cook and clean.'

'How long have you worked here?'

'Oh, it must be . . . forty years or more.'

'When did you leave Algeria?'

'At the time of independence, when I was a baby.'

Taleb decides to ask no more about the circumstances of her family's departure from their homeland. The likeliest explanation for it is that they were *harkis* – those Algerians who served or supported the French administration. If so, leaving with the French was the difference between life and death. Brutal slaughter was the fate of many thousands of those who remained.

There is nothing to be gained by discussing such terrible things in the warm and tajine-scented kitchen of the Villa des Ormeaux. Taleb gazes up at the bags of onions and herbs suspended from the rafters. The atmosphere is soothing. But he can't afford to surrender to it.

'Do you know why I'm here?' he asks.

'Yes,' Noussa replies. 'My husband and I both hope you will be able to free Agent Mokrani.'

'Do you know why *he* was here?'

'The conference, you mean? We have no idea what that is about.'

'But you see the participants from day to day?'

'We see them. As you will. Why they come – what they discuss – is none of our concern.'

'Do your employers – the Elasses – often host such events?'

'No. There has been nothing like this before.'

'Do you live here – at the villa?'

'We live over the garage and workshop. You will be able to see it from the window of your room.'

'You know the area well?'

'Oh yes.'

'Have you noticed anything . . . unusual . . . recently?'

'The conference is unusual. Having DSS agents here is unusual. Beyond that . . . no.'

'Have any of your neighbours reported seeing . . . strangers moving around?'

'Our neighbours are few. And they generally keep themselves to themselves. Besides . . .'

'Yes?'

'They do not know there has been a kidnapping, so would see no need to report such sightings.'

'Perhaps you think it would have been wiser to alert the local police to what has happened?'

'I do not think about such matters. They are for others to decide.' She lifts the lid of the tajine, dips the spoon in the sauce and samples it. 'Ah. That is very nearly ready.'

Culinary perfection, it seems, lies within Noussa Rezig's grasp. Taleb envies her that. There is no hope of perfection in his profession. And even adequacy may prove to be beyond him in this case. But at least there will be a fine meal to savour before he has to confront that possibility.

'Are you hungry, Superintendent?' Noussa asks.

He smiles and nods. 'I am now.'

*

'Hello.'

'Rochdi Abidi here. You left a message for me, I think.'

'Ah yes. I'm glad you've called.'

'Who are you?'

'You can call me Halima.'

'Halima?'

'Yes.'

'As in Chadli's wife?'

Hidouchi is gratified her teasing pseudonym has hit the mark. During the dying days of Chadli Bendjedid's presidency in the early 1990s, rumour had it he was no better than a eunuch, dominated by his wife Halima. She, it was said, took all the important decisions. Hidouchi only knows this because Taleb once told her about it. But Rochdi Abidi, a man steeped in the conspiracy theories of the past, may see in the reference a promise of genuine revelations.

'What do you know about the DRS . . . Halima?'

'Enough.'

'And the DSS? Do you work for them?'

'I can say nothing on the telephone. I think we should meet.'

'I'm only interested in meeting if you have something valuable for me.'

'And you'll only find out if I do by meeting me.'

There is a brief silence. She hears him sigh. Then: 'All right. But I get to say where and when.'

'It has to be tomorrow. But the *where* is up to you.'

'You drive a hard bargain.'

'I'm taking a lot of risks by reaching out to you.'

'And you think I'm not taking risks by responding?'

'Just name a time and place tomorrow, Rochdi. If you're interested in the kind of information a journalist like you *should* be interested in.'

Another pause. Then Abidi says, 'The Cinéma Splendide.'

'I don't know it.'

'Well, its splendid days are behind it. As are its film-showing days. Many years behind, in fact. But you'll find it if you look hard enough. Eleven o'clock tomorrow morning. Don't be late.'

Waking in the Provençal countryside is very different from the first encounter of the day Taleb normally has with consciousness, in the familiar surroundings of his apartment in Algiers as the city stirs noisily around him. All at the Villa des Ormeaux, by contrast, is still and silent, the light greyer and paler than he's used to.

He struggles out of bed, coughing as he goes, shrugs on his dressing-gown and moves to the window. He pulls back the thin curtain and peers out. The view is of soft, misty green fields sloping up into the hills behind the villa. Below him he sees the glazed roof of the gallery connecting the house at ground level only with a two-storey annexe, which looks of more recent construction than the main part of the villa. This, he assumes, is where the conference room mentioned by Lydia Seghir is located.

Away to the right he can also see a garage with rooms above which he takes for the Rezigs' living quarters. There's a paddock beyond that. Behind the annexe are gardens and the wall of what he guesses is a kitchen garden. He lights a cigarette and checks the time. Just gone eight. He's surprised by how soundly he's slept, considering the unpredictability and possible dangers of the day that lies ahead of him.

The phone Kadri gave him, which he kept on overnight, hasn't rung, for which he's grateful. But he's sure it *will* ring at some point, when the kidnappers choose to make contact. The timing of that is in their hands. All Taleb can do is wait for the moment to come.

After a shower and a shave, he dresses and heads down to the kitchen in search of breakfast. Noussa is there, dicing carrots.

She's happy to break off and serve him something she describes as muesli but which tastes a great deal better than Taleb expects. He follows this with a croissant and jam and a bowl of excellent coffee. He finds himself envying the Elasses for having such a wonder to cook for them.

The kitchen has windows set high in the walls at the level of the courtyard outside. As Taleb is drinking his coffee and smoking his second cigarette of the day – to which Noussa considerately raises no objection – he hears the sound of car engines outside and glimpses movement through the windows.

'There is to be more meeting today,' says Noussa. 'And talking, of course. Lots of talking. Which makes men hungry, I find.'

Taleb stands up and cranes for a view through the windows, but he isn't tall enough to see anything. 'What sort of men are they?' he asks.

'Serious men,' Noussa replies. 'They do not laugh.'

'Are they French?'

'They speak French. Also Arabic, which I don't. But some of it is Darija, I think. I would say most of them are North African.'

Those who are communicating in Darija – Algerian dialect Arabic – must in fact be Algerian. The nature of this secret conference becomes ever more intriguing to Taleb. He has been told to keep his nose out of it, of course, but that has only piqued his curiosity. 'Do you have a stepladder, Noussa?' he enquires with what he hopes is a winning smile.

She admonishes him with a shake of the head, but says nothing and fetches a stepladder from the scullery. He hurriedly sets it up and climbs to the top platform for a view of the courtyard.

Three cars have newly arrived – a couple of black Mercedes saloons and a large grey people-carrier. From one of the Mercedes three men have emerged – their chauffeur is just closing the doors behind them – and are walking towards the villa. They are late-middle-aged or older, sombre-faced, two of them portly and heavily mustachioed in the style of *pouvoir* placemen, the third leaner and darker-skinned and with a more obviously Arab cast to his features.

They move out of Taleb's eyeline as they enter the villa, leaving only the chauffeurs for Taleb to watch, which promises to be unrewarding. He climbs down from the stepladder and folds it up, then passes it back to Noussa, who still says nothing.

'If you've heard them talking . . .' he begins.

'I hear, but I do not listen.' She gives him a stern look. 'You understand?'

He understands. There is more she could say, but she isn't going to say it. And to press her on the point would be unwise. He moves back to the table and sits down.

'More coffee?' Noussa asks brightly.

After his third coffee, Taleb goes back up to his room, where he finds Irmouli waiting for him.

'Your day seems to have started slowly, Taleb.'

'There's nothing I can do until the kidnappers make contact.'

'Then make sure waiting is all you engage in until they do.'

'Oh, it will be.'

'We'll be alerted as soon as General Mokrani has spoken to them.'

'And you'll let me know at once?'

'Of course. Oh, you should find a photograph of Agent Mokrani on your phone next time you check.'

Taleb takes out his phone and checks. Sure enough, what looks like a standard DSS staff mugshot of Karim Mokrani has been sent to him. He's thinner in the face than in the snapshot his mother supplied, maybe ten years older, duller-eyed and pencil-moustached. He's become a harder man, determined to conform to what is required of him, decisively set on his course: success the Algerian way.

But success, for Karim Mokrani, has come at a price. 'We don't want you to bring us the wrong man, Taleb,' says Irmouli with a smile.

'I won't do that,' says Taleb. And he doesn't smile back.

The Cinéma Splendide, judged by outward appearance, hasn't been a functioning business for about three decades. The plaster on its Art Deco frontage is peeling, the relievo lettering of its name heavily scarred and mottled with decay. The tattered fragments of a poster are still visible in a broken frame beside the double-doored entrance, but there is not enough to reveal the title of the film it once advertised. The hanging sign visible through the wired-glass door panel – *Fermé* – hardly seems necessary.

Hidouchi presses the cobwebbed bell-push nonetheless. She is a few minutes early for her appointment with Abidi, but suspects he will already be inside, waiting for her.

Sure enough, after some delay, a latch is pulled back and the door edges open. Abidi – looking markedly less spruce and sure of himself than when he graced the nation's TV screens the previous Sunday – squints out at her.

'I am Halima,' Hidouchi announces.

'Of course you are. Come in.'

He moves back and she follows him into a dusty foyer. To her right is a redundant ticket cubicle, ahead a broad curving flight of carpeted stairs. Dust floats in the musty air.

'No matinée today,' says Abidi. 'We have the place to ourselves.'

He leads her through a set of double doors into the ground-floor auditorium. The light is low, as if in preparation for the showing of a film. But the screen is obscured by ceiling-high sheets of chipboard. And there is no expectant audience filling the ranks of seating.

'Shall we sit down?' Abidi plonks himself in an aisle-side seat.

'Why have you brought me here?' Hidouchi asks.

'It's convenient. And I can be sure we won't be interrupted. My brother, who technically owns the building, spends most of his time abroad. It was our father who ran this as a cinema. In the seventies and eighties it did quite well. Then it did less well. And then he was murdered for the crime of trying to entertain people. So it went in this country during *la décennie noire*, which you are surely too young to remember.'

'I know what happened back then.'

'In that case, you must tell me. I and many others who lived through those years would dearly like to know what really happened. But please sit down. I get nervous when people stand over me.'

Hidouchi takes a seat on the other side of the aisle from Abidi, the hinge creaking loudly as she pulls it down.

'So, I have explained why I brought you here . . . Halima. Perhaps you'd like to explain why you came.'

'As I told you in my message, there are secrets I think should be brought to public attention. Judging by what you said on television, you're the man to do that. And I'd like to help you . . . if I can.'

'You work for the DSS?'

'Yes.'

'In what capacity?'

'The specifics of what I do there don't matter. All you need to know is that I have access to the records. Including those of the DRS which the DSS has inherited. I just need you to tell me what to search for.'

'You don't look like a clerical officer to me. Something closer to a field agent, I'd say.'

'I'm taking a big risk by contacting you. The question isn't what my job title is. It's whether you want me to help you or not.'

'What makes you think I want help from a DSS officer? You could be setting me up. It's what people like you generally do to people like me.'

'Why did you agree to meet me, then?'

'Because I need hard facts to back up my suspicions about General Mokrani's activities during *la décennie noire* – and later.'

'OK. So, where are you going to get those facts from – if not a DSS insider?'

Abidi falls silent for a moment. He takes out a pack of cigarettes and lights one. Hidouchi sees the smoke spiral like a lariat in the dim light. She waits, knowing he must be the next to speak. As eventually he does. 'Fair point.'

'You made your opinion of General Mokrani and the DRS pretty obvious on *Microscope*. I don't really see how I could set you up any better than you've already set yourself up.'

'I was trying to get that rat Taleb to tell what he knows.'

'What do you think he knows?'

'The truth about the Boudiaf assassination. Or more of it than I know, anyway. He discovered that Mokrani's assistant, Ghezala, had hidden copies of internal DRS documents at his apartment – documents connecting Mokrani to the hit on Boudiaf. And you know what he did when he found the documents? He surrendered them to a DRS agent called Zoubiri. Who now works as Mokrani's bodyguard and fixer. Now, I doubt Taleb handed those documents over without looking at them. But, even if he did, he must have known – just as he must still know – that they hold the key to what happened to Boudiaf.'

'You think they still exist?'

'It's possible. There's a balance for someone like Mokrani between retaining evidence that implicates others and destroying it because it implicates him. *Les pouvoiristes* won't hesitate to blackmail each other if it's a question of self-preservation. You surely don't suppose they have any genuine sense of solidarity, do you? These people are gangsters. They run this country as a Mafia state. And you – I regret to have to say – are one of their servants.'

'So was Ghezala.'

'Yes. Some of you have a conscience, I admit. You may be one of them.'

'How can I prove to you that I am?'

'Ideally by finding those documents – and any other records Mokrani kept of his murderous activities.'

'That's asking a lot, considering he'll have taken anything truly damaging with him when he left the service.'

'Maybe. But the DRS was a bureaucracy like any other. Which means they left a trail of paper behind them whenever they made a move. Expunging every written trace of what Mokrani did wouldn't have been easy. It's hard to believe there's nothing lodged in the archives about Unit ninety-two, for instance. That would be a good place to start.'

'Unit ninety-two? I've never heard of it.'

Abidi sighs. 'Of course you haven't. It was set up by Mokrani on orders from above in the year it was named after: 1992. How old were you in 1992, Halima?'

'Three.'

'There you are, then. Which means you weren't even alive on October fourth, 1988, when inflation, food shortages and mass unemployment sparked the first popular uprising since independence – and protesters were gunned down in their hundreds by the army on the streets of this city. The legitimacy of the FLN as guardians of the republic's soul was shot down that day too – and never recovered. That led to the political rise of the FIS and the possibility that we might end up as a hardline Islamist state, which seemed to be coming true when the FIS won most of the seats in the first round of legislative elections in December of ninety-one. They made no secret of what life would be like under a government run by them: women in burkas, men with beards and shaven heads, strict sharia law. I didn't want that. No one I knew wanted it. And as a woman you should be especially grateful it never happened. *Le pouvoir* didn't want it either, because their days as cocks of the walk would have been over. So, a few weeks later, in January of ninety-two, they came to our rescue. They cancelled the second round of voting, put the army back on the streets and declared a state of emergency.'

'I'm not as ignorant of our nation's history as you seem to suppose,' Hidouchi objects mildly. She has in fact become much better informed about Algeria's past than she once was thanks to her collaboration with Taleb. This is partly because he has often talked of such episodes as those Abidi is describing and partly because the crimes and conspiracies she has investigated with him have all too often been linked to the grimy workings of *le pouvoir*'s many decades in control of events. 'Chadli Bendjedid was forced to resign as president and Boudiaf was recalled from exile to take his place.'

'Yes he was. But though he considered suppression of the FIS essential for Algeria's future he also believed the people's faith in the FLN could only be restored by rooting out the corruption that had sapped the nation's finances and trashed the party's reputation. That was a naive and hopeless aspiration. *Le pouvoir* was never going to let it happen.'

'Is that where Unit ninety-two comes in?'

'As far as I can establish the prime movers in *le pouvoir*'s January ninety-two coup set up Unit ninety-two, with Mokrani in charge of it, before Boudiaf even stepped off his plane from Morocco. It operated in complete isolation from the rest of the DRS, often directly recruiting secret service candidates before they were formally appointed. Mokrani's brief was to do anything and everything to ensure that the Islamists never came to power and that the primacy of *le pouvoir* was never threatened again. For nearly a quarter of a century, he had *carte blanche* to do whatever it took to maintain the status quo.'

Abidi takes a couple of long draws on his cigarette. 'I could recite all the mysteries, big and small, surrounding Boudiaf's assassination, but it would serve little purpose. It was our Dallas sixty-three moment, complete with disappearing acts, imposters, patsies and cover-ups of cover-ups. All you need to understand is that the man they still have mouldering in prison for killing Boudiaf was just a pawn in a conspiracy organized and overseen by Mokrani.

'Solving *le pouvoir*'s Boudiaf problem earned Mokrani a lot of credit. He became their go-to man for dealing with the ongoing and steadily escalating Islamist threat. There were atrocities on both sides during *la décennie noire*, but the situation became truly diabolical when Mokrani began implementing a strategy of undermining public support for the FIS and its armed offshoot, the GIA, by infiltrating them and encouraging them to carry out ever more extreme acts. Unit ninety-two also perpetrated massacres and bombings themselves which they blamed on the GIA. You must know the saying that period made famous. *Qui tue qui?* Who is killing who? And why? The GIA were pitiless murderers, no question. But Unit ninety-two made them look like amateurs. Who really beheaded the French monks abducted from their monastery at Tibhirine in 1996? The GIA – who appeared to claim responsibility? Or the DRS in the form of Unit ninety-two, working on the assumption that such barbarity would prompt the French government to back their suppression of Islamism and quite capable of generating a GIA communiqué if they needed to? And that's before we consider the bloody wave of massacres that swept the country the following year. It seemed at one point as if they would never stop. We were locked in a nightmare. But an end was coming – on *le pouvoir*'s terms. It was terror fighting terror. And the greater terror – *their* terror – won.

'What lesson did Mokrani and his kind take from their victory? That their strategy worked, of course. That it had worked then and would go on working, whenever the need arose for it to be deployed. As far as they were concerned nothing changed with Bouteflika's election as president in 1999. It was . . . business as usual.'

Hidouchi says nothing, hoping her silence will imply shock at what Abidi has said, whereas in truth she is already well aware of the probability that false flag operations lay behind some of the bloodiest episodes of *la décennie noire*. She knows Taleb believes the massacre that claimed the lives of his wife and daughter in December 1997 was one such operation. Mokrani's supposedly central role in Boudiaf's assassination is new to her, however, as is his creation of Unit 92. If such a unit truly existed, it has been expertly hidden from view. But perhaps, in view of what it may have engaged in, it had to be.

'After Nine Eleven the Americans began supplying us with high-grade weapons systems to use against Islamist insurgents operating just over or sometimes inside our southern border,' Abidi continues. 'The Bush White House had convinced itself – encouraged by our government – that the Sahara was infested with terrorists linked to al-Qaeda who'd fled Afghanistan when the US invaded. Bouteflika wanted more sophisticated hardware than they gave him, however. So, Mokrani obliged with evidence that the terrorist threat was even greater than the Americans thought: the kidnapping of thirty-two European tourists in the Algerian Sahara in early 2003. They were eventually released, of course, but not until *after* the US invaded Iraq.'

'You're suggesting the DRS somehow provoked the Americans into invading Iraq?' To Hidouchi this sounds absurd. She isn't altogether surprised that Abidi's gone too far. It's what tends to happen to conspiracy theorists. The problem she's going to have, she realizes, is distinguishing fact from fantasy in his allegations.

'I'm suggesting it was in *le pouvoir*'s long-term interests for the US to believe the Sahara-Sahel region was swarming with Islamist terrorists,' he goes on, undaunted, 'who posed such a serious security threat to the West that Algeria had to be amply supplied with money and weapons to suppress that threat – and a blind eye had to be turned to whatever repressive measures Bouteflika took to neutralize domestic opposition to his government. We sit on a sea of oil, Halima. The Americans weren't about to let control of it fall into the wrong hands. Neither were the French, come to that. I've no doubt the DGSE traded intelligence with the DRS on a regular basis. They'd have been happy to collude with them in encouraging the US to pour money into counter-terrorism programmes in the region. And if Mokrani had to . . . manufacture . . . some of that terrorism to keep the dollars flowing? Where's the harm? Plenty, of course, if you happened to be one of the thirty-nine foreign workers killed in the In Amenas raid, which you certainly *are* old enough to remember.'

Hidouchi does remember, very well. The terrorist seizure in January 2013 of a natural gas plant near In Amenas, in the Algerian Sahara, close to the Libyan border, saw dozens of foreign and Algerian workers taken hostage. When the army attacked, at least eighty people were killed, most of them hostages. At the time it strengthened her determination to contribute in whatever way she could to the fight against Algeria's enemies, both within and without. But the event has since been enveloped in a murk of suspicion about who planned it and why. Her idealism of nine years ago is painful to recall now. Nothing is ever as simple in Algeria as she thought it was then.

'In Amenas was the DRS's fatal overstep,' Abidi continues. 'Their role in setting up the assault on the plant was just too widely known. And the death toll of foreigners couldn't be overlooked. Bouteflika concluded that Unit ninety-two was becoming a liability. He began reining the DRS in. And within two years Mokrani was out. Unit ninety-two was history. Except that it *wasn't* history. Not the chronicled and acknowledged kind. Not the official kind in any sense. Not only did Unit ninety-two no longer exist. It never *had* existed. Well, I'd like to put that right. I'd like to shed some light – the best disinfectant, so they say – on Mokrani's murderous outfit and what it was responsible for. Can you help me?'

Hidouchi is unsure how she could help Abidi even if she wanted to. Investigating a secret outfit of killers sub-contracted by the DRS to commit atrocities for the purpose of blaming those atrocities on 'terrorists' of one kind or another would be a suicidally risky undertaking. Which may be why Abidi himself wants to sub-contract the task to her. 'Are you aware Mokrani's son is a DSS agent?' she asks.

'Yes. I'm aware.' Abidi busies himself for a moment extinguishing his cigarette on the stubber fixed to the back of the seat in front of him.

'He won't have welcomed what you said on *Microscope*.'

'Can we forget about him?' Abidi sounds irritable. 'He's irrelevant to this.'

'Is he?' Clearly he isn't, as his kidnapping proves. But Hidouchi can hardly mention that.

'You offered to help. And I've told you how to do that. Find any records that still exist of Mokrani's stewardship of Unit ninety-two and bring them to me. I'll do the rest. The international media will run with this story when I give it to them. But it has to be verifiable.'

'When did you first hear about Unit ninety-two?'

'I'm not sure. Twenty years ago. Maybe more.'

'Who did you hear about it *from*?'

'There was no specific source. Just a tangle of rumours and whispers. Nothing I could back up.'

'Is that why you did nothing about it for so long?'

Abidi sighs. 'I guess so. The invitation to appear on *Microscope* and the discovery that Taleb was to be one of the other guests made me think there was a chance I could make a breakthrough.

And when you contacted me . . .' He turns to look across the aisle at her. 'If you want to make a difference – a real difference – to the way this country is run, this is your opportunity. You say you have access to DRS records passed on to the DSS. If evidence of the truth about Mokrani's activities is to be found anywhere, that's where to look. Looking may be dangerous. You don't need me to tell you that. But if you don't look . . . you won't find it. And it'll never be brought into the open. So, now you've heard me out . . . what are you going to do?'

SIX

TIME HANGS HEAVY ON TALEB'S HANDS AS THE MORNING PASSES AT the Villa des Ormeaux without word from Karim Mokrani's kidnappers. Instructed to stay out of sight while delegates to the mysterious conference Lydia Seghir has convened continue their deliberations, he sits in the small attic room made available to him and tries to refrain from constantly checking his phone for messages which have clearly not arrived.

He has already worked his way through half a pack of cigarettes and is wondering whether the six packs he brought with him are going to be enough, doubtful as he is that any local tobacconist is likely to stock his beloved Nassims.

Superintendent Meslem used to say waiting for something to happen was one of the hardest tasks for a policeman to master. He resorted to Maigret novels to kill time during prolonged stakeouts and bequeathed a drawerful of them to Taleb when he retired. There are actually a couple stuffed into the glove compartment of Taleb's car. But his car is in Algiers, he is in France . . . and Maigret cannot help him.

Around midday Agent Irmouli looks in with a situation report, which he delivers in a tone that suggests he isn't personally bothered whether *les souveniristes* ever make contact or not. 'General Mokrani's heard nothing. His guy Zoubiri – you met him, right? – reckons the kidnappers are tightening the screw by making him wait. Tough for you, I guess.'

'I'll cope,' says Taleb.

'Good. Just stay put here. Greed will get the better of these bastards sooner or later. I mean, they want the money, don't they?'

'I imagine they do.'

'Then it's only a matter of time.'

'As you say: only a matter of time.'

Time is also on the mind of Souad Hidouchi. After leaving Abidi at the Cinéma Splendide, she rides out to Pointe Pescade and walks on the beach under a grey sky, gazing out at the rolling, spume-flecked Mediterranean. According to Taleb, who is sometimes actually right, if you're uncertain what to do for the best then it's best to bide your time.

Such, it seems, is the accumulated wisdom of a police officer after forty years' service. And it's certainly true Hidouchi isn't certain what to do in response to Abidi's revelations. No one who knows anything significant about Unit 92 is likely to confide in her voluntarily, and extracting information coercively will set alarm bells ringing in places where she really doesn't want them ringing, certainly not while Taleb is trying to secure the release of Karim Mokrani from his kidnappers in France.

Offering to help Abidi has yielded a sobering insight into the death-dealing career of Karim Mokrani's father. There's no reason why she has to go ahead and deliver on her offer, despite giving Abidi the impression she would. In fact, there are plenty of reasons not to. The blood-soaked history of Unit 92 – assuming Abidi is to be believed – tells her General Hamza Mokrani is a brutal and ruthless operator she'd do well to avoid confronting. Besides, Taleb is in an exposed position as chosen negotiator with *les souveniristes*. She's not about to do anything that will make his assignment more dangerous. The most sensible course of action is to follow his counsel . . . and bide her time.

She really has no choice in the matter, anyway, she acknowledges to herself as she prowls the beach. Because survival in the world she moves in requires her to be selective about the battles she fights. And this battle, if it *is* to be fought, has to be left to another day.

From the vantage point of his attic window at the Villa des Ormeaux, Taleb observes the delegates leave the conference room and make their way into the main part of the villa for lunch. He's finished his own lunch – a cheese baguette delivered by Irmouli – and has nothing to occupy his thoughts but speculation about who the delegates represent and what they are conferring about. The presence of a senior Algerian civil servant and several DSS agents indicates that the proceedings must be taking place with the knowledge and consent of their government. And it's hard to believe the French government doesn't know about them as well. The delegates themselves – judging by the glimpses Taleb's had of them – are probably Algerian or at least North African, though what groups they represent he cannot begin to guess. Conferring here, in an obscure corner of the French countryside, suggests none of them wish it to be widely known that they're meeting, let alone what they're meeting *for*. He's been explicitly forbidden to pry into what's going on, but he can't help wondering – and worrying – that it's connected in some way with the abduction of Karim Mokrani. He hopes he's wrong about that, but his experience of 'need to know' operations is that he's all too often the one who needs to know – but doesn't.

Lunch appears to mark the end of proceedings for the day. Taleb is roused from a shallow doze by an echoing of voices down in the hall, followed by the sound of doors opening and closing, footsteps on the courtyard flagstones, car engines rumbling into life. From a window on the landing downstairs from his room, he observes limousines and SUVs pulling away along the drive.

And then they're gone. Silence descends on the house. Leaving Taleb with nothing to do but wait for his phone to ring – which it stubbornly refuses to do.

With the conference suspended, he is at least free to go for a walk. He steps out into the hollow grey afternoon. There's a mountain range away to the east which he couldn't see the previous night. The summit is patched with snow. The sight of it makes him feel colder than he already does. He walks round the deserted garden, smoking a cigarette. Far from home and nothing like as well informed as he'd like to be about what he's in the middle of, he feels both impatient *and* anxious, a disagreeable combination of sensations which he's experienced before in his career – and never as the prelude to a happy outcome.

He hears a drill operating in the workshop and heads in that direction, hoping a few minutes' conversation with a normal human being – Noussa's husband is surely the driller – will make him feel a little better.

The double doors of the workshop are standing open. A man in a dark blue boiler suit is sitting on a stool in front of a bench that runs the length of one wall. He's so thin it's hard to be sure there's a body inside the boiler suit, but the presence of hands and head proves there must be. His face is hollow-cheeked. Grey hair peeks from beneath the rim of a beret. A cigarette hangs pendulously from his lips. He drills another neat hole in a wooden rail held in a vice as Taleb watches. Then he notices his visitor and stops to look at him.

'You're the guest my wife told me about?' he enquires with a furrowing of bushy eyebrows. 'Arrived last night?'

'That's me,' Taleb replies.

'So, you would be Mouloud Taleb.'

'Not if I could help it.'

'But you can't?'

'No.' Taleb shapes a smile. The man's use of his first name has disconcerted him. He's surprised Noussa knows what it is.

'I am Abdou Rezig.'

'Pleased to meet you.'

'It's good to see you also.' The man's tone is strangely effusive. He pulls off his beret to reveal a full head of iron-grey hair. 'Which of us carries our years the lighter, do you think?'

'I . . . I'm sorry. I don't . . .'

'Don't recognize me?'

'Should I?'

'You should, Mouloud. Yes, you should. But I probably wouldn't have recognized you if I hadn't known you were coming. So . . . you are forgiven. It's been a long time, after all. Though what is sixty years between friends?'

'Sixty years?' Memory stirs in Taleb's head. Abdou Rezig. *L'haricot*, as he was known to his schoolmates on account of his extreme thinness. 'It's really you, isn't it?'

'Oh yes, Mouloud. It's really me.' Rezig plucks the cigarette from his mouth and grins. 'No one would go to the bother of impersonating an unimportant old *harki* like me, would they?'

Taleb recalls that the Rezigs left Algeria in a hurry the summer the country gained independence from France. Abdou's father served as an auxiliary in a French army unit and would have been marked for a gruesome death if he'd remained. All this was lost on seven-year-old schoolchildren, of course. They only knew that Abdou and several other classmates vanished from the school – along with many of the staff who were French – in July 1962. Those who fled were condemned as traitors, for reasons

Taleb did not understand at the time. And the traitors' children were condemned by association.

Rezig stubs out his cigarette, stands up and advances towards the workshop doors, arms outstretched. A few seconds later, Taleb is astonished to be enveloped in a hug. He is even more astonished to find himself welling with emotion. It is as if time has suddenly reversed itself and he is a child again, dwelling in a world of light, the sadnesses and misfortunes of his life lifted from him – for a moment.

'*Haricot.*' Taleb chokes slightly as Rezig releases him and he returns to the present. 'It's . . . wonderful to see you again.'

'And unexpected, right?' Rezig steps back. He's still grinning. It's a long time since anyone has looked so pleased to see Taleb.

'Well . . . yes.'

'A policeman, hey? I'd never have predicted that. And a senior one too. Superintendent, no less.'

'Promotion's inevitable if you stay long enough.'

'Shouldn't you have retired by now?'

'I could say the same to you.'

'Oh, what I do here is . . . pretty undemanding. Whereas you . . .' Hesitancy enters Rezig's tone. His grin falters. 'We know why you're here, Mouloud, Noussa and I. Negotiating with kidnappers? Is that a game a man of your age – *our* age – should be playing?'

'No one else volunteered.'

'I don't suppose they did. Do you . . . er . . . have a wife worrying about you back in Algiers?'

'I'm a widower.'

'Sorry. That's tough.' Rezig pats Taleb on the shoulder. 'Children?'

'No.'

'That's even tougher. We have a daughter . . . married to a

lawyer, would you believe? They live in Paris. There's a grandchild on the way.'

'Congratulations.' The glimpse Rezig has given him of the life he might have had – growing old contentedly with Serene, dandling Lili's children on his arthritic knee – sends a lance of pain through Taleb's soul. But he is armoured against the sensation through long practice. And he is mysteriously immune to envy. 'I'm pleased for you, Abdou. That's good to hear. And you and Noussa . . . seem happily established here.'

'We are. To be honest, I think leaving Algeria may have been the best thing that ever happened to me.'

'You could be—' Taleb breaks off at the trill of his phone. He plucks it out of his pocket and, raising his hand to excuse himself, moves away from the workshop. He puts the phone to his ear. 'Hello?'

'Superintendent Taleb?'

'This is Taleb.'

'I speak for *les souveniristes.*'

'I've been expecting to hear from you.'

'I've just spoken to General Mokrani. He says the money is in place and so are you.'

'I'm here.'

'And the money?'

'Available.'

'How very cooperative.'

'I'm instructed to pay you what you've asked for.'

'I know. And you're not even tracing this call, are you?'

'No.'

'That must rankle with you, as a policeman. Abject compliance is an encouragement to the likes of us.'

'I have my orders.'

'Yes, you do. So, here are some more. From me. I want to meet you, Taleb, *before* the exchange.'

'Is that necessary?'

'I'm not sure I can trust you. Or General Mokrani. This is all . . . too good to be true.'

'Nevertheless, it *is* true.'

'No conditions?'

'Just one. Prior proof that Agent Mokrani is alive and well.'

'I'll supply his father with that shortly before the exchange. As for you and me, we meet tomorrow. To ensure there are no . . . slip-ups . . . on the day. Be at Aix TGV station at nine a.m. Stand outside the east entrance. You'll be collected.'

'How will you recognize me?'

'You're a veteran Algerian police detective, Taleb. We'll recognize you even before we see you.'

The call ends. Taleb turns back towards the workshop.

'That was them, I'm guessing,' says Rezig.

Taleb nods. 'It was.'

'Everything going according to plan?'

'Everything's going according to *their* plan, certainly.'

'Does it involve you doing anything this evening?'

'No.'

'Then you can come to dinner. Noussa always cooks more than I can eat. It'll take your mind off . . . whatever you're going to have to do to get Agent Mokrani released.'

'Thanks.' Taleb smiles. 'That's kind of you.'

'You'll come, then?'

'I certainly will.'

Taleb finds Irmouli waiting for him back at the villa, doing little to hide his irritation.

'Where were you when they called?' he demands.

'I went for a stroll.'

'I told you to stay put.'

'Did you? Well, if I was one of your juniors I suppose I'd have taken some notice. As it is, it seems to me unimportant where I was when I spoke to them.'

Irmouli closes on him. 'I was told you'd agreed to abide by our directions.'

'You were misinformed. I agreed to do whatever is necessary to secure Agent Mokrani's release. And I'm sticking by that.'

Irmouli gives him a long hard look. It has no effect. Taleb has greater challenges ahead of him than this – far greater, he suspects. 'What did they say?'

'That they'd spoken to General Mokrani and were willing to go ahead. They want to meet me tomorrow morning to settle arrangements for the exchange.'

'Why not make the arrangements over the phone?'

'Trust issues.'

'What does that mean?'

'I get the feeling they've been spooked by the speed with which we've given in. Maybe they were expecting a lengthy negotiation. General Mokrani's supposed to be a hard nut. But he's cracked at the first application of pressure.'

Irmouli simmers. 'The priority is to get Agent Mokrani back before he discloses any damaging information.'

'Just how damaging might that information be?'

'None of your concern.'

'OK. The less I know the less I can be forced to disclose, I suppose. I'll talk to them tomorrow and try to wrap this up as quickly as possible. Meanwhile, can I assume you recorded their conversation with the general and are running the voice of the caller through your databases?'

'You can assume that, yes.'

'And you'll let me know if you identify him?'

'Of course.'

Taleb strongly suspects they've already lifted a recording of his conversation with the kidnappers' representative from the phone he used, supplied by them. There's nothing in it to make them doubt his commitment to the task in hand for the simple reason that he *is* committed to it. Even though he's certain Irmouli isn't telling him anything like the full story. He decides to test him on the point. 'Tell me, why had Agent Mokrani gone into Aix on his own the evening they grabbed him?'

'I don't know. He doesn't answer to me.'

'But he wasn't just taking the night off? He was . . . on duty at the time?'

'You seem more interested in issues that are none of your business than in doing the job you were sent here for, Superintendent. You need to curb your curiosity.' Irmouli prods Taleb in the shoulder. 'Got it?'

Taleb smiles, which he calculates will rile the other man. He knows doing so may be counterproductive, but he can't seem to help himself. 'Working with you is proving to be a real tonic, Agent Irmouli. I'm sure we'll miss each other when we go our separate ways.'

Seeing the last of Agent Irmouli is still a long way off as Saturday evening sets in. Taleb sends text messages to Bouras and Hidouchi telling them everything is proceeding as well as can be expected – which is almost true – then instructs himself to take a break from the cares of his mission. He resolves before setting off for dinner with the Rezigs to ask them no leading questions about Agent Mokrani or the conference being hosted at the villa. Not only does he want to avoid embarrassing them but he's actually relishing the prospect of discussing almost anything *but* Agent Mokrani and the conference.

It soon becomes apparent that the Rezigs feel much the same way. Their apartment is much more homely and more genuinely lived in, it seems to Taleb, than the cheerless salons of the villa. There are numerous family photographs on display, many charting the life of their beautiful daughter. Abdou has dug out a Cheikha Rimitti album to play on the stereo. He reckons it reminds him of the Algeria of his childhood more than anything else. Noussa apologizes for the Frenchness of the food she's serving – *daube de boeuf* – but, as she points out, they're far more French than Algerian after all these years. Taleb basks in their hospitality and feels a transitory contentment creeping over him.

He suspects this might be related to a French habit the Rezigs confess to succumbing to – wine with dinner. Taleb drank wine and beer as a young man, but Serene disapproved – and her mother even more so – which obliged him to give up. He could have drowned in a sea of alcohol after Serene and Lili were killed, but obtaining the stuff at that point in *la décennie noire* was formidably difficult and he never summoned the energy to seek it out. Now he sips a local red appreciatively as Rimitti belts out *Er-Raï Er-Raï* at suppressed volume and wonders what course his life would have taken had his parents left Algeria when Abdou's and Noussa's did. No Serene and no Lili, of course – but no agony of losing them. No police career, in all likelihood – but something else instead, something safer and saner.

Abdou recounts without any obvious bitterness the privations of his existence after arriving in France: an isolated and overcrowded repatriation camp in the Camargue, followed eventually by a move to cramped and squalid accommodation in Marseille. For Noussa the story was much the same. They were children, so coped as children do, but their parents were evidently scarred by the experience.

Abdou also reveals that their employer, Monsieur Elasse, came from *pieds noirs* stock. His parents too struggled after leaving Algeria, though they faced fewer difficulties than the *harkis*. He married well, however, and through his wife inherited a large and successful furniture business. The villa is hers. The business is now run by their son and daughter-in-law, who live in Avignon.

The Elasses have departed for a skiing break in the Alps, leaving the mysterious Lydia Seghir to run her equally mysterious conference at the villa in their absence.

The Rezigs simply do as they are told by Madame Seghir. Monsieur Elasse has obscure political connections which appear to explain how the use of the villa came to be broached to him and Madame Elasse. They were apparently happy to oblige. 'What it's all about,' Abdou says, 'we neither know nor want to know.'

To which Taleb can only say, quite genuinely, 'Very wise.'

At the end of a long and enjoyable evening, Abdou walks some of the way back to the villa with Taleb. They are smoking cigars. The scent of the tobacco plumes around them in the chill air. Taleb doubts Abdou has accompanied him just to ensure he makes it safely to his room after drinking more glasses of wine than he should have. And he's right.

'How you do your job is obviously up to you, Mouloud,' he begins hesitantly. 'You're a policeman and I'm . . . not. But . . .'

'But?'

'I wouldn't like you to . . . run into trouble . . . because I didn't . . . say something.'

'Probably best to say it then.'

Abdou lowers his voice to something close to a whisper. 'It's about . . . the kidnapping.'

'I assumed it was.'

'And what . . . happened . . . the night Agent Mokrani was taken.'

'Go on.'

'Well, it was last Wednesday night. Noussa and I weren't told about the kidnapping until the following day. Madame Seghir informed us. I think she felt she had no alternative. She didn't want us to do or say anything that might draw the delegates' attention to Agent Mokrani's absence. On Wednesday, Agent Mokrani drove into Aix, apparently. I don't know why. When he hadn't returned by midnight, Agents Irmouli and Jahid went looking for him and found his car abandoned at the roadside a few kilometres from here. According to what Madame Seghir told us, the kidnappers contacted his father next morning.'

'That tallies with what I've been told.'

'Right. Well, this is about Wednesday night. I took a look around the grounds at about ten o'clock – it's what I normally do, to make sure everything's as the Elasses would want it to be. It was pitch dark – no moon. So, when I came along the kitchen garden wall, Jahid, who was on the terrace between the main part of the house and the annexe they're using for the conference, couldn't see me. Irmouli emerged from the villa – I heard him open and close the door from the rear drawing room – as I approached. And Jahid said, "Is it time to go?" I stopped, wondering where they might be thinking of going and why. And I heard Irmouli reply. "Not yet," he said. "We wait for the word." That was it. They lit cigarettes then and started complaining about their duties and having to do what they were told by "the Seghir bitch", as they called her. I retreated – taking care they didn't hear me. I didn't want them to think I'd been listening to them. Even though what they said didn't seem to amount to much. But next morning, when Madame Seghir put us in the picture . . . I wondered what that exchange really meant.'

Taleb is wondering now as well. '*Is it time to go?*' '*Not yet. We wait for the word.*' Go where? And at whose say-so? 'Did they go anywhere, Abdou?' he asks, already sure he knows the answer.

'I can't be certain. But I don't think they left the villa until quite a bit later – when they drove off to look for Mokrani.'

'Because they'd had word . . . it was time?'

'How can I say? It just seems . . . odd.'

'Odd? Yes, it seems that all right.'

'It was as if . . . they knew Mokrani was going to be—'

Taleb silences his old friend with a hand on his shoulder. 'Don't say that. It's the kind of thing that can't be unsaid once you've uttered the thought. And you shouldn't utter such a thought, believe me.'

'But if I'm right . . .'

'If you're right, I needed to know. And now I do. Thank you.'

'I had to warn you, Mouloud.'

'You didn't warn me. We never spoke of this. And you should never speak of this to anyone else.'

'I won't. I only told you . . . because we were children together once.'

'That was long ago.'

'Yes. But we're still those children. Whether we want to be or not.'

Taleb doesn't sleep well that night. He can see no way round keeping his appointment with *les souveniristes*' representative, but Abdou's revelations have solidified a suspicion that was already forming in his mind. The kidnapping of Karim Mokrani is looking more and more like a put-up job. Its purpose is obscure to him. Maybe Irmouli and Jahid have been promised a cut of the ransom money in return for setting Mokrani up. Or maybe some deeper and more devious ploy explains what has happened. Taleb just has to hope he is simply part of the scenery that is being moved around the stage: the stooge who hands over the cash. If that is his role, then he has little to worry about. But if not . . .

He falls asleep eventually, but wakes well before the alarm on his phone goes off. To add to his woes he now has a sandpapery throat and a hangover. He gulps down a couple of paracetamols with half a litre of water and heads for the bathroom.

He decides to leave as soon as he can. There is no sign of

Noussa in the kitchen, but he makes some coffee for himself and finds a large bowl of homemade muesli in the fridge which supplies him with breakfast. Then he's ready to go.

But, early or not, he can't elude Irmouli, who is prowling around at the front of the villa, as if waiting for him.

'All set, Taleb?'

'I'm as ready as I'll ever be.'

'I've had a report back on the voice recognition analysis of the phone recording of the *souveniriste* guy you spoke to. Thought you'd like to know.'

'Is there a match with anyone known to the DSS?'

'No.' Irmouli smiles. 'Nothing to go on there, I'm afraid.'

'Well, thanks for telling me.'

'No problem.' Irmouli holds his smile. 'I'll see you later.'

'You will.' And with that Taleb turns and heads for his car.

Taleb passed Aix TGV station on Friday evening when he followed Spühler from Marseille airport to the villa, so he knows where it is, out in the middle of the countryside south-west of the city. The roads are largely empty so early on a Sunday and he makes good time, reaching the station with a full half hour to spare before he's due to be collected.

During the drive he's been debating with himself whether he should alert Hidouchi to the turn the case has taken. He reaches a final decision as he smokes his way through his third cigarette of the morning standing in the station car park. He pulls out his reserve phone and makes the call.

She answers promptly, her voice echoing slightly. 'Taleb?'

'You're in the parking basement of your apartment block, aren't you?'

'How d'you know?'

'The acoustics are right. Plus it's about the time you normally set off for DSS HQ.'

'Where are you?'

'Aix-en-Provence TGV station.'

'Catching a train?'

'No. Not sure what I might be catching. I'm supposed to be meeting the people holding our man to agree arrangements for the handover. But . . . information's come my way that this whole deal might be . . . not what it seems.'

'What kind of information?'

'I can't go into the specifics. But you should know, if things turn sour here, that your department's agents on the scene . . . aren't to be trusted.'

'Maybe you shouldn't go ahead with the meeting.'

'That would only make them suspect I'm on to them. And it would leave our man high and dry. I *think* this morning's going to go OK. But just in case it doesn't . . .'

'He isn't worth getting killed for, Taleb.'

'I'm not planning on getting killed.'

'No one ever is.'

'Look, if I'm being set up, it's possible they have something in mind for you as well. So . . . watch your back.'

'You should do the same.'

'Oh, I intend to, believe me.'

Like Taleb, Director Bouras has a headache. But his is of the metaphorical variety. And Taleb is the cause. The superintendent's disastrous TV appearance has set in motion a chain of events that pose Bouras the sort of problems he has spent much of his career seeking to be spared. But seniority within the DGSN carries responsibility as well as privilege and there is no way he can shake off his department's share of the blame for what has happened to Karim Mokrani. He is pinning his hopes now on Taleb negotiating Mokrani's release by his kidnappers before there are any further developments of a disturbing nature.

But his hopes are destined to be dashed that Sunday morning. As he drives away from his home, heading for what according to his diary should be a quiet day, his phone rings. And he hears the voice of Lieutenant Lahmar.

'So very sorry to call you like this, Director.' Lahmar is, as ever, annoyingly obsequious. 'But we've had a report I thought you'd want to know about as soon as it came in.'

'What is it?' snaps Bouras.

'It concerns the journalist Superintendent Taleb got tripped up by on *Microscope*. Rochdi Abidi.' Lahmar has predictably taken the opportunity to criticize Taleb, a man whose place in the hierarchy he has long aspired to.

'What about him?'

'Reported found dead. Probably murdered.'

'*What?*' The news could hardly be worse. Abidi alive was a nuisance. Abidi dead has the potential to become something much worse. 'Murdered, you say?'

'Looks that way. I wasn't sure . . . how you'd want to handle it.'

'Where are you now?'

'On my way to the scene. Disused cinema. The Splendide.'

The Splendide? A memory stirs in Bouras of cinema-going in his youth. The Splendide had a reputation for showing avant-garde French films, which appealed to his intellectual image of himself but sealed its fate during *la décennie noire*. 'I'll join you there.'

'You're going to the scene?'

'Yes, Lahmar. I am.' And he is – much though he would prefer not to have to. But in this matter Bouras senses he has no choice. He needs to know how Rochdi Abidi came to die.

Taleb smokes his fourth cigarette of the morning and sits in the car as the time ticks down to his appointment. With ten minutes to go, he walks into the station and buys an espresso at the refreshment kiosk, which he knocks back before heading out to wait where he's been told to.

The morning is grey and cool, the station quiet. Traffic is thin on the road he drove along from Aix, which he can see below him. He gazes out across the orderly French countryside. There are no portents in the air. But something is coming. And it's coming his way.

Lahmar and his deputy, Sebti, are already at the Splendide when Bouras arrives. The cinema's mouldering Art Deco frontage is instantly familiar to him as he approaches, as are the decayed and dusty furnishings of the interior. He can remember it well in all its original smartly maintained glory of bright lights and plush seating. But its glory is long gone.

Sebti is waiting by the entrance to let him in. 'Lieutenant Lahmar's up in the projection room, chief. That's where the body is. The stairs are to the left of the ticket-box.'

'Who else is here?'

'Doctor Chabba and his assistant.' Chabba is the pathologist they usually call on for suspicious deaths. 'And Abidi's wife. She found him. We've got her in the auditorium with Sabeur.' Sabeur is a female officer often chosen when female witnesses need coaxing or comforting.

'What has she said?'

'She came here this morning because Abidi didn't return home last night and wasn't answering his phone. She hasn't seen him since yesterday morning. She knew he used this place for confidential meetings – it's in the family, apparently, belonged to his father – and couldn't think where else to try.'

'How is she?'

'Not as upset as you might expect.'

That was good news in a way. It might make it easier to get some sense out of her. But she could wait. Bouras needed to see what had happened. 'Where are we on forensics?'

'The team's en route. Delayed by Sunday morning in-service training.'

Bouras lets that pass. 'Send them straight up when they arrive. But don't let anyone else in without my say-so.'

'OK, chief. There's a scene-of-crime kit just inside.'

Bouras enters the musty foyer and locates the kit, lodged on the shelf of the old ticket-box. He clambers into the zippable paper coverall and puts on the gloves and overshoes. Then he heads up a narrow flight of dimly lit stairs. He can hear voices and movement above and, turning a corner, sees an open doorway ahead.

The projection room still has its interior window looking out into the auditorium, but the projectors have long gone, replaced by a desk, a couple of upright chairs and a threadbare armchair. There's a filing cabinet in the corner.

It's not a big room and seems smaller still thanks to the presence in it of four people. Three of them are dressed in coveralls, though they are also distinguishable from the fourth by the fact that they are alive, whereas Rochdi Abidi is very obviously dead.

He's lying face downwards on the floor with a plastic bag tied round his neck. His head is twisted sideways. There's a large blood-clotted wound at the back of the head. It looks instantly to Bouras as if he's been knocked unconscious and then asphyxiated. Murder, quite obviously.

Dr Chabba is crouching beside the body. He looks up as Bouras enters and nods a greeting. 'We are honoured to see you, Director. It's surely unusual for you to turn out for something like this.'

'We live in an age when our priorities are governed by the media, Doctor. And the media are going to make as much as they can of Rochdi Abidi getting himself murdered within a week of airing explosive allegations on national television.'

'Ah. You've already decided it's murder, have you?'

'Are you going to tell me it isn't?'

'Assuredly not. Rendered unconscious by a blow to the head and then asphyxiated using a plastic bag. That would be my preliminary opinion. The bag without the head injury might suggest suicide or some kind of autoerotic act gone wrong. The bag *with* the head injury indicates murder, as you suggest.'

'Have you ever actually dealt with an autoerotic act gone fatally wrong?' Bouras has risen to the bait. But *why*? Why has he let himself be drawn in?

'No, Director. But the possibility that I might gets me up in the morning.'

Bouras resolves to stick to the script from here. 'Can you estimate the time of death?'

'*Rigor mortis* is well established. That plus the temperature of the body suggests he died . . . about twelve hours ago.'

'That tallies with something I found, chief,' says Lahmar.

'What is it?'

'Abidi's phone.' Lahmar holds it up, eyes gleaming with pleasure at his discovery. 'I checked the filing cabinet. It's stuffed with old letters and documents dating from when this was a working cinema. But his phone had been slipped into one of the cradles in the third drawer down. And it's unlocked.'

Bouras moves across to join Lahmar by the cabinet. He takes the phone from him and looks at the screen, on which is displayed a text message.

'Drafted at fourteen minutes past eight last night,' Lahmar explains. 'But never sent. The intended recipient was the *Microscope* production team.'

Bouras reads the message – what there is of it. *You need to know I am in danger dss agent hidouchi on way to see me I fear she*

'That's all there is,' says Lahmar. 'The log shows phone calls made and received earlier in the day. But nothing after eight fourteen.'

'And your thinking is?'

'The woman he was frightened of arrived before he could finish and send the text, so he hid the phone in the cabinet. And then . . .'

'Come downstairs with me.'

'OK, chief.'

They leave the room and descend to the foyer. The draft text makes Hidouchi an obvious suspect in Abidi's murder. But that, of course, may be its purpose. Anyone could have composed the message if the phone was in their possession. They may have done so with Abidi lying dead on the floor beside them. Bouras doesn't suppose for a moment that Hidouchi killed him. But he does suppose others will think she did – if they see the message.

'What are we going to do, chief?' asks Lahmar.

'Well, we're certainly not to going to press *send*. Give me a sample bag.'

Lahmar pulls a ziplock plastic bag out of his pocket and hands it over. Bouras drops the phone into the bag and carefully seals the zip.

'Potential DSS involvement means we have to tread very carefully, Lahmar. You understand?'

'Yes, chief.'

'I'll deal with this side of the case. You don't need to know any more about it. OK?'

'Yes, chief.' Lahmar looks relieved to have been told to leave the problem in the director's hands. No mere lieutenant wants to tangle with the dreaded security service.

'Go back up and stay with Doctor Chabba until the forensics team arrives. I want a full sweep of the projection room, the stairs and this foyer. Got that?'

'Yes, chief.'

'I'll have a word with the wife before I go. And I'll see you back at HQ. Don't mention the phone – or the message – to anyone. Is that clear?'

'Yes, chief.'

Lahmar heads back up the stairs, leaving Bouras to pause for a moment – and think.

But this leads him nowhere beyond a forest of difficulties, some foreseeable, some inevitably not. Exasperated with the situation he finds himself in, he slides the bagged phone into his jacket pocket and turns towards the doors leading to the auditorium.

An anonymous silver car pulls up beside Taleb, who advances cautiously towards it. The front passenger window slides open. The driver, a hunched, bearded figure in jeans, fleece and baseball cap, calls, 'Get in the back.'

Taleb obeys and the car moves off. As it does so, the driver tosses something over his shoulder into Taleb's lap. It's a mask – the kind supplied to passengers trying to sleep on planes. In fact, there's a small label attached bearing the *Air Algérie* logo.

'Put that on,' says the driver.

It isn't a request. And Taleb knows he'd have to comply even if it were. He puts the mask on, covering his eyes.

The car moves slowly, describing, as far as Taleb can tell, a wide circle. It pulls up and he hears the door to his left open. It clunks shut as someone climbs into the rear seat beside him. Then the car moves off again.

The newcomer says nothing as the car picks up speed.

And Taleb waits for the silence to be broken.

Abidi's wife is a portly headscarfed woman of sixty or so, slumped in one of the cinema seats beside Lieutenant Sabeur. Sabeur stands up as Bouras approaches along the aisle. 'Hala Abidi, Director,' she whispers, making way for him to sit down beside the older woman should he wish to do so.

But he decides to remain standing. He bows his head as the woman looks up at him. There are no tear tracks on her cheeks. She is solemn but calm in the face of what has happened.

'My condolences,' he murmurs.

'Thank you,' she says. 'You are?'

'Director Bouras.'

'Did he suffer much . . . Director? They have not told me.'

'I believe death came to him swiftly.'

'That is a mercy.'

'You last spoke to him yesterday morning, I understand.'

'No. I last *saw* him then. But I spoke to him by phone yesterday evening . . . at around six o'clock. He called to say he would be home late. He said he had a meeting.'

'A meeting with . . . ?'

'He didn't say. I didn't expect him to. My husband . . . told me little of his work. He said it was safer for me that way. And I never pressed him.'

'Did he say he was here?'

'No. I assumed . . . he was out in the city somewhere. And that the meeting would be . . . in a restaurant, maybe. I wasn't surprised when he still wasn't back when I went to bed. That was . . . normal. My husband . . . kept late hours. He had many friends, many . . . acquaintances.'

'But this is where you came when you couldn't contact him this morning?'

'I couldn't think where else to try. Sometimes . . . when he drank alcohol . . . he would sleep here . . . up in that . . . projection room . . . to avoid . . . offending me.'

'Had he seemed . . . anxious lately?'

'He always lived on his nerves. That TV programme . . .' Her words peter into silence.

'You mean the *Microscope* broadcast?'

A spasm passes across Hala Abidi's features. 'He was a fool to do that. After I saw it . . . I said to him . . . you have made yourself a target. He did not deny it. He just said . . . "The truth has to be known."' She sighs. 'Such stupidity. As if the truth can ever be known. I loved him once for his idealism. But eventually it exhausted me. I knew it would be the death of him. And now . . .' She shrugs. 'It has ended as it was bound to, I suppose. He was always too trusting.'

'Who did he trust?'

'Oh, his . . . informants. His . . . sources. It was through one of them he was lured into saying the things he said on that TV programme. It was supposed to be part of something bigger. Some scoop that would finally get him the respect he thought he deserved. But instead . . .'

'You've no idea what this "scoop" was about?'

'Everything he'd ever worked for rolled into one – to hear him talk. But what that meant . . . if it meant anything . . . he never said. And I didn't ask him to. I never really wanted to know what he was mixed up in. Something dangerous, though. That's obvious now, isn't it? Because whoever he met here last night . . . came to kill him.'

'It seems so.'

She looks away. 'And kill him they did.'

'Does the name . . . Hidouchi . . . mean anything to you?'

She shakes her head. 'No. I never heard him speak of anyone by that name. But he never spoke of his sources by name anyway. He kept me out of all that.'

There seems to be nothing more to say. Rochdi Abidi's murder has saddened his wife, but not surprised her. She has done much of her grieving in advance of the event. And now here she is, resigned to the reality of what she has long foreseen.

'Thank you for being so . . . helpful,' says Bouras. 'I'll leave you now. Lieutenant Sabeur will make sure you get home safely.'

'Will you catch my husband's murderer?' Hala Abidi asks as Bouras moves away.

He turns back to look at her. 'We'll do our best.'

She holds his gaze for a moment, then says, 'Of course you

will.' And her mournfully phlegmatic tone leaves Bouras in no doubt as to what she thinks will happen.

The clicking of the car's indicators and the change of tone between one road surface and another tells Taleb they've left the station complex and joined the D9, heading east, he thinks. But not for long. The car slows, the indicators click again and they turn off onto a side road.

The going now is slower and more sinuous. And the second passenger speaks at last.

He's the man Taleb spoke to on the phone. His voice is distinctively gravelly. He sounds as if he might be a heavy smoker. And his accent is clearly Algerian. 'Thank you for coming, Superintendent.'

'Did I have a choice?'

'You did. And this is the choice you made.'

'Who are you?'

'The man you have to deal with.'

'What should I call you?'

'Major. That was my rank in the army. You can call me by it.'

'Well . . . Major . . . what can I do for you?'

'Agree the terms for Karim Mokrani's release.'

'The terms are already agreed. I can't change them. The practical arrangements for an exchange are a different matter, however. I'm—'

'Listen to me, Taleb. Listen carefully. I have nothing against you personally. A man who devotes more than forty years of his life to the DGSN – as you have – has my respect if not my understanding. It seems perverse, but it suggests you can at least be relied upon to follow orders. As the representative of those holding General Mokrani's beloved son, I am the one who will be issuing the orders in this matter. And you are the one who will be following them. Is that clear to you?'

'It is.'

'Tomorrow morning at eight you will drive into the car park near the dam on the west shore of Lac du Bimont. You will have the ransom money with you. I will make phone contact with you at that point and supply visual proof that Karim Mokrani is alive and well. You will then proceed as directed by me to a second location, where the money will be swapped for Mokrani. And then you will drive him back to the Villa des Ormeaux. Understood?'

'Yes. I can do that.'

'You *will* do that.'

'OK.'

'But there is a further condition.'

'I'm not authorized to agree anything beyond payment of the ransom in exchange for Agent Mokrani's release.'

'Ah, but this is a condition only you can fulfil, Taleb, so the authorizing party . . . is you.'

'I . . . don't understand, Major. A condition only I can fulfil? What would that be?'

'Tomorrow afternoon at three, following payment of the ransom and Karim Mokrani's release, you will visit the offices of a lawyer in Aix – I will supply you with their name and address when the time comes – where you will record a full account of your investigation of General Mokrani's involvement in the Boudiaf assassination. By full I mean precisely that. Every detail of your contact with Youcef Ghezala and your surrender of documents secreted by him at his apartment building to DSS agent Khaled Zoubiri.'

How does the Major know about such things? Zoubiri wasn't mentioned during Taleb's cross-questioning by Abidi on *Microscope*. Taleb is struggling to keep pace with the implications of this new demand. Has the Major been in touch with Abidi? If so—

'And that is not all. We know everything about you, Taleb. We know more than you can possibly imagine. Boudiaf wasn't the last top politician to be assassinated during the DRS's killing spree in the nineteen nineties. We'll need you to disclose what contact you and your late superior Superintendent Meslem had with a representative of Kasdi Merbah shortly before *his* assassination in 1993.'

Merbah? Taleb stiffens with shock at mention of the name. According to Meslem, an intermediary acting for former prime minister and security service chief Kasdi Merbah sounded him out in the summer of 1993 about opening a police inquiry into documents allegedly supplied to Merbah by Ghezala shortly before his death. Merbah was a perversely honourable man who harboured deep suspicions about how Boudiaf had met his death and it was difficult for Meslem to refuse to look at such evidence, even though he knew it would be highly dangerous.

Taleb's memory carries him, like an LP on a jolted record player jumping tracks, back to Meslem's office at Police HQ on a clammy August evening in 1993. More than a year on from Boudiaf's assassination, the descent into civil war had steadily gathered pace, though the worst horrors of *la décennie noire* still lay in wait in the future, unimagined because unimaginable.

Meslem had asked Taleb to stay late, so they could discuss a matter of pressing concern in confidence. He was smoking a cigarette as Taleb entered his office and the air was thick with the smoke of the many others he'd already reduced to crumpled stubs in his overflowing ashtray. His cigarette consumption rate had always been a sure guide to his state of mind and there could be no doubt in this instance that he was a troubled man.

He asked Taleb to sit down and offered him a cigarette, only then noticing that Taleb was already smoking one of his own. He smiled and raised a hand in acknowledgement of his distraction.

'Did you ever tell your wife about the business with Youcef Ghezala last year, Taleb?' he asked.

'Er . . .'

'It's all right. Speak freely. I don't expect my officers to keep secrets from their wives. I don't keep any from mine. Well, not many.'

Taleb relaxed. 'I . . . told her, yes.'

'How did she react?'

'She was appalled by the implication that the DRS could have had a hand in the President's assassination. But she was also . . . relieved that I didn't have to pursue a case with such . . . hazardous ramifications.'

Meslem nodded. 'Much the same as my own wife's feelings on the matter. Our conscientiousness worries them. They fear it may lead us . . . to a fate similar to Ghezala's. As it was, there was nothing for us to investigate.'

'If I'd held on to the documents I found . . .'

'The DRS wouldn't have let you. And if they'd even thought you'd studied their contents before surrendering them . . . I would probably have been consoling your wife at your funeral a few weeks later. So, let's not waste time rehearsing the might-have-beens of that.' Meslem stubbed out his cigarette and immediately lit another. 'We need now to address the might-yet-be of a related development.'

'What's happened, Super?'

'What's your opinion of Kasdi Merbah?'

Merbah was an ambivalent figure in Algerian politics. Head of the security service when it was still called the SM rather than the DRS, he'd subsequently served as a government minister and briefly prime minister during the presidency of Chadli Bendjedid. He'd never seemed happy with the manoeuvrings and machinations of *le pouvoir*, however, and had set up a party advocating moderate liberal policies which had attracted pitifully little support in the 1991 parliamentary elections. 'I think . . .' Taleb began. 'I think . . . he might be that rarest of things, an honest politician . . . or a naive one.'

'Rumour has it, Taleb, that Merbah is trying to broker peace between the government and the Islamists.'

'Someone should.'

'Indeed. And perhaps he will succeed. Meanwhile, however, he has . . . reached out to me through an intermediary.'

'To you?'

'Yes. Because he knows you and I had some dealings with Ghezala. And Ghezala, it transpires, also had some dealings with him.'

'What sort of dealings?'

'Ghezala appears to have supplied Merbah with top secret DRS documents pointing to General Mokrani's involvement in the Boudiaf assassination. Perhaps the very documents – or some of them – you found copies of on the roof of Ghezala's apartment building.'

'Merbah has them?'

'So I'm led to understand. Presumably Ghezala thought Merbah, with his security service background and surprisingly enlightened character, was the obvious person to disclose such material to. Now Merbah, I'm told, wants me to use that material to pursue a criminal case against Mokrani for Boudiaf's murder. He has despaired of the government seeing sense where its arm-wrestling with the Islamists is concerned and proposes to use the evidence he has against Mokrani to attack the entire rotten edifice of *le pouvoir*.'

'Through us?'

'You have it, Taleb. Through us.'

'But . . .'

'But we would never be allowed to and would pay for trying with our lives. Was that the objection you were about to express?'

'It's not an objection, Super. It's a statement of fact.' As he spoke, Taleb was sickened by the truth of what he was saying and by the fear he could feel bubbling within him. It didn't matter what he thought or believed in or hoped for. *Le pouvoir* would crush them like beetles if they crawled into view.

'You're right.' Meslem sighed. 'That is the reality of the country we live in. So, what am I to do? If I refuse to entertain Merbah's request, I am turning my back on one of the worst crimes that has ever been committed in our history. And I am a policeman, Taleb, as you are. We are sworn to uphold the peace and to bring criminals to justice. If we do not do these things, what is the point of our existence? What claim do we have to the respect of anyone?'

All Taleb found by way of response to that was a helpless shrug. He stubbed out his cigarette and gazed forlornly at Meslem across his desk.

'It is a sad day when we avert our gaze from the truth,' said Meslem musingly.

'We are living through sad days,' said Taleb.

'Yes, we are.'

'Whatever you decide to do, Super . . . I'll back you.' Taleb had spoken the words for the simple reason that he could not imagine saying anything else.

Meslem looked at him with genuine appreciation. 'You are a good man in a bad world, Taleb – not a recipe for happiness.'

'I didn't join the police in search of happiness.'

'That was wise of you.'

'Do you know what you're going to do?'

Meslem nodded. 'I haven't made my mind up yet. This requires careful consideration. And that is what I will give it.'

As far as Taleb knew, Meslem was still giving the problem careful consideration when, less than a week later, Kasdi Merbah died in a hail of machine-gun fire when his car was ambushed near his home in Bordj el-Bahri. The GIA claimed responsibility – or had it claimed for them. Whatever threat Merbah posed to *le pouvoir* had been neutralized. And next morning, at Police HQ, Meslem called Taleb into his office and drew his attention to the names listed in *El Watan* of those who'd died in the car along with Merbah: his son, his brother, his driver, his bodyguard . . . and an assistant called Yassin.

'That was the man Merbah sent to speak to me,' said Meslem. 'We will hear no more of Ghezala's documents now. *Le pouvoir* must have realized Merbah was preparing to move against them. You will note it is reported that his dying words were, "I was betrayed." That is easy to believe in these treacherous times. Clearly, there is nothing to be done. Which is as well for you and me. Any documents Merbah had will be in General Mokrani's hands by now – if he hasn't already incinerated them. The Ghezala case will stay closed. And our courage will remain untested.'

'I'm sorry, Super,' said Taleb.

'So am I. Though neither of us should be. We're off the hook.'

'It doesn't feel as if we are.'

'No.' Meslem nodded in sympathy. 'It doesn't, does it? I suppose that's because this is a hook we can never truly be off in this world. We must learn to live with that. You think you can?'

'I expect so, Super.'

Meslem patted him on the shoulder. 'Good man.'

'Are you listening to me, Taleb?'

The Major's words cut through Taleb's recollections. He realizes the car has stopped moving. A sliver of sunlight lances between the edge of the mask and his left cheekbone as his arm is jostled.

'You understand what we require of you?'

'I'm sorry, Major. I . . .'

'You will record a statement disclosing everything you know concerning Youcef Ghezala and General Mokrani, including details of Kasdi Merbah's involvement. And you will sign a transcript of that statement for us to use in any way we deem appropriate.'

'If I do that . . .'

'You fear the consequences?'

'Of course I do. Mokrani will kill me.'

'As he will if you fail to secure his son's release. The general's wrath will surely be lessened by having his son returned to him, for which happy outcome you will be responsible. If the ransom is paid and Karim Mokrani is freed but you fail to provide the statement we require . . . we will come after you. Your chances of survival are therefore higher if you do as we ask.'

'It's suicide.'

'Not if you stay out of the general's clutches for as long as it takes us to bring him down, which is our firm intention. I recommend you help bring that about by telling us where the documents Merbah sent to Meslem are to be found.'

'He didn't send any. It's true he contacted Superintendent Meslem through an intermediary and claimed to have incriminating material supplied by Ghezala. But he was assassinated before it ever reached us.'

'Don't lie to me, Taleb. We have spoken to a surviving member of Merbah's staff. He told us something he'd not revealed to the DRS under questioning: that crucial documents were handed to Meslem two days before the assassination by a trusted assistant of Merbah's who died with his boss in the ambush. The DRS seized all Merbah's records after his death, of course, but they didn't know – luckily for you and Meslem – that some of the material supplied by Ghezala had already reached you.'

'That's not true. Your . . . informant . . . is mistaken.'

'Is he? I don't think so. I think you're trying to cover your tracks. Either that or Meslem didn't tell you the documents had reached him.'

Of course. That was it. Meslem hadn't told him.

Within two months of Merbah's assassination, they'd lost Lieutenant Dif – boyish, ever enthusiastic and eager-to-please young Dif – to a GIA murder squad and another officer to a sniper's bullet at Dif's funeral. They were harsh and awful times. And they weighed heavily on Meslem.

'For as long as this madness continues,' he announced at a squad meeting he convened shortly after Dif's murder, 'officers answering to me will observe a new minimal risk protocol. No one will operate alone. No one will visit scenes of reported crime without my approval – or, in my absence, Inspector Taleb's. No one will rely on undertakings given to them by representatives of other government departments, however senior those representatives may be. We will trust each other and no one else. We're on our own, boys. There's a war going on and we're not an army. The only victory we can hope for is survival.'

Perhaps that was the moment when Meslem's thinking had revealed itself. He had the documents – some of them, anyway. But he wasn't prepared to waste his life or Taleb's on trying to use them against General Mokrani. Survival had become his primary objective.

'He never told me,' Taleb says mournfully. 'He must have decided it was a battle we couldn't win. And he was right.'

'What about the documents?' the Major demands.

'He must have destroyed them. Keeping them would have been too risky.'

'I don't believe you, Taleb.'

'I'm telling you as much of the truth as I know. I never saw any documents apart from those I glimpsed at Ghezala's apartment building before Agent Zoubiri took them from me.'

The Major says nothing for what feels to Taleb like a long time but is probably less than a minute. Then he says to the driver, 'Back to the station.' And the car starts to move.

'Let me spell it out for you, Taleb,' the Major continues after another pause for thought. 'We will release Karim Mokrani on payment of the ransom and on condition that you make the statement we require from you. Do I have your agreement on that?'

Taleb isn't yet sure what he means to do after Karim Mokrani has been released. All his choices are bad ones. But he knows what the Major needs to hear from him. So he delivers it. 'You have my agreement.'

'And do I have your word that you'll honour the agreement?'

'You do.'

'If you break your word or if we think what you say in your statement falls short of the truth . . . we will show you no mercy.'

'I realize that.'

'But if you keep your word and we're satisfied that you've cooperated fully . . . there'll be a reward.'

'I don't want any reward.'

'You haven't heard what it is yet.'

'With all due respect, Major, I don't think there's anything you can offer me that I want.'

'How about the name and current whereabouts of the man who organized and approved the operation that resulted in the deaths of your wife and daughter at Tamel Chaabat on the night of December eighteenth, 1997?'

Taleb feels his innards twist. Not that. Please not that, from a quarter of a century ago. He has lived with it, he has died with it, he has lived again, in the pared-down existence that has been his since Serene and Lili were taken from him. Dreams of revenge once tormented him. He cannot bear such torment again. 'How would you know his name, Major?'

'We know everything. We remember everything.'

'And what would I do with such information?'

'You would seek the man out and visit retribution upon him.'

'Is that what you would do?'

'Most certainly.'

'You and I are not the same.'

'I think we are, Taleb. I think you want to know who it was. And when you do . . .'

'This is your idea of a reward?'

'A reward or a curse. Only you will know which. When you learn the truth.'

'They died. That is the truth. Perhaps I don't need any more truth.'

'Then you can refuse the reward. If that is really what you want. I can give you that choice if no other. For the rest . . . you must do what you have sworn to do. That is now settled between us. And I will hold you to it.'

SEVEN

THERE'S ONLY ONE VEHICLE IN THE LAY-BY AHEAD AND HIDOUCHI recognizes the number plate. She pulls in behind it, props her bike, takes off her helmet and gloves and walks towards the car. She anticipates Bouras has bad news for her. Otherwise he would never have contacted her and proposed an urgent meeting far from prying eyes in the city, out here on the coast road near Aïn Benian, where the only audience comprises a couple of stunted Aleppo pines and a few seagulls circling speculatively over the still, grey Mediterranean. The only question is – and it's been worrying her the whole way – *how* bad?

She opens the front passenger door of the Mercedes and slips into the seat. Bouras nods a silent greeting.

'I was surprised to hear from you, Director,' she says.

'You wouldn't have if I could have avoided it,' he responds glumly, which she finds easy to believe. 'But . . . something's happened.'

'Concerning Taleb?'

'Not directly. Have you spoken to him since he left?'

'Earlier this morning. He was about to meet a representative of the kidnappers in order to agree arrangements for payment of the ransom and Agent Mokrani's release.'

'How did he sound?'

'Apprehensive.'

'As well he might.'

'He warned me to be on my guard.'

'How very prescient of him.'

'Why? What's happened?'

'Did you meet with Rochdi Abidi yesterday?'

'Yes. I did. But I assumed you preferred to know as little as possible about my activities.'

'Ordinarily, that would be true. When and where did you meet him?'

'Late morning. At a disused cinema he's part-owner of.'

'The Splendide?'

'That's the one.'

'Well, Abidi was found dead at the Cinéma Splendide this morning. Knocked unconscious and suffocated with a plastic bag.'

Hidouchi should be shocked, but her profession has inured her to such events and their unpredictability. Besides, a man as outspoken as Rochdi Abidi was always at risk of such a fate. 'He was alive and well when I left him.'

'I don't doubt it. This happened some time last night. His body was discovered in the projection room. By his wife. She says he claimed to be on the brink of some . . . big scoop.'

'He probably thought he was. He wanted me to help him by digging out material from DSS records he could use against General Mokrani.'

'Did you agree to help him?'

'I let him think I'd agreed. My objective was to find out as much as I could about what he was looking into. It sounds as if it's just as well I talked to him when I did.'

'Not necessarily. We found his phone – with a draft text on it mentioning you. Take a look.' Bouras passes her a smartphone enclosed in a sealed plastic evidence bag. 'Don't open the bag. Just press any key. The draft will come up.'

Hidouchi pushes a button through the plastic. And the words appear on the screen in front of her: *You need to know I am in danger dss agent hidouchi on way to see me I fear she*

'The intended recipient was the *Microscope* production team,' Bouras continues. 'If you believe what you see. The message was drafted at eight fourteen last night. Around the estimated time of death.'

'I didn't kill Abidi, Director.'

'I'm sure you didn't. The phone was concealed in a filing cabinet, to make it look as if Abidi had hidden it there when you arrived, with the message naming you unfinished. You don't happen to have an alibi for eight fourteen last night, do you?'

'No.' Hidouchi was alone in her apartment at that time, taking a bath, as she recalls. Whoever tried to frame her for Abidi's killing wouldn't have known where she was, of course – unless her apartment is under surveillance.

'I assume we're likely to find your fingerprints and DNA at the cinema?'

'Mine and many others, no doubt.'

'Indeed. All of which would take us nowhere – unless we had your name on his phone as an imminent visitor he feared ... meant him harm.'

Hidouchi passes the phone back to Bouras. 'What are you going to do, Director?'

'That is what we're here to discuss. If I retain the phone as evidence recovered from the crime scene then investigation of your dealings with Abidi becomes unavoidable. Naturally, I would have to notify Deputy Director Kadri. I imagine you would be suspended from duty pending the outcome of our inquiries. Although they might rapidly become DSS inquiries.'

'Oh, they certainly would. Especially if all this was orchestrated by Kadri in the first place.'

'You're suggesting your departmental superior has tried to frame you for murder?'

'Well, Director, many people may have had a motive for killing Abidi, but none of them bar Kadri has any reason to link me with the crime. General Mokrani probably wished Abidi dead, but he surely wouldn't have taken such drastic action until his son was freed. That leaves Kadri, who has long suspected me of working with Taleb to ends not necessarily in the best interests of the DSS. And the DSS, I have to say after talking to Abidi, might have had good reason to consider him a threat to national security. His murder, blamed on me, would kill two birds with one stone.'

Bouras says nothing for a moment. Then: 'How big a threat was Abidi to national security?'

'His basic allegation was that General Mokrani ran a secret unit that staged covert and false flag operations. It was called Unit ninety-two – after the year it was set up – and was responsible, so Abidi claimed, for President Boudiaf's assassination and numerous other killings, including massacres of whole villages during *la décennie noire*. He laid the execution of the Tibhirine monks at their door, for instance, as well as the In Amenas attack. According to him, the worst terrorist outrages of the past thirty years were all carried out or arranged by Unit ninety-two. It was closed down when Mokrani was sent into retirement in 2015, but if any of Abidi's allegations could be substantiated and made public . . . that would certainly be regarded by the DSS as a threat to national security, simply because *le pouvoir* would regard it as a threat to their position. And you and I both know how they react in such circumstances.'

Another lengthy silence follows. Eventually, Bouras speaks. 'This is turning out to be a strong candidate for the worst day of my professional life, Agent Hidouchi. I am not an enemy of the status quo. I did not design the system that governs our affairs. I am not responsible for the compromises and accommodations we all have to make to thrive in this country. I have made my share of those, perhaps more than my share. I have also sought to moderate the worst effects of *le pouvoir*'s way of doing things. But I have no wish to be a hero, far less a martyr. Abidi was crazy if he ever thought he would be allowed to make such matters public. If this is true, the only surprise is that he wasn't killed a long time ago.'

'Perhaps the *Microscope* broadcast opened some powerful people's eyes to what he was capable of.'

'Perhaps so. And you suspect, presumably, that Kadri, having been ordered to eliminate Abidi, decided this was an opportunity to get rid of you as well.'

'I do suspect that, yes.'

'Leaving me with an awkward problem. Either I play my part in framing you or I suppress the planted evidence and thereby alert Kadri to where my loyalties lie, which isn't something I can afford to do.'

'That's very frank of you, Director. Is there . . . a solution to this problem?' Hidouchi can only hope there is. Her future hinges on how their meeting ends. And so does Bouras's.

'There may be. Perhaps you returned to the cinema late last night, broke in, discovered Abidi's body, found his phone and realized you were being set up. You then left the way you'd come, taking with you the phone, which you later destroyed.'

'But I didn't return to the cinema.'

'What if we have a witness who says they saw someone – maybe a man, maybe a woman – entering the rear of the building through an ill-fitting window? There's actually no sign of a break-in, so I imagine Abidi let his murderer in. Kadri would know that and therefore assume you were the person seen breaking in later.

In that scenario, you removed the phone, frustrating his attempt to frame you. It's galling for him, but it's a story that makes sense. It leaves you no worse off than you already are where he's concerned and it leaves me . . . in the clear.'

'Except that you don't have a witness.'

'I'm a policeman, Agent Hidouchi. Witnesses are my stock-in-trade. You can leave me to find one.' Bouras drums his fingers on the steering wheel. 'Yes, I think that will serve the purpose.' He passes the phone back to Hidouchi. 'Don't delay destroying it.'

'I won't.'

'I blame Taleb for this, of course.'

'You do?'

'He's lured me into a number of small rebellions against *le pouvoir* which have amounted over time to taking more risks with my career than I ever intended to. And he's introduced you into my life, which is another level of risk altogether. A stubbornly principled police superintendent and a DSS agent with her own agenda: company I definitely shouldn't keep.'

'I'm sorry if I've . . . put you in an awkward position, Director.'

'Are you?' Bouras looks at her and sighs. 'Take the phone and go. Make sure it's never seen again. And say nothing to Kadri that undermines the credibility of the version of events I'm going to serve up to him.'

'You have my word on all of that. Thank you, Director.'

'Can I ask you to inform Taleb of what's happened? I think he needs to know.'

'I'll tell him.'

'One other thing. This isn't going to be the first in a succession of favours I do you, OK? This is strictly a one-off.'

Hidouchi nods. 'Understood. But if there's ever anything I can do for *you* . . .'

Bouras says nothing. He doesn't want to acknowledge the debt she owes him. It establishes the possibility of more debts to be incurred and owed between them in the future. He knows this. It's unavoidable. It is the way of the world – particularly the Algerian corner of the world. He and she are linked now, whether they like it or not.

Hidouchi slips the phone into a zipped pocket of her jacket and gets out of the car. She hears the engine of the Mercedes start as she walks back towards her motorbike. Before she reaches it, Bouras pulls out of the lay-by onto the far side of the road and accelerates away in the direction of Algiers.

Taleb drives slowly on his way back to the Villa des Ormeaux. His encounter with the Major has left him shaken and uncertain. He knows he has to go through with delivery of the ransom money. Otherwise Karim Mokrani will not be freed and he will take the blame. But once Agent Mokrani *is* free Taleb has to supply his statement for *les souveniristes* to use as they see fit. He will take the blame for that as well. If General Mokrani thinks he's going down, he'll lash out like the petulant brute he is beneath his gold epaulettes and his chestful of unmerited medals. If he's going down, he'll be sure to take Taleb with him.

For the moment, Taleb can see no escape from his dilemma. He certainly can't withdraw from negotiating Agent Mokrani's release. What excuse could he give, after all? Illness? A family bereavement? Besides, the consequences would hardly be any less severe than honouring his agreement with the Major. He is playing poker with no cards in his hand.

Except one. The documents Kasdi Merbah may have supplied to Superintendent Meslem shortly before his murder in August 1993. If they still exist . . .

Meslem told Taleb nothing about such documents. And he certainly made no use of them. But did he destroy them, assuming he ever received them? He was a cautious man who thought ahead and wouldn't lightly have disposed of hard evidence relating to a presidential assassination. It would have gone against his nature and better judgement. It would have offended his policeman's soul.

But if he kept them, he must have hidden them so well no one ever came to know of their existence; so well, in fact, that they are probably – eleven years after his death – still where he originally concealed them.

The only conclusion Taleb can draw with confidence is that they would not have left Algeria. But he is in France. And he won't be going home until Karim Mokrani is free and *les souveniristes* have what they want – five million Swiss francs *and* Taleb's statement. He has no choice but to go on.

Irmouli is waiting for him at the villa, looking no more pleased with life in general and Taleb in particular than when they parted earlier. He too is playing a double game, as Taleb knows from what Abdou overheard the night of the abduction. Perhaps the strain is telling on him, but he deserves no sympathy. Taleb suspects he is under far greater strain himself.

He briefs Irmouli on what he agreed with the Major, but only up to a point. Naturally, he makes no mention of his scheduled visit to a local lawyer. He confines himself to the need to have the money ready for delivery at eight o'clock the following morning. And Irmouli immediately calls Spühler.

It's a short conversation with a simple outcome. 'Spühler will be here this evening,' Irmouli reports.

'With the money?'

'What do you think?' Irmouli frowns menacingly at Taleb. 'Of course he'll bring the money. You don't need to worry about that. He'll bring it. And you'll hand it over to the kidnappers tomorrow in exchange for Agent Mokrani. Nothing's going to go wrong. Unless you somehow bungle the swap. And you're not going to do that, are you? Because if you do . . .' He draws a finger across his neck in a throat-slitting gesture. 'It'll be the end of you.'

Taleb shapes a grim smile. 'Thanks.'

'What for?'

'Letting me know where I stand.'

Hidouchi doesn't leave the lay-by straight away. She needs to put in an appearance at DSS HQ in case Kadri decides to check on her whereabouts, but she can't risk taking Abidi's phone with her, so she starts checking through its contents as soon as Bouras's car has vanished from sight.

She deletes the draft text mentioning her, but is well aware it will remain in the phone's memory, from which the DSS technical team are quite capable of retrieving it. The same applies to all the other deleted material. Abidi appears to have been sedulous in deleting texts, emails and voicemail – implausibly so, in fact. The log shows various messages received prior to his death, from numbers and email addresses Hidouchi has no way of tracing without assistance, but the messages themselves have vanished. She suspects his killer was responsible for purging the material, with the intention of limiting the evidence the police could lift from the phone to the draft text implicating her.

A couple of emails have arrived today, however. One is from the *Microscope* team, asking if they can pass on his contact details to journalists and researchers interested in what he said on air. The other is from the editor of a current affairs website inviting him to expand on his claims for the benefit of their users.

There's also one voicemail message. And Hidouchi is surprised when she listens to it that she recognizes the caller: Professor Hachemi Difala of the University of Algiers, who was, twelve years in the past, her academic supervisor and the man who suggested she explore working for the security service – at that time the DRS.

'I got your message. Not sure how I can help you. I think your TV appearance was unwise, but I'd be willing to meet you and answer your questions as far as I'm able to. It would have to be on a completely confidential basis, you understand. I can't be publicly associated with you in view of your controversial profile. Call me back and let's see what we can arrange.'

What questions did Abidi want to put to Professor Difala? It's too late to ask Abidi, but perhaps Difala has some idea. Hidouchi transfers his number to her phone, then takes a wrench out of the toolkit in her saddlebag, sets Abidi's phone on the ground and smashes it into several jagged chunks of plastic and metal. She walks across to the fence separating the lay-by from a patch of clifftop scrub, climbs over the fence and advances to the edge of the cliff, from where she hurls the chunks into the sea.

Then she returns to her motorbike and pulls out her reserve phone to make the promised call to Taleb.

She finds a text message from him waiting for her. *Returned safely from rendezvous indications of hidden agenda remain watchful.* She calls him straight away.

And he answers promptly. 'You got my text?'

'Yes. Where are you now?'

'The villa. But I'm alone. We can speak freely.'

'There's been a development at this end. Abidi was found dead this morning.'

'*No!*'

'Yes. I'm afraid so.'

'Murdered?'

'How did you guess?'

'He was making a lot of trouble for a lot of people. Murder's a common cause of death for someone like him. I'm not sure what his elimination means, but we're not just dealing with a kidnapping. That much is clear to me.'

'And to me.' Hidouchi decides it's best to spare Taleb the

details of the planted material on Abidi's phone. 'We both have to tread very carefully.'

'I'm already doing that. But it's starting to get complicated, with an additional condition for our friend's release.'

'What sort of condition?'

'A statement from me backing up Abidi's accusations.'

'You mustn't give them that, Taleb.'

'Well, I'm not expected to supply it until *after* the release, so there may be some way to work round it. Meanwhile, I hope you're heeding my warning about uncertain allegiances within your department.'

'I am. When do you anticipate the release happening?'

'Tomorrow morning.'

'OK. Maybe I should hold off on any action until then.'

'What kind of action were you thinking of taking?'

'I have a lead on what – or who – Abidi was mixed up with prior to his death.'

'Follow it up right away. The more we know – and the sooner we know it – the better.'

Bouras is sipping coffee and trying to cultivate a composed frame of mind in his office at Police HQ when DSS Deputy Director Kadri returns his call.

'Did you want to speak to me about Superintendent Taleb's handling of negotiations in France, Director?' Kadri languidly enquires. The man exudes arrogance even in his tone of voice, which somehow suggests he is constantly seeking to suppress a yawn. 'My understanding from our agents on the ground is that everything is proceeding satisfactorily. Have I been misinformed?'

'Not as far as I know,' Bouras replies. 'I called regarding Rochdi Abidi. I regret to have to inform you that he was found dead this morning.'

'That is . . . disturbing news. Not natural causes, I'm guessing?'

'It would appear he was murdered.'

'Terrible for his family, of course, and unfortunate timing, but he can't have been short of enemies. Do you know who did it?' Kadri is purveying the impression that this is the first he's heard of Abidi's demise. Bouras would have expected nothing less. It could even be genuine – theoretically.

'We don't yet have a suspect.'

'Really? That's . . . disappointing.' And perhaps surprising if the phone evidence was planted on Kadri's orders. 'Where did this happen?'

'A disused cinema he part-owned. The Splendide. We think he was murdered around nine o'clock last night.'

'And you've turned up nothing at the scene to suggest who might be responsible?'

'Not yet. Investigations are ongoing.'

'I can place some of our resources at your disposal if you require . . . expert assistance.'

'That won't be necessary, thank you. Our forensics team know what they're doing. What I want to suggest to you is that there should be a media blackout on the news until Agent Mokrani has been released. I don't know if you have any reason to believe Abidi was involved with *les souveniristes*, but in the circumstances . . .'

'No direct involvement is suggested by the little we know, Director. But I agree it would be wise to hold back any announcement in case it somehow . . . spooks the kidnappers.'

So far so textbook. Kadri is giving nothing away. 'Very well. It won't be easy to prevent the news leaking out, so I hope we won't have to keep the lid on it for very long. Publicity can yield valuable information, after all.'

'In addition to your on-scene investigations.'

'Quite so.'

'How was Abidi murdered?'

'Knocked unconscious, then suffocated with a plastic bag.'
'Interesting.'
'How so?'
'It's, er . . . a professional method, that's all. Quiet, simple and effective. Not the sort of thing an aggrieved subject of one of Abidi's scoops would do in a temper.'
'Well, that's . . . a valuable observation, Deputy Director. I'll bear it in mind.'
'Please do. And please alert me . . . as soon as you make any significant discovery.'
'I certainly will.'

The call ends moments later. And Bouras immediately speaks to his secretary on the internal line. 'Ask Lieutenant Lahmar to come up here right away, please.'

Lahmar arrives within minutes, in his customary condition of breathless eagerness to please, heightened by a recent perception on his part that promotion is in the offing. And so it is, though not because of the retirement of Superintendent Taleb that he has so keenly anticipated.

'Sit down, Lahmar,' says Bouras, leaving Lahmar to perch himself awkwardly on the sofa that has discomfited many a visitor to his office. 'Any news from forensics regarding Abidi's murder?'

'Nothing significant, Director. Multiple fingerprints, most of them Abidi's. We're running a check on the others to see if we have a match on our database. None yet.'

'Any developments you will bring directly to me.'

'Understood.'

'This is a highly sensitive matter. I'm not issuing a press release. There's to be a media blackout for the next forty-eight hours. Be sure that's clear to all officers involved. And keep the number of those officers to an absolute minimum.'

'I will, Director.'

'We operate on a need-to-know basis where this is concerned. And hardly anyone needs to know.'

'You can rely on me, Director.'

'I *am* relying on you, Lahmar. In Superintendent Taleb's absence, I look to you to handle this case with discretion and effectiveness. If you satisfy me that you're able to, I believe the time will have come to elevate you to inspector level.'

'You won't regret putting your faith in me, Director.'

'I'm glad to hear it. Let me emphasize that the possibility of DSS involvement we discussed earlier – in particular the discovery of a phone at the scene – must remain unmentioned except between us. You will leave that aspect of the case for me to manage and you will say nothing about it – not a word – to anyone else. Regard that as a test of your loyalty to me. And bear in mind that loyalty is what I prize most in my senior officers.'

Lahmar nods furiously. 'I am loyal, Director. And dedicated.'

'Good. Demonstrate that in the days ahead and your future in this department will be a rewarding one.' Bouras confers a smile of blessing on the lieutenant. 'Now, back to work, I suggest.'

There's no conference business scheduled for Sunday, so the hours pass slowly and quietly at the Villa des Ormeaux. Taleb can find nothing to distract him from fruitless rumination on how to avoid making the statement about General Mokrani he's agreed to supply without being hunted down and killed by *les souveniristes*. The Major's suggestion that Mokrani might overlook Taleb blackening his name out of the sheer joy of having his son set free gives him little comfort. He feels as if he's caught in a vice, the jaws of which are slowly tightening. He refrained from telling Hidouchi how grim his prospects were simply because he knew there was nothing she could do to help him. He keeps telling himself he isn't going to provide the signed statement demanded of him. And most of the time he believes that. But what is he going to do instead?

When Noussa invites him to join her and Abdou again for supper that evening, he is more grateful than he can say. A few hours of good food and friendly conversation will drain some of the anxiety out of him, at least temporarily.

Before then, however, he has to renew his acquaintance with Lydia Seghir, Irmouli having informed him that she requires his presence in the conference room. Taleb reports there at the appointed time and finds *la dame formidable* sitting working at her laptop at the far end of a long table flanked by empty chairs. She glances up at him over the tops of her half-moon glasses as he makes a sheepish entrance, fails to ask him to sit and spends a full couple of minutes finishing whatever she is doing on the computer before closing it down and giving him her fixed attention.

'You met a representative of the kidnappers this morning, Superintendent?'

Taleb nods. 'I did.'

'Agent Irmouli tells me you have arranged for the ransom to be paid and Agent Mokrani released tomorrow morning. Is that correct?'

'In principle, yes.'

'In principle?' She looks unamused by such language. 'What is to happen *in practice*?'

'The same. But the kidnappers set the rules. And they can change them without notice. There is nothing certain in such an operation.'

'Certainty is what you were sent here to supply.'

'I was sent here to negotiate an exchange and that's what I'm doing. But negotiations are never truly ended until the desired outcome has been arrived at.'

Seghir gives him a scowling glare. 'Are you confident of that outcome, Superintendent?'

'I would describe myself as . . . cautiously optimistic.'

She removes her glasses, props an elbow on the table and sucks thoughtfully on one of the arms of her spectacles as she stares at Taleb. 'If you deliver a satisfactory result, you will have earned my appreciation, a sentiment likely to prove highly advantageous to a public servant such as yourself. An *un*satisfactory result, however, is something you will have cause to regret. You understand?'

'I do.' Oh yes, Taleb understands. Like many others in positions such as hers, Lydia Seghir believes threatening subordinates with dire punishment for failure will somehow force success into being, even if it is in reality unattainable.

'This must *not* become a problem for me. If it does, it will be a far bigger problem for you.'

It seems there will be people lining up to tear the flesh from Taleb's bones if he does not somehow achieve a happy resolution of the Karim Mokrani kidnapping case. He does not have the heart to tell Seghir that she is likely to find herself several places back from the front of such a queue. 'Is there anything else I can do for you?' he asks, devoutly hoping the answer is no.

And this one hope of his is fulfilled. 'You may go,' Seghir says with a haughty sweep of her hand.

What Hidouchi intends to be no more than a token appearance at DSS HQ is elevated in significance as soon as she arrives by a summons to Kadri's office.

Meschac Kadri is a creature of the security service hierarchy, elevated to deputy director status thanks to family connections and shameless adherence to the organization's priorities whatever his personal view as to their desirability. Actually, though, he doesn't have personal views, except in the non-professional arenas of fashion, interior design and male grooming. His large wide-windowed office features Italian furniture of the low-slung tubular steel and black leather variety. The suits he's required to wear have an expensively unstructured look to them. His moustache and half-beard are always exactly the same meticulously trimmed length. And his cologne precedes and succeeds him in wafts of what he clearly believes to be the very essence of irresistibility.

His carefully cultivated air of relaxation, often edging towards boredom, is not present this morning, however. One of his lapels is slightly caught up at the neck and his hair is fractionally disarranged. This would betoken very little in most people. In Kadri it instantly tells Hidouchi that something has rattled him.

'Take a seat,' he says, uncharacteristically failing to summon a smile.

'Thank you,' says Hidouchi, seating herself at one end of his largely empty desk, no chair having been positioned directly opposite Kadri.

'You are one of our most expert agents, Souad.' He swivels his chair to face her. 'It's a cause of regret to me that we've never enjoyed what I would call a fruitful relationship.'

Kadri's idea of a fruitful relationship with the young women of the department centres, according to the office gossip-mill, on the long sleek-lined couch imported from Venice which Hidouchi can see out of the corner of her eye. She doesn't glance towards it. 'I am sorry you feel that, Deputy Director.'

'I doubt you truly are. We both know you insist on following your own conscience, even when – perhaps especially when – a demonstration of unconditional loyalty to the needs of the service would serve your career much better.'

'Is there something I've done wrong?'

'There is much. There is also much you have done right. They exist more or less in equilibrium. But I didn't ask you here to review your performance as a DSS agent. Your record speaks for itself, both on the plus side and the minus.' Kadri sighs and examines his fingernails. This relieves him of the need to look at her as he continues. 'I know you've maintained informal working connections with Superintendent Taleb of the DGSN since you and he conducted a joint operation in Paris eighteen months ago. This I have . . . tolerated . . . because there's been no conflict with your DSS assignments . . . and because there was always the possibility that such a connection would one day . . . prove valuable to me. To us, that is – the service. And that day has come.'

Hidouchi must weigh her every word now. If Kadri was responsible for planting the evidence implicating her in Abidi's murder, this encounter is part of the same manoeuvre. He doesn't yet know, of course, that the attempt to frame her has failed. But, strangely, his behaviour – his conciliatory tone – suggests he does. Or perhaps, she is disarmed to reflect, he actually knows nothing about the frame-up at all. 'I don't quite . . . understand,' she says, accurately enough.

'I suspect you're well aware of the mission Taleb has been sent on to France. I suspect you're also well aware of what has happened to Rochdi Abidi. If you insist on pretending otherwise, I'll have to waste my time explaining that mission and the gruesome discovery made this morning at the Cinéma Splendide. I'd appreciate it, I really would' – now he looks at her again – 'if I didn't have to do that. Because I have an assignment for you. One I think you'll want to take.'

'I am always happy to discharge my duty as a DSS agent.' This response leaves all that Hidouchi wishes to leave unsaid – and hopes Kadri is willing to leave unsaid as well – safely in the realm of the implicit.

'Of course you are.' He smiles for the first time. 'Director Bouras has insisted the DGSN will handle the investigation into Abidi's murder without our involvement. That's not an arrangement I can accept. Abidi's outburst during the *Microscope* broadcast and subsequent events suggest very strongly that there's an intelligence dimension to all of this we can't ignore.

Who killed Abidi and why? Who are *les souveniristes* and what is their objective? I want you to exploit your DGSN connections and explore all other avenues in search of the answers to those two questions. And before you respond, let me emphasize that there are ample grounds for suspending you pending a full disciplinary inquiry that would undoubtedly lead to the termination of your service.'

The conversation has suddenly taken a threatening turn. 'What grounds are those . . . Deputy Director?' Hidouchi asks, not allowing her gaze to falter in the slightest degree.

'Unapproved contact with a DGSN officer and sharing sensitive intelligence information with him; unapproved assistance afforded to said officer in the pursuit and prosecution of criminal suspects that amounts to a breach of your conditions of service; failure to seek permission from your line manager – that would be me – for these and various other actions carried out by you over the period in question.' Kadri pauses. He might have been quoting from an internal document detailing his charges against Hidouchi. Perhaps he's already drafted one in his mind. But he won't have gone any further. Because the message he's really conveying is that disciplinary proceedings remain moot. Assuming she does what he's asked of her. 'Bearing all of that in mind, Souad, I would advise you to accept the assignment I have for you without quibble or hesitation.'

There'd be no way out of this even if Hidouchi wanted to find one. As it is, the assignment serves her purposes as well as Kadri's – as he's probably well aware. 'Naturally,' she says softly, 'I will do everything I can to establish where the truth lies in this matter.'

'Thank you.' Kadri holds his smile. 'So, what are your . . . preliminary thoughts?'

'Well . . . Abidi had many enemies who might have wished him dead. And *les souveniristes* . . . are an Islamist terrorist group looking to avenge some of the suffering inflicted on them during *la décennie noire*. I would start from those two premisses.'

'We need to know *which* of Abidi's enemies killed him. And we need to satisfy ourselves that *les souveniristes* are what they present themselves as.'

'Do you doubt it?'

'I do.'

Kadri has just admitted to doubt about the composition and motives of *les souveniristes* and hence the true purpose of Karim Mokrani's abduction. He's either perpetrating an elaborate pretence of ignorance or he suspects there's more going on than he knows about – which is a lot to admit for a DSS deputy director. Hidouchi feels the ground moving beneath her feet. If Kadri didn't try to set her up, who did? And who – *what* – are *les souveniristes*? 'If I am to accomplish anything,' she says slowly, 'I need to understand why Agent Mokrani was in France.'

'Ah, the secret conference at the Provençal villa. Is that what you're referring to?'

'If it is why he was there, then . . . yes.'

'And it is. Unfortunately, I don't know the purpose of the conference – who the delegates are; what they are discussing; and what the desired outcome is. I'm in the dark on all of that. Which I don't like being.'

'Yet DSS agents have been assigned to the event.'

'Yes. At the insistence of our ministerial superiors. The order came down the line. And I had to obey it.'

'Who's actually running the conference, then?'

'Lydia Seghir. Special adviser at both the Ministry of Energy and the Ministry of Foreign Affairs.'

'Both ministries?'

'Yes. A strange arrangement, isn't it? A *suspicious* arrangement, you might say. The bottom line is: what Seghir wants Seghir gets. She has the highest level of authorization. The Villa des Ormeaux conference is a top governmental priority. Unquestioning assistance is to be afforded by all departments.'

'But you *are* questioning it.'

'I am now, yes. Following the abduction of Agent Mokrani and the latest turn of events where Rochdi Abidi is concerned, it would be negligent of me to do otherwise.'

In reality, Kadri would be more than happy to practise negligence if he thought it served his interests. His concern isn't about doing his duty. It's about – as it always is – self-preservation. 'Why was Mokrani assigned to the conference team?' she queries.

'Seghir asked for him.'

'Ah.'

'Yes. *Ah.*'

'Have you heard from her since he was kidnapped?'

'I've *never* heard from her. She keeps us at arm's length. She has stipulated to Agent Irmouli, who's leading our team on the ground, that efforts to free Mokrani mustn't interfere with the smooth running of the conference. That has been her only reaction.'

'Does Irmouli have any sense of what the delegates are discussing?'

'He says not.'

'*Says* not?'

'Obviously, I instructed him to do everything he could to establish what the purpose of the conference is. He reports it's been impossible to do so.'

'And you believe him?'

Kadri sits back in his chair and slowly shakes his head. 'Not . . . altogether.'

'One of our agents kidnapped. Another whose loyalty is in question. That's . . .'

'Not good for my peace of mind, Souad. Not good at all. Which is why I want you – someone whose . . . dedication . . . I know I can rely on – to find out what's behind all this.'

'You really have no idea?'

'None.' If that's true, as Hidouchi senses it is, Kadri must be a seriously worried man. He is famed for his wealth of contacts in influential circles, although those contacts aren't quite what they were. There was a time when he was notorious for his habit of trying to intimidate people by showing them a photograph of himself chin-wagging at a garden party with senior statesman Abdelkader Bensalah, particularly after Bensalah served as acting president between the resignation of Bouteflika in April 2019 and the election of a successor eight months later. But Bensalah has since died and if Kadri has managed to acquire a living and breathing godfather in the upper reaches of *le pouvoir* he's keeping quiet about it, which would be uncharacteristic. 'Although I have heard a whisper . . .' he hesitantly resumes, 'that might . . .' His voice tails off.

'A whisper about what?'

'Something called . . . the White Leopard project.'

'What is it?'

Kadri shrugs. 'I don't know. I've heard it mentioned precisely twice, in muttered conversations I've caught snatches of in corridors at the Ministry of Defence while I've been on my way to or from meetings. The parties to those conversations have been senior figures it wouldn't be wise for me to question. And there's nothing to link White Leopard – whatever it may be – to Seghir's conference. But still . . . when two mysteries coincide . . .'

'They may be the same mystery.'

Kadri nods. 'They may.'

'And it is for me to find out whether they are.'

'Yes. In any case, whatever you find out . . . you will bring to me first. If I discover you're feeding information to others before me . . .'

'I think we understand each other, Deputy Director.'

'Good. There'll be nothing in writing about this, by the way. No emails confirming your assignment; no record of anything we discuss. It will all be . . . under the radar.' And therefore, of course, from Kadri's point of view, completely deniable. 'Minimal communication – until and unless there's a breakthrough.'

'If that's to be so, I may have to . . . act on my own initiative quite extensively.'

'Well, Souad . . .' Kadri plants his elbows on the desk and folds his fingers together as he looks at her. 'All in all, I don't think you'll find that difficult.'

Supper that evening with the Rezigs bathes Taleb in the transitory comforts of good food and congenial company. They don't press him to reveal what progress he's made in his efforts to negotiate Karim Mokrani's release. In fact, they refrain from questioning him at all. They simply dwell in their own space of domestic harmony and invite him to share it with them. For the few hours he spends with them he's almost a happy man.

Not much of that happiness remains when he makes his way back to the villa. He knows he should be relieved to see Spühler's Citroën parked out front, but somehow he isn't. It means there really can be no excuse for not delivering the ransom tomorrow morning and doing whatever he's told to do in order to secure Karim Mokrani's freedom.

As he approaches the building, he sees Jahid waiting for him in the porch, smoking a cigarette. Irmouli would probably demand to know where he's been, but all Jahid says is, 'They're in the salon on the right.'

They turn out to be Spühler and Irmouli, seated in high-backed armchairs either side of a blazing log fire. Taleb's not been in this room before. Its corniced ceiling, wood-panelling and smattering of heavy oil paintings gives it an air of provincial French landowning affluence, reminding him – not that he needs to be reminded – that he is a former colonial subject on the territory of his former colonial masters.

Spühler isn't French, of course. And neither is Irmouli. But both look much more at their ease than Taleb feels. Irmouli's smug little grin in his direction he finds particularly irksome – but also worrying. Shouldn't a DSS agent be keeping his distance from the moneyman of a disgraced onetime DRS bigwig?

'You spend too much time with the Rezigs, Taleb,' says Irmouli sneeringly.

But Spühler instantly strikes a more reasonable note. 'I'm glad to see you're here now, Superintendent.' He takes a sip from a glass of red wine. 'I have the money as promised.'

He points towards a silver-grey suitcase standing to the right of the fireplace. It's stoutly constructed, of aluminium by the look of it, reinforced with steel at the sides. There's a combination lock, handles top and side and wheels on the base. It resembles the kind of case used by film crews when transporting camera equipment. But this case doesn't contain camera equipment, of course. It contains the small matter of five million Swiss francs.

'It's all there,' Spühler continues. 'But you'll want to see it, I imagine. Allow me.'

He springs out of the armchair, lays the suitcase flat on the floor and kneels in front of it to operate the combination lock. Taleb can't see the numbers from where he's standing. The catches snap open and Spühler raises the lid.

'The Swiss franc has the highest top-value denomination note of any currency in the world,' he says with a hint of pride in his voice. 'Rendering portage a great deal easier than it would be for dollars or euros. So, we have here five million francs in banded wads of thousand-franc notes.' He stands up and steps away, gesturing with his hand for Taleb to take a closer look if he wishes.

Taleb moves past Irmouli and crouches next to the open suitcase. There is the money in front of him. He picks one wad off the top and leafs through the crisp new notes. Then he picks another from the next level down. He has never seen so much money before, in any currency. There is a smell drifting up from it which he could hardly put a name to. Perhaps it is the smell of wealth itself – in its purest Swiss-distilled form.

'Each wad comprises a hundred notes,' Spühler purrs. 'And there are fifty wads. 'It is the specified sum.'

'Besides,' puts in Irmouli, 'General Mokrani isn't going to try and short-change the kidnappers with his son's life on the line, is he? Finished drooling over the cash, have you?'

Taleb replaces the wads and stands up. Spühler drops down beside the suitcase, which he swivels to one side, then closes and locks in a swift, practised movement.

'I'll need to know the combination,' says Taleb.

Spühler stands up again. 'I'll supply it in the morning. You'll appreciate, I'm sure, that General Mokrani wishes to ensure every precaution is taken with such a very large sum of money.'

Taleb is too tired to argue. 'All right. In the morning. But tell me, are these all new notes?'

'Not exactly.' Spühler frowns slightly. 'The circulation of thousand franc notes is necessarily limited.'

'But there'll be a record of the serial numbers.'

'I have brought what I was instructed to bring.'

'That's right,' says Irmouli. 'And we all have our instructions, Taleb, don't we? I suggest you concentrate on carrying out yours.'

Taleb looks round at Irmouli, who he suspects is trying for some reason to rile him – in which he will be unsuccessful. 'I know what I have to do. And I intend to do it.'

'Good. The car park at Lac du Bimont is about five kilometres north-east of here. Your SatNav will lead you straight to it. How long will you allow for the journey?'

'There can't be any question of turning up late. So, I'll be gone by seven thirty.'

'I suggest I meet you by your car at seven fifteen,' says Spühler 'Will that be satisfactory?'

Taleb nods. 'Seven fifteen it is.'

'Don't let us keep you any longer, then,' says Irmouli. 'You'll need to be well rested.'

Taleb doesn't rise to the bait. He simply says, 'Goodnight,' and leaves the room.

He climbs the stairs through a house filled with silence. If Irmouli and Spühler are talking about him back in the salon, they must be conversing in whispers. He hears a distant spit of the fire, but no human voice. The stairs creak faintly beneath his feet. He isn't alone in the building, but he may as well be. He doubts he will be well rested come the morning. There is every reason to suppose he isn't going to sleep soundly. The preparations are complete. The ransom is ready. And somewhere the hostage is ready too. All Taleb has to do is bring them together. And all he has to do until then is the hardest thing of all. He has to wait.

EIGHT

TALEB WAKES WELL BEFORE DAWN AND VENTURES DOWN TO THE kitchen in search of breakfast. To his surprise, Noussa is already up and about. She says nothing about the task she knows lies before him this morning, but seems to acknowledge it by plying him generously with coffee, omelette and croissants. It's a lavish breakfast by his standards. He only wishes he could savour it more.

He's out by his car well before seven fifteen. It's still dark, and chilly with it. There are spits of rain in the air. He smokes a cigarette from his dwindling supply of Nassims and seeks to organize his thoughts. This part of the operation should go smoothly, after all. *Les souveniristes* want the money and without releasing their hostage they won't get Taleb's promised statement. As far as he's concerned, they're not going to get it anyway, but they don't know that. And he doesn't know *how* he's going to avoid supplying it either. The afternoon of this day is actually more troubling than the morning. But the morning has to be lived through first.

Spühler appears on the dot of seven fifteen, carrying the suitcase. He's wearing an expensive-looking camel overcoat over his doubtless immaculately cut suit. To Taleb's relief, there's no sign of Irmouli.

The only greetings they exchange are cursory nods. Taleb opens the boot of the car and Spühler places the suitcase inside, then turns to face him. He takes a silver cigarette case out of his pocket, selects a cigarette and lights it. It smells like a *Disque Bleu* to Taleb.

'There's time for one smoke before we go, I think,' says Spühler.

The remark catches Taleb unawares. '*We?*'

'I'm going with you, Superintendent.'

'No. That's not part of the arrangement. Just give me the combination for the suitcase and I'll handle things from here.'

'I'm afraid I have to insist on accompanying you. General Mokrani – how can I put this? – doesn't feel he can trust you absolutely.'

'What does he think I'm going to do – steal the money?'

'That's exactly what he thinks you might do. It's not probable, of course. In my judgement it's highly *im*probable. But any degree of risk is unacceptable with five million Swiss francs at stake. So, as I have informed Agent Irmouli, I am to go with you and ensure that the money is paid to the kidnappers in return for Karim's release.'

'They're only expecting me. Your presence will disturb them. It's just the kind of thing that could cause a delicate operation like this to go badly wrong.'

Spühler shrugs and takes a long draw on his cigarette. 'I have my instructions. You have yours. They are not incompatible.'

'You coming along doesn't reduce risk, it creates it. Phone General Mokrani now and explain to him that I must be allowed to handle this on my own.'

'If I did that, he would think you were definitely trying to cheat him and he would still insist I go with you, so I strongly recommend . . . we simply do what he wants.'

'Why didn't you tell me about this last night?'

'It was late for arguing. And I didn't want you to retire to bed on a sour note.'

'I'd have told you then what I'm telling you now. I should go alone.'

'Your opinion is noted. But without the combination for the case you are in no position to effect an exchange. And I will only supply the combination when everything is in place. So, I suggest you accept the reality of the situation.' Spühler smiles. 'It's always best to do that, in my experience.'

It's too early for students to be seen in any number at the University of Algiers. Hidouchi paces along a silent arch-ceilinged corridor that she hasn't traversed for more than a decade. Her destination is the room where she often participated in economics seminars run by Professor Hachemi Difala. In those days, which feel to her even more distant than they actually are, Difala would have been asking the questions and she would have been trying to find the answers. Today their roles will be reversed.

She's confident she'll find Difala in his room. He was always noted for early starts. And for late finishes, come to that. He was rumoured to have an unhappy home life, from which the university and his comfortable accommodation there constituted a refuge he'd come to treasure. Which might explain why he still hasn't retired from his post.

His door is half open, as was always his custom. She knocks and enters and sees him, older and leaner than she remembers, slightly stooped and whiter-haired, rolling up his prayer mat. He has obviously just finished *Fajr* – the first prayer of the day.

'Excuse me,' she says. 'I am sorry to interrupt.'

'Do not be concerned.'

He turns towards her, smiling, his eyes gleaming. He retains his brightness of expression, despite the ravages of time. The sinews of his neck are visible as stretched cords. His beard has thinned. He moves to his desk, which stands in the shadow of a crammed bookcase covering the entirety of one wall, and locates his glasses, which he carefully perches on his nose, using both hands, before peering more closely at her.

He frowns for a moment, then says, 'Souad Hidouchi. It is you.'

'Yes.' She's surprised by how pleased she feels that he recognizes her.

'I am honoured by your visit. Please . . .' He draws out a chair for her. 'Be seated.'

'Thank you.'

'Can I offer you tea? I was about to prepare some.'

'Then I will join you.'

'Excellent.'

Difala busies himself behind a screen in a corner of the room as Hidouchi gazes around. Little has changed since she came here regularly – the piles of books and working papers, strewn about in what appears to be a disorderly fashion, though as she recalls he could always place his hand on whatever he wanted whenever he wanted it; the threadbare upholstery of the furniture; the faded, curling rugs: it is all much as it ever was.

'You must be a very busy woman,' says Difala as he brews the tea. 'You *are* still with the DSS, I assume?'

'I am.'

'So I thought. You have not . . . married?'

'No, Professor, I have not married.'

'I suspected you wouldn't. You always had the same . . . determination . . . I see in you now.'

'Is that why you suggested I consider the intelligence service?'

'Essentially, yes. You were obviously patriotic as well.'

'I don't remember ever being in the habit of saying anything particularly patriotic.'

'That's what gave it away. The fact that you didn't speak of it.'

Hidouchi laughs. 'I do remember you saying economics was

more about psychology than profit and loss. It sounds as if that hasn't changed.'

'Do you regret following my career advice?'

'No.'

'Then psychology wins.' Difala delivers the tea and sits down at his desk, facing her. 'It is good to see you again.'

'It is good to see *you* again.'

'I somehow suspect, though, that you haven't come here because you missed my company.'

'You're right. Though now I'm here I realize I have missed it. You were always able to sum up the state of our economy in a few pithy sentences.'

'I like to think I can still do that. Algerian politics may be complicated, but its economy is very simple. It's all about the price of oil, which for a long time now has been falling. The government had foreign currency reserves ten years ago of two hundred billion dollars. Today that's down to less than fifty billion. Which tells you all you need to know about our future.'

'Grim, I take it?'

'Perhaps. But all the government needs is a big international crisis to push up the price of oil and we're saved. There's speculation in the media that Putin may invade Ukraine. That would certainly qualify.'

'Surely he's not going to do that.'

Difala smiles. 'Maybe he will, maybe he won't. I am in no position to gauge his intentions. We'll just have to wait and see.' He takes a sip of tea and looks intently at her. 'Now, please don't make me wait any longer to know what has brought you here. DSS business, would it be?'

'I'm afraid so.'

'Should I be worried?'

'I hope not. Did you catch the *Microscope* broadcast last week about the thirtieth anniversary of the start of *la décennie noire*?'

'I did.'

'The contribution of Rochdi Abidi was quite ... striking, I think you'll agree.'

'Oh, Abidi has always been something of a stormy petrel. He delights in being provocative.'

'It seems he was provocative one time too many. I have to tell you Abidi was murdered the night before last.'

Difala freezes in the act of raising his tea glass to drink. 'Murdered?'

'Yes.'

'But . . .' He puts the glass back down. 'This hasn't been . . . reported.'

'The police have implemented a media blackout on the news for operational reasons. But it's true. Abidi is dead. And amongst the messages on his phone . . .'

'Was one from me.'

'Yes. Exactly.'

'Will the police be coming to see me?'

'Not if I can assure them you have given me all the relevant information in your possession.'

Difala drinks some of his tea, pondering as he does the situation he finds himself in. The calm rationalism for which he's noted soon leads to candour. 'He called me, as I assume you know from the message I left for him yesterday. I'm not sure when he called. I didn't pick up his message until some time on Saturday, though.'

'Do you still have it?'

'Er ... yes.' Difala locates his phone and activates it. 'I'm rather careless about monitoring messages ... and replying to them. But ... here it is.' He sets the phone on the desk between them and presses *play*.

'This is Rochdi Abidi. I don't know if we've ever actually met, Professor, but I expect you're familiar with my work. You probably

saw me on television last Sunday. If not, you've probably read about about what I said. And what I got out of the police officer they wheeled on. The thing is I'm reliably told you used to act as an informal recruiter for the DRS amongst the students you taught at the university. I got this information from a former student of yours, Taha Semmar, who went on to join the DRS and came to regret it. I believe he's told you about his experiences. So, could you and I talk about what happened to him? It's worrying, I think you'll agree. And I want to give you the opportunity to answer the questions I have for you before I put anything more into the public domain. So, give me a call as soon as you can. I'll look forward to hearing from you.'

'I don't know what questions exactly Abidi had for me,' Difala explains. 'But I thought it would be better to engage with him than let him put out whatever he'd got from Semmar . . . undiluted, as it were.'

'Semmar *was* a student of yours?'

'Yes. In the early nineteen nineties. He struck me as promising material for the intelligence service, so I . . . pointed him in their direction.'

'How long had you been a DRS recruiter at that point?'

'Oh, not long. I had contacts – friends from earlier days – within the DRS, but only started recommending students to them when it looked as if the country might turn into an Islamist republic, a prospect I viewed with horror considering what was happening in Iran at the time. It seemed to me the DRS was dedicated to defeating the Islamists and I wanted to help them do that. I had no idea then of the methods they were planning to employ. I didn't believe the rumours that started circulating that they'd penetrated the GIA and were responsible for some of the worst outrages of *la décennie noire*, although not believing took more and more effort as the years passed.'

'Do you believe the rumours now?'

Difala nods mournfully. 'Yes. Though I'm hopeful the DSS

has put all that kind of thing behind it.' He looks at her with his head lowered. 'Can you assure me they have?'

'Much has changed for the better. But not all. Which is partly why I'm here.'

'Are you . . . acting on your own initiative in this, Souad?'

'I'm acting with my line manager's authority.'

'I'm relieved to hear that. Relieved for you, I mean.'

'What about Taha Semmar?'

'I didn't stay in touch with him. But I learnt later he resigned from the DRS some time in the late nineties. I never expected to hear from him again. But about five years ago he turned up at one of my free public lectures and spoke to me afterwards. He was clearly deeply troubled. He was working as a street cleaner. He'd abandoned his previous life as a privileged servant of the state. I encouraged him to tell me what had gone wrong – what had prompted his resignation from the DRS. I wish I hadn't. Because he told me. And what he told me . . . I'd rather not have known.' Difala sighs. 'Are you sure you want to hear this?'

'I'm sure.'

'OK. Well, according to Semmar he was recruited into a top secret section of the DRS called Unit ninety-two, run by General Hamza Mokrani – the man Abidi accused on air of involvement in the assassination of President Boudiaf. Have you ever heard of Unit ninety-two?'

'Yes.'

'Maybe you know what he told me, then.'

'Or maybe not. I need to hear it, Professor.'

'All right. Unit ninety-two – according to Semmar – carried out a series of violent outrages during *la décennie noire* that were blamed on – and hence severely damaged the public image of – the Islamists. Semmar and other Unit ninety-two operatives infiltrated GIA cells and steered them in ever more extreme directions. He said that, acting on General Mokrani's orders, he helped organize the infamous hijacking of an Air France Airbus in December 1994 and a wave of bombings in Paris the following summer. A lot of innocent blood was shed, a lot of terror was sown. And the Islamists were blamed, just as Mokrani intended. But Semmar was sickened. For him, protecting the Algerian state couldn't justify killing innocent passengers on the Métro. And back here in Algeria worse – much worse – was to follow. So, he quit. To save his own sanity, he said. Though it was clear to me his sanity was far from . . . unimpaired.'

'And he subsequently spoke to Abidi?'

'Evidently so. How Abidi tracked him down I don't know. Unless Semmar contacted him after the TV debate. But somehow I doubt he would have done. It didn't seem to me he wanted to broadcast the details of what he'd been involved in.'

'What were you planning to say to Abidi?'

'As little as possible. But refusing to speak to him at all didn't seem wise. That's why . . . I responded to his message. Who do you think might have killed him?'

'Not sure. Maybe Semmar could tell me. Do you know how to contact him?'

'No. But I suppose he may still be working for the municipality.'

'I'll try them.'

'I've told you all I know.' Difala drains his glass. 'Is it enough to spare me a visit from the police?'

'I think so, Professor.' Hidouchi stands up. 'I'd appreciate it, though, if you didn't mention our conversation to anyone.'

'I won't. You have my word. To be honest . . . I'd prefer to forget I ever heard the story Semmar had to tell.'

'So would I. But unfortunately . . . I can't do that.'

The Lac du Bimont is a flat and motionless body of water beneath a slowly brightening sky. Taleb stands beside the car, smoking a cigarette, which he lit as much for an excuse to get away from

Spühler as for the consolations of nicotine. The hills around are folded in greenery. The still air seems to expand the silence in which he waits. He does not pull out the phone to check the time. He feels oddly free for the moment of all responsibility. The Major will call when the Major calls. Until then . . .

The phone rings. It was always going to, of course. There is business to be done.

Taleb answers. 'Hello?'

'*Bonjour*, Taleb.' It is the Major, as it was bound to be. 'You are at the lake?'

'Yes.' Taleb sees Spühler emerge from the other side of the car and hurry round to join him.

'And you have the money?'

'Yes.'

'Then we can proceed.'

'I need to see evidence that Karim Mokrani is alive and well.'

'I'm sending you a video.'

A link appears in the corner of the screen. As Taleb moves his thumb to click on it, Spühler reaches where he's standing. Taleb angles the phone so the other man can see what's on it and switches to loudspeaker mode. Then he clicks on the link.

Karim Mokrani appears, instantly recognizable from the DSS mugshot Irmouli supplied. He has acquired a bruise over his left eyebrow and a split lip and he's unshaven, his growth of beard catching up rapidly with his existing moustache. There are bags under his eyes. He looks worried, as well he might. *'I am Karim Mokrani,'* he says, looking directly into the lens. *'They say you'll see from the time and date that I'm speaking to you live.'* He's right. There's a display at the foot of the video inset, showing *24.01.22* and a running timer. *'I'm OK. Follow their instructions and I'll stay that way. Just do exactly what they tell you to. I—'*

The video cuts out. 'Alive and well,' says the Major. 'You agree?'

'He appears to be.'

'So, let's not waste any more time. You're going to drive out of the car park and turn right. I'll give you further directions as you need them. Understood?'

'Yes.'

'Keep the line open. Off you go.'

Taleb raises a finger to his lips, signalling for Spühler to say nothing, then climbs back into the car and starts up. Spühler gets in the other side and Taleb reverses, then heads for the exit.

'Another early call, Lahmar?'

'I'm sorry, Director, but I thought you'd want to know about this right away. There's been a development in the Abidi case.'

'Tell me.'

'A witness has come forward who saw someone breaking into the Cinéma Splendide on Saturday night, around the time Abidi was murdered.'

'How did this witness know there'd been a murder?'

'He lives near the cinema and saw our officers coming and going. He also saw the removal of Abidi's body, though he doesn't know the identity of the deceased. As far as I can tell, he was just trying to be helpful.'

'And it sounds as if he has been. Breaking in, you said. I haven't heard that you found any sign of a forced entry.'

'We haven't. The witness says the intruder got in through a small window that may not have been properly secured. My guess is they secured it after climbing in and left by the front door after killing Abidi.'

'Which doesn't fit with the theory that Abidi let his killer into the building.'

'No, Director, it doesn't.'

'Very well. Good work, Lahmar. Take a detailed statement from the witness and file it in the normal way.'

'Yes, Director. Are you, er . . . considering when to lift the news embargo on this?'

'Yes, Lahmar. I am considering it.'

A brief silence follows. Then Lahmar says lamely, 'OK, Director. Thank you.'

'Thank *you*, Lahmar.'

Bouras ends the call and returns his attention to the road ahead. He allows himself a small smile of satisfaction at a plan that seems to be working exactly as he intended. The witness who's so conveniently come forward is a former organizer of illegal gambling on sheep-fighting contests whom Bouras treated leniently when dealing with him as a young lieutenant, acting on the sound advice of his senior at the time, who extolled the advantages of having members of the public out there who owed you a favour. 'You never know when you might need a favour, Bouras, as you'll realize when you've been in this game as long as I have.'

How right he was.

Taleb describes his progress to the Major as he goes, with the phone on loudspeaker, responding to each change of route as it is dictated to him. He rapidly loses all sense of direction, as he suspects he's intended to. He doubts Spühler, whose tense posture suggests he has plenty to say but knows he mustn't speak, has any clearer idea of where they are. There's no sun to tell east from west and neither of them knows the area. They are generally climbing, though, into the hills ranged ahead, with roadside habitations falling away. Wherever they're bound seems likely to be an isolated spot.

And so it proves. The Major has Taleb turn off a winding tarmac road onto a rough track that leads into a hillocky stretch of scrub and brush and stunted trees, with high wooded country looming above. As the scrub thins, Taleb also glimpses ahead some kind of building – a barn or cottage, perhaps, with a half-ruined tower beyond.

'Stop the car,' comes the instruction.

Taleb brakes to a halt.

'I can see you now.'

'Then show yourself,' says Taleb, doing his best to retain control of the situation, though aware all the advantage is with the kidnappers. He takes comfort from the fact that the Major expects him to supply a statement later damning General Mokrani. Logically, that should guarantee Karim Mokrani's release will go smoothly.

'There's someone with you.'

'That doesn't matter.'

'I told you to come alone.'

'No, you didn't.' Taleb is reasonably certain the Major never actually said he was to come alone. Perhaps he didn't think he needed to.

'Who is he?'

'He's, er . . . General Mokrani's accountant.'

'Mokrani's *accountant*? I would certainly like to hear from him. Speak, whatever your name is.'

Spühler scowls at Taleb as he twists in his seat to bring himself closer to the phone. 'My name is Spühler.'

'Why are you here, Herr Spühler?'

'I have brought the money you demanded. General Mokrani wishes to be certain it is properly handed over in exchange for his son.'

'Doesn't he trust Taleb? Don't answer. He trusts no one, I'm sure.'

'The money is here. If you bring Karim to us, you can check the amount and we can conclude this transaction.'

'Transaction? Is that what you call it?'

'We can call it anything. But it's payment on our side, delivery on yours.'

The Major says nothing for a worryingly long moment. Taleb

notices a rivulet of sweat working its way down Spühler's temple. Maybe he's regretting agreeing to participate in the exchange. Taleb certainly wishes he'd refused. His presence is already causing problems.

And they're only mounting. 'So, General Mokrani doesn't trust Taleb,' says the Major at last. 'And he shouldn't, of course. Do you know what Taleb has agreed to do later today, Herr Spühler? Has he told you about the statement he's going to make to a lawyer in Aix this afternoon?'

Spühler frowns. 'What . . . statement?'

'I thought not. General Mokrani isn't going to like what he has to say. He isn't going to like it at all.'

Spühler glares at Taleb. 'What is he talking about?'

When Taleb replies, he is effectively addressing both Spühler and the Major. 'We should get on with the exchange. Sitting here arguing accomplishes nothing.'

'The voice of reason,' says the Major. 'But reason must always be the servant of justice. General Mokrani doesn't trust Taleb. Well, I don't trust him either. But I trust General Mokrani and his number-crunching lackey in a sharp suit – who's probably already calculating how to write the ransom off against tax – even less. Your presence is a breach of the agreement we made with Taleb, Herr Spühler. Get out of the car. You can be collected after we've finished with Taleb.'

'Why? What—'

'*Get out of the car.*'

Taleb gestures to Spühler, urging him to obey, and silently mouths a request. *Combination.*

'I left it unlocked,' Spühler snarls as he gets out. Then he slams the door shut and steps away.

'You really shouldn't have brought him,' says the Major in what sounds like the mildest of rebukes.

'It wasn't my decision.'

'No. I'm sure it wasn't. But decisions have consequences, both for those who make them and those who don't.'

'Shall I drive on?'

'No. You don't need to do that. We have you where we want you.'

The remark puzzles Taleb – and disturbs him. Then he realizes, even more disturbingly, that the Major has ended the call.

His meaning becomes clear a second later. Spühler is standing near the front of the car, looking ahead along the track. Then he stops looking and turns round. The frown on his face suggests a worrying thought has come into his mind. But it's not there for long. Taleb hears a whirring noise through the open window and recognizes what it is. Simultaneously, blood and fragments of bone burst out of the back of Spühler's head and he falls forward – dead before he hits the ground.

For a couple of seconds time is suspended. Then gunfire comes in a loud, rattling burst. Bullets ping off the bonnet of the car. One pierces the windscreen and plugs itself into the passenger seat-back. Another takes a chunk out of the wing mirror. *We have you where we want you.*

They've killed Spühler and now they're going to kill him. Taleb has no doubt of it. The ransom payment; the release of the hostage: all that's been abandoned. Why, he doesn't really understand. But he does understand that it's happened. All he can do now is save himself. He jams the car into reverse and accelerates back along the track. Another few bullets strike the bonnet and roof with a sound like pelting hailstones.

Taleb stares over his shoulder as he careers backwards. The car pitches and bounces on the uneven ground. He can only hope the suspension holds. He steers as best he can, but runs off the track at various points, crashing through the scrub until he rejoins the track. He doesn't slow down, though.

Suddenly, the brush clears. He lurches out into the road,

wrenching the steering wheel to the right to avoid going straight across. The car skids and jolts. He takes his foot off the accelerator. That and the uphill slope brings him to a standstill.

Everything's gone wrong – disastrously wrong. Taleb doesn't understand why. Spühler's presence shouldn't have provoked such an extreme response. What were the kidnappers thinking? What *are* they thinking? He doesn't know. All he knows for certain is that he's still alive and he wants to stay that way.

He puts his foot down again and takes off down the road.

The Algiers municipal services depot is largely empty of both vehicles and staff, with morning cleaning and refuse collection rounds under way. In a Portakabin office in the corner of the yard Hidouchi finds a harassed supervisor taking a phone call from someone he seems to have to make excuses to. Above him on the wall hangs a large street map of Algiers, with coloured lines dividing the city into assorted zones, some with overlapping boundaries. She assumes it all makes sense to him if to no one else. There's a gridded chart next to the map showing staff down one side with dates along the top. At first glance she can't see Taha Semmar listed.

The phone call ends and the supervisor massages his eyes wearily. His day already appears to be going badly. And his reaction to Hidouchi's DSS ID card doesn't suggest her arrival constitutes any kind of improvement.

She decides to take pity on him by coming straight to the point. 'I'm looking for a member of your cleaning crew: Taha Semmar.'

'You're too late. Semmar left us last week.'

'What do you mean – "left us"?'

'He died.' The man twists round and points to a crossed-out name on the chart. Hidouchi peers at it and deciphers Semmar's name beneath the crossing-out. 'Last week.'

'When last week?'

'Er . . . we heard Thursday. So, Wednesday night.' A few days after the *Microscope* broadcast, then, which Hidouchi doubts is a coincidence. 'Suicide, apparently.' The man turns back round and frowns at her. 'Did he know you people were after him? That could explain it, I guess, though he was never what you'd call cheerful, so maybe it was just standard issue depression.' He rubs his eyes again. 'Scraping rubbish off the streets all day can take some people that way.'

'How did he kill himself?'

'Overdose, I was told.'

'Overdose of what?'

The man shrugs. 'No idea. I didn't know much about him. I mean, he's been here all the time I have, which is a lot of years, but he always kept himself to himself.'

'Is there anyone on the staff who was . . . friendly with him?'

'Er . . . there's Karef. He was on chatting terms with Semmar, which is more than most were.'

'Where can I find Karef?'

'Right now?'

'Right now.'

The man turns round again and looks up, first at the chart, then the map. 'Port Saïd Square. Or nearby. Look for a fat guy in orange overalls leaning on a broom and smoking a cigarette. That'll be Karef.'

Taleb anxiously watches the rear-view mirror throughout the journey back to the Villa des Ormeaux, but sees no sign of pursuit. It's only when he spots the grey expanse of Lac du Bimont between folds of land to the south that he's able to navigate with any confidence. As it is, he drives more slowly than he's tempted to, praying he won't be stopped by a traffic cop on account of the splintered windscreen.

By the time he reaches the villa, his hands have been gripping the steering wheel so tightly for so long that cramp has set in. He stops just inside the entrance gate, turns off the engine and sits for a while, listening to the silence, flexing his hands and trying to breathe less quickly and shallowly. The fear of imminent death is giving way to the creeping realization of just how catastrophically wrong everything has turned out. No ransom paid; no hostage released; the kidnappers antagonized; Spühler dead. In terms of consolations, the only one that occurs to him is that he didn't share Spühler's fate.

Then he sees a figure walking towards him along the drive: Agent Jahid.

Taleb slowly climbs out of the car as Jahid approaches. He lights a cigarette to calm himself, though the effect is marginal at best. Jahid stops and stares. 'What happened?' he gasps.

Taleb summons a reply. 'We were shot up, as you can see.'

'Where's Agent Mokrani?'

'Still held captive. I never saw him.'

'What about Spühler?'

'You knew he was with me, then?'

'He told Irmouli he'd be going too.'

'Right. Well, Spühler's dead. *Les souveniristes* didn't react well to his presence. They'd probably have killed me too, if I hadn't got out of there.'

Jahid puffs out his cheeks and runs a hand through his hair. 'This is bad.'

'You're right. I warned Spühler that coming along with me was a mistake.'

'This is bad.'

'You just said that.'

'I'd better go and let Irmouli know.'

'Do me a favour. Drive the car up to the villa. I'll walk. I need some air.'

'You want me to drive the car?'

'Why not? You'll get there before me. You can break the news. Hold on, though.' Taleb moves round to the boot, opens it and lifts out the suitcase. He has to maintain as much control of the situation as he can. And he doesn't trust anyone else to take charge of five million Swiss francs in an unlocked case. 'The car's all yours.'

Jahid frowns deeply. He doesn't really understand the turn of events. Neither does Taleb, come to that. But they're both going to have to live with it. He starts walking, pulling the case behind him.

He hasn't gone far when he hears the car start. It drives past him and heads on up the drive.

Taleb keeps walking. One foot in front of the other. He finishes the cigarette and pauses to stub it out on the ground. Then he moves on under the grey French sky. He can hear a pigeon cooing somewhere. If he had to choose a word to describe the sights and sounds around him at this moment he'd opt for *peaceful*. But there's no peace waiting for him at the villa. He's well aware of that.

Sure enough, as the curve of the drive delivers a sightline to the area in front of the villa, he sees Irmouli standing with Jahid beside the car. There's a third man with them Taleb recognizes as Touati, Lydia Seghir's smartly dressed, bland-faced assistant, who he's encountered on a couple of occasions without it leading to anything that could be called a conversation.

Taleb doesn't quicken his pace. If anything, he slows it. But that isn't going to win him much of a breathing space. Irmouli stalks towards him, Jahid and Touati straggling behind.

'What have you done?' Irmouli shouts.

The accurate answer would be nothing – except survive. But Taleb favours silence until they're at closer quarters, which only angers Irmouli.

'Explain yourself.'

'They had us under observation as we approached the

rendezvous on a track off the road somewhere north of the lake. As soon as they spotted Spühler, things went wrong. They reckoned him being there was a breach of the agreement – which in a sense it was. I tried to talk him out of coming with me, but he insisted he had to supervise the handover of the ransom money. Apparently, you knew he was going to do that.'

'He told me, yes. General Mokrani's orders.'

'Well, General Mokrani's orders wrecked the plan. They shot Spühler and they'd have shot me too if I'd hung around.'

'Are you sure about that?'

'Of course I'm sure. Look at the car.'

'I have. Lots of bullet-strikes. But none of the bullets hit you. And they didn't shoot at the tyres, did they? So, you were able to drive away. Or were *allowed* to drive away.'

'What's that supposed to mean?'

'Did you sabotage the exchange, Taleb? Is that what you did?'

'Why would I?'

'Who knows? You might have had your reasons. You haven't done more than the bare minimum to get Agent Mokrani released. And now this.'

'You seemed on pretty friendly terms with Spühler last night, Irmouli. You must have realized it was a stupid idea for him to accompany me to the exchange. As for doing the bare minimum, I met the kidnappers' representative yesterday and I put my life at risk this morning.'

'So you say. But, like *I* say, why did they let you live?'

It is, in its infuriating way, a reasonable question. Taleb hasn't thought the issue through until now. When he does, there's only one answer that comes to mind. And it's a strangely hopeful one. All may not be lost. 'Maybe they still want to go through with ransoming Agent Mokrani. But it has to be strictly on their terms. They made a point by killing Spühler. We have to follow their instructions to the letter.'

'What instructions? They haven't issued any since you left the scene, taking the money with you, have they?'

'No. But they will. They'll let the dust settle . . . and then call to fix another rendezvous.'

'You think so?'

'Why wouldn't they?'

'I don't know, Taleb. I don't know what's in their minds or in yours. But I do know I have to explain this fuck-up to General Mokrani.'

'His decision to send Spühler along with me explains it. That plus your decision to let him.'

Irmouli glares at Taleb for several long seconds. He's confused as well as angry. He doesn't know what to do – for the best or for the more compelling cause of covering his back. But he has to inform the general that his son is still missing and his Swiss moneyman is dead. There's no way round that. 'Give me the case,' he says suddenly. 'I'll make sure the money's safe until we know what's going to happen next.'

'No. I'll hang on to the case.' Taleb doesn't actually suppose Irmouli means to steal the money. But he isn't about to base anything on supposition. The money is his salvation as much as Karim Mokrani's.

Irmouli's gaze narrows. 'You're pushing your luck, Taleb.'

'I'm not handing the money over to anyone other than the kidnappers – in return for Agent Mokrani's release.'

Irmouli simmers a moment longer. Then Touati steps forward. 'This . . . misfortune,' he says quietly, as if reminding them of something they should be aware of, 'cannot be allowed to interfere with the final stages of the conference. I speak for Doctor Seghir on this.' Ah, so it's *Doctor* Seghir. 'Your operation, Superintendent, is a secondary consideration.' How pleased, Taleb reflects, General Mokrani would be to hear that. 'Obviously you will do everything you can to bring it to a satisfactory conclusion, but the discussions being chaired by Doctor Seghir are of far greater significance and I must insist on her behalf that you proceed with maximum sensitivity. We cannot have . . . intemperate behaviour . . . by anyone present that might disrupt her work. Is that understood?'

Taleb nods his agreement, which he is in no position to withhold. Irmouli clearly doesn't like being pulled into line by a civil servant. But he has no authority to resist either. 'Yes,' he concedes.

'The car must be moved out of sight. And any communications you need to have with interested parties in the matter of Agent Mokrani must be conducted discreetly. Can I leave you to ensure that is the case, Agent Irmouli?'

'Yes,' Irmouli reluctantly replies.

'Thank you.'

With that, Touati walks briskly away towards the villa. Irmouli turns to Jahid and instructs him to drive Taleb's car round to the workshop. 'Tell Rezig to make space for it in the garage. And tell him to say nothing to anyone. Got it?'

'Got it.' Jahid beetles off.

'Follow me to my car, Taleb,' says Irmouli. 'We're not done yet.'

What Irmouli has in mind isn't clear, but he seems cowed by Touati's intervention and doesn't speak as Taleb follows him over to one of the parked SUVs. The wheels of the suitcase crunch in the gravel as he goes.

Irmouli fishes a map out of the front of the car and spreads it flat on the bonnet. It's big and covers the surrounding area in considerable topographical detail. 'The scale's four centimetres to a kilometre,' he explains. 'We're here.' He points to a dot that Taleb assumes represents the villa. 'And Lac du Bimont is here.' His finger moves to a vaguely dragon-shaped stretch of water. 'So, show me where you ended up.'

Taleb peers at the map, struggling to reconstruct the route

they followed from the lake based on the turns he can remember taking and the roads and tracks and contour lines shown. 'It isn't . . . easy,' he murmurs.

Irmouli sighs heavily. 'I'm going to have to send out a team to verify your story, Taleb. And to pick up Spühler's body. We can't have the gendarmerie getting there first. I suspect the kidnappers will have left the area, but we can't be sure. It's potentially dangerous. I need you to be as accurate as possible.'

'Well . . .' Taleb places a finger tentatively on a dotted line which he guesses is the track where they were ambushed. 'I reckon this is where . . . it happened.'

Irmouli brushes Taleb's finger away and bends over the map, studying it closely. He nods. 'OK.' He folds the map up.

'When will your team leave?' Taleb asks.

'As soon as possible. Meanwhile I'll have the pleasure of informing General Mokrani that his son is still a captive of *les souveniristes* and the man he trusts with his money is dead. Which leaves his money in the hands of someone we know he *doesn't* trust. You.'

'I never wanted this to go wrong.'

'But it did. And we have to deal with the consequences of your failure, don't we?'

'It wouldn't have been a failure if I'd been allowed to manage the exchange without interference.'

'Listen to me, Taleb. If this ends badly – and it's going pretty badly right now – I mean to ensure you take the blame. OK? Fair warning.'

'No need to warn me. It goes without saying that would be your tactic.'

'Yeah? Well, now I've said it. So, we know where we stand, don't we? I'll leave you to babysit the suitcase. Don't leave the villa until you hear from me.'

*

Hidouchi parks her motorbike at Gare d'Alger, planning to walk to Port Saïd Square from there and keep an eye out for orange-clad street-cleaners as she goes. As it is, she's barely left the station when a call comes through on the phone for which only Taleb and Bouras have the number. And this call is from Taleb. She answers straight away.

'Where are you?' is his opening question.

'Downtown. Following up a clue left by Abidi. What's the situation with you?'

'Not good. The exchange went wrong. General Mokrani insisted Spühler go with me, apparently because he didn't trust me with the money. The kidnappers didn't react well. They shot Spühler and I had to get out fast. I'm back at the villa, hoping they'll call to rearrange. Irmouli is trying to blame me for what's happened, naturally.'

'Springing Spühler on them was asking for trouble.'

'I know. But he left me no choice. The money was in a combination-locked case and only he knew the combination.'

'Does that mean you'll have to force the lock to get at the ransom now?'

'No. It turned out he'd unlocked it himself before we set off.'

'I'm beginning to think your only sensible choice is to walk away, Taleb. You're lucky still to be alive.'

'I can't walk away. The kidnappers won't deal with anyone else. And General Mokrani will come after me if I abandon his son.'

'But it was his fault his son wasn't released this morning.'

'His kind blame other people for their mistakes, Souad. I can only appease him by making sure it goes right second time round.'

'But will there be a second time?'

'*Les souveniristes* want the money. And I have it. Right in front of me.'

'Nothing about this is straightforward, Taleb, as I'm learning.

We don't know what's really going on. Until we do, every move you make is loaded with risk. Maybe you should play for time.'

'I'll try. But I can't stall *les souveniristes*. The next move is theirs to make.'

'Then just . . . be careful.'

'I will be. You can count on it.'

Taleb ends the call. He checks the other phone to see if any message has come in from the Major, even though the phone hasn't left his side and hasn't beeped once. Naturally, there is no message. Taleb suspects General Mokrani's response to the turn of events will be transmitted to him by Irmouli long before the kidnappers are in touch again. The Major may have decided to let Mokrani – and Taleb – stew. He doesn't have to hurry, after all. He still holds his hostage. And the hostage is his ace.

Taleb crosses to the dormer window in his room and looks down at the roof of the annexe, where, according to Touati, Lydia Seghir's conference is entering a conclusive phase. It is another unknown in the forest of unknowns through which he's trying – and so far failing – to find a path.

At least he still has the ransom – and therefore the means to secure Karim Mokrani's freedom. And it is grimly consoling that Spühler won't be around to spook the kidnappers next time. In truth, though, the Major didn't sound spooked. To judge by his tone, Spühler's presence was a breach of faith he'd foreseen and prepared for.

The money represents certainty, however. The money is an asset that can be traded. All Taleb has to do is manage the trade if and when the time comes.

He walks back to where the suitcase is standing beside the bed and lays it on the floor. He wants to see the wads of Swiss francs again, to remind himself of the tangible wealth they represent. He flicks the latches.

But nothing happens.

He tries again. Nothing. The case is still locked. And he can't unlock it without the combination.

Spühler's last words to him – to anyone – were a lie.

When Hidouchi first went into the field as an agent, she was advised by her trainer always to concentrate on herself – her effectiveness, her safety, her management of any situation she found herself in. One of his maxims was that worrying about colleagues was not just a waste of mental energy, since she couldn't control what they did, it was a loss of focus. And a loss of focus was to be guarded against at all costs, since in some circumstances it could prove fatal.

Hidouchi had taken the advice to heart. She always left her fellow agents to look out for themselves, as she assumed they would her. She is faintly irritated to discover, however, that this doesn't apply to Taleb. She's genuinely worried about him, because, of course, she cares what happens to him. And she knows he cares what happens to her. They depend on each other. Her trainer would say dependency creates vulnerability. And he'd be right. But there's nothing she can do about it now.

Except try as best she can to put Taleb out of her mind as she enters Port Saïd Square and immediately spots a man exactly matching his supervisor's description. Rotund and looking rotunder still thanks to his unflattering tangerine boiler suit, street-cleaner Karef is not currently doing any cleaning, but is, as predicted, propped on the handle of a wide-headed broom next to his wheeled rubbish bin under a palm tree near the bandstand. He isn't actually smoking a cigarette, but he is in the act of preparing a roll-up.

He suspends the procedure when Hidouchi shows him her DSS ID, but otherwise reacts with considerable sangfroid. 'I know you lot aren't what you were when you called yourselves the DRS, but are you sure a humble bin-pusher like me is worthy of your attention?'

'Let me be the judge of that.'

'Fair enough.'

'Your name is Karef?'

'That's right. Karef. Though it sounds better when you say it.' He grins leerily.

'I'm told you were acquainted with the recently deceased Taha Semmar.'

The leeriness dissipates. 'Poor old Semmar? Yes. I knew him.'

'You worked together a long time?'

'We did. But, as you see, clearing up after the litter-happy citizens of this city isn't a collaborative business, so from one day to the next . . . Semmar and I didn't do much more than nod to each other in the locker room at the depot.'

'Were you surprised when you heard he'd committed suicide?'

'It was the kind of shock that isn't a shock, if you know what I mean. The guy wasn't happy in the head.' Karef taps his temple. 'Demons had taken up residence there. Demons from his past. Which involved . . . well, your department, as a matter of fact. Semmar was a DRS man in his younger days, right?'

'Right.'

'So, you must know more about him than I do.'

'Not necessarily. Did he talk much about what he did while he was a DRS agent?'

'He didn't talk much about anything. But I got the impression there were . . . things he'd done . . . or been involved in . . . that troubled him. He wasn't far off retirement. Maybe he didn't fancy having a load of spare time on his hands to think about those things. I have being run ragged by my grandchildren to look forward to. Semmar had no one and nothing. And he wasn't in the best of health. There was an old injury that gave him gyp. He never said how he got it, but I know he was on painkillers because of it. I guess it all got too much for him in the end. Although that was kind of . . .' Karef hesitates. He's engaged in some fairly obvious calculating about what it's wise to say and what it's wise not to. 'Hey, what do I know? Semmar had his problems. Don't we all? But some have bigger problems than others and I reckon Semmar was one of those. Can I get back to my work now?'

Hidouchi eyes him coolly. 'You weren't exactly overstraining yourself when I arrived, so let's not worry about your work rate. What were you going to say? "Although that was kind of . . ." Kind of what?'

Karef squirms. 'Look, I don't want any trouble.'

'And you won't get any – if you tell me everything you know.'

'Is the DSS really interested in a washed-up ex-agent like Semmar? He was just . . . getting by the best way he could. Like the rest of us.'

'But he wasn't like the rest of you, Karef. You know that. And it's not for you to decide what the DSS is interested in and what it's not. There's something you're not telling me. And if you go on not telling me I may have to recommend the department gives you some close attention, which you won't enjoy, believe me.'

Karef grimaces. 'You people . . . are all the same, aren't you?'

'Are you going to tell me what you know?'

'Do I have a choice?'

'Yes. But the smart choice is to tell me.'

'OK. You win. The likes of me are only here to be pushed around by the likes of you, after all.'

Karef's given in. But he's in no hurry to act on it. Hidouchi gives him a stern look that warns him her patience is wearing thin. 'So?'

'Well, over the last few months, Semmar actually seemed happier – or less *un*happy – than he had in years. He'd bumped into an old agent he'd served with in the DRS and this guy was . . .

helping him. With money, with . . . other things. He said being able to talk to someone who understood what he'd been through was . . . making life easier. Until . . . until it wasn't, apparently.'

'This other former DRS agent. Did Semmar ever name him?'

'No. But a few weeks ago I was at the depot when a phone call came through for Semmar. He had no phone of his own. He said they were too easy to track. Like anyone would be trying to track him, was my thought. But maybe I was wrong about that. Anyhow, Semmar wasn't around and I took a message asking him to call this guy, who said he was a friend of his. I assumed he was the former agent Semmar had mentioned. He didn't say so when I gave him the message. But . . . it seemed likely.'

'And the caller left his name?'

'Yeah. Zebarri, Zerrabi, something like that.'

'Zoubiri?'

Karef thinks for a moment, then nods. 'Yeah. That's it. Zoubiri.'

Taleb's still staring helplessly at the locked suitcase in his room at the Villa des Ormeaux when, without knocking, Irmouli walks in and tosses him his phone. 'General Mokrani wants to talk to you,' he announces, with a sneering twist to his mouth. 'He's on the line.'

'Now?'

'Right now.'

Taleb raises the phone to his ear. 'General?'

'Where is my son, Taleb?' Mokrani's voice is knotted with fear and fury. He expects to be in control of people and events. In this case he's in control of neither. And his son's life is on the line, as opposed to the lives of countless others he regarded during his DSR career as of no account.

All of which is of little help to Taleb. 'Has Agent Irmouli told you what happened this morning?' Irmouli himself walks slowly across to the window and gazes out, his back turned.

'He has told me.'

'I'm sorry, General, but insisting Spühler go with me was bound to be risky. There was always a chance the kidnappers would react badly.'

'Do you take me for a fool, Taleb? Do you seriously think I wouldn't have been aware of such a risk?'

'Then why—'

'I gave Spühler no instruction to accompany you. And he wouldn't have acted without my authority. What you and Irmouli are telling me makes no sense.'

'He said you didn't trust me to handle the money alone.'

'Of course I don't trust you. With the money or anything else. But trust isn't required between us. You know what I will do to you if you betray or disappoint me. That is enough.'

Taleb's thoughts are racing to accommodate the significance of what Mokrani has said. Spühler was playing a double game, lying at every turn. But what kind of game? Not a very smart one, evidently, since it got him killed. What did he expect to happen at the exchange? To be given a cut of the ransom? Maybe he thought it was Taleb for the chop, not him. If so, he must have been in secret communication with the Major and struck a deal the Major spectacularly broke. But why? What objective was being served?

'It must have been at your request that Spühler went along, though why he didn't consult me I don't understand.' Mokrani too has been trying to make sense of something that neither he nor Taleb is equipped to comprehend. 'Explain yourself.'

'I didn't ask him to go with me, General. I didn't want him to be there. I was worried about what the kidnappers would do when they realized there were two of us. With good reason, as it turned out.'

'Then why did you allow him to go?'

'I had no choice. He wouldn't tell me the combination to open the suitcase.'

'You're saying this was all his doing?'

'Yes.'

'But he was risking his life. Why would he do that?'

'He obviously didn't think he *was* risking his life. I can only assume he'd been negotiating with the kidnappers himself, maybe for a share of the money.'

Mokrani says nothing for a moment. Taleb senses he's only now considering the possibility that Spühler betrayed him. From that it's but a short step to a host of other disturbing possibilities.

'I think we can still secure your son's release, General,' Taleb continues in what he hopes is a calming tone. '*Les souveniristes* want the money. They'll make contact to arrange another exchange. They've made their point. If we do exactly what they tell us to next time, there's no reason why we can't pull this off.'

'That is your considered opinion, is it, Superintendent?'

'Yes. It is.'

'Tell me this. Why didn't they kill you as well as Spühler this morning? They'd have the money then, wouldn't they?'

'I was just lucky to get away.'

'Implausibly lucky, according to Agent Irmouli.'

It was inevitable, Taleb supposes, that Irmouli would choose to cast suspicion on him, the better to divert any from himself. The fact is, though, that the kidnappers probably could have killed him if they'd wanted to – and helped themselves to the money. But then, of course, Taleb wouldn't have been alive to supply the promised statement – the second condition for Karim Mokrani's release. It's an explanation of sorts for what happened. But it's not one Taleb can afford to volunteer. He has to devise another – quickly. 'It may sound odd, General, but I think these people are abiding by a . . . code of honour.'

'Honour?'

'They didn't blame me for Spühler's presence, so they let me live. Which was also a message to you: don't use unreliable intermediaries who try to cut deals on the side.'

Irmouli, who's been listening intently to Taleb's side of the conversation, turns round and silently applauds. He's evidently impressed.

But is Mokrani? 'My son is safe so long as I let you handle everything. Is that what you're telling me, Superintendent?'

'I'll do my best to secure his release, despite this . . . setback. We know he was alive and well this morning. Have you seen the video?'

'Yes. Irmouli sent it to me. It is . . . some comfort to Karim's mother.'

'We just have to . . . hold our nerve.'

'For how long?'

'I don't know, General. After this morning, they may make us sweat.'

'So, your recommendation is . . . wait for their call?'

'What else can we can do?'

'If my son comes to any harm, I will hold you personally responsible, whether or not it was technically your fault. You understand that, don't you?'

'All I can do is my best.'

'I expect to hear as soon as there's any news.'

'You will. I—'

The line is dead. Mokrani has heard enough. Taleb offers the phone to Irmouli. As Irmouli takes it from him, it rings again.

The call that follows involves Irmouli listening far more than he speaks. Taleb sits on the edge of the bed, staring once more at the suitcase. He's going to have to open it soon, in order to confirm that the money is actually inside. The chance that it isn't – that Spühler's trickery had one more twist to it – has to be eliminated before the Major makes contact. Hidouchi's suggestion that he simply walk away from this lingers alluringly in his mind, even though he knows that in reality there is for him no escape.

The call ends. 'Spühler's body has been discovered,' says Irmouli.

'Where I showed you on the map?'

'No. And not by us. The kidnappers evidently decided to move the body. It was found by a man walking his dog in woods near Venelles, north-west of here. We've been monitoring local police communications and heard the report. It's their case now, which is unfortunate, to say the least. He was carrying ID, of course. They already have his name and citizenship. We just have to hope nothing on him leads them here. We checked his car over and found nothing to tell us what his plans may have been.'

'You'll tell General Mokrani?'

'In due course. He's got enough on his mind right now. You're cleverer than you look, Taleb, I'll say that. The kidnappers' code of honour was a nice touch.'

'Maybe it's true.'

'And maybe you really know what you're doing. But maybes won't help you. As I see it this . . . Major . . . has your life in his hands as well as Agent Mokrani's. And the way he dealt with Spühler suggests . . . he isn't the indulgent type.'

NINE

DIRECTOR BOURAS APPROACHES THE CINÉMA SPLENDIDE IN deepening dusk, the shadows merging with the twilight in this crumbling quarter of Algiers. From one of those shadows steps Agent Hidouchi, who has requested they rendezvous here. Bouras has spent much of the afternoon questioning the wisdom of collaborating with Hidouchi, especially since Taleb reported the failure of his attempt to secure Karim Mokrani's release, suggesting as it does that they are contending with forces and objectives of which they have dangerously little knowledge. But it is too late to back out now. Bouras is involved whether he likes it or not.

'Thank you for agreeing to this,' says Hidouchi.

'You hope to find something my officers missed?'

'Perhaps. It's a question of knowing what you're looking for.'

'And what is that?'

'Let's talk inside.'

Bouras unlocks the door of the cinema. They stoop beneath the *POLICE – DEFENSE D'ENTRER* tape and enter the dark, dusty and echoingly empty foyer.

Bouras closes the door carefully behind them and locks it. 'We will not be disturbed,' he assures her. 'What is it you didn't want to say outside?'

'I wasn't set up by Kadri, Director. He's as much in the dark as we are and, if anything, more worried on that account. He's authorized me to do whatever is necessary to establish who killed Abidi and why, who *les souveniristes* are and what their aims are and what the purpose is of the conference at the Villa des Ormeaux. According to him, Lydia Seghir, who's running the show, is an adviser to two ministries: Energy and Foreign Affairs. But her remit . . . is unknown to him.'

'Has he also authorized you to share any discoveries you make with me?'

'Let's just say he wants to hear everything I uncover before anyone else – such as you – hears about it.'

'Have you been able to report any progress to him yet?'

'No. Maybe I'll be able to after this visit.'

'In which case I'd know what it was.'

'You would. Can we go up to the projection room?'

'This way.'

Bouras leads Hidouchi up the narrow stairs to the room where Rochdi Abidi met his end. Aside from the removal of his body, everything has been left exactly as it was found. The filing cabinet has been searched, revealing nothing but letters and invoices dating from the years when the Splendide was a functioning cinema. The drawers of the desk contain assorted stationery of similar vintage. Abidi seems to have taken pains to leave little trace of himself, unless it is the depression in the cushion of the armchair.

'What are you looking for?' Bouras asks as Hidouchi looks about her.

'Something – anything – linking Zoubiri to the scene.'

'You think he killed Abidi?'

'I do. Abidi was on a one-man mission to wreck General

Mokrani's reputation. Ideally, get him charged with involvement in the Boudiaf assassination. The stakes rose after the *Microscope* broadcast and the kidnap. Maybe Mokrani was worried about what his son might reveal to his captors under torture. So, precautions had to be taken. Last week a former DRS agent called Taha Semmar who was a member of Unit ninety-two killed himself. Except I don't believe it was suicide. There was a danger Semmar might speak out about the unit's activities, specifically terrorist outrages in France in the mid-nineties blamed on the GIA but which Semmar said were the work of Unit ninety-two operatives. Zoubiri had befriended him recently, which we can be sure wasn't because he enjoyed chatting about old times. He was trying to close off Abidi's avenues of inquiry. Mokrani must have decided drastic action was called for. So, Semmar was killed in a faked suicide, then Abidi was murdered, with evidence planted on his phone to implicate me.'

'We checked all fingerprints we found against the database, which would include Zoubiri as a former intelligence service employee. There was no match.'

'Zoubiri is an experienced killer, Director. He knows how to defeat forensics.'

'Then there isn't going to be anything to show he was ever here.'

'Probably not. But it's worth checking.'

'Check away.'

Hidouchi slides open the top drawer of the filing cabinet and begins thumbing through the contents of the files. 'Thank you for supplying that witness, by the way,' she says as she proceeds.

'You're welcome.' Bouras sits down in the swivel chair positioned in front of the desk. It squeals as it swivels and foam has burst through the fabric of the cushions in several places.

He studies Hidouchi as she searches and falls to wondering – despite knowing that these days he shouldn't be wondering such things – whether there is anyone in this strikingly attractive woman's life. He suspects not. He suspects she has no tolerance for emotional dalliance. He muses regretfully on the possibility that her life would in fact be a happier one if she were less dedicated to her profession – or at any rate her conception of what her profession involves.

'This is all old stuff, isn't it?' she sighs.

'Lieutenant Lahmar assures me he checked every piece of paper in that cabinet and none of them is less than twenty-five years old.'

'So I see.'

Bouras swivels the chair and idly slides open one of the drawers under the desk. Pens, pencils, unused envelopes, a stapler, a hole-punch and a wad of unissued entry tickets: nothing Zoubiri is likely to have touched or tampered with, but checked for prints along with everything else.

Hidouchi is on the next drawer down in the filing cabinet now, working busily through the yellowing documentation of the cinema's past. Bouras opens the other desk drawer as he waits for her to finish.

It contains only an appointments diary for 1994, apparently imported from France. He flicks through the pages. Most days are blank. Maybe business was bad by that point in *la décennie noire*. Maybe Abidi senior had little to record, with closure looming as the terrorist threat steadily ratcheted up. The ribbon marker never made it beyond the week commencing 17th January.

By chance, the days of the week in 1994 matched those in 2022, so the date of Abidi's murder, 22nd January, was a Saturday then as well. Or is it chance? There are a couple of entries made using what looks from the ink to have been a fountain pen – Abidi senior's fountain pen, he assumes – but several others appear to have been made with a ballpoint in a different hand, including two on Saturday 22nd. The first of them catches Bouras's eye at once. *Halima, 11 a.m.*

He turns back to Hidouchi. 'You said you used an assumed name when you arranged to meet Abidi here, didn't you?'

She stops searching the cabinet. He has her attention. 'Yes. I called myself Halima.'

'Look at this.'

She steps across to the desk and he points out the entry. 'Abidi must have written that,' she says at once. 'What is this?'

'A 1994 appointments diary, which, coincidentally or not, matches this year in terms of which dates fall on which days.'

'He's been using it for this year. Disguised as an old diary left behind by his father. Which means he—' She draws a sharp breath.

Because it's a French diary, the working week is shown as beginning on a Monday rather than a Sunday. Accordingly, Saturday and Sunday are allotted only half a column each. In the lower half of Saturday 22nd there's a note scrawled in ballpoint diagonally across the column. Bouras leans forward to decipher it. With some difficulty, he makes out '*ce soir à propos du léopard blanc*'.

'"This evening regarding the white leopard."' He looks up at Hidouchi. 'What does it mean?'

Hidouchi frowns. 'White Leopard is a secret government project Kadri mentioned to me. He has no idea what its purpose is, but he suspects the conference at the Villa des Ormeaux is related to it in some way.' She picks up the diary and sits on the edge of the desk as she studies it. 'If I'm right and it was Zoubiri who killed Abidi, then he knows about White Leopard as well.'

'Why?'

'Because that's how he persuaded Abidi to wait for him here and let him in. Abidi must have been digging into White Leopard. Maybe that was the scoop he mentioned to his wife. He phoned her and said he'd be late home because of a meeting, remember? It was a meeting with Zoubiri. He knew what Abidi was up to and phoned him, offering information about White Leopard. See how Abidi put inverted commas round what he wrote?' She puts the diary down in front of Bouras and taps the page with her index finger. 'I think he wrote those words as they spoke on the phone. I think they're a direct quote from what Zoubiri said to him. Maybe it went, "I can talk to you this evening about White Leopard . . . if you're really interested." Something along those lines. And Abidi jotted down part of the phrase.'

There's no denying her argument is persuasive. 'That could be,' Bouras agrees.

'Which means everything – Abidi's allegations during the *Microscope* broadcast, the conference in France, the kidnapping, White Leopard – is somehow connected.' Hidouchi falls silent. She's still frowning, thinking through the implications and consequences of her reasoning.

'You may be right,' says Bouras. 'But I don't see what we can do about it.'

Hidouchi thinks a moment longer, then stands up. 'Could you take Zoubiri in for questioning, Director?'

'In connection with Abidi's murder? I suppose so. He's a logical suspect. But we have no real evidence against him. And he's too wily to give himself away. We couldn't hold him for long.'

'A few hours would be enough.'

'Enough for what?'

'Whatever Zoubiri knows General Mokrani knows. And probably more besides. I need to question Mokrani in the absence of his bodyguard. It's our best chance of finding out how precarious Taleb's position – and ours – really is.'

'I doubt you'd get any more out of Mokrani than we would out of Zoubiri.'

'Ah, but my methods are a little more extreme than yours, Director. Mokrani would answer my questions. I'm confident of that.'

'I imagine I'm better off not knowing how you can be so confident?'

'Much better off.'

'When . . . would you want to do this?'

'Early tomorrow morning.'

'I see. Well . . .'

'Can you get Zoubiri out of the way for me?'

Bouras turns the idea over in his mind. Questioning Zoubiri is reasonable in the circumstances. It's a legitimate step to take in the investigation of Abidi's murder. As for what might happen at General Mokrani's villa while such questioning is under way at Police HQ, he can't be held accountable.

Or can he? Mokrani is a diminished figure in *le pouvoir*, but he is still part of the system, which functions to protect his kind of people whatever their transgressions. Running the risk of incurring such a man's enmity isn't something Bouras would normally consider. But he may well already be in Mokrani's sights, along with Hidouchi and Taleb. And Hidouchi is going to take such action as she deems necessary with or without his help. Nor can he allow himself to be outmanoeuvred by Kadri. He needs to know what's really going on before – or at least as soon as – Kadri does. To guarantee that, he has to ensure Hidouchi trusts him more than she does her DSS superior. He has to commit himself.

'Yes.' He looks up at Hidouchi. 'I can get him out of the way.'

'Thank you.' She smiles at him. 'Tomorrow morning it is.'

Rezig is waiting in his workshop, as Taleb asked him to in the message he sent via Noussa. What Taleb is about to ask Rezig to do is risky, but he can see nothing else for it. He has to know what is inside the case. Turning up to a rendezvous with *les souveniristes* empty-handed would be suicidal. The Rezigs are worthier of his trust than anyone else at the villa. In fact, they're the only people there he's remotely inclined to trust with anything.

'Working late, Mouloud?' Rezig asks as he takes a drag on his cigarette.

'Early, late. It's all work for me here. And none of it easy.'

'Did things go badly with the kidnappers?'

'About as badly as they conceivably could, with the proviso that, as you see, I'm still alive.'

'And Agent Mokrani? Is he still alive?'

'I'm certainly operating on that assumption.'

'But the Swiss banker?'

'You won't be seeing him again.'

'So I gather.' Rezig shrugs, half apologetically. 'Noussa gets the latest news from Agent Jahid. He's addicted to her *marrons glacés*. As a result, not a lot happens here that we don't know about.'

'Perhaps you could tell me what Doctor Seghir is aiming to achieve, then.'

Rezig shakes his head. 'Jahid's as much in the dark about the purpose of the conference as you are. Assuming, I mean . . . that you are in the dark.'

'Oh yes. I'm in the dark.'

'Noussa said you'll be joining us for dinner.'

'It's good of you to invite me.'

'It's a pleasure. But evidently . . . something can't wait until then.'

'I need to open this.' Taleb nods to the suitcase beside him.

'Ah, right. Noussa said you were carrying it when you visited her in the kitchen. The ransom money is inside, is it?'

'I hope so. But I need to be sure. I don't know how deep a game Spühler was playing beyond the fact that it was obviously deeper than was good for him. And I don't know the combination to open this. But before the kidnappers make contact again, as I expect them to do quite soon . . .'

'You want me to open it?'

'I thought you'd have a jemmy or something we could break it open with.'

'We don't have to resort to anything as drastic as a jemmy. I didn't spend a year working as a baggage-handler at Marseille airport without learning how to open combination-locked suitcases. Got a piece of paper?'

'A piece of paper?'

Rezig grins. 'That's all it takes.'

Taleb pulls out his notebook, tears off a sheet and hands it to Rezig, who carefully folds it in half, then lifts the case onto the bench. He slides one end of the folded edge of the paper into the crevice between the first of the combination dials and its housing, then turns the dial. Then he turns it again. And again.

'Two, I think,' he announces with evident satisfaction. 'Let's try the next.'

He repeats the process with the second dial, progressing from one number to the next until he detects something that tells him he's reached one of the pre-set numbers. It's 2 again.

'The rod the dials are mounted on is smooth except for the ridge fixing the combination,' he explains as he proceeds. 'Where the paper catches on that gives us the number. Not exactly rocket science.'

He arrives at the fourth number. 'There you are, Mouloud. Two two one eight.' He stands up and steps away. 'See if I'm right.'

Taleb lays the case flat and flicks the latches. They spring open.

As Taleb raises the lid, Rezig moves away. He apparently doesn't want to see just how much money the case contains.

The answer is most – but clearly not all – of the original five million Swiss francs. Some wads are missing. Taleb's guess would be that they amount to around ten per cent of the total – half a million francs, skimmed off by Spühler prior to the handover. His commission, maybe, agreed in advance? As it's turned out, though, he was never destined to spend any of it. Which raises the obvious question: where is it now?

Taleb closes the case and turns the combination. 'Thank you, Abdou. I'm obliged.'

'You're welcome. Everything as it should be?'

'Everything as I might have expected it to be.'

'Ah ... Never trust a Swiss banker, Mouloud. That's my advice. Of course, I've never needed to, so it's easy for me to say. Are you going back to the villa before dinner?'

'I am.'

'Well, we're expecting you at seven thirty.'

'I'll be there.'

Taleb makes his way back to the villa. He doesn't know which room Spühler spent the night in, but he doubts he would have left the half million there. His car is a likelier place. The Citroën is a vintage model, so opening it using the car thief's favourite tool, a straightened coat-hanger, should be possible. Taleb knows much more about that than the opening of combination-locked suitcases.

He walks round to the front of the villa to confirm the Citroën is still parked there. It is. And all is quiet, the conference having adjourned for the day. He appears to have a clear run.

He goes up to his room, fetches one of the utilitarian metal coat-hangers from the wardrobe and makes his way down again.

He's been carrying the suitcase everywhere with him. It doesn't exactly make him inconspicuous. And walking around alone with it after dark doesn't do much for his peace of mind either. But he has no choice in the matter. Without the ransom – what remains of it – Karim Mokrani won't be freed and Taleb himself won't be off the hook. A lot is riding on the contents of the case.

As he emerges from the villa and heads through a gulf of deep shadow towards Spühler's Citroën, two figures emerge into view round the corner of the house: Irmouli and Jahid – Taleb knows them now just by their silhouettes.

They take a course converging on Taleb's route to the car. They don't hurry. They don't even pretend to look surprised. For his part, Taleb doesn't divert or slow down. He's not about to start pretending either.

The two men reach the car at more or less the same time as Taleb. The tip of Irmouli's cigarette glows red in the darkness as he draws on it.

'Taking the evening air, Taleb?' he asks. 'Or planning to search Spühler's car, perhaps?'

'What if I were?'

'Well, in that case I'd help you out by explaining that we searched it earlier. He left the keys in his room, which we also searched. The searches . . . turned up nothing of any significance.'

Several possibilities present themselves at this point. Irmouli and Jahid found the money and decided to keep it for themselves. Spühler hid the money somewhere else, planning to collect it later. Or Spühler and Irmouli were in league from the start and skimmed off the half a million last night or early this morning and split it between them. Whichever it is, Taleb knows he will gain nothing by confronting Irmouli. Wherever the money is now, it's not going to be handed over to Taleb.

'Do you want us to open the car for you? Or would you prefer to impress us with the old coat-hanger trick?'

'There's no need for me to look in the car if you've already checked it over.'

'As we have.'

'There we are, then.'

'Are you really as confident as you let General Mokrani believe you are that the kidnappers will be in touch again?'

'Why wouldn't they be?'

'Oh, maybe because Spühler showing up today has made them suspect you'll pull some other stunt next time.'

'But they have all the advantages. All we have is the ransom money. Which they want.'

'*Should* want, I agree. Money's important, after all. Especially to underpaid government employees like you and us. Sometimes, when you see an opportunity . . . you should grab it.'

'What opportunity do you see here, Agent Irmouli?'

Silence falls. Irmouli finishes his cigarette and drops the butt, grinding it out in the gravel. 'General Mokrani is a magician who's lost his wand. Without Spühler, he has no representation here. Doctor Seghir regards the kidnapping of Agent Mokrani as a nuisance. Would it be more of a nuisance – or less – if he . . .'

Irmouli doesn't finish the sentence. He doesn't have to. Taleb has the very distinct impression he's being offered his own cut of Spühler's commission – or maybe his own cut of a still larger sum. He's carrying a lot of money around with him – enough to make all three of them rich beyond any dreams they've ever seriously entertained.

'You have a tough job on your hands, Taleb,' Irmouli continues. 'Sometimes you must wonder whether you're being adequately rewarded for all the risks you run. I know I wonder that about myself.'

'So do I,' says Jahid, as if on cue.

Taleb isn't going to allow himself to be drawn down this road any further. 'You found nothing significant in Spühler's room or his car?'

'That's right,' Irmouli smoothly replies. 'Nothing at all.'

'Then there's no more to be said. Have a pleasant evening.'

With that Taleb turns and walks back towards the villa.

They don't call after him. And they don't follow. The overture has been made. Now he will be left to dwell on it.

But dwell on it he doesn't. Of all the mistakes he could make in his current situation doing a deal with Irmouli would surely be the gravest.

He also has the benefit of an agreeable distraction in the form of dinner with the Rezigs. Police work creates the illusion that everyone in this world is venal or violent or both. It's a joy and a relief to be reminded that there are actually decent, honest, loyal people you can choose to mix with. Abdou and Noussa accept without needing to spell it out that Taleb is doing his best in a virtually impossible situation. His reward is their company, their wine – to which he succumbs again – and Noussa's delicious chicken *à la niçoise*.

In the end, it is Taleb, not his hosts, who mentions the intractability of his position. 'It's kind of you not to have mentioned the . . . kidnap problem,' he says reflectively as he accepts another glass of wine to accompany the cheese course. 'I'm sure you know more or less everything that's happened so far, which means you know I'm no closer to achieving Agent Mokrani's release than I was when I first arrived.'

'We also know that's not your fault,' says Noussa, patting his hand consolingly.

'You may be the only two people around here likely to take that view of the situation.'

'We just see what we see,' says Abdou. 'And we hear what we hear. You remember what I told you I overheard Irmouli and Jahid saying the night of the kidnapping? It's made me wonder if this was ever . . . a real kidnapping.'

'I've wondered that too. But I have to work on the assumption that it was.'

'Perhaps you don't have to. Perhaps you could—'

He stops abruptly. And Taleb realizes a glance from Noussa is what's stopped him. 'What's wrong?'

'Nothing.' Abdou looks sheepish.

'Please go on with whatever you were going to say. The more information I have the better my chances of success.'

A silence falls, broken by a clock in another room striking ten. Abdou looks at Noussa. Eventually, she nods. 'Tell him, then,' she says quietly.

'All right.' Abdou lowers his voice, as if worried someone might be listening, though the only other living creature within earshot is their dog, who is dozing. 'If I wanted to check on a group like *les souveniristes* – to find out if they're what they claim to be – I think I'd ask . . . a professional kidnapper.'

Taleb smiles bemusedly. 'Do you know one?'

'In a sense . . . yes.'

'What sense is that?'

'There was a guy I met in the repatriation camp back in sixty-two. He was a schemer even then, finding ways to make life easier, trading one group off against another. But he never cheated me. I helped him learn to read and write. He could outwit anyone, but he couldn't write much more than his own name. Only I knew he was illiterate. Trusting me with that secret made us the firmest of friends. When we got settled in Marseille, he drifted into crime and although I made it clear I wanted nothing to do with that kind of thing we stayed in touch. He helped me out on several occasions, so I can't deny I benefited indirectly from his illegal activities. He got me the job at the airport, where naturally he had a lot of contacts. As the years passed, he prospered. His racketeering slowly turned into a criminal empire. He's a semi-legendary figure in the Marseille underworld now – a real *gros bonnet*. He's had his hand in bank raids, art heists, gangland hits, people smuggling . . . and drug dealing, obviously. Plus kidnapping. His name's been linked with several abductions of high profile businessmen and heirs to fortunes. Linked, but never proven. He's clever, like I say – street clever. And well organized. He's probably got a long list somewhere of magistrates, judges and senior police officers he's bribed to stay out of his way.'

'Farabi Merzouk,' says Noussa. 'That is his name. I wish sometimes . . .'

'She wishes I'd never met him,' says Abdou. 'She doesn't approve of our friendship and neither, to be honest, do I. But it's better to have him as a friend than an enemy. Le Merz, as they call him, is feared by almost everyone who knows him. But I don't fear him. I don't have to.'

'And this is who you suggest I ask for advice?' Taleb looks sceptically at Abdou.

'I do. If you want to know who you're really dealing with. The kidnapping of a DSS agent in what Le Merz regards as a fiefdom he shares control of with just a few other long-established operators . . . is something he'd expect to know about and approve beforehand. If he wasn't consulted . . .'

Taleb grasps what Abdou is hinting at. It might be possible to force *les souveniristes* into releasing Karim Mokrani sooner rather than later by setting the local *gros bonnet* on their tail. And the *gros bonnet* in question might supply valuable information about exactly who they are. But surely . . . 'I can't imagine he'd want to help out an Algerian police officer.'

'It's me he'd be helping out, Mouloud.'

'What are you proposing – a meeting?'

'If you want.'

Taleb sits back in his chair and sips his wine. It would be easy to dismiss the idea as too risky. But Taleb is currently operating at such a profound disadvantage that the greater risk might lie in not accepting Abdou's offer of help. 'You'd be willing to . . . act as an intermediary . . . between me and Merzouk?'

'You won't get to speak to him otherwise. And if I were you . . . I'd want to speak to him.'

'What he is saying makes sense,' says Noussa. 'I wish it didn't, because I don't like him having anything to do with this man. But in the circumstances . . .'

Taleb looks at her earnestly. 'If you have no objection . . .'

She returns his look. 'I have no objection.'

'Well . . .' Taleb shrugs. 'It seems I'd be a fool to turn you down, *Haricot*.'

His old schoolfriend nods solemnly. 'Then it is settled. I will call Le Merz in the morning.'

Tuesday morning is grey and cool. Algiers stirs late on winter mornings such as this, denied its customary rousing warmth and glare. The streets are quiet, particularly in Hydra, where most of the residents can afford to make leisurely starts to their days.

Lahmar has made good time on the drive to General Mokrani's villa. He draws up in front of the entrance gates, the patrol car pulling in behind. Then he winds down his window, stretches out his arm and presses the button on the intercom panel set in the pillar beside the gate.

Bouras, sitting in the passenger seat smoking a cigar he hopes will project more self-assurance than he actually feels, recognizes the voice that responds through a crackle of static. It is Zoubiri, Mokrani's aide in all things, including – Bouras believes – multiple murder.

'Yes?' comes Zoubiri's curt greeting.

'Lieutenant Lahmar, DGSN. I'm here with Director Bouras. Let us in please.'

'We weren't expecting you.'

'Just open the gate. This is official police business.'

'You don't have an appointment. General Mokrani sees no one without an appointment.'

'We're not here to see the general. It's you we've come to speak to. Open the gate.' Lahmar glances round at Bouras – for approval, Bouras senses, which he bestows with a reassuring nod.

'Give him a moment,' he murmurs. 'He has no choice but to let us in. He just has to be allowed to realize that.'

Several moments pass, in fact. But then the gates swing open.

The two cars drive through and round to the rear of the villa, where Bouras and Taleb were received when they came to meet General Mokrani the previous Friday. Zoubiri is waiting for them beneath the portico of the rear entrance to the building, black-suited as before, but unshaven – and scowling ominously.

The cars come to a halt. Bouras and Lahmar get out, as does one of the uniformed officers in the patrol car. Zoubiri looks as if he's uncertain what to make of all this. As well he might be.

'News from France?' he asks, drawing on a cigarette.

'None you don't already have,' Bouras replies.

'Then why are you here, Director?'

'I am concerned with many potentially significant crimes in this city on an ongoing basis. Often their ramifications ... overlap. As in this case.'

'What's that supposed to mean?'

'Rochdi Abidi was found dead two days ago. We believe he was murdered on Saturday night.'

'You've kept that quiet.'

'You don't look surprised.'

'The guy wasn't short of enemies.'

'Enemies who included your employer, General Mokrani.'

'Are you seriously suggesting the general killed Abidi?'

'Not personally, no. It's you I want to discuss the particulars of the crime with. Along with the particulars of another death, that of Taha Semmar, a former DRS agent.'

'Never heard of him.'

'That is a pointless lie. We know you were acquainted with him.'

'Semmar, you say?' Zoubiri frowns theatrically. 'Well, maybe I *have* heard of him.'

'Where were you Saturday night?'

'Here. In my room. Watching football on the television and eating a pizza.'

'Zero points for originality, Zoubiri. You're coming with us. We're going to discuss your dealings with Abidi and Semmar at HQ.'

'The general won't like that.'

The proof of Zoubiri's words arrives in the same instant, as General Mokrani emerges from the villa, breathless and bustling, clad, as for their previous meeting, in a tracksuit.

'What is happening here?' he shouts at Bouras.

'I'm taking Zoubiri in for questioning in connection with the deaths of Taha Semmar and Rochdi Abidi.'

'Have you lost your mind? You can't do this.'

'You'll find I can, General. There are reasonable grounds for suspicion that he was involved in both deaths.'

'Abidi is dead?'

Bouras is unimpressed by Mokrani's pretence that he has until this instant believed Abidi to be alive. 'Zoubiri will be questioned with full regard for his rights, General. We are the police. He has nothing to fear from us.'

'What evidence do you have against him?'

'I do not propose to discuss that here.'

Mokrani moves in on Bouras, seeking to intimidate him with a close-quarters glare. 'You dare do this while my son is still in the hands of kidnappers thanks to the incompetence of one of your officers?'

'We both know what happened yesterday resulted from Herr Spühler's intervention. It was no fault of Superintendent Taleb. He is still working to free your son. And I am supporting him in that. Meanwhile, I have no choice but to investigate the murder of Rochdi Abidi. And formal questioning of your aide is part of that investigation.' Bouras signals to the uniformed officer to load Zoubiri into the patrol car.

Zoubiri says nothing and does not resist. But he holds Bouras's gaze as he walks over to the patrol car and climbs in. His lip curls faintly and his eyes narrow. His silence somehow succeeds in being altogether more threatening than Mokrani's bluster.

'You will regret this, Director,' growls Mokrani.

'I am sorry for any inconvenience you may suffer as a result of Zoubiri's absence, General. It is unavoidable.'

'Sorry? You will be, believe me.'

'My business here is concluded, but I should explain that we've been accompanied by a DSS agent who has some questions for you and so the intrusion on your morning is unfortunately not yet at an end.'

One of the rear doors of Bouras's Mercedes opens and Agent Hidouchi steps out. She has in fact accompanied Bouras only a short distance, from where she left her motorbike. She bids Mokrani an unsmiling '*Sabah al-khair*.'

He does not reply, but continues glaring at Bouras.

'I will leave Agent Hidouchi to explain the reason for her visit,' says Bouras. 'I will of course advise you if it proves necessary to detain Zoubiri on an extended basis. Beyond that, I can only remind you that we are all working to reunite you with your son. And I hope for good news on that score very soon.' He essays a respectful nod, the only response to which is a flaring of Mokrani's nostrils.

The general's day has not begun well.

Nor has Taleb's, though his problem is the opposite of General Mokrani's: nothing is happening. He expects a call from the Major with every passing hour – if not every passing minute. But no such call comes. And it is impossible not to consider the possible implications of the kidnappers' continuing silence.

Logically, he persistently reminds himself, there is bound to be a call. They want the money. If they didn't, they would never have demanded it in the first place. Therefore, a call will come.

Until it does, Taleb has to take the phone he will receive the call on wherever he goes, fully charged. And he has to take the suitcase containing the ransom money with him as well. Which means it is impractical to stray far from the villa, where Dr Seghir's conference is about to resume.

He manages a pre-breakfast excursion to the kitchen garden, where he sits on an old roller and smokes one of his precious Nassims. It is a measure of his state of mind that he finds himself thinking that if Abdou arranges a meeting with Le Merz, and that meeting is in Marseille, as would seem likely, it would be worth investigating whether there is a tobacconist somewhere in the city that stocks Nassims, which there may well be given the number of Algerians who live there.

It's the most hopeful thought he can come up with. All in all, the day ahead does not promise to be one of his better ones.

Predictably, Mokrani demands Hidouchi leave immediately, otherwise he will call Kadri and complain about her invasion of his privacy. 'Go ahead' is her response. As she explains, Kadri has authorized her to investigate *les souveniristes* to establish the scale of the security threat they pose as well as the murder of Rochdi Abidi in view of its intelligence implications. And he has given her a free hand in doing so.

Technically, this is true, though Hidouchi is not sure how much support Kadri would actually give her if backed into a corner. He will always choose to protect himself over his staff. But Mokrani is no longer a power in the land. He still wields influence, but others wield more. He is one of yesterday's men. And Kadri thinks only of today – and tomorrow.

In the end, Mokrani does not call Hidouchi's bluff, presumably because he is himself bluffing. Claiming he has no wish to humiliate her, he tries to gain the upper hand by attributing his surrender to concern for his son. 'I do not wish to give your department any excuse to abandon Karim. Question me if you must. We will go to my study.'

This is no more effective a tactic than his earlier pugnacity. Hidouchi is confident she will soon have him where she wants him. They enter the villa.

The study is a large room, as it needs to be to accommodate a vast desk that looks as if it might be made of sandalwood: a preposterously extravagant indulgence if true, dating, Hidouchi assumes, from the apogee of Mokrani's career. It has gilt edging and decorations that resemble the epaulettes that would adorn his army uniform. There's a huge lamp as well, designed in the likeness of a three-masted schooner, and an elaborate gold inkstand. Mokrani may treasure these emblems of his success, but their old-fashioned appearance only serves to underline how far from the heart of *le pouvoir* he has drifted. He still has the swagger of his prime, but he no longer wields a cudgel to go with it.

He flops into the leather-upholstered swivel chair behind the desk. Above him on the wall hangs an enormous framed map of southern Europe and North Africa. It is of some vintage, since Burkina Faso is still shown on it as Haute Volta, a name several decades out of date.

He extends a hand, inviting Hidouchi to take the only other chair, set some way back from the desk. Then he folds his hands over his paunch and looks at her directly. 'How *exactly* can I help you, Agent Hidouchi?'

She does not answer at once, nor take the offered seat. She noticed as Mokrani closed the study door behind her that it's fitted with a bolt. It is at first sight a strange precaution for a man to take in his own home, but perhaps, for such a man as he is, not so strange after all.

She walks back to the door, slides the bolt across, then returns to the desk and sits down.

Mokrani glares at her. 'What do you think you're doing?' He sounds as if he can hardly believe what she's done.

'We will require privacy,' she says, returning his glare with a placid gaze. 'As to how you can help me, I want you to tell me all about Unit ninety-two.'

'I don't know what you're talking about.'

'That is odd, since, as I understand it, you created Unit ninety-two in the year it's named after, having been instructed to combat the Islamist threat the then government believed existed. And to combat it in any way you saw fit.'

'I was a loyal officer of the DRS. There certainly was an Islamist threat to the stability of the nation at the time of which you speak. I carried out various orders at various times to neutralize the threat in compliance with the laws under which the department operated.'

'So, you admit to running Unit ninety-two?'

'I admit nothing beyond what I have just said. *If* a secret unit existed and *if* I oversaw its activities, I would consider myself bound by the confidentiality that applied to most of the duties I performed whilst serving the department and wouldn't feel free to say a word about it.'

'Even if what Unit ninety-two engaged in was often criminal in its own right?'

'Nothing the DRS did was criminal. By definition.'

'If so, you can have nothing to fear from the activities of Unit ninety-two becoming public knowledge.'

'There is very little I fear, Agent Hidouchi.'

'You feared Rochdi Abidi, I think. That's why you ordered Zoubiri to eliminate him.'

'I gave no such order. Abidi's accusations were no more than a minor irritant to me.'

'Really? So you weren't worried at all when you discovered that Abidi had extracted information about Unit ninety-two's activities from a former member of the unit, Taha Semmar?'

'I've never heard of Taha Semmar. What has he told you?'

'Nothing. Semmar is dead. As of last week. As I'm sure you're aware, since Zoubiri was in contact with him. And contact with Zoubiri has a tendency to lead to fatal results.'

'This is ridiculous. Even if Abidi had "extracted information" as you put it from this man Semmar and even if Semmar was a former DRS officer, it's of no consequence. Abidi couldn't publish or broadcast allegations against me relating to my period of service in the DRS without violating the National Reconciliation Law, which, I surely don't need to remind you, makes it a criminal offence to lodge a complaint against any state security official regarding episodes of violence that took place during the national tragedy of *la décennie noire*. So, Abidi has never posed any kind of threat to me.'

'The amnesty doesn't apply to the Boudiaf assassination.'

'The man responsible for that act is serving a life sentence in prison. I have no connection with the event.'

'Your connection is that your then assistant, Youcef Ghezala, appeared to know about Boudiaf's assassination before it happened. And you're not going to pretend you've never heard of Ghezala, are you?'

'He was my assistant, yes. And a rank incompetent. Also mentally disturbed. As his subsequent suicide demonstrated.'

'Semmar also committed suicide – officially.'

'Sadly, it's not uncommon. Now, is that all? I've answered your questions, Agent Hidouchi. Perhaps you'd like to unbolt the door . . . and leave.'

'You've answered nothing. So far. Perhaps I can persuade you to be more revealing where White Leopard is concerned.'

Mokrani frowns. Hidouchi's impression is that she's surprised him for the first time. 'White Leopard?'

'What is it, General?'

'A rare wild animal. Beyond that . . . I have no idea.'

'You expect me to believe that?'

'What you believe or disbelieve is of no interest to me.'

Hidouchi decides to capitalize on Mokrani's slight but detectable discomfiture. 'Your area of responsibility at the DRS was pre-emptive operations, wasn't it?'

'Who told you that?'

'It's listed in personnel files the DSS have inherited from the DRS.' Well, maybe it's listed in such files, maybe not. Hidouchi doesn't know. But she's betting Mokrani doesn't know either. She certainly has no intention of naming Fatima Remichi as her source. 'Are you denying it?'

'Where such matters are concerned, I offer neither confirmation nor denial.'

'I imagine you had authorization to operate over a wide area. Presumably not confined to this country.'

'Imagine what you like.'

'Maybe that map on the wall behind you represents the area you ranged over.' Hidouchi springs out of her chair and walks round one side of the desk to examine the map at closer quarters.

'It's just a map, Agent Hidouchi,' Mokrani growls, without looking round at her. 'Showing, amongst other things, the borders of our republic that we in the army have successfully defended since the French were sent on their way.'

'Indeed.' Hidouchi slips the binding wire out of her pocket. It requires swift and dexterous application to pinion the subject effectively. But she's done so with younger and fitter men than General Mokrani. She has the measure of him. And of what she needs to do.

She whirls round, stretching the wire from the holder, and loops it round Mokrani's chest and arms and the chair he's sitting on before he can react. Then she yanks it tight, pinning him in his seat, and secures the end.

'What are you—' Mokrani doesn't get out more than three words before he realizes what's happened. He tries to stand, but with his arms trapped at his sides he can't manage it. Hidouchi crouches behind him, pulls his right ankle back and ties it to the leg of the chair with a second loop.

Mokrani lets out a curse and pushes against the desk with his free leg, trying to drive the chair back against Hidouchi. But she dodges left, grabs his left ankle and ties that to the chair with a third loop.

'Let me go,' Mokrani shouts. But shout is all he can do. He's helpless now.

Hidouchi circles round to her chair, pulling out her gun as she goes. She sits down and levels the weapon at Mokrani. He stops shouting. 'I've no doubt you have a gun of your own in one of the desk drawers, General,' she says, slowly and quietly. 'If necessary, I can fix things up so it seems as if I shot you in self-defence. Zoubiri isn't the only one who can stage-manage a murder scene to look like something else.'

'I'm not going to tell you anything,' says Mokrani, his mouth setting in a stubborn line as he struggles unavailingly against the ties.

'Are you sure about that? Like you say, you have the amnesty to fall back on. And *le pouvoir* won't allow the Boudiaf case to be reopened whatever happens. Why get yourself shot when you have nothing to lose but your reputation, which in the eyes of most Algerians could hardly be any lower?'

Mokrani squirms and scowls. He has no immediate response. Then there's a tapping at the door. 'Husband?' comes the call from the other side in a nervous, quavering voice. 'I heard . . . a shout.'

'Go away,' Mokrani calls back. 'There is nothing wrong.'

'Are you sure?'

'Go away, woman. Leave me alone.'

There's a sound of pattering feet. At least Mokrani can still command his wife.

He glares at Hidouchi. 'You will suffer for this.' He spits out the words. 'Once I've secured my son's release, I'll come after you. You can be sure of that.'

'You've already come after me, General. But Zoubiri's attempt to frame me for Abidi's murder went awry. So, here I am, coming after *you*.'

'I don't have to account to the likes of you for actions I took in the service of the nation. Whatever I did was necessary and proportionate. Yes, I ran Unit ninety-two. We did good work. We did what we had to do to ensure the survival of the republic as we knew it and as we wanted to go on knowing it. You should thank me. The nation as the Islamists were set on remaking it would have had no place in it for you.'

'What is White Leopard?'

'I don't know.'

'I don't believe you.'

'Then shoot me and see if you can get away with it. I can't tell you what I don't know. White Leopard is a mystery.'

'We'll see about that.'

She stands up, holsters her gun and pulls out of her pocket a clear plastic bag. Then she advances on Mokrani.

'This is how Zoubiri killed Abidi, as I'm sure you know. Do you want to go the same way?'

'I want to live long enough to see my son freed by the devils who are holding him. Beyond that I don't care. I can't tell you what White Leopard is because I don't know.'

She stands beside him, the bag stretched in her hands. 'But you've heard of it?'

'As a rumour. A whisper. It has something to do with those damnable *souveniristes*. Something cooked up between them and the Seghir bitch.'

'You think the kidnappers are in league with Lydia Seghir?'

'There's nothing else I *can* think. The kidnapping is a blind – a distraction. But it's effective. While Karim remains in their hands there's nothing I can do. If I dig into White Leopard it could be fatal for him. Abidi knew something, but . . .' Mokrani stares balefully up at her. 'You can mistime suffocation as an interrogation technique, you know, even when the subject has the information you want, which I don't. What I do have is a heart condition that makes oxygen deprivation a risky ploy. So you should think twice about putting that bag over my head.'

He seems to be telling her Abidi died thanks simply to a misjudgement by Zoubiri. Hidouchi considers the possibility that the plan was actually to extract from Abidi whatever he knew about White Leopard rather than kill him. If so, framing Hidouchi was just Zoubiri's way out of the problem after he'd botched the interrogation. Reluctantly, she finds herself inclined to believe Mokrani on the point.

She has no doubt his fears for his son are genuine. Fatherly love is probably the only kind of love he genuinely knows. Which means she should probably believe him about White Leopard as well. She takes a step back. 'If Seghir's involved, whatever she's up to must be government-approved.'

'Probably. But there may be bigger players involved.'

'Bigger than the government?'

'Bigger than *our* government.'

'Who, then?'

'I don't know.'

'And to what purpose?'

'I don't know that either.'

'How can a man with all your connections *not* know?'

'Because connections wither if they're not lubricated. I'm out of the game. I can't do favours for people any more. And the only favours I can call in are from those too far from the centre of things to know what's really going on. I just want my son back. You've somehow managed to avoid being suspected of killing

Abidi. Don't push your luck. Obstruct Karim's release and I can promise you I still have enough power and influence to make sure you and your friend Taleb pay dearly.'

'Only if you're still alive.'

'Yes. *If*. Which at the moment seems to be up to you.' He looks her in the eye. 'So, what are you going to do?'

Bouras devoutly hopes Hidouchi's interrogation of General Mokrani has yielded something of value. At Police HQ he is rapidly running out of questions to put to Zoubiri, who is so well informed about the football match he claims to have been watching on television at the time of Rochdi Abidi's murder – extending to a virtually word-for-word recollection of an argument between two of the commentators during half-time analysis – that it would be possible, if Bouras didn't know better, to believe he really had been relishing their exchanges in his room at Mokrani's villa rather than torturing Abidi to death in the projection room at the Cinéma Splendide.

He isn't really surprised. Zoubiri still operates by the rules the DRS drilled into him. For whatever he does there will always be a cover story to supplement the lack of forensic evidence. He is a professional.

As such, he can't be intimidated by eyeballing and table-thumping. And he can't be outwitted. Try as Bouras might, he's made no progress whatever in breaking down Zoubiri's account of himself. 'I never went to the Cinéma Splendide, Director,' has been the man's untiring refrain. 'I didn't even know Abidi owned the place. The guy was a pain, sure, but I didn't kill him. He wasn't worth the effort. Of course, he made enemies sticking his nose into other people's affairs. I'm not exactly surprised one of them decided they'd had enough. But I had nothing to do with it.'

The same, to hear him tell it, applies to the death of Taha

Semmar. 'I can't be blamed for every suicide amongst ex-DRS men. The service asked a lot of them and it was too much for some – Semmar included, so it seems. But that was nothing to do with me either.'

And so it has continued. Until Bouras notes that the clock on the interview room wall tells him Hidouchi has had the hour alone with Mokrani she demanded – in fact closer to two hours. It's time to bring his questioning of Zoubiri to a merciful close.

'Very well,' he declares, allowing none of the relief he feels to seep into his voice. 'That will be all – for now. You remain a suspect in this case and you may be called in again. But for the present . . . you can leave.'

Zoubiri smiles. 'Thanks, Director. It's been a privilege to see you at work. I suppose seniority means you get a little . . . out of practice at this kind of thing.'

Bouras remains impassive. 'As I say, you can leave now.'

'How about a ride back to the villa?'

And now it is Bouras's turn to smile. 'You'll have to make your own way, I'm afraid. All our drivers are busy.'

Time has thickened around Taleb into something he can almost feel pressing against him. Patience is a must for a police detective and he has never lacked in that department. But even his considerable reserves of it are running short as he waits and waits . . . and goes on waiting . . . for word from *les souveniristes*.

He descends to the kitchen for an early lunch. Noussa is busy preparing food for the conference delegates, who are present in full force to judge by the number of cars parked in front of the villa. She already has something set aside for him.

She also has a message from Abdou. 'He has news for you. You can find him in the workshop. But I suggest you eat this slice of *pissaladière* first. It's just come out of the oven.'

*

The *pissaladière* is predictably delicious. Taleb only wishes he was sufficiently relaxed to enjoy it properly. He leaves with a slice for Abdou and makes his way to the workshop.

'That smells good,' his old friend declares, grabbing the slice from him and wolfing it down without bothering to clean the dirt off his hands or even to extinguish his cigarette, which he balances on one jaw of the bench-vice.

'Noussa said you had news for me.'

'I do. Le Merz texted in response to my phone message. He can spare us half an hour this evening. We're to meet him at nine thirty. I have the address – outskirts of Marseille. You still want to do this?'

'Yes.' Taleb is weary of having terms dictated to him. He isn't about to pass up the opportunity of turning the tables on the supercilious Major. 'I still want to do this.'

'I wouldn't take that with you.' Abdou nods at the suitcase. 'Le Merz is a criminal, Mouloud. Give him a whiff of a load of money and he's likely to help himself. Our friendship only wins me so many favours.'

'There's nowhere secure here where I can leave it.'

'There's my tool-chest.' Abdou directs Taleb's attention with a *pissaladière*-greased finger to a large steel trunk under the bench. An open padlock is dangling from the bar behind the hasp. 'We can lock it inside that and you can keep the key until we get back.'

For an instant Taleb wonders whether Abdou can be trusted with the case. Then he rebukes himself for letting his professional scepticism infect their relationship. Abdou and Noussa aren't going to decamp with the money. And the tool-chest is just about the safest place to store it. 'Good idea. Though I'll hang on to it for now. I don't want Irmouli or Jahid to see me without it.'

'Have you figured out yet what they're really up to?'

Before Taleb can answer, Abdou holds up his hand. 'It was

stupid of me to ask you that, Mouloud. Forget I did. The less I know the better.'

'You're right. Stay well out of it. That's my advice. I speak as someone who knows too much for my peace of mind and too little to get my job done properly.'

'Do you ever regret becoming a policeman?'

Taleb nods. 'Every other day at least. Sometimes more frequently. The trouble is . . . it's the only thing I've ever been any good at.'

'It was your destiny, then.'

Taleb nods again. 'So it seems.'

Bouras pulls into the lay-by on the coast road near Aïn Benian that is in danger of becoming a regular rendezvous for him and Agent Hidouchi. She is waiting for him, prowling back and forth by her motorbike. He stops beside her, turns off the engine and leans across to push the passenger door open.

'Director,' says Hidouchi expressionlessly as she slides into the seat beside him.

'What did you get out of Mokrani?' He is too impatient for news to bother with niceties.

'He doesn't know much more about White Leopard than we do.'

'You're sure of that?'

'I am. He picked up whispers about it from others in his circle – back-numbered DRS contemporaries for the most part – and the gist was that it represented some kind of threat to them but nobody knew exactly what *kind* of threat. Then, around the same time, Abidi started asking awkward questions about Unit ninety-two. Mokrani suspected he'd been tipped off by someone. And he feared Abidi would publish whatever he learnt in the French press, where he couldn't be gagged. That's why Semmar was got rid of.'

'Mokrani admitted ordering Semmar's murder?'

'No. But his denial was pretty half-hearted, unlike when it

came to Abidi. It seems killing Abidi wasn't part of the plan, even after the *Microscope* broadcast. Mokrani wanted to learn what he knew about White Leopard, so he sent Zoubiri to extract whatever information he possessed. Unfortunately, Zoubiri overdid the persuasion tactics and Abidi ended up dead. It was just . . . a mistake.'

Bouras sighs disappointedly. He was hoping Hidouchi had laid bare the facts of a devious conspiracy. Instead they have no useful facts at all. But the conspiracy remains.

'Mokrani believes his son was kidnapped to stop him digging into White Leopard. He blames Lydia Seghir. Apparently she's responsible for delivering the project.'

'Which must be the purpose of the conference at the Villa des Ormeaux.'

'Mokrani assumes so, yes.'

'If he's right, they won't let his son go until Seghir has completed her task.'

'Which he thought she must have done when arrangements were made for Karim to be released. But now it looks as if he was just being strung along.'

'So, Taleb's wasting his time.'

'It could be worse than that. Abidi manoeuvred Taleb into making comments critical of Mokrani on national television. I worry he's being lined up to take the blame for sabotaging negotiations with the kidnappers to work off a supposed grudge against Mokrani.'

That sounds all too plausible to Bouras. Taleb as scapegoat. What else are veteran police officers good for, after all? 'We should warn him.'

'I intend to. Without delay.'

Bouras lights one of the slim cigars he finds a comfort in moments of professional perplexity. He offers Hidouchi one as well, but she declines with a brisk shake of the head. He draws on the cigar as he contemplates the assorted difficulties he has been drawn into. 'I suspect Taleb already distrusts the motives of the kidnappers. He won't be unduly surprised by what you tell him.'

'He's never unduly surprised by anything. I will also have to inform Deputy Director Kadri, of course. Though naturally I won't be mentioning this conversation to him – or saying a word about alerting Taleb to the peril of his position.'

'How will Kadri react, do you think?'

'He'll decide to stay uninvolved. If White Leopard is a secret government project – as it certainly appears to be – he won't risk being suspected of obstructing it. That wouldn't be a smart career move.'

'More like a career-*ending* move. We must be sure not to obstruct it ourselves for the same reason – or at least not to be seen to obstruct it.'

'But what about Taleb?'

'I can't pull him out without giving Seghir cause to suspect I know what she's up to. Even though, in reality, I don't.'

'An unenviable dilemma for you, Director.'

'Thank you for pointing that out.' Bouras gazes through the window at the cold blue Mediterranean. 'We're sailing in treacherous waters.'

'It seems we are.'

'We'd be much better placed if we knew what White Leopard is all about.'

'True enough.'

'We need the counsel of a senior insider at one of the two ministries Seghir advises. Energy or Foreign Affairs.'

'You know such a person?'

Bouras does. And the person in question owes him a favour. Has done, in fact, for many years. Has the time finally come to call in the favour? The question will need to be pondered. 'I may do, Agent Hidouchi, I may do.'

TEN

THE ONE LUXURY HIS CONFINED IDLENESS AT THE VILLA DES Ormeaux has afforded Taleb is the opportunity to think. If and when the Major nominates a new time and place for surrendering his hostage, Taleb will have to decide what to do about the small problem of being short of about half a million Swiss francs in ransom money. Informing the Major that he'll have to settle for significantly less than he demanded doesn't promise to end well. Spühler had nothing with him beyond the suitcase itself when they embarked on their fateful first attempt to buy Karim Mokrani's freedom. So, if he stole the half a million, it would have been found either in his car or in his room at the villa. But, according to Irmouli, there was nothing there.

Irmouli is lying. Nothing else makes sense. He has decided to help himself to the money Spühler skimmed off, share it – probably unequally – with Jahid and let Taleb suffer the consequences. He doesn't care about Karim Mokrani and he certainly doesn't care about Taleb, particularly not after virtually offering to cut him in and having his offer rejected. All he sees is a comfortable early retirement – a very comfortable one, considering what the Algerian dinar is worth against the Swiss franc.

Taleb is going to have to deal with Irmouli. He's going to have to get the money back from him. Assuming the Major ever calls, of course. There's no point in confronting Irmouli until he knows he has to. Until he does, he can think – long and hard – about how best to play the few cards he holds in his hand.

The small matter of his reluctant agreement to make a statement to a lawyer of the Major's choosing detailing the crimes he believes General Mokrani to be guilty of also occupies his thoughts. Obviously, he can't go through with it. The Major's offer to name the man responsible for the raid that claimed the lives of Taleb's wife and daughter is no incentive to someone who has too often seen, as Taleb has, the bloody consequences of vengeance for the wrongs of the past. Serene would tell him, if she could, that seeking revenge would be godless folly. And he obeys her as much in death as he did in life. Besides, attacking Mokrani so directly would be suicidal. He'd never live long enough to take revenge against anyone.

He lies on the bed in his room at the villa, contemplating these intertwined dilemmas during the eventless passage of the afternoon. A clear and simple path through the thicket of difficulties does not present itself to his mind. But maybe if he persists long enough . . .

Then there's the trill of an incoming phone call. For a fraction of a second Taleb thinks it's from the Major. But it's actually his reserve phone, kept for communications with Hidouchi and Bouras, that has rung. He grabs it from the bedside table.

'Yes?'

The voice he hears is Hidouchi's. 'Still at the villa, Taleb?'

'Still here. And still waiting.'

'Any news?'

'Not from the kidnappers.'

'The conference is continuing?'

'As we speak.'

'Then you won't hear from *les souveniristes*. I've had a . . . frank discussion . . . with General Mokrani. It seems Lydia Seghir is in charge of something called the White Leopard project, to which the conference is crucial. He believes his son was kidnapped to stop him trying to find out what White Leopard is all about, because, evidently, it poses a threat to him and his kind.'

'You're saying Seghir is behind the kidnapping of Karim Mokrani?'

'To the extent that she may have pointed the kidnappers in his direction . . . yes.'

'So handing over the ransom money isn't going to solve the problem?'

'Not in itself, apparently. But, Taleb, you should be aware of the possibility that your role in all this is to take the blame if and when negotiations for Agent Mokrani's release collapse or miscarry in some way. Abidi may have been set up by Seghir to lure you into making those statements about General Mokrani on television.'

Taleb falls silent. There's no lack of supporting evidence for the theory that Karim Mokrani's abduction has never been a straightforward kidnapping. If what Hidouchi's said is true, and he has little doubt it is, then he's been sent on a mission that can't succeed – that isn't even intended to succeed. He's a pawn destined to be sacrificed.

'Taleb? Are you listening to me?'

'I've heard every word, Souad. Does Bouras know about this?'

'Yes.'

'What does he want me to do? Sit tight?'

'He can't pull you out without tipping off Seghir that we're on to her. So . . . yes. For the moment.'

'According to Seghir's assistant the conference is in its final stages, so maybe I won't have to sit tight for long.'

'You can't rely on anything you're told by Seghir or her people.'

'So it appears. And I suppose you have no idea what White Leopard is all about?'

'None. Although Bouras is hoping to learn something from a contact at the Foreign Ministry.'

'I could do some digging at this end.'

'That could easily turn out very badly for you.'

'What other options do I have?'

'You could pull *yourself* out. Bouras can't force you to stay.'

'Abandon Karim Mokrani to his fate, you mean? I promised his mother I wouldn't do that.'

'Sometimes you have to think of yourself.'

'And his father wouldn't be best pleased either. I think I have to see this through.'

'I don't like the way it's shaping up, Taleb.'

'Neither do I. Which is why I'm not just going to sit here and wait to see what happens.'

'Don't take any unnecessary risks.'

'I'm not about to. These risks will be of the strictly necessary kind.'

Dinner is under way for the conference delegates when Taleb leaves the villa by the back stairs. He hears the distant burble of their conversation from the direction of the dining room as he exits, suitcase in hand. Fortunately, there's no sign of either Irmouli or Jahid as he makes his way to the workshop, where Rezig is waiting for him, smoking listlessly and apparently entranced by crackly football commentary on an old transistor radio that sits on a shelf high above the workbench.

'No second thoughts, old friend?' Abdou asks, arching his eyebrows.

'Plenty. But let's go anyway.'

'You're the boss.' Abdou bends down and opens the lid of the tool-chest. 'I've made room for the case.'

'Thanks.' Taleb loads the case into the chest.

Abdou closes the lid, padlocks it shut, then hands the key to Taleb. 'Don't lose that.'

'I won't.'

'OK, then.' Abdou frowns as the commentary relays an attempt on goal that ends in a kick way over the bar. Then he reaches up and switches the radio off.

It's not difficult to interpret the silence that follows as ominous. But Taleb says nothing to break it.

Neither does Abdou as he shrugs on an anorak and heads for the door.

And Taleb follows.

Despite – or perhaps because of – all the worries crowding in around him, Taleb falls asleep during the drive to Marseille. Rezig wakes him as they near the city, a jumble of neon beneath the inky night sky. They are still on the autoroute, a long way from the centre, but Rezig reports their destination is close.

They exit the autoroute and drop down into a sprawl of factories and warehouses which Rezig navigates his way through to the darkened premises of a mineral water distributor that no longer appears to be in business.

There are a couple of big black SUVs parked in the loading bay, however, and a dim glimmer of light towards the rear of the dock. Someone is waiting for them.

Rezig pulls up beside the cars and stops. 'Here we are,' he murmurs.

Taleb rubs his eyes. 'Any last words of advice?' he asks.

'Don't make him angry. He has a temper like . . . Vesuvius.'

'I'm not planning to make him angry.'

'It could happen without you meaning it to.'

'Thanks, Abdou. That's . . . very useful.'

They get out of the truck. The air is chill and clear. And the only sound is a rumble of traffic on the autoroute. Closer to there is only silence. He considers lighting a cigarette, then reconsiders.

Rezig walks towards the steps that lead up onto the dock. Taleb falls in behind. Before they reach the bottom step the doors above them slide noisily open. Light splashes out.

'You can stay there,' booms a voice.

A broad-shouldered, corpulent man in a voluminous overcoat strides forward and looks down at them, his face cast in deep shadow. A couple of figures move behind him, but do not draw near.

'Good to see you, Abdou,' the man says. He is smoking a cigar. Taleb catches the pungent smell of it wafting down to him.

'Good to see you too, Farabi,' Rezig replies. 'And thank you . . . for agreeing to this meeting.'

'Anything for you, *mon ami*.'

'This is Mouloud Taleb. Mouloud, this is . . . Le Merz.'

'*Bonsoir*,' says Taleb in what he judges to be a respectful tone.

Le Merz nods. Taleb can see little of his features. He appears to be bald, possibly mustachioed. There's a jowly thickness to his throat. 'You're a policeman, Abdou tells me.'

'That is correct.'

'I hate policemen.'

Taleb can think of no obvious response to that. He opts for silence.

Then Le Merz laughs. 'Fortunately for you, the policemen I hate are all French. You are the first Algerian policeman I've encountered since I was a child in Algiers back before independence.' He turns and waves to someone behind him, who brings out a chair for him to sit on. He settles and takes a few puffs on his cigar. 'You were at school with Abdou, right?'

'I was.'

'And he vouches for you. Don't you, Abdou?'

Rezig also nods. 'I know Mouloud to be . . . an honest man.'

'Hah!' Le Merz laughs again. He seems to be enjoying himself.

'An honest Algerian policeman. You have brought me a miracle. Are you honest, Taleb?'

'That's not for me to say.'

'What rank do you hold?'

'Superintendent.'

'Really? Quite senior, then. How do you explain that, if you're as honest as Abdou seems to believe?'

'Promotion's inevitable if you stay long enough.'

'And if you *live* long enough, of course. There must have been quite a high death rate in the DGSN during *la décennie noire*, which you surely served through.'

'It wasn't an easy time.'

'I'll bet it wasn't. But here you are and not yet retired. Why haven't you been pensioned off?'

'I have my uses, apparently.'

'Someone obviously thinks so. What's brought you to Provence?'

'A kidnapping. Of the son of a leading figure in *le pouvoir*.' Taleb sees no need to mention Mokrani by name, or dwell on the recent decline in his influence.

'Kidnapped here?'

'Yes.'

'By?'

'A group calling themselves *les souveniristes*.'

'*Les souveniristes*?'

'Yes.'

Le Merz sends up a plume of smoke. 'I've never heard of such a group.'

'Me neither. Until this . . . development.'

'Well, the intelligence deficiencies of the DGSN are not my problem, Taleb. The point is that I don't share those deficiencies. Kidnappings on my territory by unknown actors? Kidnappings by third parties, more to the point, without my sanction? That is . . . a very serious matter. Would I have heard of the victim's father?'

'I believe you would.'

'Are you willing to identify him?'

'I can't do that.'

'Was his son involved in this conference Abdou tells me is being held at the Villa des Ormeaux?'

'He was part of the security detail.'

'Who is attending the conference?'

'It's been organized by an Algerian government representative. But I don't know who's attending. Or what they're discussing.'

'Tell me something you *do* know.'

'I've met a man who speaks on behalf of *les souveniristes*. The Major. From what he said to me, it's clear the objective of the group, apart from extracting ransom money to fund their activities, is the exposure of those responsible for some of the worst outrages of *la décennie noire*.'

'Aren't such outrages all covered by an amnesty?'

'In Algeria, yes. Perhaps that's why they've struck in France.'

'Describe the Major.'

'I never saw his face. From his voice I'd say he's middle-aged . . . and definitely Algerian.'

'How have your negotiations with him gone?'

'Not well. At present, they're . . . frozen.'

'Are they asking for too much money?'

'It's not that. I'm beginning to get the impression . . . the money doesn't really matter.'

'People who don't care about money are dangerous. I can't have such people upsetting the rules of commerce in my territory.' By 'commerce' Taleb takes Le Merz to mean organized crime. 'In normal circumstances, I'd let *le pouvoir* clean its own stable.' The remark suggests he has dealings with members of *le pouvoir*, which Taleb somehow doesn't find surprising. Their offshore investments are very likely to have intersected with those of a *grand bonnet* of the Marseille underworld. 'But this all sounds potentially worrying. I may have to take . . . direct action.'

'What might that involve?'

'Hah! You think I'm going to reveal the way I work to a policeman? I'm grateful to both of you for bringing this to my attention. The conference, the kidnapping, *les souveniristes*? I don't like the sound of any of it. Elasse shouldn't be involving himself in such matters.' So, Taleb notes, it seems Le Merz is acquainted with Elasse as well as Rezig. 'As for you, Taleb, watch your back. That's my advice to you. I'll be looking into *les souveniristes* and the mysterious Major. Where was your meeting with him?'

'I was picked up by car from Aix TGV station and blindfolded, then driven in circles while he and I talked.'

'Well, you negotiate with him as you please. But he has my eye on him now, so . . . circumstances could change quickly. How much have you agreed to pay him to release the hostage?'

Taleb suspects disclosing the sum involved would be unwise. 'We, er . . . haven't settled on a final figure.'

'No?' Le Merz chuckles. 'If you say so. But if I lay hands on the hostage, I'll charge you a retrieval fee. The going rate for that kind of thing, given his connection to a leading member of *le pouvoir*, runs into seven figures – in cash. Will that be a problem for you?'

'It shouldn't be.'

'Good. I'm glad we had this chat.' Le Merz stands up. His flunkey moves into view and removes the chair. Le Merz takes a puff on his cigar and gazes down at Taleb. 'If I have any news, I'll let Abdou know. Then you and I can talk again. If we need to. Fair enough?'

Taleb nods. 'Fair enough.'

'Go carefully in the meantime. You too, Abdou.'

With that, *le grand bonnet* turns and strides away.

*

'Was that helpful?' Rezig asks as they drive away from the depot.

'It might have been,' Taleb replies. 'Only time will tell, I suppose.' He reaches for his cigarettes, only then remembering how short of Nassims he is. 'Hold on. You must know which area of the city most Algerians live in. Is it far from here?'

'You want to go there?'

'Yes – if you know a late-night *tabac* where I might be able to get my favourite brand.'

'Those are Nassims, aren't they?'

'That's right.'

'You should buy decent tobacco and roll your own.'

'What about the *tabac*?'

'Well, it's quite a diversion. We'll have to go into the centre. There's a place I used to go near the Porte d'Aix that might stock them. It'll probably still be open.'

'Let's go. I'll think better for knowing I'm not about to run out of Nassims.'

They get back on the autoroute and head south into the heart of Marseille. Taleb smokes as they go, reflecting on their encounter with Le Merz, a man whose happiness to oblige an old friend had swiftly transformed itself into a determination to bear down hard on interlopers in his criminal domain. His motives are less important to Taleb than what he is likely to accomplish – which promises to be far more than Taleb can hope to manage on his own. And his contacts, which are presumably innumerable, happen to include Rezig's employer.

'You never mentioned Le Merz had dealings with Monsieur Elasse, Abdou,' Taleb says after they've driven in silence for a while.

'I work for the guy, Mouloud. It's not for me to gossip about who he does or doesn't do business with. They've probably just . . . met socially.'

'*Socially?*'

'Well, Le Merz puts himself about. Charity events and such like. That could be how they've come across each other.'

Charity events? Taleb is wholly unconvinced. But Rezig's done him a big favour this evening. He doesn't deserve to be interrogated. 'OK, Abdou, let's forget about that. I'm not in France to investigate your boss. Or Le Merz, come to that. For now, let's concentrate on what's really important: my cigarette supply.'

The street where Rezig decants Taleb could easily be in Algiers. Most of the other pedestrians and cruising moped riders would fit right in. The *tabac* is still open, as promised, and doing brisk trade, though in what exactly isn't clear, since many of the customers are loitering rather than buying. Taleb has only one objective in mind, however, and the proprietor is able to oblige. 'Nassims, monsieur? You are obviously a man of discernment. Buy five packs or more and you get a discount.'

Taleb opts for the discount. It's only when the packs are stacked on the counter that he remembers he left his bag in Rezig's truck, containing the phone supplied to him by Kadri for communications with the kidnappers, along with his official DGSN phone. It's late and he's tired. His concentration is fraying. He's not worried, however. He'll soon be back in the truck. And the discount turns out to include a bag for his cigarettes.

He exits onto the street and spots Rezig double-parked a short distance away. Stepping off the pavement, he is narrowly missed by a moped. An insult is flung back at him which he's glad he doesn't catch.

'You should be more careful, Mouloud,' Rezig informs him as he clambers into the truck.

'You're right. I should.'

'You left your phone – well, one of your phones – here.'

'Been searching my bag, Abdou?'

'No. It rang. Gave me quite a fright.'

'It *rang*?'

'Yes. And I thought . . . I ought to answer . . . in case it was important.'

Important? Taleb doesn't doubt it was that. 'What happened?'

'The caller said he was the Major. He asked what you were doing in Marseille.'

'How did he know where we are?'

'People can track your location from your phone if you don't know how to block it, Mouloud. You must know that.'

'I'm not really . . . up to date with technology.'

'Obviously not.'

'What did you tell him?'

'The truth. That you were here to buy cigarettes. It seemed to amuse him.'

The Major amused? Perhaps that was a good thing. 'What else did he say?'

'You're to go to the same place as before, tomorrow morning at eight o'clock.'

'Just that?'

'Well, he . . .'

'What?'

'He said this was your second and final chance. And . . .'

'*And?*'

'I'm not sure I . . .'

'Just spit it out, Abdou.'

'He said that if you didn't do exactly as you were told this time they'd kill Mokrani . . . and you.'

'I suppose you don't actually have to go tomorrow,' says Rezig as he contrives to roll and light a cigarette while rattling back up the autoroute.

Taleb is already puffing on one of his replenished supply of

Nassims. The same thought has already occurred to him. But every time he thinks through the real-world consequences of bailing out of the operation he realizes they'd actually be far worse than whatever risks he'll be running by turning up to the handover, alone and with the ransom money, ready to be surrendered in exchange for Karim Mokrani.

The coincidence that the Major called so soon after his meeting with Le Merz – almost as if he knew they were meeting and decided he needed to move before Le Merz could take any action – is also weighing on Taleb's mind. In reality, it can't be anything other than a coincidence. But reality is proving a little hard to keep a firm grasp of.

At least there's one thing he can be certain of. 'Actually, Abdou,' he says at last, 'I do have to go tomorrow. Though before then I need to have a serious conversation with Agent Irmouli.'

'It's just that I was thinking . . .'

'What were you thinking?'

'Well, you're past normal retirement age for a policeman and you don't have any family waiting for you in Algeria, so you could just . . .'

'Take the money and run?'

'Something like that.'

'Ah, but you've forgotten the Nassims.'

'What do they have to do with it?'

'Smoking's bad for the lungs, Abdou. And I've smoked a lot over the years, so running's out of the question. Besides, like you told Le Merz, I'm an honest man. I sometimes wish I wasn't, but . . . you can't change your nature.'

'So, you *are* going?'

'Unless you write both of us off in a crash on the way back to the villa tonight. Is there any chance you could steer with your hands rather than your elbows?'

*

When they reach the villa, there are still several delegates' cars parked out front, at an hour when they're normally long gone. Taleb spots a prowling Jahid by the glow of his cigarette. He asks Rezig to drop him there. 'I'll leave the suitcase in your tool-chest overnight if that's all right with you, Abdou.' He has the sense that it'll actually be safer there than inside the villa. How Irmouli is going to react to what Taleb has to say to him is hard to predict.

Rezig pulls up and Taleb clambers out of the cab, his bag over his shoulder, with the plastic carrier bag containing his precious Nassims clutched in his hand. As the truck moves away, he walks over to where Jahid is standing.

'You never said you were leaving the villa tonight,' says Jahid. Irmouli would have made the statement sound like a reproach. Jahid just drawls out the words inexpressively.

'Where's Irmouli?' Taleb asks, deciding he really doesn't need to point out that he's not required to log his movements with them.

'Inside. With Seghir, I think. Everything's wrapping up.'

'What do you mean?'

'The conference is over. Mission accomplished – whatever the mission was.' Jahid shrugs. 'I don't know anything. Except that Seghir and her team are flying home tomorrow. And we'll be leaving soon after. Can't say I'll be sorry to see the last of this place. I haven't felt warm one single day I've been here.'

'I need to speak to Irmouli.'

'He won't thank you for interrupting him while he's persuading Doctor Seghir her comfort and convenience are all he thinks about.'

'That can't be helped.' Taleb heads for the front door of the villa.

'Where's the suitcase?' Jahid calls after him.

'I checked it into left luggage at the railway station in Aix.'

Contemplation of whether Taleb is joking or not reduces Jahid to silence. Either that or he's struck dumb by the appearance of Lydia Seghir, resplendent in a glittering evening gown.

She walks slowly out of the villa and stands in the porch, flanked by two men, one balding and portly, the other younger – slimmer and taller, with crewcut hair. The porch lantern lights his face from above, catching the harsh line of a scar running down over his left eyebrow and cheekbone.

Taleb stops dead. They aren't looking in his direction. They're absorbed in their conversation, smiling and laughing in a quietly celebratory manner. He moves back into the shadow between the lights cast from the windows at the front of the villa. He must not be seen. Not at this moment. Not by the young man with the scar on his face.

Because they have met before – five months before, one broiling hot night in Algiers.

Connections and conclusions are piling up in Taleb's mind as he retreats round the side of the villa, out of sight of Seghir and the young man with the scar. He enters the building at the rear and heads up the stairs towards his room. He won't be lingering there, however. He has to speak to Irmouli. But he thinks it prudent to lie low for half an hour or so.

As it happens, he doesn't have to wait half an hour to hold a conversation with Irmouli, who emerges from the corridor leading to Taleb's room just as Taleb reaches the landing.

'There you are,' says Irmouli, frowning. 'I was looking for you.'

'Why?'

'I thought you ought to be made aware that the conference is over. Lydia Seghir's team will be leaving tomorrow.'

'So Jahid told me.'

'Then you'll know the DSS detachment is also being pulled out. You'll be on your own.'

'Unless Agent Mokrani is released before you all leave.'

Irmouli smiles weakly. 'Is that likely?'

'It might be. By the way, who was the young man with the conspicuous scar I saw with Doctor Seghir just now?'

'Her son. Urtan. He's something junior at the Energy Ministry. How's that for nepotism? He's here to be impressed by his mother's ability to manage sensitive negotiations, I imagine. But he's more than just a trainee pen-pusher, if that scar's anything to go by. It's certainly not a paper cut, is it? Now, where's the suitcase you're never parted from?'

'In a safe place.'

'I certainly hope so.'

Taleb steps closer to Irmouli. They stand in the doorway leading from the landing into the darkened corridor. Taleb lowers his voice to avoid it carrying down the stairwell. 'You'll be glad to know an exchange with the kidnappers is imminent.'

Irmouli raises his eyebrow. 'Really?'

'Good news, don't you think?'

'Obviously.' Nothing in Irmouli's tone or expression suggests he actually thinks it *is* good news.

'As a result, I need the balance of the ransom money.'

'The balance?'

'Spühler skimmed off what I estimate to have been ten per cent – half a million francs. He didn't have it with him when he was killed. So, he must have left it here.'

'We found nothing.'

'I don't propose to debate the issue with you, Irmouli. If I don't get the half million back by six o'clock tomorrow morning, I'll tell General Mokrani it's missing – and why I'm more or less certain you and Jahid have it. Well, *you*, actually. I imagine Jahid's just on a promise. I'll tell *les souveniristes* as well.'

'You intend to meet them with some of the ransom money missing?'

'If necessary.'

'I don't believe you. It would be suicide.'

'You think I'm bluffing?'

'I don't care whether you are or not. I don't have the money.'

'You virtually offered me a cut of it last night.'

'You must have misunderstood me.'

'General Mokrani may not be the man he once was, but he still has the means to make you – and me – suffer for abandoning his son. I'm not about to do that. And I *will* accuse you of stealing what Spühler was already planning to steal. Will Mokrani believe me? Who knows? The question is: can you afford to assume he won't?'

Irmouli says nothing for several long moments. Then he brushes past Taleb and sets off down the stairs, tossing back his answer over his shoulder. 'You're crazy. I can't help you.'

Taleb retreats to his room. He's glad he decided to leave the suitcase in Rezig's tool-chest. There'd be a chance otherwise Irmouli might go for broke and try to steal all the money. As it is, he may suspect Taleb is bluffing, but he can't be certain. And he'll need time to appreciate the invidiousness of his position. Admitting defeat is a process that can't be hurried. Accordingly, Taleb has to be patient as he waits for his opponent to acknowledge to himself that he has to back down.

While he waits, there is much else to occupy Taleb's thoughts. It's just as well he's replenished his stock of cigarettes, since smoking has always been good for his powers of reasoning. Why was Urtan Seghir in his office that hot night last August? What was he looking for? And was he looking for it on his mother's behalf?

The Major spoke of documents supplied to Meslem by a representative of Kasdi Merbah, documents supposedly originating from Youcef Ghezala and containing hard evidence linking General Mokrani to the Boudiaf assassination. Meslem had told Taleb at the time – in 1993 – that the documents, though mentioned to him, hadn't arrived prior to Merbah's own assassination and that – unsurprisingly – no more had been heard of them thereafter. Taleb's suspicion, based on the Major's assertion that the documents were known to have been delivered to Meslem, was that Meslem had decided, following Merbah's violent death, to destroy them. And who could blame him?

But perhaps Meslem *hadn't* destroyed them. Or perhaps there were grounds to *suspect* he hadn't destroyed them. If so, they might have been what Urtan Seghir was looking for that night, an informant having told him there was a box with Meslem's name on it sitting atop a cupboard in Taleb's office.

It seems to Taleb that anyone who believed Meslem had retained the documents would check many other more obvious hiding places before raiding Taleb's office. That would surely be a last resort. Meslem's own home would be the logical place to start. Yet Taleb knew of no report from Meslem's widow of a break-in at their apartment.

He still has Meslem's home phone number recorded in his notebook. Acting on impulse, he calls it. The man who answers says he and his family took over the lease from Chahira Meslem five years ago. They don't have an address or new phone number for her. She must be drawing a widow's pension, however, so Bouras could trace her through the personnel department. Taleb decides to leave that for another day.

Meanwhile, there is the puzzle of the timing of the Major's latest contact to ponder. He can't have known about Taleb's meeting with Le Merz. And yet . . .

There is so much Taleb doesn't know and so little he can be sure of. It's a situation he's not unfamiliar with. But that doesn't make it any easier to bear.

He places his gun on the bed beside him when he lies down and turns out the light. If he has to use the weapon, things will have taken a desperate turn. But that's a possibility he can't rule out.

He's roused from a shallow doze by a tap at the door. He's instantly alert. He checks his phone for the time: 2.20 a.m. Then he lies motionless, waiting for a second knock that never comes.

Did he imagine the sound? Did he dream it? He lies still, ears straining to detect movement on the other side of the door. He hears nothing. Then, in the distance – it's hard to tell how far away – a click. That's all. Another door closing somewhere along the corridor? Maybe.

He sits up, lowers his feet to the floor, waits through another few soundless moments, then grasps the gun, stands up and moves cautiously to the door. He lowers the handle and edges it open.

There's something on the floor – something bulky and darker than the enveloping shadows: a black plastic bag, fastened at the top with a knot.

He picks up the bag and retreats into the room, closing the door behind him. He carries the bag back to the bed, sets it down and switches on the bedside lamp, then waits a moment for his eyes to adjust to the glare.

He unties the knot and opens the bag. And there they are: five neatly banded wads of thousand Swiss franc banknotes. He already knows there are a hundred notes in each wad, so this is all of what Spühler took. And this is all Taleb needs. Irmouli has given in.

Maybe, Taleb reflects, this really is going to end well after all.

ELEVEN

IT'S JUST BEFORE SEVEN O'CLOCK ON WEDNESDAY MORNING WHEN Taleb knocks on the door of Irmouli's room. There's an instantaneous response. 'Who's there?'

'Taleb.'

A few seconds later, the door opens. Irmouli is fully dressed, though unshaven. He looks at Taleb blankly. 'What do you want?'

He knows, of course, what Taleb wants. But the game they are playing now means there will be no reference by either man to their stand-off of the previous night. Taleb never gave Irmouli an ultimatum. Irmouli never delivered a bag of money to Taleb's door in the small hours. None of that happened.

'I need you to contact General Mokrani,' Taleb says emolliently. 'Notify him that I am meeting the kidnappers this morning in the hope of securing his son's release.'

Irmouli nods. 'I'll notify him.'

'Tell him I'll be complying exactly with the kidnappers' terms.'

'Nothing can go wrong, then.'

'Just tell him.'

'Anything else?'

'I'll need to use Spühler's car. I can't drive the Renault with all those bullet-holes in it.'

'Hold on.' Irmouli retreats into the room, returning a few seconds later with a set of keys attached to a Citroën fob. He drops them into Taleb's hand.

'Thank you, Agent Irmouli.'

'Thank you, Superintendent.' With that Irmouli closes the door.

Rezig is waiting for Taleb at the workshop. He offers him a cup of coffee from his Thermos. It tastes good. 'I hope all goes well for you this morning, Mouloud,' says Rezig as they sip their coffees.

'There's no reason it shouldn't,' Taleb reassures him. 'This time.'

'Visiting Le Merz was pointless, then.'

'Not necessarily. If he chooses to make life difficult for *les souveniristes*, I won't be sorry.'

'Well, I'll certainly be grateful to have the ransom money off my hands. I didn't sleep well last night.'

'Me neither.'

Taleb drains his coffee and pulls the tool-chest out from beneath the workbench. He unlocks it and raises the lid. The sight of the suitcase inside is reassuring. He lifts it out and lays it on the bench. Rezig wanders off discreetly towards the door and gazes out into the darkness. Dawn is still a little way off.

Taleb opens the case. The money's there, of course, as he knew it would be but occasionally during the night contrived to imagine it might not be. He takes the five wads from the black plastic bag and adds them to the pile, then closes and locks the case.

'Time I was on my way,' he announces.

'Good luck, my friend,' says Rezig.

'Let's hope I don't need any.'

Rezig smiles at him. 'Let's hope.'

Taleb arrives at the Lac du Bimont car park nearly half an hour early for the exchange. Dawn is creeping slowly over the mountainous surroundings, the cloud-filled sky revealing itself in grey-black contusions, the water of the lake still and dark beneath it.

There's one other vehicle in the car park, an anonymous silver Volkswagen. There's no sign of the driver and the windscreen's beaded with rain, which suggest it's been there all night. Taleb walks over and peers into the interior, but sees nothing suspicious. Then he returns to the Citroën and checks the phone he's expecting the Major to call him on for a good signal. It's fine. He lodges the phone in his pocket.

All he has to do now is wait.

Hidouchi sets off for DSS HQ that morning in a mood that is both apprehensive and frustrated. She's anxious about how the Mokrani kidnapping will end and how Taleb will come out of it. But she's aware that there's nothing more she can do for the present to help him. All she can do in fact is wait upon events.

She reaches the top of the ramp out of the apartment block's underground car park and flicks down the visor on her crash helmet, ready to weave her way through the Algiers traffic. A high speed ride won't solve any problems. But the concentration required will at least distract her.

The road's clear as she pauses and looks both ways. She swings right, preparing to throttle up.

Suddenly, as if from nowhere, a black car pulls across her path from the other side of the road. It's coming straight at her. She swerves left, into the road, rather than right towards the kerb, where there's a rapidly closing gap. She feels the wing of the car brush a fold of her leathers as they pass. A few millimetres are all that saves her.

She brakes to a halt by the opposite kerb and glares back at the car, which has also stopped. A truck rumbles between them, the driver gesticulating at her as he goes.

Then she locks eyes with the driver of the car, who's looking at her, elbow propped in the open window. He's smiling. In that instant, she realizes who he is. Khaled Zoubiri.

'You should be more careful, Agent Hidouchi,' Zoubiri shouts across at her. 'The way you're going you could get yourself killed.' Before she can respond, he accelerates away, swinging back across the road to the correct side.

This is Zoubiri's answer to what happened yesterday. And Hidouchi doubts it's his last word on the subject.

But if his intention was to intimidate her it's failed. All she feels is regret that she can't go after him. Not yet, anyway. 'I'll be seeing you,' she murmurs.

Checking his watch, Taleb reckons there's time to fit in a call of his own before he hears from the Major. He takes out his reserve phone and keys in the code for Hidouchi's number.

'Taleb?' She answers promptly, with a breathless flutter in her voice.

'Have I interrupted your morning run?' he asks.

'No. I just had a . . . Never mind. Is there news?'

'I heard from the kidnappers last night. We've agreed to an exchange this morning. I'm at the rendezvous.'

'You think they mean to go through with it?'

'I do. The conference is over. Seghir is leaving today. And money's money, when all's said and done, so why wouldn't they? Maybe this is their reward for helping her out where General Mokrani is concerned.'

'I hope you're right. If you bring his son back with you, he can't complain.'

'That sounds good to me. I'd certainly like to come home.'

'There are still a lot of unanswered questions, though.'

'We can talk about them when I've got this part of the job done.'

'OK. But—'

'I've got to go,' Taleb interrupts. The phone in his pocket has started to trill. 'I'll call you later.'

He rings off and answers the other phone. 'Hello?'

'Are you at the lake, Taleb?' It's the Major's voice.

'Yes. I am.'

'Early, eh? I thought you might be.'

'I'm alone. And I've got the money.'

'Good. And you're well rested, I hope, after your trip to Marseille.'

'I'm ready, Major.'

'You went all the way to Marseille just for cigarettes?'

'My favourite brand isn't available locally.'

'Persist with that story if you like. I have no doubt you went there for some other reason. What were you looking for? Insurance?'

'Hardly. I've been uninsurable for many years.'

The Major chuckles. 'You probably have. Now, listen to me very carefully. A car will shortly join you there. There'll be three men in it. The driver and the front seat passenger are my operatives. The rear seat passenger will be Karim Mokrani. Got that?'

'Yes. So, we're doing this here, are we?'

'We are. I thought we'd keep it simple. There's no one else around, is there?'

'Nobody that I can see.'

'Any other cars?'

'One. But it's empty. No idea where the driver is.'

'OK. Let's not worry about that. When the car with my people in it arrives, the front seat passenger will get out. Then you will get out. He will walk towards you. You will meet him by the boot of your car and show him the money. I take it you're carrying it in the boot?'

'Yes.'

'Right. So, at that point Mokrani will get out of our car. My man will then take the money back to it as Mokrani walks over to you. They will pass on the way. My men will then leave. And you . . . can do whatever you like. Except follow them, of course. That would be a serious mistake.'

'I won't follow.'

'Very wise.'

So far the Major has said nothing about his earlier requirement that Taleb make a sworn statement to a lawyer in Aix detailing General Mokrani's assorted misdeeds. To secure Karim Mokrani's freedom, Taleb will have to confirm he'll make such a statement, even though, in reality, he'd be mad to go ahead and do it. He hopes *les souveniristes* will be content with the money once they have it in their hands and won't pursue the matter. But he's too preoccupied with the challenges of this stage of the proceedings to dwell on the point.

'You do have the sum agreed with you, don't you, Taleb?'

Taleb is relieved the Major is concentrating on the question of the ransom. 'I do.'

'The *full* sum?'

'It's all here, Major. Waiting for you.'

'Good. As regards the lawyer in Aix I wanted you to speak to . . .'

'Yes?' It was too much to hope, of course, that the idea would have been dropped.

'That may no longer be . . . appropriate.'

'What do you mean?'

'You'll understand soon enough.'

'Understand what?' The Major's ambiguity is beginning to worry Taleb.

'You don't have long to wait, I assure you.'

He's right. From the corner of his eye Taleb catches a movement and, turning, sees a black Tesla glide silently into the car park. It comes to a halt about halfway between the Citroën and the empty VW.

Taleb looks across at the vehicle. He can see the profiles of the two men sitting in the front. The one closer to him is dark-haired and bearded. Behind him is the other passenger. Is he Karim Mokrani? There's no way to be certain. Perhaps because he's been forbidden to, he doesn't look in Taleb's direction.

But at this point the bearded man in front of him does. His complexion is swarthy, his hairline low, his beard full. He doesn't smile or frown. He just stares at Taleb for a long moment. Then he opens the door and steps out. He's dressed in boots, jeans, sweater and a zipped jacket. There's no conspicuous indication that he's carrying a gun, though Taleb reckons it's virtually certain he is.

So is Taleb, of course. It would be crazy not to. He opens his door and climbs carefully out of the Citroën.

The bearded man starts walking slowly towards Taleb, who moves, also slowly, round to the boot of the car. He opens it and pulls the case forward. It's already set on its combination.

The man reaches him and stands at his shoulder. Taleb opens the case and raises the lid, revealing the piled wads of thousand Swiss franc notes. The man reaches past him and picks up one of the wads. He fans through it, then does the same with another two wads, chosen at random. Taleb says nothing. He knows it's all there. That's one thing – perhaps the only thing – he doesn't have to worry about.

The man appears satisfied. He closes the case and lifts it out of the boot, transferring it to his left hand as he does so. He looks at Taleb and ever so faintly nods. Then he turns round and seems to exchange a look with the driver of the Tesla, who is leaning forward to catch his eye. A second later, the rear door of the car swings open and their passenger steps out.

It's Karim Mokrani. Taleb knows him from the video message the Major supplied prior to the first, abortive exchange. He's had a shave since then, but the bruise over his left eyebrow is still visible. He's dressed in a badly creased dark suit and a crumpled white shirt: the clothes he was wearing when they grabbed him, presumably. He raises one hand slightly. He looks less apprehensive than Taleb would have expected. He's on the brink of freedom, but if he's worried that freedom might be plucked away from him at the last moment he doesn't show it.

The bearded man starts walking towards the Tesla at a steady pace, the signal for Mokrani to move as well, matching his pace as he heads towards the Citroën. Taleb closes the boot and moves back to the driver's door to meet him. Everything's going smoothly, just as smoothly as could be. Taleb's beginning to believe it's going to be all right this time. There doesn't seem to be anything that can go wrong now.

'It's good to meet you, Agent Mokrani,' says Taleb. He extends a hand. Mokrani grasps it. He smiles, then glances over his shoulder. The bearded man is loading the suitcase into the Tesla.

'You're Superintendent Taleb?' Mokrani asks, looking back at him.

'Yes. DGSN Algiers.'

'Thank you . . . for playing your part.'

'You're welcome. I suggest you get in.'

'OK.' Mokrani heads round to the other side of the Citroën. As he does so, the bearded man slips into the front passenger seat of the Tesla. The car starts to move, once again in disarming silence. It reverses in a slow turn, then swings out of the parking area and accelerates smoothly away.

The kidnappers have gone. And the money's gone with them. But Taleb has the hostage, alive and well. He takes a second to savour his success, then, hearing the passenger door of the Citroën close behind him, turns, opens the driver's door and climbs in.

'We should give them a head start before we leave,' he says to Mokrani. 'Do you want to phone anyone – your father, your mother – while we wait?'

'I don't think so,' Mokrani replies in a strange, distant tone of voice that doesn't seem to match the momentousness of the occasion.

'Up to you. Cigarette?' Taleb proffers his pack of Nassims.

Mokrani shakes his head dreamily. 'No thanks.'

Taleb lights one for himself. Then Mokrani asks, 'How long will you wait here?'

'Oh, five minutes or so.' Taleb takes a satisfying draw on his cigarette.

'That sounds about right, although . . . I won't be waiting with you.'

'What?' Taleb's first thought is that he's misheard.

'I had plenty of time to think while I was being held. There's no one I can trust back in Algeria. My DSS colleagues set me up on Seghir's orders. And my father? The Major said you know most of the terrible things he's done over the years. Now I know them too. What would I be going home to? I'm just a pawn in other people's power plays. Well, I won't be that. Not any more. The Major's made me an offer and I think I'll probably accept.' Suddenly Taleb understands why the Major said he was no longer expected to make a statement to a lawyer. Recruitment of Karim Mokrani to their cause is more damaging than anything Taleb could have supplied.

'What kind of offer?'

'I'd be serving a good cause, Taleb. Any idea what that would feel like? You must dream of it occasionally yourself.'

'Are you saying . . . you're going to help *les souveniristes*?'

'The Major has given me a choice. A *free* choice. That car over there? I have the key to it. He had it left here for my use. But where I go . . . and what I do . . . is up to me. You see? It's for me to decide. I'm not being forced to do anything. He even returned my gun.' Mokrani flicks back his jacket to reveal the weapon lodged in his belt-holster.

'You can't trust the Major either,' says Taleb, struggling to frame an argument that will change Mokrani's mind.

'It would be a gamble, I agree. But it would be *my* gamble.'

'Whatever you do, I need proof you've been released.' Taleb pulls out the phone he's been speaking to the Major on. The call, he sees, has been ended.

'What are you after? Some kind of videoed statement by me you can show my father? Forget it. He can think whatever he likes.' With that Mokrani pushes the door open and gets out of the car.

Taleb climbs out himself, fumbling to switch the phone to camera mode as he goes. He's unfamiliar with the settings and is still thumbing between them as Mokrani strides off towards the VW. 'Wait,' he calls.

And Mokrani does wait. He stops, turns round and pulls his gun out of its holster. 'Sorry,' he says, raising the gun. 'I can't take any chances.'

Taleb thinks for an instant that he's about to claim some small part in DGSN history by becoming the first police officer to be killed by a hostage he's just rescued from his kidnappers. And when Mokrani fires he thinks it's really happened.

But he's still standing there, still breathing, when the echo of the gunshot fades from the surrounding mountainsides. And then he hears the hiss of air escaping from the front tyre of the Citroën.

'I can't risk you following me, Taleb,' says Mokrani. 'This has to be a clean break.'

'You're putting me in an impossible position,' says Taleb,

already imagining the difficulties Mokrani's disappearance is going to plunge him into.

'I know. I'm afraid it can't be helped.'

Mokrani turns back and hurries over to the VW. Taleb, still fumbling with the phone, hears the door locks release. Mokrani jumps into the driver's seat and starts the engine.

At last, though too late to make much difference, Taleb locates the camera function and trains the phone on the car as it reverses towards him, capturing a clear view of the number plate but nothing of the driver.

Then Mokrani puts his foot down. The VW skids slightly as he spins the wheel and accelerates out of the car park, dust thrown up by a scatter of gravel swirling in its wake.

Taleb keeps videoing, but to no purpose. The car is just a blurred, receding shape. Mokrani has gone.

As have the kidnappers. And the ransom money. Only Taleb remains, with a dead man's car, a flat tyre and the taste of ashes in his mouth.

Taleb has thought often of late of his old boss, Superintendent Meslem, source of many a wise maxim. One of those, which Taleb acted on before leaving the Villa des Ormeaux, is that in any field operation the prudent detective should have a fallback position. There was always a chance the exchange would go wrong, though Taleb never foresaw it going wrong in the way it has. But the man on the spot inevitably takes the blame for mishaps, whether fairly or not. And so there has always been the possibility that he might need to make himself scarce. Accordingly, he brought along everything he travelled from Algeria with. It's in his bag in the boot. He can make a run for it if that's his only option – though where he would run *to* is unclear.

Everything hinges now on General Mokrani's reaction to what has occurred. Taleb doubts his account will be believed.

Mokrani will suspect treachery because it is in his nature to do so. But delay in rendering the account will only deepen the general's suspicions, so the sooner he hears it the better. Taleb calls Bouras, but gets no response. He leaves a message. It's the same when he tries Hidouchi. At that time of day, they might both be travelling. He knows they will respond as soon as they can.

That leaves him with no excuse but to fetch the spare wheel and the jack from the boot-well and start trying to get the Citroën back on the road. His cack-handedness when it comes to such undertakings ensures progress is slow, and he's done no more than jack the car a few centimetres off the ground when Hidouchi calls.

When he tells her what has happened, she goes at once to the nub of the matter. 'Will Karim Mokrani contact his parents and inform them of his release?'

'I'm not sure,' he admits. In fact, that's putting it too optimistically. 'Actually, I don't think he's going to. He wants to punish his father. And he may think silence is the best way to do it.'

'Can you prove he was actually released?'

'I have video of him driving away, but there's no clear view of him at the wheel. I, er . . . didn't operate the phone quickly enough.' Taleb thinks he can hear a sigh of exasperation from Hidouchi. His technological shortcomings have always been a bone of contention between them.

'Even if he does call his father,' she says after a pause, 'there would be no proof he wasn't being forced to do so by the kidnappers.'

'I suppose that's true.'

'But they've been paid the ransom?'

'Of course.'

'So, what's to stop General Mokrani jumping to the conclusion that you've taken the money and fabricated the whole story of an exchange – or that you've done some kind of deal on your own account with *les souveniristes*?'

'Nothing,' Taleb bleakly admits.

'Does Bouras know about this?'

'Not yet. But he soon will.'

'And he'll inform Kadri. He has to. Then they'll both have to face General Mokrani.'

'Yes.'

'Bouras will express his full confidence in you. But Kadri will do whatever he thinks is in his own best interests. Unless Karim Mokrani catches the next flight to Algiers and reports directly to DSS HQ . . .'

'He isn't going to do that. He believes his DSS colleagues betrayed him. As I think they did.'

'What is he going to do, then?'

'Throw in his lot with *les souveniristes*. Or just . . . disappear. I don't know.'

'You may have to disappear yourself if that's the case. Bouras will instruct you to return to Algiers. He'll have no choice. But if you do . . .'

'It won't go well for me.'

'It will go as it's intended to. You've been set up, Taleb.'

'I'm aware of that.'

'What are you going to do?'

'After I've finished fitting this tyre . . . I'm not sure. I need to think.'

'I suggest you call on the services of our mutual friend.'

The friend Hidouchi is referring to is Amed Sidhoum, born like Taleb in 1955 and who grew up in the same neighbourhood of Algiers, sadly killed by a stray bullet during the riots sparked by de Gaulle's visit to the city in December 1960. When Taleb began collaborating with Hidouchi in off-the-books operations in the summer of 2020, she advised him to acquire an alternative identity he could make use of if and when the need arose. So it was that Amed Sidhoum was magically reborn, complete with identity card and passport. And now the need foreseen by Hidouchi has arisen for Sidhoum to do some travelling.

'He is with you, isn't he?' Hidouchi clearly fears Taleb might have left his emergency documents in Algiers. She has a low opinion of his day-to-day competence.

'He's here,' Taleb reassures her.

'That's something. Until we know how things are likely to play out you should lie low.'

'I intend to.' At that moment a message appears on the screen of Taleb's phone indicating Bouras is trying to contact him. 'The director's calling me back, Souad.'

'I'll ring off, then. Remember: *lie low.*'

Hidouchi ends her call and Taleb switches to Bouras. 'Director?'

'What's happening, Taleb?'

'A lot. I've secured Karim Mokrani's release, but I can't prove it.'

'How can that be?'

Taleb explains. Bouras listens to him in silence, a silence that only seems to intensify as the explanation continues. Taleb is well aware the turn of events places the director in an awkward position, though rather less awkward, he reflects, than the position he's in himself.

In the end, Bouras asks the same question Hidouchi posed. 'Do you think Karim Mokrani will contact his parents?'

'I don't know. Considering what he said about his father . . . I rather doubt it. I'm sorry, Director. He caught me off guard. I never thought he would just . . . leave.'

'But he did. And that's the version of events I'll have to present to General Mokrani.'

'It's the truth.'

'I don't doubt it for a moment. But Mokrani will doubt it. In fact, with his five million Swiss francs gone and his son nowhere to be seen, he'll suspect you've betrayed him.'

'Perhaps you could tell him Karim said he'd be in touch with his mother . . . soon. That might . . . give us some breathing space.'

'But he didn't say that, did he?'

'No.'

'And there's no reason to think he'll do it?'

'None.'

'And nothing short of Karim's appearance in the flesh is likely to satisfy his father anyway. Nevertheless, as you say, it might stay his hand for a while. I'll think about it. Meanwhile, the conference is over?'

'Yes. Lydia Seghir and her team are leaving today.'

'The conference wraps up and the kidnappers release Karim Mokrani. Coincidence, you think?'

'I'm not sure it is.' Briefly, Taleb relates what he knows of Urtan Seghir.

Bouras groans. 'That only makes the situation even more delicate. We have no clear idea who is manipulating us, but that we are being manipulated is beyond doubt. I don't like this, Taleb, I don't like this at all.'

'I'm not exactly enjoying myself either, Director. But I have some hopes of establishing what Urtan Seghir was looking for at HQ last summer. For that I need the current address and telephone number of Superintendent Meslem's widow.'

'You think she may know something?'

'Perhaps without knowing she knows it, yes. Based on what I remember of her, she won't be easy to draw out, but she'll be inclined to trust me because of my long association with her husband. If she's still alive, of course. I don't actually know whether she is or not.'

'I'll check with Personnel. Anything else?'

Taleb has decided against mentioning his dealings with Le Merz, of which he suspects Bouras would disapprove. 'I think I've covered everything.'

'Very well. You will hold yourself available on the phone Kadri supplied in case General Mokrani wishes to speak to you direct. I will inform him of the situation immediately. I imagine I will have to meet him. It will not be an easy encounter.'

'I regret putting you in this position, Director.'

'Indeed. I am trying to remind myself that it is not actually – or at least principally – your fault. I will be meeting someone tomorrow who may be able to enlighten us where Seghir's . . . agenda . . . is concerned. Meanwhile, stay out of trouble.'

'I'll do my best, Director.'

'Everything from your disastrous TV appearance onwards suggests you have been allotted the role of scapegoat in this matter. For that reason I recommend you make yourself . . . elusive.'

'That was my intention.'

'But you will communicate with me regularly and frequently. Understood?'

'Clearly understood, Director.'

'I suppose it is a blessing you are the officer who's handling this.'

'Is it?'

'Yes. If it were anyone else I would entertain the notion that you have fabricated this story in order to steal the ransom money. But I don't know anyone less equipped to start spending five million Swiss francs than you, so . . . you continue to have my full confidence.'

The best part of an hour passes before Taleb manages to fit the spare wheel. He is exhausted by then, but only allows himself the space of one cigarette to consider his options before driving away. He has decided to risk a brief return to the Villa des Ormeaux, reckoning a failure to show his face there will count against him when General Mokrani starts asking questions. He also wants to give the Rezigs some kind of explanation of what's happened and to establish some means of communicating with them so that he can continue to monitor events at the villa once he's taken refuge elsewhere.

As to where that elsewhere might be, he will think about that when the time comes, aware though he is that the time will come very soon.

He's only covered a few kilometres when he has to pull over to take a call from Bouras.

'Have you spoken to General Mokrani, Director?'

'Yes. It wasn't an easy conversation. My questioning of Zoubiri yesterday didn't help. To be honest, I'm not sure he didn't believe your account of what's happened. Perhaps it tallies with what he knows of his son's character. But he's not going to admit that. He's already thrown out some accusations in your direction – prejudice, incompetence and so forth – but there may be worse to come when I meet him. I'm about to set off for his villa. I've informed Kadri of developments and he's going to meet me there. From a departmental point of view, Taleb, this has the makings of a major reverse. Kadri will be happy to load blame onto us in order to avoid consideration of the DSS's role in the original kidnapping. If the exchange had been managed more adroitly, I might be much better placed. As it is . . .'

'I am truly sorry, Director.'

'I have no doubt you are. And not for the first time. It would be nice to believe this will be the last.'

Bouras rings off, leaving Taleb to ponder what exactly he meant by his parting remark. And none of the possible interpretations is reassuring.

There are fewer cars than usual parked out front at the Villa des Ormeaux. Touati is loading boxes – presumably containing conference paperwork – into the boot of one. He is so engrossed in what he's doing that he doesn't look up as Taleb drives past. There's no sign of Lydia Seghir – or her son. Or Irmouli, come to that. The coast is comfortingly clear for Taleb's flying visit.

He drives on round to the workshop and pulls up outside. But the door's closed. Rezig must be busy elsewhere. Taleb goes in search of him.

The search leads to the kitchen garden, where Rezig is repairing a crumbling section of the wall. He looks round and smiles cautiously as Taleb approaches. 'Success, *mon ami*?' he asks.

'Yes and no,' Taleb replies, pitching his voice low. 'Agent Mokrani has been freed.'

'Excellent.' Catching Taleb's frown, Rezig lowers his voice too. 'Not excellent?'

'He's headed off on his own. And I'm not sure he's going to contact his family. He doesn't seem to trust anyone.'

'Who can blame him for that?'

'Not me. But it puts me in a bind. Will his father believe he's been released if he only has my word for it?'

Rezig grimaces. 'From what you have said of his father . . .'

'Exactly.'

'Will you go back to Algiers now?'

'Not right away. But I'm not staying here. In the circumstances, it would be . . . unwise. Can you say goodbye to Noussa for me?'

'You're leaving right away?'

'I have to, Abdou. If anyone asks, you know nothing. OK?'

Rezig forms a finger and thumb into the shape of a zero. 'Total blank.'

'Thanks. Listen, that phone on the wall in the workshop. Does it work?'

'Oh yes. It's the same line as the phone in our kitchen. Hardly ever rings, but . . . it would if you dialled the number. You want it?'

'I'd be grateful. Then I can check in with you . . . to see if anything's happened I should know about.'

Rezig takes out one of his cigarette papers, plucks a pencil from above his ear and writes the number down, then hands the paper over. 'You want to give me your number?'

'Safer not to, on balance.'

Rezig nods. 'Understood.'

'I'll be off, then.'

'When this is all over, Mouloud, it would be great to see you again. You could come for a holiday.' Rezig's tone is wistful, as if he knows – and knows Taleb knows too – that such a thing is never going to happen.

'I'd like that,' says Taleb nevertheless.

They shake hands and he turns and hurries back towards the car.

And so Bouras finds himself seated once more at the long table in General Mokrani's villa. Kadri sits beside him, forever fiddling with his phone while Bouras relays what Taleb has told him of Karim Mokrani's release – his frustratingly unconfirmed release, that is, the general having stated as if it condemned Taleb as a liar that he has heard nothing from his son since he was supposedly set free.

Mokrani's expression is a semi-permanent scowl. Bouras makes allowance for what he must be feeling as a father, delight at the news undermined by doubt about its veracity and perhaps ashamed that his son does not wish to contact him. Somewhere in the building his wife will be torturing herself with similar oscillations between relief and anxiety. No one can pretend the situation is satisfactory.

Bouras himself stands by Taleb's version of events. He has in fact not the slightest doubt that Taleb is telling the truth. But the other two people in the room do not share his confidence. Kadri contrived to arrive first and what he said to Mokrani prior to Bouras's arrival can only be guessed at. It will have been self-serving and of little help to Bouras, however. That much is certain.

'I feel sure you will soon hear from your son, General,' Bouras declares, though in truth he feels far from sure on the point. 'Then all your misgivings can be set aside.'

Mokrani's scowl darkens. 'I want to see my son stepping off a plane from Marseille, Director. I want to embrace him and look into his eyes. My "misgivings" will vanish in that event, I assure you. As matters stand, all we have is the word of an officer known to bear me a grudge that Karim has been set free.'

'Superintendent Taleb is completely reliable, General. I have no doubt he has accurately reported what took place.'

'Your lack of doubt is hardly the point. Where is my money? In the hands of *les souveniristes*. Where is my son? We do not know.'

'If you wish to speak to Taleb, we can phone him now. He will answer all your questions.'

'He's never short of excuses for his blunders, if blunders is what they really are. If he's to be questioned, it should be in a setting where he can't hide behind evasions and misrepresentations.'

'I'm sure he hasn't misrepresented anything.'

'You are sure, or so you say. But I am not. Nor will I be until I set eyes on Karim and he tells me all is well. You must recall Taleb and subject him to proper interrogation.'

'Interrogation?'

'I think the general means,' Kadri interrupts in his syrupiest of tones, 'that unless and until his son's freedom can be properly verified, Superintendent Taleb's account must be regarded as . . . unproven.'

'Yes.' Mokrani points a stubby forefinger at Bouras. 'I do mean that. We need the truth from that man, whatever it may be.'

'As far as I am concerned,' says Bouras, 'we have the truth.'

'Forgive me, Director.' Kadri smiles thinly. 'Agent Irmouli, my senior man on site, reports that Taleb's behaviour in recent days has been erratic and his intentions often suspect. There are clearly grounds for subjecting him to intensive questioning if Agent Mokrani's whereabouts remain unknown.'

Bouras cannot let this pass. 'I did not propose to disclose in this meeting what Taleb has told me of Agent Irmouli's own behaviour in view of how badly it reflects on the DSS, but you leave me no choice in the matter.' Bouras looks Kadri in the eye. 'When Taleb opened the suitcase containing the ransom money following the abortive first exchange, he discovered that approximately ten per cent was missing – removed, presumably, by the late Herr Spühler.'

Mokrani's expression darkens. 'Why was I not told of this?'

'Because Agent Irmouli insisted no such cache of Swiss francs was found amongst Spühler's possessions. Taleb challenged him on the point when the second exchange was arranged and threatened to report the matter. The money was then returned.'

'You're suggesting Irmouli tried to steal the portion of the ransom Spühler kept for himself?' snaps Kadri.

'Draw your own conclusions. After Taleb spoke to Irmouli last night, a bag containing the money was placed outside his room.'

'Taleb has made this story up in a transparent attempt to discredit my officer. I have full confidence in Agent Irmouli. In fact . . .' Kadri stabs at his phone. 'Let's speak to him now and hear what he has to say about this.'

'I hardly think he's likely to admit it,' Bouras says drily.

Kadri tosses his head at him and holds the phone to his ear. A silence falls in the room. Mokrani visibly seethes in his chair. His thunderous expression suggests he finds no comfort in their squabbling. Bouras wonders if he will add to his complaints a protest about how he and Zoubiri were treated the previous day, but senses he won't. He can't be sure Hidouchi has shared everything he said with either of them or how much they know about White Leopard.

Irmouli isn't answering. That becomes obvious when Kadri speaks, leaving a message for Irmouli to call him back immediately. He rings off. 'It is a busy time for him,' he says, unconvincingly. 'He will respond shortly, I'm sure.'

'We *can* speak to Taleb,' says Bouras.

'Having him repeat what he's already told you won't convince me,' growls Mokrani. 'I want to question him face to face.'

'That would surely be the best course of action in the circumstances,' says Kadri, scrabbling to make up the ground he's lost by theatrically phoning Irmouli and then getting no answer. 'There's nothing for him to do in France now anyway, is there?'

'There isn't,' Bouras concedes. 'I will certainly recall him.'

'I want him in custody,' Mokrani declares, 'until such time as I am satisfied as to my son's wellbeing.'

'He will not be placed in custody unless I have reason to suspect him of misconduct – which I don't.'

'My son is still a serving officer in the DSS,' Mokrani looks meaningfully at Kadri. 'Will you place Taleb in detention, Deputy Director, pending a full investigation of what has occurred?'

Kadri seems surprised by the question. 'Well, I . . .' He glances at his phone, perhaps hoping to be rescued by a call from Irmouli. But there is no help from that quarter. 'If Agent Mokrani remains missing and Superintendent Taleb's account continues to be unverified, then . . . taking into consideration his allegations against another of my officers . . . I will probably judge it necessary to . . . call him in.'

'That,' says Mokrani with great emphasis, 'is all I'm asking for.'

So, there it is. When Taleb returns, he will be pulled into the maw of the DSS. And Bouras will not be able to help him then.

'When will he return?' Mokrani puts the question directly to Bouras.

'He can travel with my detachment,' Kadri suggests. 'They will leave no later than tomorrow.'

'He will make his own arrangements.' Bouras isn't going to allow the DSS to get their man before he's actually within their jurisdiction. 'He won't require the assistance of the DSS.'

'*When?*' Mokrani's tone is insistent.

Bouras can't dodge the issue, although he's already debating with himself what he will actually instruct Taleb to do. 'Tomorrow. Though by then I'm sure—'

'I want no more platitudes,' Mokrani cuts in. 'I want Taleb here in Algiers. And I want the truth extracted from him.' The truth, as he speaks of it, sounds rather like a rotten tooth. 'The truth, do you hear?'

Bouras nods. He hears.

The meeting ends. Bouras and Kadri exit together. Their drivers are waiting for them outside. The only mercy Bouras can identify is that Zoubiri, who greeted him earlier in deadpan fashion, is nowhere to be seen.

'I'd hoped our departments could continue to cooperate in this matter,' he says to Kadri. His tone is of mild reproof, but he knows Kadri will receive it as rather more than that.

'We must serve our respective priorities,' says Kadri, smiling brazenly. 'Cooperation, alas, can only take us so far.'

'For the DSS to move against a senior DGSN officer without my agreement would be . . .'

'Unfortunate?'

'Extremely.'

'Then we must hope we don't need to move against him.' Kadri is still smiling. 'Or, if we do, that you realize your agreement is . . . inevitable.'

Taleb has driven to Aix TGV station, where he's parked the Citroën and done his best to wait patiently for word from Bouras.

Coffee and a croissant at the station café has made him feel more human, if hardly more optimistic.

The call comes as he wanders back into the car park. It's on the phone reserved for communications with Bouras and Hidouchi rather than the phone supplied by Kadri. It seems he's at least to be spared an earful of abuse from General Mokrani.

'Director?'

'I've just left Mokrani's villa, Taleb. The meeting didn't go well, even allowing for my low expectations before it began.'

'I'm sorry to hear that, Director.'

'Lieutenant Lahmar is currently gazing quizzically at me from the car, wondering why I've stepped out to make this call.'

'General Mokrani doesn't believe me, I assume.'

'He's claiming not to believe you, certainly, and has the lack of word from his son to back him up.'

'There's nothing any of us can do to force Karim Mokrani to contact his parents.'

'I'm aware of that.'

'What do you want me to do?'

'Officially, I'm instructing you to return here tomorrow to assist with inquiries into events at the Villa des Ormeaux following the kidnapping of DSS Agent Mokrani. *Un*officially, I'm advising you to do no such thing. Kadri will fasten all responsibility for what has happened on you in order to avert blame from his own officers, who clearly he's not completely sure of – particularly Irmouli. You would find yourself in DSS custody as soon as you got off the plane and frankly what I could do to extract you from their clutches if Karim Mokrani remains missing would be . . . minimal.'

'I appreciate your candour, Director.' Bouras's assessment of the situation in fact largely matches Taleb's own.

'I suggest you lie low and await further word from me. My

meeting tomorrow may yield valuable information about White Leopard, which would put us one ahead of Kadri *and* General Mokrani. Beyond that . . .'

'There is Chahira Meslem. Do you have her address and telephone number?'

'Not yet. Doubtless the information is waiting for me back at HQ. I will send it on to you as soon as I have it.'

'Thank you, Director.'

'You're taking all this very calmly, Taleb, I must say. Your reward for freeing Agent Mokrani is to be targeted by the DSS as a scapegoat. It hardly seems fair.'

'To be an Algerian policeman and expect fairness from life is a recipe for despair.'

'And you are not about to despair?'

'No, Director. Then they really would win. And I don't intend to let them.'

Lying low is what Hidouchi has already urged Taleb to do and he's had enough time now to decide how best to set about it. It starts in his mind with laying a false trail. After Bouras ends his call, Taleb collects his bag from the Citroën and returns to the station. There, using his credit card, he buys a ticket for the next train to Paris. Then, after a strategic cigarette break, he buys a second ticket, this time using cash, for the next train to Marseille. If the DSS check, it'll seem he's fled to the French capital. But he's going in exactly the opposite direction.

Hidouchi isn't surprised to be summoned to Kadri's office. The bizarre twist in the Mokrani kidnap case – Karim Mokrani no sooner released than vanished of his own accord – will only have heightened his anxiety about Lydia Seghir's true agenda and how it may impact on his career. Since the death of the man he liked to imply was his patron, former acting president Bensalah, Kadri has been less sure of himself and his prospects. He has looked at times – and this is one such time – a worried man.

It soon transpires that there is much for him to worry about – even more indeed than Hidouchi imagined. He hooks his finger in and out of the handle of his espresso cup as he waves impatiently for her to sit down.

'I set you three specific mission goals, Agent Hidouchi.' It is rare for him to use her surname. He usually addresses her as Souad, hinting at the intimacy he's deluded himself into believing they could profitably and pleasurably develop – if only she would open her mind to the possibility, which she will never do. 'What progress have you made?'

'My questioning of General Mokrani established that Rochdi Abidi died at Zoubiri's hands in a botched interrogation. The interrogation was aimed at extracting information from Abidi about White Leopard. As it is, General Mokrani has no better idea than us of what White Leopard is.'

'So, progress on one goal, none on another. What about the third?'

'*Les souveniristes* are not a conventional terrorist group. They appear to be working in collaboration with Lydia Seghir. Their kidnapping of Agent Mokrani served to limit his father's probing of White Leopard. She has steered the conference we must assume was central to the White Leopard project to a successful conclusion and Agent Mokrani has been released because he is no longer of any use to them.'

'Success all round for Lydia Seghir, then.' Kadri frowns.

'It seems so.'

'Leaving your friend Taleb to take the blame for how the kidnapping has ended.'

'Unless and until Agent Mokrani reappears as a free man.'

'Taleb is a natural scapegoat, Souad. You know that. In the ecosystem you and I inhabit, there are predators and there are prey. He is the latter. You must understand that the time may be fast approaching when you need to abandon him to his fate. Choose your allies wisely.'

'I always try to.'

Kadri draws a deep breath, letting her see in his gaze the warning his words embody. 'I require you to carry out your instructions without regard to Taleb's interests. And what I next require of you he must never hear of. Is that clear?'

'It is clear, Deputy Director.' There is nothing else she can say, even though she does not feel bound by such an undertaking – and she suspects Kadri knows that.

'Seghir's conference is at an end. White Leopard, we must suppose, is moving forward on all fronts. And we here at the DSS don't appear to be among those trusted with the details of what it involves. That worries me. It should worry you as well. What *is* Seghir's objective?'

Kadri taps a button on his desktop keyboard and swings the screen round for her to see. He has called up part of the department's file on Lydia Seghir. There is a recent photograph of her – a middle-aged woman, not beautiful, somewhat coarse-featured in fact, but whose bearing conveys an air of authority. Born 1972; a degree in petroleum engineering; a spell at Sonatrach, the national oil and gas company; a junior advisory position at the Ministry of Energy that became a senior advisory position; a recent simultaneous attachment to the Foreign Ministry. Married to Yanik Seghir, a Sonatrach official, now divorced. One child, Urtan, born 1997, recently appointed to a trainee position at the Ministry of Energy despite two arrests during the *Hirak* protests of 2019.

'There she is,' says Kadri. 'And there is the little we have on her.'

'Transition from the oil industry to direct government employment isn't unusual,' says Hidouchi.

'No, it isn't. But we should have more on her. It troubles me that we don't. And it's not just her. The son? Well, straightforward nepotism, I guess, with youthful participation in street protests conveniently overlooked. But the husband? The ex-husband, I should say. Not a career Sonatrach man, as you might imagine. Hired 2002, aged thirty-eight. So, born around 1964. Pre-Sonatrach career . . . a total blank. And no longer with the company. Current activities? Nothing on file.'

'If they're divorced, he's probably . . . dropped out of her life.'

'Maybe so. But these are the scraps of information we have to work with. I'd hoped Irmouli might come up with something more substantial. I instructed him to find out everything he could about the conference. All I've had back from him so far is bullshit about the impenetrability of the security protocol devised by Seghir's assistant, Touati – a man she personally appointed, incidentally, not allotted to her by the ministry.'

'You should have sent me over there.'

'Perhaps I should. And perhaps I would have if Taleb hadn't already been there, dealing with the kidnapping. You're compromised by association, Souad, that's the truth you prefer to ignore.'

'Am I to blame for Irmouli's incompetence?'

'You're to blame for me having to rely on him. And now . . .' Kadri grimaces. 'Now it seems he may have been worse than incompetent.'

This sounds bad. Hidouchi softens her tone, offering a milligram of sympathy to her beleaguered boss. 'How so?'

'I tried to contact him when Bouras and I met General Mokrani earlier. He wasn't answering, which made me look an idiot. Eventually, I spoke to his number two, Jahid. It seems . . .' Kadri puffs out his cheeks. 'It seems Irmouli has vanished from the Villa des Ormeaux. He wasn't due to leave until tomorrow, with the rest of our detachment. But he's already left. Room cleared out, car gone, destination unknown.'

'Taleb believes Irmouli aided and abetted Agent Mokrani's kidnapping.'

'In other words, he's been working for Seghir all along?'

'It looks that way.'

'Like just about everyone else, it seems.'

'Taleb isn't working for Seghir, Deputy Director. Neither am I.'

'No. That I believe.' Kadri leans back in his chair. 'Which is why I want you to discover as much as you can for me about Seghir and White Leopard. But you can start with Irmouli. Go to his apartment. He lives at the service block. I'll call ahead and instruct the supervisor to give you a key. See if you can turn up anything that'll tell us how long he's been working for Seghir and what she's had him doing.'

'I'll go right away.' Hidouchi stands up.

'Irmouli is one of ours, Souad.' Kadri catches her gaze and holds it. 'I wouldn't react well if I discovered you were sharing dirt on him with others that I didn't get to hear about first.' Curiously, perhaps in an acknowledgement of Hidouchi's other loyalties, he's not demanding exclusivity on her discoveries, only priority. It's a sign to her mind of his desperation. 'You follow?'

She nods. 'I follow.'

Taleb exits the Gare St-Charles into a bright and gusty Marseille afternoon. He explores the surrounding streets in search of a cheap hotel and has no difficulty finding one, booking into the far from glittering Saphir as Amed Sidhoum. A text arrives from Bouras as he's making his way to his room, supplying Chahira Meslem's address and phone number.

He calls her as soon as he's unpacked. She's living in Cherchell, which Taleb dimly recalls Meslem referring to as her hometown. Maybe she moved there after his death to be close to her relatives, having no children of her own.

Her phone rings for so long he thinks she isn't going to pick up. No answering system cuts in. Then, suddenly, there's a response. A woman recites the number. But Taleb can't be sure it's her.

'Excuse me,' he says hesitantly. 'I'm trying to contact . . . Chahira Meslem.'

'Is that you, Taleb?' It seems she has no difficulty recognizing his voice despite the lapse of years since they last met.

'Yes, it is. I . . . didn't think you'd . . .'

'All those times when you'd phone after Samir had come home – an emergency, you'd always be deeply apologetic to say, an emergency requiring his particular attention – and you didn't think I'd know you at once?'

'Well, of course, now you . . . put it like that . . .'

'Besides, you were on television the weekend before last. *Microscope*.'

'Ah, that. You saw it.'

'Who didn't? Have you called to apologize for naming Samir during the broadcast? My nephew and his easily shocked wife were horrified that you mentioned his role in the investigation of President Boudiaf's assassination. Why reopen old wounds, they wailed? Why dredge up the past? They weren't pleased, Taleb, they weren't pleased at all.' Widowhood and a move away from Algiers don't seem to have dulled Chahira's spirited approach to life, which Taleb only now recalls was one of her most memorable features.

'I'm sorry if that . . . upset you,' he mumbles.

'I wasn't upset at all. A fine and dedicated officer, you called him. It was lovely to hear him spoken of again by one of his colleagues. He always had a high opinion of you, Taleb. He would have used just those words to describe you.'

'I'm not sure about that.'

'Well, I am. Now, if you haven't called to apologize – and you have nothing to apologize for, I should emphasize – why have you?'

'It concerns . . . a current investigation.'

'Of course it does. Why else would I hear from you? I must say I'm surprised you haven't retired.'

'I'm surprised by that myself.'

'I'm also pleased. For your sake.'

'You are?'

'Samir should never have retired. He had nothing to live for when he ceased to be a policeman. It would be the same for you, I think.'

'I may soon have no choice in the matter.'

'But that day evidently hasn't come yet. So, how can I help you?'

'Well, last summer, there was an ... incident ... at HQ ... one night. An intruder. He seemed to be searching for something Superintendent Meslem may have ... left in his office when he retired.'

'He wouldn't have left anything important behind.'

'He didn't.' Taleb thinks of the Maigret novels and the Russian chess magazines. 'The intruder left empty-handed.'

'What do you think he was hoping to find?'

'I don't know.' Taleb isn't going to risk mentioning Kasdi Merbah over the phone. 'But I wondered if ... he might have come looking for it ... at your home.'

'You wondered that, did you?' Her response strikes an odd note.

'Was there perhaps a break-in ... or attempted break-in ... last summer?'

Chahira doesn't answer immediately. She seems to be thinking. Then she says, 'There was a break-in, yes. Early August. During the worst of the heat.'

'You didn't report this to us.'

'I notified the local station. Nothing was taken or even damaged, however, so they didn't pursue it. I'm not sure they believed there'd been a break-in at all, but I'm quite capable of knowing when my possessions have been disturbed – drawers and cupboards searched and so forth. I suspect the front door lock was picked, which suggests the intruder knew his business.'

'But nothing was taken?'

'He evidently didn't find what he was looking for.'

'You say that as if you know what he was looking for.'

There's another pause. Then she says softly, 'I don't think we should discuss this over the telephone. Why don't you visit me? Then we could talk face to face.'

'I'm out of the country at present.'

'Really? Somewhere nice, I hope.'

'France.'

'Mmm. Nice country. Not sure about the people. When will you be back?'

'It's hard to say. Perhaps . . . I could send someone trustworthy to speak to you on my behalf.' Taleb is thinking of Hidouchi.

Chahira deliberates silently, then says, 'I'm sorry, Taleb. I trust no one I'm not personally acquainted with. Besides, Samir said you were the only one of his colleagues he could rely on absolutely. What goes for him goes for me. I'll speak to no one except you. If you want to know any more you'll have to come here.'

Taleb has the distinct impression she's not going to be talked round. But he decides to give it a go. 'I can guarantee the reliability of the person I have in mind. She is my closest confidante.'

'But not mine. It has to be you, Taleb. You and no one else.'

TWELVE

ACCORDING TO KADRI, IRMOULI MOVED INTO THE DSS'S APARTMENT block after the collapse of his marriage. Moved *back* into would be more accurate, since Hidouchi assumes he started out his DSS career living there. Certainly she did, leaving as soon as she had the wherewithal to lease an apartment of her own. It's baffling to her that Irmouli voluntarily reverted to such an existence, although he probably didn't suffer the succession of unwelcome sexual advances from other residents that she did.

The block's supervisor is the same as in her day – a melancholic old DSS hand called Makhlouf, essentially unaltered save for the acquisition of an extra patina of ageing. He gives her the spare key to Irmouli's apartment without asking what she's looking for or why Irmouli has become the subject of internal investigation. His greatest gift is perhaps an innate ability not to ask questions about anything. He's not an enthusiastic answerer of them either.

Hidouchi climbs the stairs to the fourth floor – the building is consumed in middle-of-the-day silence – and lets herself into Irmouli's apartment. Her first impression is that no one actually lives there at all. Personal possessions are notable for their absence. There's a closet containing a minimal quantity of clothes. The kitchen is sparsely equipped. The bathroom cabinet holds a few basic toiletries. Of Irmouli himself – of any sense of his personality or interests – there's little or no trace. It really does seem as if he knew he wouldn't be returning from France.

Undaunted, Hidouchi commences a search of all drawers and cupboards. Doing so meticulously takes time, but the effort is eventually rewarded with the discovery of a car key taped to the underside of a shelf at the back of one of the kitchen cupboards. The building has an underground car park and she at once suspects Irmouli has a vehicle stored there.

She hurries down to Makhlouf's office. He confirms Irmouli keeps his car in the basement and supplies the bay number. She sets off.

It's a 4WD Jeep, its colour hard to determine in the stark overhead basement lighting. There's a layer of dust obscuring the windows and number plate, which Hidouchi soon identifies as sand when she opens the driver's door. A quick check of the glovebox and the storage bin between the seats reveals nothing except some spare batteries, a pen torch and some loose change. She gets out and opens the hatchback. A tool-kit, a jack, a threadbare blanket, a waterproof – pockets empty – and a short-handled shovel: it looks as if he likes to be prepared for travel in adverse weather. Beyond that, nothing.

She checks under the seats and turns up the edges of the mats and carpet. Again, nothing. Which only leaves . . . the SatNav. It should hold a record of where he's driven recently – as far back as the system's memory allows. Irmouli ought to know that and maybe he also knows it won't reveal anything significant, but it's certainly worth having it analysed by HQ's tech specialist, Nadour. She unscrews the SatNav from its bracket and yanks out the wiring.

It's as she's climbing out of the Jeep that she glimpses a movement somewhere near the ramp down into the basement from the street outside. A shadow, a shape: it's hard to tell. Instinctively, she flicks back her jacket and lowers her hand towards her waist-holstered gun.

There's no more movement. She waits, steadying her breathing, watching intently. Then a door opens and closes somewhere at the far end of the car park. And she senses she's alone once more.

Makhlouf, checking on what she's doing? It seems unlikely. But he smokes too much to get back to his office without still being short of breath by the time she catches up with him, so she'll soon know.

In the event, Makhlouf is breathing quite normally, smoke pluming lazily from the cigarette he's propped in the ashtray on his desk. He nods to the array of closed-circuit TV screens on the wall ahead of him as she enters his office and remarks matter-of-factly, 'You're being followed.'

'Show me,' says Hidouchi, stepping closer to the screens.

Makhlouf uses a remote to display different streams of video. 'He seems to know where the cameras are, but he can't stay completely out of the picture. See?'

Hidouchi sees various grainy images of herself moving around the building. Then a second figure appears, never captured clearly – lean, male, baseball-capped. It's never more than a glimpse, and then only from the rear. Identification is impossible, although Hidouchi feels certain who he is. 'He was in the basement,' she says. 'Vanished when I noticed him.'

'This is the fire escape from that level.' Makhlouf calls up video footage showing the man passing through a doorway leading to a flight of stairs, head down, moving fast. 'Looks like he's left the premises. But that doesn't mean he's stopped trailing you.'

'He probably thinks he knows where I'll be going from here.'

Makhlouf picks up his cigarette and takes a drag on it. 'Just so long as you're aware.'

'I'm aware.'

Makhlouf looks at the SatNav she's carrying under her arm, wires trailing loose beneath it. He says nothing. He doesn't need to. She knows he thinks she's engaged in the dirty business of probing the loyalty and/or honesty of a fellow DSS officer and he's right. She knows he also thinks there are consequences to undertaking that kind of work. The man on the video, dogging her footsteps, is just one of them. He's right about that as well.

'Thanks for your help,' she says, dropping the key to Irmouli's apartment on the desk and turning to leave.

'No problem,' he wearily intones.

Taleb sits in a café near Marseille's Vieux Port, sipping coffee and munching a pastry as the winter afternoon passes, the lowering sun gleaming on the chop in the harbour stirred by the passage of the ferry from the north side to the south and back again. He's surprised by how calm he feels, how unworried by the uncertainties hanging over his future. The explanation, he realizes as he orders another coffee, is that there's nothing he can do, at least until Bouras contacts him again with instructions, which will probably not happen until after his meeting tomorrow with a highly placed informant. Until then, Taleb has only empty time in a city where he's totally unknown and has no official status. He has no power and no responsibility. He actually feels relieved that for once all that is required of him is to wait upon events outside his control. He believes he may sleep better tonight than he has since his ill-fated appearance on Algerian national television ten days ago. He's not looking far ahead – the view is unappealing. But for the rest of today and some of tomorrow he can enjoy something that he's tempted to regard as . . . peace.

His reverie is interrupted by the chirp of his secure phone. There's a text message from Hidouchi: *Irmouli gone missing am investigating.*

Taleb is tempted to reply *Good luck to him*, but contents himself with *ok standing by*. Irmouli going on the run doesn't altogether surprise him. Maybe he didn't relish answering the questions General Mokrani might want to ask him. Taleb obviously isn't the only one in the firing line, which is comforting in a way.

He'd very much like to light up at this moment, but smoking isn't allowed inside the café and it's too cold to sit outside. Ah well, it's nice to have a first-world problem for once.

Bouras's rendezvous with Hidouchi late that afternoon is briefer than those that have preceded it. He's not sorry to hear Kadri has Irmouli's disappearance to worry about. He deserves any troubles that come his way after trying to divert all the blame towards Taleb – and hence Bouras – during their meeting with General Mokrani. The actual significance of Irmouli dropping out of sight is hard to gauge. White Leopard is an enigma wrapped in a riddle concealed by a crime. And Bouras hasn't yet got further than the crime.

'Do you think your Foreign Ministry friend has the answer?' Hidouchi asks as they prepare to part.

'If he has, he's not likely to divulge it to me. But a hint? A clue? A pointer in the right direction? I might get that much from him.'

'We need something, Director.'

Bouras is well aware of that. Stifling a tetchy response, he says simply, 'I know.'

Hidouchi took several detours en route to her meeting with Bouras as a precaution against being followed by Zoubiri. There was, as it turns out, no sign of him tailing her. She suspects he may have gone to the service apartment block after learning from an informant of Irmouli's disappearance and only caught up with her there. He probably doesn't see the need to follow her every move. But she'll be watching for him now wherever she goes.

Nadour has promised a report on what he can extract from

Irmouli's SatNav in the morning. Meanwhile, Hidouchi has an empty evening ahead of her. It's Wednesday, when she often contacts Zico. The consolations of his uncomplicated company – he never makes the mistake of supposing he should try to engage her on any level beyond the physical – are a powerful draw after the day she's had. But she can't risk alerting Zoubiri to Zico's place in her life. That would be a dangerous error.

And so her evening will be solitary as well as empty.

Bouras always endeavours to separate his private and professional lives. His wife, Rihana, with whom he co-exists in a state of complete domestic harmony, observes the distinction almost as sedulously as he does. But this evening she makes an exception to the rule. After their two daughters have gone to bed and they are relaxing in the lounge, she cautiously expresses concern about the case he is currently involved in. She knows none of the particulars, of course. What she does know is that since Superintendent Taleb made his unfortunate appearance on the TV current affairs talk show *Microscope* her husband has been a preoccupied and deeply worried man. And she doesn't like it.

'You think highly of Taleb, don't you, my darling?' is her opening gambit.

'Taleb?' Her darling frowns at her. 'He is an honest and competent officer. Why do you mention him?'

'Why do you think?'

Bouras shifts uncomfortably in his armchair. 'The situation regarding Taleb is . . . difficult.'

'Because it is drawing you into dangerous territory?'

'Some challenges cannot be avoided.'

'My father allowed me to marry you because he believed you would be a loyal husband and could be trusted to take no risks in your career. Success in the service of the state, he said, requires circumspection above all else.'

'He was right.'

'Is there a chance, my darling, that you are not being . . . circumspect . . . at present?'

Bouras considers the question for several long moments before he replies. 'A loyal subordinate deserves to be supported . . . as far as possible.'

'And how far is that in Taleb's case?'

'I'm not sure.'

'That is what troubles me. That you are not sure. You are a father as well as a husband. Your daughters need your love and protection. As will your grandchildren in the fullness of time, if we are so blessed. But Taleb has no family. And he should surely have retired by now anyway. You should not support him, however loyal he may be, at our expense.' She reaches out and lays her hand on his knee. 'I won't speak of this again. But if the choice is forced upon you . . . you will do the right thing for those closest to you, won't you?'

'Yes, Rihana.' He pats her hand. 'I will.' Which is easy to say. But . . .

Hidouchi arrives earlier than usual at DSS HQ the following morning and goes straight to Nadour's office. Nadour himself, a thin, prematurely bald man who compensates for his baldness with a bushy moustache, is hunched as ever over one of several desktop computers, sipping weak tea while a soothing hum emanates from a ceiling-high cabinet of back-up hard drives behind him.

'Agent Hidouchi,' he says, adjusting his rimless glasses as he switches his focus from the computer screen. 'I was expecting you an hour ago.'

'You've been here an hour already?'

'Longer, actually, eager as I am to assist you with your priority request. Although of course' – he smiles thinly – 'all your requests tend to be priority, don't they? You seem to operate on a higher level of urgency than most people in this building.'

She smiles blithely in return. 'This is certainly urgent.'

'No doubt. And it's been interesting to unravel Agent Irmouli's movements over the past six weeks, I'll admit. That was as far back as the SatNav memory took me: mid-December. A busy period for him, it must be said. I wonder if his fuel claim was paid without demur.'

'What have you got for me?'

Nadour slides a memory stick across his desk towards her. 'That's the full record. You said you didn't want it emailed to you through the office network.' Nothing in his tone suggests he regards the arrangement as questionable. Such issues simply do not concern him. 'Would you like to know the highlights?'

'I would.'

'Well, Irmouli has travelled around greater Algiers extensively, as you'd expect. Beyond the city there was a journey to Mers-El Kébir on the twentieth of December.'

'The naval base?'

'Yes. Perhaps that signifies something to you.' It doesn't, which only makes Hidouchi more suspicious. 'He parked his car close to the entrance gate, so I can't tell you where in the base he actually went.'

'Has he gone on any other long journeys?'

'One. *Very* long at that. He left his apartment block early on the morning of the twenty-fourth of December and proceeded to the airport, where he stopped for nearly an hour before heading south on the N1. He stayed on it all day and into the evening, stopping at Ghardaia overnight, then carried on the next day, reaching Tamanrasset that evening.'

'Tamanrasset? That's deep in the Sahara. It must be fifteen hundred kilometres or more from here. And it has an airport. Why didn't he fly there?'

'Such questions lie beyond my area of expertise. What I can say is that the next day, the twenty-sixth, he drove south-west from Tamanrasset to a location quite literally in the middle of nowhere, about halfway to the Malian border. He stayed there for a couple of hours, then returned to Tamanrasset. Next day he drove back north, stopping again at Ghardaia overnight before returning to Algiers, again via the airport, on the twenty-eighth.'

Hidouchi thinks for a moment. Irmouli actually went to the airport, but didn't fly to Tamanrasset. If he'd needed the use of a car once he'd got there, he could have hired one on arrival. The gruelling two-day drive made no sense. Unless . . . he was taking someone south who didn't want any record of their journey. 'The stops in Ghardaia and Tamanrasset were at hotels?'

'Yes. The details are on the stick.'

If Irmouli had company, the hotels they stayed in might be able to supply a name. Hidouchi picks up the stick and pockets it. 'What about the "middle of nowhere" location south-west of Tamanrasset? What details can you give me of that?'

'I can give you the grid reference. But there's nothing there. It's an arid, uninhabited plain.'

'There must be *something* there.'

'You'd think so, wouldn't you? But there really doesn't appear to be.' Nadour smiles with what seems to be a hint of mischievousness. 'A tantalizing mystery for you to tussle with, Agent Hidouchi. I almost envy you.'

Hidouchi goes straight to her desk and studies the contents of the stick. They tally with what Nadour has already told her. Irmouli drove between his apartment and HQ virtually daily. He took various other drives around the city and beyond it that don't seem unusual for an active DSS agent, including two visits to El Harrach prison, probably to question a prisoner about an ongoing case. The trip to Mers-El Kébir is undoubtedly odd, though it would look less odd if it hadn't been followed within a week by his long drive south.

She notes the names of the hotels in Ghardaia and Tamanrasset where he stayed and considers phoning them, but hesitates, wondering if it might be safer to ask Bouras to deal with that side of things. Investigating a fellow DSS agent is an inherently risky business. He may have allies or confederates in the building. Alerting them to her activities would be unwise in the extreme.

She exits into the winter sunshine and calls Bouras from the roadside. She's already told him Irmouli has gone missing, so he's not surprised by this latest development. 'Text me the details of what you require and I'll put the local stations on to it. We should meet later. Maybe I'll have an answer by then. Usual time and place?'

'Yes.' Hidouchi will take all necessary precautions to ensure Zoubiri doesn't follow her. 'I'll look forward to hearing how your lunch went.'

'Informatively, I hope.'

'I hope that also, Director. Information is what we need.'

Bouras sets Lahmar the task of contacting the DGSN stations in Ghardaia and Tamanrasset before departing at noon for his lunch with Hammou Chenna. The venue – the Sheraton restaurant at the exclusive Club des Pins resort on the coast west of the city – was insisted on by Chenna. It's to be his treat. 'Such a pleasure to hear from you, Farid,' he said when Bouras called him. 'It's been far too long.'

Bouras considers the possibility that Chenna's enthusiasm may falter when he's pressed on the subject of White Leopard. As someone elevated in the Foreign Ministry hierarchy, it's hardly likely he knows nothing about it, but whether he'll disclose any of what he knows is quite another matter. Still, an obligation is an obligation. Ensuring Chenna's financial consultant brother didn't join those arrested and jailed after the collapse of the Khalifa banking group in 2003 wasn't entirely risk-free for Bouras, but, taking Chenna at his word that his brother was simply a credulous fool, he decided to do what he could, mindful of the possibility that one day he might need to ask for a favour in return. And nineteen years later . . . the day has come.

Valet parking, tinkling fountains and grandiose architecture greet him at the Club des Pins, where the palm trees are barely stirring in the breeze and the sky is clearer and bluer than in the city he's left behind. The centre of Algiers seems much more than fifteen kilometres away in this oasis of affluence. He feels instantly soothed by deference and privilege. If only he could always dwell in such agreeable settings. He feels he could become a well-practised hedonist if only he had more spare time.

Chenna is waiting for him in the hotel's vast and comfortable bar, sipping a fruit juice. Bouras asks for the same. There is back-slapping and a comparing of career notes. Each expresses more admiration than they actually feel for the other's progress. Bouras knows Chenna to be idle and self-indulgent by nature – as his waistline and double chin confirm – and such a man would undoubtedly regard choosing to join the police service as a serious misstep in life. No matter. They retain an easy familiarity from their college days and doting descriptions of their children is safe ground for them to share.

They move to their table in the spacious restaurant, which appears to Bouras to be one of the best, commanding a fine view through the window of the deep blue Mediterranean and a limitless horizon that reflects the Club des Pins' prevailing sense of infinite and rewarding possibilities.

The food is equal to the surroundings. Chenna is well known to the staff and service is attentive without verging on the obsequious. Bouras regrets ever more keenly as the meal proceeds that he can't relax enough to enjoy himself. Chenna, on the other hand, appears in his element, discoursing happily on subjects as varied as yachts (he owns one), Lamborghinis (he dreams of owning one), golf (the country's dire need of better courses) and daughters (how to find suitable husbands they will actually agree to marry).

Bouras takes advantage of the mention of family matters to enquire subtly after Chenna's brother, prompting a despairing shake of the head. 'There was a time when I thought Imad might learn from his mistakes. But all he has learnt is how to repeat them. His latest folly is to have invested in a company manufacturing face masks just as the pandemic has fizzled out.'

'We cannot choose our relatives, Hammou.' Bouras smiles sympathetically. 'It is to your credit that you have not abandoned Imad.'

'Don't think I've forgotten the help you gave him, Farid. I remain grateful, even if he does not.'

'What are friends for but to help in such situations?'

'And what a situation. It would have done my career no good for my brother to be caught up in the Khalifa scandal. But for your . . . intervention . . . I probably wouldn't be as well placed as I am now.'

'I was glad to do what I did. And glad to be able to.'

'Well, as I've said more than once, if there's ever anything I can do for you . . .' Chenna grins. 'But what can a civil servant do for a policeman?'

'Actually, you may be able to assist me . . . with a problem I'm currently dealing with.'

If Chenna is displeased by being taken at his word, his expression doesn't even hint at it. He cocks his head and engages Bouras with a man-to-man smile. 'What sort of problem might that be, Farid?'

'I can't go into details – this touches on an ongoing criminal investigation – but it seems there may be an indirect connection between that investigation and a government project I can't find out anything concrete about. I was wondering . . . if you could . . .'

'An *indirect* connection, you say?'

'Yes. Very much so. The project itself is, I'm sure, entirely reputable and above board. But if I knew what it concerns it would be valuable background information. And without such information I'm currently at a dead end.'

'Are dead ends unusual in your line of work?'

'Not at all. But I have a valued senior officer in an exposed position and I'm anxious to do everything I can to protect him.'

'That's commendable. Loyalty is a two-way street, after all. But what makes you think I'm likely to know anything about this project?'

'The suggestion is that it's being overseen by your ministry.'

'Really?'

'It goes by the codename of . . . White Leopard.'

There's a flicker of reaction in Chenna's gaze, so slight it would be easy to miss. But Bouras doesn't miss it. 'White Leopard?'

'Does that . . . mean anything to you?'

Chenna sits back and takes a sip of sparkling mineral water. 'It might.'

'I would treat anything you can tell me in the strictest confidence.'

'Of course. That applies, I trust, to this entire conversation on both sides. We are talking here . . . as friends.'

'Indeed.'

'So, as your friend, I would recommend you . . . leave White Leopard out of your inquiries.'

'I'm not sure I can do that.'

'On account of this . . . exposed senior officer?'

'Yes.'

'Then a hard choice may confront you, Farid. Him . . . or you.'

'I hope it won't come to that.'

'So do I. But if it does . . .'

'Whatever happens, Hammou, nothing I learn about White Leopard would ever be traceable to you.'

'I understand. But you should also understand. We who serve the state must serve the state's priorities. Some matters – of which White Leopard is one – are embargoed at the highest level. I want to help you. But . . . my hands are tied.'

'I'm sorry to hear that.'

'As I am sorry to say it.'

'There's nothing – absolutely nothing – you can . . .' Bouras opens his hands, as if to receive a gift, however meagre – a gift of information.

Chenna ruminates for a few moments, then leans across the table towards him and lowers his voice. 'There is nothing I am free to tell you, Farid. However, I could suggest you . . . consult the French national companies register. It's the sort of thing you might think of doing yourself, after all, without any prompting from me. Thoroughness is the hallmark of good police work, isn't it?'

'It is.'

'There's information everywhere in this interconnected age. You just have to . . . sift it.'

Bouras is tempted to take out his phone and start sifting right now. But that would be indelicate. Chenna is trying to tell him something while saying nothing. Bouras's role in the exchange is to pretend it hasn't actually happened.

'The food here really is superb,' says Chenna, savouring a mouthful of grilled tuna. 'What's in this sauce? Hazelnut oil?'

'Sesame, I think.'

'Ah yes. Sesame it is. You have a sensitive palate, Farid.'

'Not according to my wife.'

'She is a fine cook, I'm sure.'

'She is.'

'I'm sorry never to have met her. We must try to put that right. A dinner *à quatre* would be delightful, I think.'

Bouras smiles. 'It would indeed.' And so they complete the

return to safe conversational territory. The favour has been repaid – to the extent it can be.

No more is said of White Leopard until they are standing outside the hotel an hour later, about to take their leave of each other. And what is said is spoken in an undertone, as they shake hands and hug.

'It is in the nature of embargoes to expire at some point.' Chenna holds Bouras's gaze. 'You only need to wait a while to learn more. And waiting is often the best policy.' He adds a wink to underline the point.

'What if I can't wait?'

'Then you can't. But you should, you really should.'

Bouras has no doubt Chenna's advice is well intentioned. He should probably heed it. A few years ago, he undoubtedly would have done. But Taleb and Hidouchi have lured him of late into questioning whether he is willing to be no more than a cog on a gearwheel in the well-oiled workings of *le pouvoir*. And the answer, it's transpired to his dismay, is that his willingness has limits. And in this matter his limit has been reached.

The valet delivers his car and he drives away from the hotel, heading back towards Police HQ, letting time and distance separate him from his encounter with Chenna.

He pulls into a shopping mall on the outskirts of the city, one of the gaudy retail emblems of the consumerist future the government professes to believe in – and wants the people to believe in as well. He parks as far as possible from the entrance to the mall, lights a cigar and calls up the French national companies register on his phone.

It is the work of a few seconds. Then the entry for *Léopard Blanc SARL* is there on the screen in front of him: an address in Toulon, with the company's business specified as *infrastructure de communication, maritime et terrestre.* This tells him little. But the page listing the company's five directors is rather more revealing.

Because two of them are known to him.

Taleb is roused from a late-afternoon doze in his hotel room by the beeping of his phone: the one reserved for communications with Bouras and Hidouchi. He grabs it off the bedside table, noting that Bouras is the caller, and answers huskily.

'Taleb?'

'Yes, Director. It's me.' He turns away from the phone to cough some of the sleep out of his throat. 'Has there been word of Karim Mokrani?'

'None that's reached me. But something else has happened that I need you to act on. It transpires that White Leopard is the name of a French-registered company specializing in communications infrastructure.'

Taleb is briefly nonplussed. What exactly is 'communications infrastructure'? He decides not to ask. 'You think the name is no coincidence?'

'Definitely not. Two of the directors are Henri Elasse and Yanik Seghir.'

'Elasse and Seghir? What . . . what's going on?'

'I don't know, Taleb. What I do know is that Lydia Seghir's ex-husband and the absentee host of her recently concluded conference sit on the board of *Léopard Blanc SARL*. It's highly suspicious. And we need to find out more about their company as soon as possible.'

'How?'

'It's headquartered at an address in Toulon. I want you to go there, dig around a bit and learn as much as you can. Too late to start today, I think. Get there early tomorrow and report back on *anything* you discover.'

'Understood.'

'I'm texting you the address now. My contact at the Foreign Ministry wouldn't be drawn on the subject of White Leopard. He spoke of an embargo on information at the highest level of government. So, whether the project itself, whatever it is, and the company that shares its name are essentially one and the same is an open question. But we must tread carefully. *Very* carefully. Don't give yourself away.'

'I won't.'

'If you do . . .'

'You didn't send me. In fact, you've ordered me to return to Algiers without delay.'

'Indeed I have, Taleb.'

'Leave this with me, Director.'

'I am happy to do so.'

Bouras ends the call, leaving Taleb to stare at White Leopard's address on the screen of his phone. Henri Elasse and Yanik Seghir. They didn't seem to be important figures in the web of secret alliances Taleb has been tangled in since beginning his attempt to negotiate Karim Mokrani's release by his kidnappers. But now they've stepped to the front of the stage. White Leopard is beginning to show its face.

Hidouchi has notified Kadri of her discoveries at Irmouli's apartment and of Nadour's report on his movements in recent weeks. The deputy director was clearly as baffled as her about what it all meant, though he did his best to imply otherwise. His attempts to suggest he possessed profound powers of reasoning were, as ever, unconvincing. Their hollowness was only emphasized by his instructions to her. 'Await the police report on who travelled with Irmouli to Tamanrasset. Otherwise, do nothing for the moment.'

She has higher hopes of Bouras and sets off for their rendezvous at the end of the working day with some relief. He can be relied upon to have news for her, though whether good or bad . . .

As it turns out, she has to wait nearly half an hour for him to join her. Pacing up and down – with the sky slowly bleaching and the sea silvering as evening encroaches – sharpens her impatience. What she has learned about Irmouli suggests a large-scale conspiracy lies behind Karim Mokrani's kidnapping. The sooner she can establish the nature of that conspiracy the better. But for the moment she has to wait for others to feed her information.

Bouras looks harassed and a touch weary when he arrives. He's smoking one of his small cigars. It seems to Hidouchi that his smoking has increased of late. The director is showing the strain of not being in control of events.

'How was your lunch?' she enquires without preamble.

'The food was excellent. The conversation was . . . delicate. My friend confirmed without actually saying so that White Leopard is a secret government project we'd do well not to pry into.'

'But we're still prying.'

'So it seems. He went so far as to suggest I take a look at the French corporate register – on which *Léopard Blanc SARL* appears.'

'Really?'

'Yes. And who should I find two of its directors are but Henri Elasse and Yanik Seghir.'

Hidouchi is briefly taken aback. A blurred vision of the conspiracy she's been hunting appears before her, as if through a fog bank. White Leopard, in the persons of Henri Elasse and Yanik Seghir. France and Algeria, the old enemies, but always joined. She doesn't like the sound of this. 'What business is the company in?'

'Communications infrastructure. They're based in Toulon. I've sent Taleb to take a look.'

'You know how it feels to walk into a spider's web you didn't realize was in front of you until it brushed across your face, Director?'

'I do. And I take your meaning. We are woefully uninformed.'

'It appears we are.'

'But I do have reports from our stations in Ghardaia and Tamanrasset. They are gratifyingly prompt to respond to requests from headquarters.'

'Do we know who was travelling with Irmouli?'

'We do. Two people. One of them was Yanik Seghir.'

'Him again.'

'Yes. He's clearly as significant in all this as his ex-wife.'

'The other person?'

'A French citizen. Female. The hotels photocopied her passport, as per regulations. Her name is Françoise Patou, resident in Paris, born 1969. The passport could be a fake, of course. I haven't checked with the French authorities yet in case it tips them off that we're on to one of theirs. I don't suppose the name means anything to you?'

'Nothing.'

'OK. So, here she is.'

Bouras calls up on his phone a scanned image of the photograph page of Françoise Patou's passport and shows it to Hidouchi.

The face looking out at her is delicately featured, high-cheeked and framed by short dark hair. She looks typically French, in appearance some years younger than her actual age. The unsmiling expression suits her. It conveys her personality very much as Hidouchi remembers it.

'You know her?' Bouras asks, catching something in Hidouchi's reaction.

She nods. 'Yes. Her real name is Erica Ménard. Assistant Director of Intelligence, DGSE.'

Bouras draws in his breath sharply. 'The woman who tried to frame you and Taleb for murder during the Zarbi-Laloul affair?'

'The same.' The same – and more. As Bouras well knows, it was actually Taleb Ménard tried to frame. Hidouchi was invited – with implicit encouragement from Kadri – to cooperate with the DGSE and hang Taleb out to dry. But she decided to stand by him. Together they went on to uncover evidence of DGSE interference in internal Algerian politics in the years following independence, potentially extending to the present day. It was dangerous evidence to be in possession of and they were lucky to escape alive.

'A senior French intelligence officer, travelling incognito with a DSS agent to the remote south in the company of Lydia Seghir's ex-husband. What are we to make of that, Agent Hidouchi?'

'Nothing good.'

'What could they have been doing down there?'

'I don't know. But we need to know.' Hidouchi looks at Bouras intently. 'If Erica Ménard is mixed up in this, Director, we have a serious problem.'

'More serious than it already was, you mean?'

Hidouchi nods. 'Much more.'

Taleb boards an early train for Toulon from Gare St-Charles in Marseille the following morning with misgivings weighing heavily on his mind. Hidouchi phoned him last night with the news that their old foe Erica Ménard of the DGSE is involved in White Leopard. In some ways he wasn't even surprised. Why would he expect her *not* to be involved? But it's a complication he only wishes he'd been spared. If Ménard discovers he's trying to obstruct her plans – whatever they might be – she will be ruthless in seeking to neutralize the threat he represents. He outwitted her last time, for which she's probably never forgiven him. If there's a next time, he wouldn't give much for his chances of emerging in one piece.

His fellow passengers appear mostly to be commuters and business types, embarking wearily on their working days. Many of them look monumentally bored by the prospect. It's a state of mind he finds himself envying even as he longs for the cigarette SNCF conditions of carriage forbid him to indulge in. In Algeria the weekend is beginning. But there is no rest for Superintendent Mouloud Taleb. It seems he is always on duty.

Duty also calls for Bouras. His suspicion that he will find little time for spiritual reflection this day of prayer is confirmed when he receives a call from Lieutenant Lahmar before he's even finished breakfast.

'Sorry to call so early on a Friday, chief. That DSS agent you put out an all ports alert for – Wael Irmouli?'

'Has he entered the country?'

'No. And he never will. Word from the Marseille police. He's been found dead.'

'In Marseille?'

'Yes. At the airport, to be exact, trussed up in the boot of a hire car. Shot through the head with a gun left at the scene – his, by the sound of it. His passport was in his pocket – there was no attempt to disguise his identity.'

'Found in a hire car, you say?'

'That's where it gets tricky, chief. The vehicle was parked in one of the bays outside the Europcar office. It's not clear how long it had been there. It was hired from them last week – by Taleb.'

Bouras utters a profanity that draws a reproving glance from his wife Rihana as she enters from the kitchen carrying a pot of mint tea.

'Will you be coming in, chief?'

'Yes. Do the DSS know about this?'

'Not yet.'

'Hold off on telling them until I get there.'

'And the Marseille police? They want to know whether Taleb travelled to France on official business – and why, if he did, they weren't informed.'

Bouras sighs. 'Of course they do.'

'What should I say?'

'Nothing. I'll deal with them when I reach the office.'

'OK, chief. How, er . . . long . . .'

'I'm leaving now.' Bouras ends the call and shrugs apologetically as Rihana catches his eye. Not for the first time – or the last – the exigencies of the service have claimed their due.

To reach the premises of *Léopard Blanc SARL* Taleb has to catch a local train from Toulon to a station the other side of the city's naval base. It hasn't escaped him that Toulon is home to the French Mediterranean fleet, and one of the journeys Irmouli is known to have taken prior to travelling to France was to the Algerian Navy's main base at Mers-El Kébir. This seems unlikely to be a coincidence, but for the present Taleb can make no sense of what it might mean.

He's standing with a clutch of other people on the platform, waiting for the train in a keen breeze that blew out three matches before he managed to light his cigarette, when Hidouchi calls. He moves away along the platform as she speaks.

'I've just heard from Bouras, Taleb. He asked me to let you know the news because he's going to be kept busy himself trying to convince the Marseille police you haven't murdered Irmouli.'

'Has someone murdered him?'

'I'm afraid so. Which wouldn't matter much except they stowed his body in the boot of the Renault you hired from Marseille airport last week.'

'I left the car at the Villa des Ormeaux.'

'Well, it seems it didn't stay there. But its theft wasn't reported, so as hirer of the car you're prime suspect in the case.'

'General Mokrani thinks I stole his five million Swiss francs. Now the French think I've murdered a DSS agent on their territory. I can't win, can I?'

'The important thing is not to lose. Who would have murdered Irmouli – and why?'

'The people he was really working for, who probably didn't approve of his attempt to filch some of the ransom money.'

'*Les souveniristes?*'

'Or whoever's hiding behind them.'

'Lydia Seghir? Her ex-husband? Henri Elasse?'

'Any or all of those. I can't pretend to have the first idea what's really going on.'

'You'll make no progress from inside a police cell in Marseille. You should leave France as soon as possible.'

'And return to Algeria, where your boss will detain me if Bouras declines to? Unless Karim Mokrani shows himself, of course. There's always that to hope for.'

'I don't hear much hope in your voice, Taleb.'

'No? Well, that's not so surprising. We're outmatched, Souad. That's the truth. We can't win.'

'You've said that kind of thing before and been proved wrong.'

'And I'll be happy to be proved wrong this time as well. I'll go back to Marseille and lie low at the hotel as soon I've taken a look at *Léopard Blanc*'s offices here.'

'OK. Just—'

'Be careful?'

'Yes, Taleb. Be careful.'

Hidouchi rings off, leaving Taleb to walk slowly towards the end of the platform, trying to figure out some explanation for what's going on. He decides to call Rezig, who may know something about the removal of the hire car from the villa grounds.

He listens to the dialling tone, imagining the phone ringing in the workshop and wondering if there'll be an answer. While he waits, he reflects on the disquieting fact that if Karim Mokrani had been willing to return to Algeria he'd have gone with him and couldn't have been framed for Irmouli's murder. He's being manoeuvred, like a pawn on a chessboard. And he's not the only pawn in the game that's being played. Irmouli was another. But he's been sacrificed now. He's off the board. For Taleb there's still a chance.

Rezig answers. 'Mouloud?'

'How did you know it was me?'

'No one else would have rung this number.'

'How is it there?'

'Quieter now the conference is over and the DSS agents have gone. But your hire car . . .'

'It's been taken, hasn't it?'

'Yes. I noticed it was gone early yesterday morning. I didn't see who took it out of the garage. Did Europcar send someone to collect it?'

'No, they didn't. And you have no idea who took it?'

'Not a one. It was there. Then it wasn't.'

'I've been set up, Abdou. Not for the first time in this whole misbegotten affair. It's probably best I don't go into details. If the police come round – as I'm sure they will – just say you don't know where I am and you haven't heard from me. Take my word for it I didn't do what they're likely to say I did.'

'Understood.'

'I have to go now.' Taleb sights his train lumbering into the station. 'When are you expecting the Elasses back?'

'Oh, they returned yesterday. A few hours after Irmouli and Jahid left.'

Did they now? 'Refreshed from their skiing trip?'

'Not so you'd notice. But Monsieur Elasse didn't stay long anyway. He headed straight off again.'

Somehow, Taleb isn't surprised. 'Do you know where he's gone?'

'No. An urgent business trip, according to Madame.'

Urgent business. Yes, that sounds right. 'OK. Thanks, Abdou.'

'You're at a station. I can hear a train coming. Going far?'
'Not far enough.'
'Sorry to hear that. Take care, my friend.'
'I always do.' It's as much a promise to himself as a response to Rezig. Taleb rings off as the train passes him, its brakes squealing, and hurries along the platform to where the other passengers are waiting.

Hidouchi is unsurprised to be summoned to HQ by a terse call from Kadri. It's clear this Friday isn't going to be a normal one. Not that she thinks Kadri will greatly mind being denied the opportunity to attend his mosque. She doesn't have him down as a devout man. He will mind having to grapple with the varied problems recent events have thrown at him, however. He is fundamentally lazy and would much prefer the whole corrupt machinery of the state to function as it always has without him being called upon to do anything.

As to that, he is out of luck. Irmouli's murder – of which Bouras has informed him – leaves him with no alternative but – for once – to perform the duties of his office. Which means Hidouchi is out of luck as well. 'I've had Jahid brought in for questioning in view of this ... unexpected ... development,' he explains. 'I'd like you to make a start with him. I'll join you when I've dealt with a few other matters.'

Hidouchi is left to guess what those other matters might be. Upon arrival at a half-empty HQ, she is directed to one of the basement interrogation rooms, where Jahid is being held in the care of a burly, expressionless guard.

Jahid looks sweaty and ill at ease, as well he might. The polystyrene cup of DSS vending machine coffee standing before him on the table at which he's seated is unlikely to have deceived him into believing his situation is promising.

He looks at her with a bemused frown. 'Hidouchi? Have they sent you to question me?'

'Well, Agent Jahid, there are certainly questions you need to answer.'

'They tell me Irmouli's dead. Is that true?'

'So the French police say.'

'I didn't know what he was up to. I had no idea.'

'You'll have to convince the deputy director of that, not me. He'll be here shortly.'

'But you can help me convince him. You know what it's like on assignment. You just do what the lead man says.'

'Is that right?'

'Of course it is. Irmouli was in charge.'

'Did he try to skim off money from the ransom payment?'

Jahid shrugs. 'He might have.'

'And there was to be a cut for you too?'

'No. I didn't want any part of whatever his scheme was. I kept my head down.'

'And did nothing to prevent a fellow agent being kidnapped?'

'That was a put-up job according to Irmouli. We were required to play our part. We did . . . whatever Lydia Seghir told us to do. Well, whatever her assistant Touati told us to do anyway. That was the assignment. Make sure the conference went smoothly. Take instructions from Doctor Seghir. Jump when she said jump. Basically that and nothing else.'

'Who gave you the assignment?'

'Who do you think?'

Kadri is the obvious answer. But claiming to have done what the deputy director told him to do isn't going to get Jahid off the hook. They both know that.

Hidouchi also knows – but isn't sure Jahid does – that there is a green light showing on the recording monitor fitted in the corner of the ceiling above and behind him, which means someone is watching and listening to their exchanges. 'Are you suggesting you were specifically authorized to facilitate Agent Mokrani's abduction?' she asks, phrasing the question with considerable delicacy.

Jahid takes the hint. 'Of course not. I wasn't present at the briefing for our assignment. Irmouli handled that. But he assured me everything we did . . . was officially sanctioned.'

'Your position is that you were just an ignorant foot soldier?'

Jahid grimaces, but doesn't argue. 'I suppose so, yes.'

'Who do you think killed Irmouli?'

'Taleb?'

'Why would Superintendent Taleb murder Irmouli?'

'Maybe they fell out over the ransom money. Taleb could have stolen it, couldn't he? Maybe he killed Spühler as well – for the same reason. We don't actually know Agent Mokrani's been released, do we? And Taleb's gone missing, hasn't he? So . . . all that would make sense.'

Jahid looks marginally less glum. The story he's improvised exonerates him and – perhaps just as usefully – Kadri. Irmouli's dead and Taleb's on the run. Neither of them is in a position to contradict him. Altogether, it sounds like a version of events that mightn't survive detailed scrutiny but might nevertheless be settled on in the interests of departmental solidarity. But Hidouchi isn't having any of it. 'I don't believe that for a moment,' she says emphatically.

'You don't?' Jahid gapes at her in apparently genuine astonishment, baffled, it seems, by her refusal to play along. 'Why not?'

'Because Taleb isn't a killer. He's just a policeman. His body in the boot of his hire car and Irmouli on the run? That would be plausible. But that isn't how it is.'

'Well, I . . .' Jahid's improvisatory abilities desert him at this point. 'I don't know . . . how to . . .'

He's rescued from his discomfort by the ringing of the internal phone fixed to the wall next to the door. Hidouchi moves past the guard and picks it up. 'Yes?'

The voice that responds is Kadri's. 'I won't be joining you after all, Souad,' he says. 'Things have . . . moved on. Come up to my office, would you? Now.'

Taleb can see the premises of *Léopard Blanc SARL*, but they're on the inner side of the perimeter fence of the naval base and he can't get any closer than the pavement on the road that runs parallel with it. He assumes access is via the nearest gate into the base, but with the police looking for the hirer of the car in which Irmouli's body was found, he doesn't think trying to talk his way in is wise, in case whoever killed Irmouli has anticipated such a move.

He smokes a cigarette and takes a surreptitious look at the building through his pocket binoculars, but all he can see is an anonymous industrial structure, with the company name discreetly signed, some cars and vans parked out front and the spur of a railway line snaking away from a loading bay. The several office windows he has a view of all have blinds angled so the interiors aren't visible. *Léopard Blanc* doesn't appear to be in the business of attracting – or welcoming – attention.

Reviewing his paltry range of options, he recalls a piece of advice from Meslem. *Never push your luck during an investigation, because, remember, policemen don't have much luck to play with.*

The decision is made. And it's one Meslem would have approved of. Taleb flicks the butt of his cigarette into the gutter and heads back towards the station.

Kadri is sitting almost horizontally in his chair and doesn't look up when Hidouchi enters his office. He appears to be focusing on the dregs of coffee in the espresso cup in front of him. For a man possessed of abundant if unwarranted self-confidence, his deflation is decidedly – and worryingly – unusual.

'Everything we do is political, Souad,' he growls. 'You are aware of that, aren't you?'

'I'm aware there's a political dimension to the department's activities, Deputy Director, yes.'

'Perhaps that dimension – to use your word – is more apparent at my level than yours.'

'Perhaps it is.'

'Word has come down the line. White Leopard must be left alone. We can tie up the loose ends of the Mokrani kidnapping and Irmouli's murder any way we like as long as doing so doesn't involve Lydia Seghir, her ex-husband, Henri Elasse – or a patch of desert south-west of Tamanrasset.'

'What about Erica Ménard?'

'I'm required to cooperate with her unconditionally.'

'That means . . . we can do nothing.'

'I'm assured this is all for the greater good. I don't have any choice in the matter. You must understand that. The powers that be know best.'

'Do they?'

Kadri pulls himself half upright. 'They know more than we do. They see the big picture.' He clearly doesn't believe what he's saying. But equally clearly he believes he has to behave as if he does. 'Now, I listened to your questioning of Jahid and I think his version of events is the best one to settle on. Obviously he was promised a cut of the slice of ransom money Irmouli tried to steal, but that hardly matters now. Irmouli and Taleb conspired together, then fell out – as thieves often do. Taleb murdered Irmouli and went on the run. If the French police apprehend him, all well and good. If he returns to Algeria, we will bring him in. Unless the DGSN catch him first, that is. I've advised Director Bouras that we regard him as the prime malefactor in all this.'

If Kadri has already told Bouras how he proposes to wrap matters up, listening to Hidouchi's questioning of Jahid was irrelevant. He'd already decided – or been instructed – how the affair had to be handled. Hidouchi feels a deep revulsion at his shameless serving of other people's priorities and his indifference to the consequences of his trade-offs, notably for Taleb. 'I'm quite sure Taleb didn't kill Irmouli or conspire with him to steal the ransom money,' she protests.

Kadri looks at her wearily. 'If the evidence against him is found to be insufficient, he'll eventually be released. After White Leopard has achieved its purpose, no one will care about a police superintendent way past retirement age. I know you feel . . . protective . . . towards him. But you should prioritize protecting yourself.'

'Erica Ménard can't be trusted. She's no friend of Algeria.'

'I'm sure you're right. On both counts. But if allowing her to become involved in White Leopard proves to be a mistake, it won't be *our* mistake. It may even be to our advantage to have expressed reservations at this stage. But it can't go beyond that. We have to cooperate. That's how the system works. I know you know that.' Kadri smiles cautiously, hoping to elicit from her a word or gesture of complicity in the compromise they're required to subscribe to.

He doesn't get one. 'You think the system works?' Hidouchi throws the question at him.

'To the extent it needs to, yes. And we benefit from it.'

'I see no benefit here.'

'I value your commitment, Souad. But there are limits to what I can allow you to do. Don't test them.'

'I won't put my name to this.'

'You don't need to. I can find another agent to draw up the report. Maybe you should . . . take a holiday. You have leave owing.'

'Are you suspending me from duty, Deputy Director?'

'Only if you force me to. But in view of your earlier run-in with Ménard our dealings with her – whatever they may amount to – are likely to proceed more smoothly . . . in your absence. So, I think you should . . . take a well-deserved break.'

'You do?'

'Yes.' He props his elbows on his desk and steeples his fingers. 'I think it's for the best.'

Bouras composes himself for several minutes before making the call. There is no way round acquainting Taleb with the reality of his situation. But saying it isn't going to come easily to him. Any more, he imagines, than it's going to be easy for Taleb to hear.

'Director?'

'Can you hear me? There's a lot of noise in the background.'

'I'm on a train. And it's quite busy. Do you have news?'

'None that's good, I'm afraid. The DSS, acting on orders from above, have decided to blame everything that's gone wrong there on you. If you return to Algeria, they'll undoubtedly take you into custody. To avoid that, we'd have to arrest you ourselves. Meanwhile, the DGSE are happy for the French police to hunt you down and charge you with Irmouli's murder – and Spühler's too. I've tried to persuade the police chief in Marseille that you're just the fall guy in all this, but he isn't willing to play along. I suspect he's had orders from above as well. Your old friend Erica Ménard will be happy to see you rotting in jail while she pursues her own agenda with White Leopard.'

'I have no idea what her agenda might be. My trip to Toulon achieved nothing.'

'So, we're both in the dark where White Leopard is concerned?'

'Forgive me for saying this, Director, but from what you've told me the place I'm in is considerably darker than the place you're in.'

'You're right, of course. I'm sorry things have turned out as they have. I'll continue to lobby on your behalf.'

'Thank you. I appreciate that. Meanwhile, any . . . suggestions?'

'Don't get caught.'

'I'll certainly try not to.'

'If I were you, Taleb . . .'

'Yes, Director? If you were me?'

'I'd leave France. But I wouldn't come back here. I'd find some . . . third country . . . to lie low in until . . .'

'Until?'

'Just until. That's really all I can say.'

Bouras turns round in his chair after ringing off and stares out at the dockside cranes that are the only interruptions to the view of the Mediterranean his office commands. None of the cranes are moving on this day of rest and reflection. The city he serves is as still as it ever gets. But that does not make it peaceful. Bouras feels a turmoil within himself. He is appalled by the decision forced upon him to cut Taleb adrift. No course of action is in truth open to him that would be of any help to the fugitive superintendent. The realities of survival within the Algerian system, by which he is governed, have enforced themselves. As they always do.

He picks up the internal phone and calls Lieutenant Lahmar.

'Yes, chief?'

'You can go home, Lahmar. Try to enjoy the rest of your weekend.'

'Aren't we expecting further contact from the Marseille police?'

'They can leave a message. If they wish.'

'But—'

'They're going to do what they want to do – or what the DGSE tells them to. We can't stop them. But I see no reason why they should have our explicit agreement to their actions. So, go home. That's certainly what I intend to do.'

'OK, chief.'

Bouras puts the phone down and listens to the silence around him for several long moments. Then he sighs, stands up and heads for the door.

Taleb exits the train from Toulon back at the Gare St-Charles in Marseille in close formation with a knot of other passengers. He doesn't think there will be police patrols on the concourse. Logically, if he'd really killed Irmouli, he wouldn't linger in Marseille, which makes it as safe a hiding place as anywhere else. Still, it pays to be cautious. He has few options and none of them are good. Bouras's advice, such as it was, hardly constituted grounds for optimism. He is on his own now, officially abandoned.

He walks slowly out into the late morning, crosses the road and starts down the grand staircase descending from the station into the heart of the city. He lights a cigarette as he goes. He has already dismissed Bouras's suggestion that he flee to a third country. He is too old to start anew somewhere else, even if he could escape detection and probable extradition. He is an Algerian and for better or worse Algeria is where he should take his stand.

Chahira Meslem has something the Seghirs would dearly like to lay their hands on – something seriously damaging to them. Taleb feels certain of that. It represents their greatest point of weakness. He has to find out what it is. To do that he has to travel to Cherchell.

But how to get there without falling into the clutches of the French authorities is the immediate challenge. Erica Ménard will have issued instructions for all ports and airports to be carefully watched. His alias will avail him little with his photograph doubtless already in circulation. He could cross the unpoliced border into Spain by train and aim for Almería. He believes there's a ferry service from there to Ghazaouet in the far west of Algeria. But it's probably only a weekly service at this time of year, and using local trains to get as far as Almería – as he'd have to – would make for slow going.

Still, no other route offers a better prospect of success. Spain it has to be. He'll pack his bag, check out of the Hotel Saphir, return to the station and start heading south-west. There's nothing to be gained by delaying his departure. And mouldering in Marseille, waiting for a knock at the door, is an unappetizing prospect.

He turns into the narrow street leading to the Saphir. His plan, though far from perfect, is beginning to appeal to him. Maybe he can outwit his pursuers after all. He isn't finished yet.

The shabby frontage of the Saphir comes into view ahead. He quickens his pace. Now he's decided what to do he's eager to set off.

The driver's door of a parked car swings open suddenly in front of him. He tries to dodge round it, but collides with a tall, broad-shouldered man who doesn't step aside. Then he's grabbed from behind by a second man and before he can take a breath a hood is pulled over his head, blanking out the city around him.

He's bundled into the back of the car, thrust head first across the rear seat. He cries out in protest, but his cries are muffled by the hood. He hears the doors of the car slam as the men climb in, one in the back, twisting Taleb's feet out of his way. There's a shout of '*Go!*'

The car's engine roars and they start away with a shriek of tyre on tarmac.

Wherever they're going, Taleb feels quite certain it isn't the Spanish border.

THIRTEEN

THE CAR BARRELS THROUGH MARSEILLE IN A SUCCESSION OF JUD-
dering switchbacks. Nothing is said by the men who have seized Taleb and he says nothing either. He knows protesting at his treatment would be pointless. He guesses, in the absence of any other explanation, that he's in the hands of *les souveniristes*, though he's hardly an obvious kidnap target. The DGSN aren't going to pay five million Swiss francs – or even five million Algerian dinars – to free him. He's a valueless hostage.

Alternative explanations for taking him captive aren't happy to contemplate. His phone – he only had one of his phones on him – and his gun have been removed. His one attempt to sit up was forcefully repulsed, accompanied by a rasped two-word instruction: 'Don't move.' Since then, he hasn't, except as an unwilling passenger in the speeding car.

The jolting journey lasts about twenty minutes by his estimate. The car slows, takes several tight turns, then halts. He's bundled out and frogmarched into a building. There is a change in the sound around him and a distinct smell of damp concrete.

They shove him down onto a plastic chair. His arms are

dragged back and his hands tied behind the chair. Then his feet are tied to the legs. They're using rope – rough chandler's rope, he reckons from the chafing against his wrists. He's fleetingly amused by his own detective instincts. The kind of rope he's been tied with is unlikely to be valuable information. But it's about the only information he has.

'OK,' one of the men says. That's all. He hears them walk away, feet scuffing on a dusty floor. A door is slammed and padlocked. Then . . . silence.

Dim light slowly seeps in through the hood. He strains his ears but hears nothing. He thinks he's been left alone. But not quite. There's a scurrying from a little way off. A rat, maybe? He doesn't like rats, especially when he can't see them.

Time passes. The rat comes nearer, then retreats. Evidently Taleb's of no interest to the creature. Even the rodents of Marseille know he's a man of little importance.

More time passes. Taleb's hearing sharpens itself in the absence of any other stimulus. He thinks he can hear vehicles moving periodically in the distance. A gust of wind rattles what sounds like a shutter-door. A dog starts barking somewhere.

Then the growl of a powerful car engine blots out the barking. He hears the vehicle pull up outside, close by. Doors slam. Footsteps crunch. A key turns in a lock.

The shutter-door he heard rattling earlier is flung up violently in an explosion of sound. He flinches involuntarily. The light strengthens. The footsteps approach. A shadow falls across him. The smell of cigar smoke comes with it.

The hood is pulled off. A flood of light dazzles him. A figure looms above him. '*Bonjour*,' comes a growl Taleb recognizes as the voice of Farabi Merzouk, aka Le Merz. 'How is the honest Algerian policeman today?'

'As you see me,' Taleb replies hoarsely.

He's in a lock-up garage. The main door is open, admitting

a wedge of bright Marseille sunlight. Le Merz, standing as ever with the light behind him, is clad as before in a capacious overcoat and is smoking a cigar. There are a couple of men behind him. One pulls up a chair for him to sit down. The other pulls the shutter-door down as a pair of fluorescent tubes flicker into life above them.

Le Merz sighs and takes a puff on his cigar, cocking his large bald head and squinting curiously at Taleb like some top-of-the-food-chain predator trying to decide whether the object before him is a worthwhile snack.

'Why am I here?' Taleb asks, trying to pitch his voice at a defiant level.

'You mean in this garage? In Marseille? Or in the world at all?' Le Merz grins. 'I can only answer for the garage.'

'What do you want with me?'

'A conversation. About matters of mutual interest. Pressing interest, that is.'

'We could have arranged to meet if you'd left a message with Abdou. There was no need to grab me off the street.'

'Wasn't there? You're a dangerous man, Taleb. If what the police say about you is to be believed. Murderer of a DSS agent in cold blood. There's another murder they seem to be trying to pin on you as well. Some fat cat Swiss accountant. Fortunately, not *my* fat cat Swiss accountant. You've been busy, haven't you?'

'I didn't kill either of them.'

'No? Well, since it's the local police who say you did I'd have to agree the chances are you didn't. Also, I know killers. I know them by the look in their eyes. You don't have the look. I do. In case you're wondering.'

'I was framed.'

'Of course you were. I never doubted it for a moment. Actually, I did you a big favour by having you brought here. The local police, incompetent as they are, would have tracked you down eventually. My man on the inside tells me the DGSE are setting the pace. You'd have been run to earth sooner rather than later with the spy-hunters from Paris on your trail. But the Saphir, like most hotels of its grade, owes me more than it does the authorities. So, I found you first. And here we are.'

'I still don't understand. What do you want from me?'

'Whatever you've got to offer. And it would be in your best interests to offer something. Otherwise you'll be on your own again.' Le Merz studies his cigar. 'Would you like a smoke of one of these? They're good for the brain.'

'I'd prefer a cigarette.'

'I don't have any.'

'I've got a pack in my pocket.'

'Which brand?'

'Nassims.'

'You have cheap tastes, Taleb, you really do. Nassims? My father used to smoke them. He had no money, of course. He prided himself on his honesty. Look where that got him. And look where honesty's got you.'

'I'd really like a cigarette.'

'OK. Out of consideration for my father's memory, you can light one.' Le Merz gestures to one of the men behind him. 'Untie him.'

Taleb's hands are released, though his feet remain tied to the legs of the chair. He flexes some mobility back into his shoulders, takes out his pack of Nassims and puts one in his mouth. While he's still fumbling for his matches, Le Merz flourishes a chunky gold lighter and leans across the gap between them. Taleb leans forward himself and meets the flame with his cigarette, catching Le Merz's eye as he does so. 'Thanks.'

'You're welcome. Maybe they'll give you a lighter like this when you finally retire.'

'You think I'll make it to retirement?'

'Hard to say at the moment. Supply me with something to use against the Seghirs and your chances will improve.'

The Seghirs. The hint of enmity towards them in Le Merz's voice gives Taleb some hope. Maybe they can cooperate against a mutual foe. 'You have some . . . issue . . . with the Seghirs?'

Le Merz sits back in his chair and puffs at his cigar. 'I spoke to the Major. It was . . . an illuminating conversation. Also a disturbing one.'

'In what way?'

'You and I had an agreement that if I secured the release of *les souveniristes*' hostage, you'd pay me a retrieval fee. Remember?'

'I remember. But he was released because I paid the ransom, not because you intervened.'

'That's not why you don't owe me a retrieval fee, Taleb. The reason is that there was no hostage. Under pressure – and you can safely assume the pressure was severe – the Major admitted that *les souveniristes* don't exist. Nor was Agent Mokrani ever kidnapped. That was all . . . make-believe.'

Make-believe? Taleb is surprised by how unsurprised he is by the suggestion. A faked kidnap by an imaginary terrorist group. And he was supposed to sort it all out. It sounds like a summary of his entire career. 'It was all . . . bogus?'

'Completely. General Mokrani paid five million Swiss francs under false pretences. His son wasn't a hostage. He was a co-conspirator with the Major. They were both acting on behalf of the Seghirs.'

'So . . . this was all about cheating General Mokrani out of five million Swiss francs?'

'No. That was just the Major's fee. The object of the exercise was to fix General Mokrani's thoughts on the survival of his only son when he should have been concentrating on the threat posed to him by White Leopard.'

'And Karim Mokrani was happy to betray his father?'

'Fathers and sons, Taleb. What can I tell you? There could be a lot going on there. I'd have asked Karim if I'd caught up with him. But he gave us the slip. The Major was slower on his feet.'

'And he's told you what White Leopard is?'

'No. He didn't know. You can be sure I tested him on the point. All he could say was that the White Leopard project – central to the conference Lydia Seghir's been holding at the Villa des Ormeaux – involves a serious assault on the privileges and prosperity of the older generation of senior figures in *le pouvoir* – General Mokrani among them. Just when he should have been doing everything he could to find out what the purpose of the conference was, he was hamstrung by his son's supposed abduction. You were part of the set-up without being aware of it. A policeman with a grudge against Mokrani sounding off on Algerian television, then – it was made to seem – abandoning Karim Mokrani to his fate and stealing the ransom money. That took the general's eye off the ball and prevented him mobilizing resistance among his contemporaries in *le pouvoir* – stopped him doing anything, in fact, that might interfere with the grand plan. He was so distracted he didn't even know there was a grand plan at all. But I know – now.'

'Why should you care what happens to General Mokrani and his kind?'

'I care because his kind – as you call them – are some of my best customers. *Le pouvoir* doesn't invest its ill-gotten gains in Algeria, Taleb. It invests them where they'll appreciate the most. And the network of enterprises I run is one of the most attractive places for them to put their money. I ensure high profits, total discretion and complete asset security. You probably think I'm some kind of gangster. Actually, I'm more of an investment manager in the black economy. I supply a service for which there's always been keen demand. My clients – like General Mokrani – rely on me. By the same token, I rely on them. Money flows in, more money flows out. Everyone's happy. It's a business model that's served me – and them – well. I can't allow it to be threatened.'

'And the Seghirs are threatening it?'

'From what the Major told me, White Leopard involves the decisive removal from the scene of many of my Algerian clients. And they're some of my very best.'

'How could White Leopard do that?'

'It's unclear. According to the Major, the people attending the Villa des Ormeaux conference included representatives of regional interest groups in southern Algeria and terrorist organizations from neighbouring countries, along with frontmen for the French energy industry and other more obscure parties. Lydia Seghir in the chair means the Algerian government are going to put their name to whatever White Leopard amounts to when it's announced – which will happen soon, apparently. And DGSE involvement confirms the French government will sign up to it as well. The conference brought together a collection of people who should logically be at each other's throats. If they're cooperating to some mutually beneficial end, it has to be something big – something game-changing. And I don't want the game to change. I like the rules we've been playing by these past few decades. I live – I prosper – by them. So, you see, this isn't a development I can afford to ignore.'

'You're aware Henri Elasse and Yanik Seghir are directors of a French-registered company called *Léopard Blanc*?'

'I am. It looks as if Yanik and Lydia Seghir are divorced largely for show. They're in this together. She's gone back to Algeria, of course. And my inside man at the airport says her ex-husband, her son and Henri Elasse flew to Algiers on the same private plane yesterday afternoon. *Léopard Blanc* are in the cable-laying and salvaging business. I can't see how that links with the kind of move against veteran figures in *le pouvoir* the Major said is in the wind. But apparently it does. So, I need ammunition to use against these people. And I think you may be able to supply it.'

'Why do you think that?'

'You make them nervous, Taleb. The Major admitted they're wary of you. That's why they went to such lengths to depict you as the villain of the piece. Any idea what exactly they're wary *of*?' Le Merz narrows his gaze. 'Looking at you, it's certainly not obvious.'

Not obvious, no. Except to Taleb. The break-in at Chahira Meslem's house, followed by the search of her late husband's office at Police HQ: the Seghirs are clearly nervous about something they suspect was in Superintendent Meslem's possession. Whatever it is represents a serious threat to them. And a serious threat to them is a valuable bargaining counter for Taleb. 'I have an idea what they're after, yes.'

'What is it?'

'I'm not exactly sure. It may relate to the Boudiaf assassination.'

'You think they're implicated in that?'

'It's more likely General Mokrani is implicated. But there's something there that troubles them, involving DSS internal documents copied by Youcef Ghezala – his name cropped up in the TV programme I stupidly agreed to appear in – and passed on by him to Kasdi Merbah.'

'Also assassinated, as I recall.'

'So he was. But those documents have never been found.'

'Do you know where they are?'

'I think I do, yes.'

'Tell me.'

'I can't do that. What I *can* do is let you see them, after I've retrieved them. But to retrieve them I need to return to Algeria.'

'You're in no position to dictate terms to me, Taleb.'

'I am to some extent, monsieur. You want dirt on the Seghirs. So do I. I know where it's to be found. You don't.'

'Why haven't you taken charge of these documents long before now?'

'I didn't know they still existed. I only discovered that after arriving in France.'

'Who's holding them?'

'I'm not going to name the person, or tell you where they live. The point to be understood is that they're only willing to surrender them to me. Me and no one else.'

'My people could change their mind about that. They're very persuasive.'

'This person is very stubborn. And I don't want any harm to come to them. So, I'll get the documents from them and you'll be able to see what they amount to. I just need safe passage to Algeria.'

'You expect me to trust you to deliver the documents to me?'

'Why not? I'm under no illusions about what will happen if I break my word. Something similar to what's happened to the Major, I assume.'

'Something similarly terminal, Taleb, yes. That would be your fate for trying to double-cross me.'

'I'm not going to.'

'I could force the name and address of the person out of you. You must know that.'

'You probably could. But, as I told you, they're exceptionally stubborn. Far more so than me. They're at an age when they may choose to defy the people you send and insist on taking the secret to their grave. Then you would have nothing – except two bodies to dispose of.'

'The bodies would be the least of my problems.' Le Merz scowls at Taleb and chews his cigar. Taleb finishes his cigarette and waits as patiently as he can for the other man to continue. Cigar smoke rises in blue whorls above Le Merz's domed head.

Then he looks directly at Taleb and gives a slow, assenting

nod. 'Very well. I will send you to Algeria. But I will send someone with you to ensure the terms of our agreement are adhered to. Also to ensure you make it to wherever you're going without getting arrested or shot by the DSS. It appears I need you alive for as long as it takes you to get hold of the documents. Serve me well and you may still get to draw your meagre pension. Betray me and you will regret it, believe me.'

'I believe you.'

Le Merz turns round and addresses one of the men behind him. 'Where is the Dutchman?'

'Genoa, boss.'

'Get him back here as soon as possible.'

'OK, boss.' The man walks away towards the shutter-door, making a call on his phone as he goes.

Le Merz tuns back to face Taleb. 'You can't go back to the Saphir, Taleb. Too risky. We'll retrieve your belongings and arrange somewhere for you to stay until we can transport you to Algeria. It won't be a luxury trip. But we'll get you there. Just make sure you deliver on our bargain when you arrive.'

'I will.'

'We have your phone and we'll be keeping it, likewise any other phones or laptop we find at the Saphir. You'll be incommunicado from now on.' Le Merz pulls out of his pocket a phone Taleb recognizes as the one taken from him and squints at the screen. 'All recent traffic on this has been deleted, I see. But you've had a text message since we picked you up from someone identifying themselves as H. Asking you to call them. Number withheld. Who are they?'

'A friend.'

'You have friends, Taleb?'

'A few.'

'Amazing. Does this one know the jam you're in?'

'She has some idea.'

'A woman in your life, eh? Who'd have thought it? Will she be worried about you?'

'She may be.'

'Well, she's going to have to go on being worried for a little while yet. You won't be calling her until this is over. You won't be calling anyone.'

'Understood.'

'Good.' Le Merz leans forward and offers Taleb his right hand. 'Time to shake on our deal, Taleb.'

Le Merz's handshake is predictably crushing and is accompanied by a wry smile. 'You're working for me now. And I am one demanding son of a bitch to work for. You'd do well to remember that.'

After Le Merz takes his leave, Taleb is escorted back to the car he arrived in and told to climb into the boot. When he looks askance, the one who seems to be in charge says, 'If the boss wanted you dead, you'd already have a bullet in your head. We're driving you to the fishing port. See? No secrets. No chance of you being spotted by the flics if you're out of sight. So, get in.' He gets in.

There's a blanket in the boot, which affords some cushioning as the car jolts and lurches around the streets of Marseille. With no light and no phone, Taleb finds the length of time he spends trying to avoid repeatedly banging his head on the fuel pipe hard to gauge. Not that it matters. Getting where they're going will take the time it takes.

Eventually, they arrive. Taleb is hoisted out of the boot, squinting in the low-angled sun, and glimpses a dock lined with fishing boats and a large shed beside it. There's a smell of fish in the air and shards of ice scattered around. This is about all he registers before they hurry him into a building and up a narrow flight of stairs.

They reach an attic from which a small dormer window looks

down onto part of the dock. The room appears to double as an office and a bedroom. There's a rickety desk and chair in one corner, with several old filing cabinets behind it. In another there's a sink, with soap and a towel, and an electric kettle standing on a shelf next to it. On the farthest side there's a low cot-bed, with a threadbare curtain rigged up round it. Beyond that an open door leads to a loo.

'Make yourself comfortable,' he's ironically advised, before being left alone. The door is locked as the escort party leaves. He's going nowhere until Le Merz arranges for him to.

The attic has little by way of entertainment to offer. The filing cabinets are locked and the desk contains nothing beyond several years' worth of local tide tables and a slew of yellowing maritime charts. There's an old transistor radio, which he tries to tune to something interesting, but gives up after finding nothing but pop music channels. After that it's simply a question of testing the cot-bed for comfort – it doesn't score highly – and struggling manfully not to smoke one cigarette after another.

The lead man returns an hour or so later with Taleb's belongings from the Saphir – minus his other two phones, of course. He has news, of a sort. 'The Dutchman will be here tomorrow.'

'What am I supposed to do until then?' Taleb asks, though he feels he already knows the answer.

'Stay here. We'll bring food later.' The man proffers a jar of instant coffee and a two-litre bottle of Evian water. 'Piece of advice: don't drink what comes out of the tap without boiling it.'

'Thanks for the warning.'

'Well, we don't want a sick man on our hands, do we? It complicates transport. As far as that goes, don't worry. We've handled hotter cargo than you and got it where it's supposed to go.' The man grins. 'OK?'

Taleb nods glumly. 'OK.'

*

Hidouchi goes to the hotel gym she subscribes to that afternoon to work off some of the frustration she feels. Kadri has ordered her to drop the case and Bouras has reached an impasse in his dealings with the Marseille police. Their strings are being pulled by the DGSE, of course, which leaves Taleb very much on his own. What he'll do next she can't guess, but his failure to respond to her latest text is far from reassuring.

She doesn't spare herself in the gym, but peace of mind fails to follow, despite the superior water pressure in the showers. She leaves the hotel by the gym entrance physically stretched but mentally still on edge.

As she approaches the motorbike bay, she sees a black car parked next to it and recognizes the vehicle as the one Zoubiri nearly drove her down in. The driver isn't visible from where she is, but as she draws nearer the tinted rear nearside window slides down and General Mokrani's puffy, mustachioed face stares out at her.

'Can we talk, Agent Hidouchi?' he asks in his gravelly voice, from which overt hostility is for once absent.

'Haven't we talked enough?' she counters. She catches a glimpse within the car of Zoubiri looking round at her from the driver's seat.

General Mokrani takes a deep breath, visibly composing himself, suppressing the instinct to bark out reproofs or demands. He presses his hand to his forehead. 'My son is missing, Agent Hidouchi. Superintendent Taleb claims he has been released by *les souveniristes*, but that can only be known if and when Karim contacts me. His mother is distraught. She fears – as do I – that he remains a prisoner – or worse. I am asking you for your help.'

'Are you serious?'

'It is a measure of my desperation that I am indeed very serious.'

'What did you find out about Irmouli?' Zoubiri cuts in. 'We know he's been killed – by Taleb, apparently.'

'Whatever I found out I'm not about to share with you. What I can say is that I'm quite certain Superintendent Taleb didn't kill him.'

'Kadri has closed you down, hasn't he?'

Hidouchi doesn't look at Zoubiri. She holds General Mokrani's gaze. 'I can't discuss internal DSS matters.'

'Kadri has knuckled under to the DGSE,' says Mokrani. 'That is what such a man would naturally do. But you are of a different calibre.'

'I follow my orders.'

'Not always, I think. You want to know what is really going on. So do I. Perhaps we can . . . help each other.'

'How?'

'If you revealed what you turned up on Irmouli, I might be willing to reveal what I know about Yanik Seghir – Lydia Seghir's ex-husband.'

'I know who he is.'

'Of course you do. Which tells me a little – but not enough.'

'Have you had dealings with him, General?'

'A long time ago, yes.'

'What was the nature of those dealings?'

Mokrani smiles thinly. 'I am, as I have admitted, desperately placed. But I am not so desperate as to give you valuable information without being sure of obtaining something in return.'

They look at one another. Hidouchi senses Mokrani has been forced by concern for his son to become genuinely reasonable. But his treacherous nature has not changed. He cannot be trusted. Doing business with him can only be a last resort. And Hidouchi has not yet been reduced to that. 'The most I can say is that I will consider your proposal.'

'Don't take too long about it. There is more than my son's life at stake. Your friend Taleb is in a vulnerable position. As a matter of fact, I think you and I are too. Do not allow yourself to be overtaken by events.'

'I have no intention of doing that.'

'Then I will hope to hear from you – very soon.'

Friday afternoon fades into evening. Taleb sleeps fitfully through the night, listening to the wind stirring the rigging in the boats moored down in the dock. The gulls wake him before dawn – a grey and breezy one, with rain spitting against the window. Breakfast is delivered to him – a small box of cornflakes, a croissant and a carton of milk. The man who delivers it ignores Taleb's questions. It's light outside now, but Taleb remains in the dark.

Saturday slowly elapses. Taleb imagines the bustle of the world from which he's sealed off. He wonders what Hidouchi has made of his failure to respond to her text. She'll be worried about him – and with good reason. He can only hope she takes no drastic action. Nothing can improve his situation bar Karim Mokrani's reappearance in Algiers, and judging by what Le Merz said that isn't about to happen. Bouras isn't going to be able to make any headway with the Marseille police. Erica Ménard will exert herself to ensure Taleb remains prime suspect in the murder of Agent Irmouli. Le Merz is in truth the only party willing and able to help him, albeit for reasons of his own. Which leaves Taleb with no option but to wait on *le grand bonnet*'s convenience.

And, as the light begins to fail on the second afternoon of Taleb's confinement, Le Merz's arrangements for him finally swing into action.

The door is unlocked. The lead man among his captors comes

into the room, wearing a yellow oilskin coat and carrying another, which he tosses in Taleb's direction. 'Put that on. Time to go.'

'Are you going to tell me what the plan is?' Taleb asks as he struggles into the coat.

'The fishing boat *Pauline* is waiting for you in the harbour. The Dutchman's already there. You'll be sailing out into the Mediterranean, rendezvousing with an Algerian vessel some time tonight east of Minorca. They'll take you to their home port, Sidi Lakhdar. Know it?'

'Heard of it.' Sidi Lakhdar is somewhere between Ténès and Mostaganem, if Taleb's geographical knowledge serves him correctly, which puts it maybe two hundred kilometres west of Cherchell. Since he hasn't revealed his exact destination as yet, he can hardly complain. His plan – if it can be called that – is to head for Cherchell and somehow contrive to give the Dutchman the slip along the way, although he doesn't rate his chances of pulling that off very highly.

'Weather forecast's reasonable, so the transfer shouldn't be a problem. You suffer from seasickness, Taleb?'

'I wouldn't say so. But then I've never crossed the Mediterranean by fishing boat in winter before.'

'Well, the crew won't like it if you throw up in the cabin, so my advice? Don't get seasick.'

'I'll be sure to remember that.'

'Right. Let's move.'

They descend the stairs and step out into the fish-tanged early evening air. Taleb puts up the hood on his oilskin as they hurry round the building and out along a quay. They pass several moored fishing boats. Taleb guesses the one ahead on which lights are gleaming is the *Pauline*. And so it is.

Boarding is swift and perfunctory. The boat's engine is already turning over. The skipper emerges from the wheelhouse for just long enough to give Taleb a cursory glance and exchange some muttered words with his minder. The other passenger, Taleb gathers, is waiting for him in the cabin. 'Go below,' is the skipper's terse instruction.

From his minder there is a farewell '*Bonne chance.*' Then, his bag thrust into his hand, Taleb heads down the narrow stairs into the bowel of the vessel.

A man dressed in jeans and a dark sweater is lying on one of the bunks on either side of the cabin, smoking a cigarette. As Taleb's shadow falls across him in the dim, yellowish lamplight, he swings his feet to the floor and sits up.

'You're Taleb?' The man is slimly built, with just a hint of muscle beneath the sweater. He looks about forty, with thinning sandy-coloured hair and a narrow pitted face. His watery blue eyes are disquietingly large, the brows above them bunched in a frown. He extends a hand in greeting. 'Good to meet you.'

'You're the Dutchman?'

'That's what they call me, *ja*. Because I'm Dutch, obviously.' He laughs.

They shake hands. As they do so, the boat's engine rumbles into reverse and the vessel backs away from its mooring.

'We're off, then. Too late to change your mind, my friend.' The Dutchman grins. 'It's Algeria or bust.'

'I'd prefer Algeria.'

'Me too. Don't worry; I guarantee everything will go smoothly. Well, the part I'm responsible for, anyway. Sea conditions aren't my province. Contraband, on the other hand – which is what you are – is my speciality.'

Taleb puts his bag down and sits on one of the low chairs set round the table in the middle of the cabin. 'Do I just call you . . . Dutchman?'

'The less you know about me the better, my friend. So, *ja*, Dutchman will do. If we go down tonight and you and I end up sharing a life raft maybe I'll let you call me by my first name. But that's not going to happen, is it? We'll make it to Sidi Lakhdar without even getting our feet wet, and then . . .' The Dutchman leans forward. 'Then what? I need to know where you want to go from there and why.'

'I'll explain when we arrive.'

'You think holding out on me will give you what – an edge of some kind? Forget it. My instructions are simple. Take you where the documents the boss requires are stored, get hold of them and deliver them to him. You'll be on your own from that point on. No harm will come to you from me provided you keep your side of the bargain, OK? But remember: I'll be armed and you won't.' Taleb has already noticed the waistband-level bulge beneath the Dutchman's sweater. 'You wouldn't be the first guy I've shot for trying to back out of a deal.'

'Telling you where we're going at this stage wasn't part of the deal I struck with Le Merz.'

'Fair enough. You go ahead and clutch that to your chest like a nervous poker player. But no nasty surprises once we're in Algeria, OK? Otherwise . . .' The Dutchman stretches out his arm and lightly taps Taleb in the middle of his forehead. 'You're dead.'

Taleb tells himself not to react. Let the Dutchman have his fun. Let him think he has Taleb where he wants him. 'If there are any nasty surprises, they won't be of my doing.'

'Then you can leave them to me.'

'On arrival, I'll need to make a phone call. And then we'll need to travel east along the coast.'

'*I'll* make the call, to the number you supply. And I'll listen to what's said. There'll be a car and a driver waiting for us at Sidi Lakhdar to take us where you need to go. We'll be sticking close together, you and I. Until the job's done.'

'Understood.'

'Good. Well . . .' The Dutchman turns and peers out through the porthole behind him. 'We're clear of the harbour. The crew will be down for their supper once we're out of French waters.' He looks back at Taleb. 'Say as little as possible to them without being impolite. They won't ask many questions. They know the drill. Carrying you is more profitable than fishing and involves much less work. I've brought a bottle of schnapps. Later on, we'll have a few glasses. Excellent for settling the stomach.' The Dutchman grins, which is something Taleb suspects he does a lot of. 'All good?'

Taleb summons a smile of his own. 'All good.'

Even as the *Pauline* makes its unnoticed passage down the roadstead of Marseille towards the open sea, with the lights of the city gleaming ever brighter against the rapidly darkening sky, on the other side of the Mediterranean Bouras and Hidouchi confer at their regular meeting place on the coast road near Aïn Benin, west of Algiers.

'Have you passed a relaxing weekend, Director?' Hidouchi asks in a deadpan tone.

'No more relaxing than yours, I imagine, Agent Hidouchi,' he replies.

'When did you last speak to Taleb?'

'Yesterday morning.'

'And since then you've heard nothing from him?'

'There's been no response to my messages.'

'Nor to mine.'

'It's worrying.'

'I agree, Director. What do you propose to do about it?'

'There's nothing I can do. He can't have been picked up by the French police. They would have notified me. Beyond that . . .'

'Perhaps the DGSE have him. Ménard wouldn't feel the need to notify anyone.'

Bouras sighs. 'I have no means of extracting information from the DGSE. That would be for the DSS to do. And Kadri has made it clear he'll be taking no action. From what you tell me, he's made it clear *you'll* be taking no action either.'

'He's instructed me to take some leave. But what I do while I'm on leave . . . is none of his business.'

'What do you have in mind?'

'Something you'd be better off not knowing about.'

'I'd advise caution.'

'Will caution help Taleb?'

Bouras sighs again. 'Probably not.'

'Then I'll do it my way. If I've still heard nothing from him by morning . . . I'll act as I judge necessary.'

FOURTEEN

TALEB CAN'T DECIDE WHETHER DRINKING SEVERAL GLASSES OF THE Dutchman's schnapps was a good idea or not. A pain behind his eyes catches up with him a second or so after every movement, it's true, but on the other hand he hasn't felt seasick at all, even during the transfer from the *Pauline* to the Algerian fishing boat *Etoile de la mer* somewhere in the lightless void of the Mediterranean back in the small hours of the morning.

Dawn has broken now and his view through the cabin porthole is of grey, rolling water beneath a silvery sky. The slashes of water against the glass could be spray or rain, he can't tell which. They're tracking south-west towards their destination at no great speed and, according to the Dutchman, the skipper plans to stop by some mussel-beds on the way. Landfall at Sidi Lakhdar is likely to be most of the rest of the day away.

The Dutchman's gone on deck to make some phone calls and take the air. He's told Taleb to stay out of sight in the cabin, even though there are no vessels nearby for anyone to catch sight of him *from*. Communication with the crew is probably the greater concern. Taleb would be able to talk to them in Darija dialect, leaving the Dutchman in the dark.

In reality, Taleb has no wish to engage with the crew. He's assuming they don't know he's a policeman and he'd like to keep it that way. Nor can they give him any help with his most pressing problem: how *exactly* is he to wrest control of the situation from the Dutchman once they're in Algeria?

He lights one of his Nassims and ponders the question once again. There's no obvious answer. But they'll be on his home ground tonight. Surely, somehow, that will give him an advantage.

'I'm glad to see you again, Agent Hidouchi,' says General Mokrani, though his careworn expression doesn't suggest he has any reason to be glad.

He's seated at the vast sandalwood and gilt desk in his study with the schooner lamp and the enormous inkstand and the outdated map of North Africa on the wall behind him. He's in his lair, surrounded by symbols of power and influence he no longer wields. And the last time Hidouchi was here she forcefully reminded him of his weakened state. It's occurred to her that he may want to exact retribution for the humiliation she subjected him to on that occasion. But she doubts it. The general is a pragmatist. And so, she would have to admit, is she. Improbable as it seems, they need each other.

Zoubiri has come into the room behind her. He closes the door and asks to see her phone to prove it's turned off. 'We don't want anyone listening in,' he says.

She shows him the phone. He signals with a nod to his boss that it's off.

'How do I know *you* don't have anyone listening in?' she asks, turning towards General Mokrani.

'I don't have any allies, Agent Hidouchi,' he growls. 'I think we established that during your last visit.'

'Maybe I should check she's not carrying a concealed recorder,' says Zoubiri.

Hidouchi's dressed in tight-fitting jeans, a black T-shirt and a high-cut leather jacket. Something in Zoubiri's expression suggests he'd relish searching her. It's not something she intends to permit, as her look at him makes clear.

'There's no need for that,' says Mokrani. 'None of us wants a record of this conversation, I'm sure.'

'Still no word from your son, General?' Hidouchi asks with a tilt of her head.

'What do you think?' he growls back at her. 'Taleb?'

'Out of contact.'

'There we are, then. I'm looking for Karim. You're looking for Taleb. It's possible we can help each other accomplish both objectives.'

'The fact that I'm here should tell you I'm open to some . . . limited . . . cooperation.'

'Your enemy's enemy is your friend.'

'So they say.'

Mokrani smiles grimly. 'So they do.'

'You offered to give me information about Yanik Seghir.'

'In exchange for information about the late Wael Irmouli. Why don't you start?'

'You came to me, General. I think it's for you to make the first disclosure.'

Zoubiri stirs behind her. She senses his anger without him saying a word. Mokrani isn't angry, though. He brings Zoubiri into line with a glance. 'All right,' he says after a pause. 'I'll indulge you, Agent Hidouchi. You accused me of running a secret outfit called Unit ninety-two, which, as I explained to you, I wouldn't be free to admit even if it was true because of the extreme sensitivity of the actions I took whilst serving in a senior capacity at the DRS during one of the darkest chapters of this country's history – when you were merely a schoolgirl.'

'Was Yanik Seghir a member of Unit ninety-two?'

'What I can tell you is that not all of the operatives I employed were serving members of the DRS. There were . . . contractors . . . we used for particularly challenging missions. Yanik Seghir was one such.'

'How long did he work for you?'

'Around . . . ten years . . . off and on.'

'Our files have him joining Sonatrach in 2002. Prior to that . . . there's no record of him.'

'There wouldn't be.'

'Was the Sonatrach job some kind of sinecure – a reward for services rendered?'

'I've said enough for the moment. It's time you told us about Irmouli. What have you found out about him?'

Pressing for more from Mokrani at this point will be futile, Hidouchi senses. She'll give him something now in order to get more in return. 'It looks as if Irmouli's motivation was basically financial. I suspect he was paid by the Seghirs to help them set up your son's abduction. He was probably killed because he got greedy and tried to steal some of the ransom money.'

'I'd already guessed that much.' Mokrani scowls. 'You're going to have to do better.'

'You took the SatNav from his car,' Zoubiri cuts in. 'What did that show?'

'OK. The SatNav. It was highly revealing. Late last month Irmouli drove to Mers-El Kébir.'

Mokrani's eyebrows twitch. 'The naval base?'

'Yes. We don't know why. A meeting with unknown parties.'

'Any other travels?'

'Yes. A few days later he set off for the far south. Tamanrasset.'

'Tamanrasset?' Mokrani frowns. 'By car? Why not fly?'

'Maybe he didn't want a record of his journey.'

'Did he go anywhere other than Tamanrasset?'

'A stretch of desert to the south-west of the city. Purpose unknown. The place he visited is a featureless plain.'

'Did he go alone?'

'There's obviously no way to tell that from the SatNav.'

'But you'll have checked the hotel he stayed in.' Mokrani is speaking briskly now, almost insistently. 'Did he book in alone?'

Hidouchi shakes her head. 'No. He didn't. There were two people with him.'

'Who were they?'

Hidouchi smiles gently. 'I think it's time for you to give me a little more about your dealings with Yanik Seghir.'

'Was he one of Irmouli's travelling companions?'

'I'm saying no more until you say more.'

'All right.' Mokrani spreads his hands compliantly. 'Yes, we arranged a lucrative position for him at Sonatrach when it was felt he'd . . . done enough for us in the field. We had only sporadic contact with him after that. We knew nothing about his marriage until Lydia Seghir came to prominence in her own right. By then they were divorced anyway. Although that now looks like a charade. I suspect he's helping her put the White Leopard project into effect.'

'Yet you claim to have no idea what White Leopard's about.'

'I didn't. Until you mentioned Irmouli's trip to the far south. Did Yanik Seghir go with him?'

Hidouchi can't see what's to be gained by holding out on the point. 'Yes.'

'And the other person was?'

'Tell me what purpose you think White Leopard may be serving.'

'Ever heard of Solahara?'

'I don't think so.'

'It was a scheme cooked up by the Sarkozy government to set

up solar energy arrays in the Moroccan, Algerian, Tunisian and Libyan Sahara to generate electricity that could be transmitted by high-voltage cables to France and other EU countries. Free power was the basic idea, given that some scientists claimed a relatively small area of desert – two hundred square kilometres or so – could provide enough energy for the entire world. The plan went nowhere after the Arab Spring took Libya out of the picture and got everyone worrying about how secure the arrays would be against cross-border terrorist activity. We had a taste of that with the In Amenas attack.'

'Good news for the petrochemical lobby, I imagine.'

'Whose agenda you doubtless think we were serving?'

'Well, weren't you?' A nexus of motivations for the DRS to stage a fake terrorist raid on In Amenas in 2013 forms itself in Hidouchi's mind. Rochdi Abidi alleged it was to feed the US narrative that al-Qaeda was active in the region after their expulsion from Afghanistan. But it occurs to her that blocking Solahara might have been an additional motive, perhaps shared with Big Oil interests worldwide.

'Why are you shaking your head, Agent Hidouchi?'

'In disbelief, I suppose, at the bottomless cynicism of your generation.'

'What you call cynicism I regard as patriotism. Algeria would not have profited from allowing the French to establish a monopoly on solar energy from the Sahara. And the terrorist threat was real, whatever you might think. Look what's happened to the countries south of us in the years since.' Mokrani turns and points to the map behind him. 'Mali is a failed state. Chad is in chaos. Niger will probably be next to implode. What with al-Qaeda, Isis, Tuareg rebels and the Wagner mercenary group on the rampage, there's no need to imagine – or fake – a terrorist threat to this country. It's all around us.'

Hidouchi takes a deep breath. Mokrani and his kind disgust

her. But there's no point arguing about his role in past events. She is here to do business with him, whether she likes it or not. 'What is the connection with White Leopard?'

'Yanik Seghir is the connection. We reactivated our links with him in order to monitor Sonatrach's involvement in Solahara-related discussions. And we used him to help sow seeds of doubt within the organization about the merits of the scheme.'

'Successfully so.'

'At the time, yes. But now it occurs to me White Leopard ... may be Solahara by another name.'

'You could be right. White Leopard turns out to be the name of a French-registered company based in Toulon specializing in maritime and terrestrial communications infrastructure. Yanik Seghir is one of the directors.'

'Then there's no doubt he's betrayed us.' Mokrani lays his hands flat on the desk, as if to steady himself. 'Toulon to Mers-El Kébir would be a logical route for the undersea section of the cabling, secured by the French navy at their end and our navy at this end. And that stretch of empty desert Irmouli visited? The site for the main generating equipment, I imagine.' He sighs. 'Who was Irmouli's second travelling companion?'

'A senior DGSE officer. Erica Ménard.'

'That clinches it.' Mokrani looks at her wearily. 'The deal's been done. It just hasn't been announced yet.'

'And is it such a bad deal? Humanity has to wean itself off fossil fuels. Many would applaud this project.'

'Don't be naive, Agent Hidouchi. If White Leopard was guaranteed to be universally popular, it wouldn't have had to be veiled in secrecy. The Seghirs wouldn't have had to plot against me – or frame your friend Taleb for murder. Who are the people Lydia Seghir spent weeks sweet-talking at the Villa des Ormeaux? Terrorists would be my guess. Enemies of the republic, some manipulated by the Russians who – let's not forget – are using the Wagner Group to infiltrate and corrupt governments throughout the Sahel. Without guarantees that the solar arrays, the generators and the transmission cables won't be sabotaged, White Leopard would have gone the same way as Solahara. The fact that it hasn't suggests concessions have been made to ensure its safety and viability. But what concessions exactly? And to whom precisely? That's what you should be worrying about. There'll be a price – a heavy one – to pay for whatever's been agreed. We have to stop this while we still can.'

'I suspect the moment for that has passed, General.'

'No. Until it becomes public – until our government and the French actually announce their joint commitment to it – we have a chance.'

In principle, Hidouchi cannot frame an objection to a vast clean energy scheme transforming the Sahara. But neither can she deny that if Mokrani is right and White Leopard can only go ahead because terrorists and insurgents – some operating in league with Russian mercenaries – have been bought off, then the question has to be asked: what have they been bought off *with*?

Mokrani grabs his phone. 'Which hotel in Tamanrasset did Irmouli and his friends stay in, Agent Hidouchi?' he asks.

'The Oasis.'

'I have an idea.' Mokrani frowns in concentration as he presses various buttons, then makes a call. A few moments pass, then the call is answered. '*Sabah al-khair.* I would like to speak to one of your guests . . . Yanik Seghir . . . *Shukran* . . . I see . . . No, no message . . . *Shukran.*' He ends the call with a measured smile. 'It is as I suspected. Yanik Seghir is in Tamanrasset. He obviously sees no need for secrecy. He displays the arrogance of one who is certain of victory. As to why he is there, I believe Lydia Seghir intends to unveil White Leopard to the world in Tamanrasset. Or to allow the Minister of Energy to unveil it, doubtless promising untold riches for the poor and oppressed peoples of the far south when he does so, while some condescending representative of the French government stands smiling beside him. I know how politicians think. This will be a set piece event.'

'I should go there, General,' says Zoubiri. 'Before Seghir is joined by the other dogs he's running with.'

Mokrani nods. 'Henri Elasse and Erica Ménard may already be there. But I agree. We should take immediate action. We've been distracted long enough. I have to forget about Karim now. This is an attack on something bigger than my family. Will you go with Zoubiri, Agent Hidouchi?'

Hidouchi turns to look at Zoubiri. Neither likes the other. There is no pretence on the point. But she senses the truth – and a way out for Taleb – will only be found by tracking down Yanik Seghir. Circumstance is forcing her into an alliance of dire necessity with Mokrani and his principal lieutenant. She'd like to refuse. She loathes the idea of working with them. But if she does refuse . . .

'This amounts to a national security emergency,' says Mokrani. 'One which your superior at the DSS is ignoring. Are you willing to let the Seghirs sell our future without knowing who the buyers are or what they intend that future to be?'

Hidouchi's answer is quiet but unequivocal. 'No.'

'We can't go by road,' says Zoubiri. 'It'll take too long.'

'And you can't fly direct to Tamanrasset,' says Mokrani. 'There's too great a risk you'll be spotted on arrival. They may be on the lookout for an intervention from us.'

'Flying commercially at all is risky,' says Hidouchi.

'It's a job for Hafsi,' says Zoubiri.

'Call him.' A decisive note has entered Mokrani's voice. 'He's a skilled pilot I used to employ for special missions,' he explains for Hidouchi's benefit. 'I still do from time to time. And this is such a time.'

'I won't be working for you in Tamanrasset, General,' says Hidouchi. 'I need you to understand that.'

'I do. And Zoubiri won't be working for *you*. We should be clear. Our interests coincide . . . until they don't. That is how it's bound to be. You'll go even so?'

'Yes.'

'Yes.' Mokrani studies her for a moment. 'Of course you will.'

Bouras has started the working week in low spirits. He's still heard nothing from or about Taleb. The Marseille police can do no better than describe their investigation of the Irmouli killing as '*en continu*', whilst Kadri has opted himself and the DSS as a whole out of the investigation. Bouras fears the worst and his secretary's attempt to cheer him with a fresh pastry to accompany his morning coffee has failed to achieve its purpose.

A text message from Hidouchi therefore comes as a welcome development. He has no hesitation in agreeing to rendezvous with her in the Parc de la Liberté at noon, despite the short notice, and takes himself off there at once.

He finds her waiting for him by one of the park's fountains, which is, like much in the city's pleasure gardens in winter, not functioning. The palm trees standing lankly around it seem to echo his despondent mood. But Hidouchi looks energized and alert.

'Has something happened?' he asks hopefully, for surely anything would be better than the nothing he is currently condemned to.

'I'm pressed for time and there's a lot to explain, Director,' she says, keeping her voice low as they stand together. 'You need to know I've agreed to accompany Zoubiri to Tamanrasset.'

Bouras is taken aback. 'Why have you done that?'

'Yanik Seghir was formerly employed by General Mokrani as a freelance operative attached to Unit ninety-two. Now he's helping Lydia Seghir set up White Leopard, which as far as I can tell is a massive solar energy scheme designed to generate electricity from the Sahara and cable it across Algeria and under the Mediterranean to France – making a fortune for the directors of *Léopard Blanc SARL* in the process. It'll be a huge project involving high-level cooperation with the French government, ultimately replacing hydrocarbons as Algeria's principal source of state revenue.'

Bouras is confused. 'This can't be all about solar energy.'

'It's not. It's about the deals and trade-offs that support the project, negotiated by Lydia Seghir during the conference at the Villa des Ormeaux. Mokrani believes concessions have been made to terrorist and insurgent elements in the Sahel to ensure the generators and cables aren't sabotaged. Exactly what those concessions amount to isn't clear and won't be unless Yanik Seghir can be persuaded to reveal what they are. He's currently in Tamanrasset, where it's reasonable to suppose White Leopard will be formally unveiled in the near future.'

'And you're going after him – with Zoubiri?'

'Yes. Mokrani's darkest suspicion – which I can't help but share – is that Russia is manipulating many of these formerly hostile parties through the Wagner mercenary group. They've already infiltrated Mali and are doubtless eyeing up Niger and its uranium mines. France has lost its influence in the region and may see White Leopard as a way of retrieving the situation as well as fulfilling its zero carbon pledges. But if Russia sees it instead as a way of obtaining a permanent stranglehold over energy supplies to Europe, with Algeria doing its bidding . . .'

'Have you put any of this to Kadri?'

'Absolutely not. And you mustn't say anything to him either. He's explicitly told me to drop all inquiries. Just having this conversation with you is an act of gross disobedience. If he knew I'd talked to Mokrani as well there'd be severe repercussions. But I can't let White Leopard go ahead without first finding out what it commits the country to. Judging by the lengths the Seghirs have gone to in order to stop Mokrani challenging them there must be far-reaching consequences. And some of those consequences may be disastrous for the future of the republic.'

'You think Yanik Seghir will tell you what they are?'

'I intend to make sure he does. He's staying at the Oasis Hotel. I can't take a commercial flight to Tamanrasset. Kadri's forbidden me to go there. My name on a passenger list would be flagged up to him before I'd even landed. I'd probably be taken into custody at the airport. So, I have to travel with Zoubiri. A pilot who's undertaken illicit flights for Mokrani in the past will fly us to an airstrip a hundred kilometres or so north of Tamanrasset and we'll drive from there. We should be in the city by tonight. That's why this has to be a hurried meeting. The pilot will be waiting for us at an airfield near Zeralda one hour from now.'

'Zoubiri is a killer, Agent Hidouchi. You know that, don't you? You can't trust anything he or General Mokrani says.'

'I'm well aware of that. But Yanik Seghir is the key to this. I need to question him – and to make sure Zoubiri doesn't put a bullet through his head before I can. Since he's in Tamanrasset and travelling with Zoubiri is the only way I can get there without being detected . . .' Hidouchi shrugs. 'There's nothing else for it.'

'How will this help Taleb?'

'As things stand, I think discovering the truth behind White Leopard is the best I can do for Taleb.'

'The journey sounds . . . risky.'

'Working for the DSS *is* risky.'

'Well . . .' Bouras frowns as he tries to accommodate all that she's told him. 'Terrorists, insurgents and Russian mercenaries are DSS business. They're beyond the remit of the DGSN. I suppose . . . you're the best judge of the situation.'

'Communication will be difficult. Mokrani doesn't want me

telling anyone else what we're doing. And Zoubiri will try to enforce that while we're together.'

'The DGSN has limits to its authority, Agent Hidouchi. But it is a national force. So, even down in far distant Tamanrasset, I have some authority. If you need me to deploy it . . .'

She looks at him with a slight start of surprise, as if he's gone further than she expected he'd be willing to. 'I appreciate that, I really do. And if it comes to it . . .' She smiles rather than finish the thought. 'But let's hope it doesn't.'

'Yes.' Bouras nods. 'Let's hope.'

And hope he does – which is all he can do. Everything else is in Hidouchi's hands.

The Algerian coast appears as a line of cliffs through the gathering murk of late afternoon. Taleb finds little to gladden him in this first glimpse of home. True, he is relieved to have left France, but the challenges awaiting him back in his native land are formidable. He realizes with some dismay that the limbo he has been held in since Le Merz took him captive was in many ways easier to cope with than the hazardous realities he is about to engage with.

'Soon it will be time for you to deliver on your promises, Taleb,' says the Dutchman with his hard-to-read smile.

Night is falling rapidly as the *Etoile de la mer* noses into the small harbour at Sidi Lakhdar. The quay is deserted. No one appears to be paying any attention to their arrival. They tie up and the crew begin to busy themselves with unloading their cargo of shellfish. The skipper barely acknowledges Taleb and the Dutchman as they step ashore, clad in yellow oilskin coats. They begin walking slowly towards the roadway beyond the sheds serving the harbour, from which lamps cast sallow light across the water slapping against the quay and stretch the shadows of the two men behind them.

'You see the car parked beyond the sheds?' asks the Dutchman as they go.

Taleb squints ahead. 'Yes.'

'That's our ride. The driver's called Mohamed.' Since that's the commonest Algerian male first name by some way, Taleb considers it as likely to be a pseudonym as the man's real name. 'He'll need directions. Where are we going?'

'As I told you, I'll have to make a phone call before we leave.'

'OK.' The Dutchman halts, takes Taleb's phone out of his pocket and hands it over. 'Tap in the number, then give it back to me.'

Taleb obeys, entering Chahira Meslem's number. The Dutchman examines it and appears satisfied. He presses a button and returns the phone to Taleb. 'It's ringing. Speak to your friend, Taleb. Any tricks – any coded warnings – I'll know. And you won't like what'll happen then.'

'No tricks,' says Taleb. And he means it. Loath as he is to involve Chahira, he can see nothing for it but to do his best to retrieve whatever it is Meslem obtained from Kasdi Merbah all those years ago. Giving the Dutchman the slip looks wildly unfeasible. Taleb's revised plan is to talk him into letting him move against the Seghirs through official channels. How realistic that is depends on the documents Chahira has said she will surrender to him and no one else. Nothing is certain. Nothing is remotely predictable.

The call is answered. 'Taleb?'

'Yes. How did you . . .'

'I logged your number last time you phoned.'

'Ah, of course.'

'Are you back in the country?'

'Yes. That's . . .'

'Why you called?' Chahira seems to be several thoughts ahead of him already.

'Exactly. I . . . my investigation has reached a crucial stage.

I'd be very grateful if you could let me see . . . the material we discussed.'

'I can do that, certainly. Now you're back. When would you like to come here?'

'Would . . . this evening be all right?'

'This evening?'

'If it's . . . convenient. The matter's become . . . rather urgent.'

'Well, luckily for you I'm not babysitting tonight, although my nephew and his wife seem to think I have no other purpose in life. So, when should I expect you?'

Taleb checks the time and swiftly calculates how long it will take to cover the distance to Cherchell. 'Around . . . nine o'clock, depending on traffic.'

'Don't worry if you're late, Taleb. I'm something of a nightbird. I'll send you the address for your SatNav. You do have one, don't you? Samir was terribly resistant to technology and I can easily imagine you being the same.'

'A SatNav?' Taleb signals his uncertainty to the Dutchman, who nods emphatically. 'Yes, of course.' Though, ironically, if Taleb were driving his own car Chahira's instinct would be correct.

'I'm sending it through now. I'll see you later.'

'Yes. Thanks so much for . . . seeing me at such short notice.'

'Anything for Samir's right-hand man, you know that.'

'Even so . . .'

'There's really no need to thank me. You may regret taking on this burden when you see what it involves.'

'I don't really have much choice in the matter. It's a question of . . .'

'Duty?'

'Yes. Duty.' The weight of the word settles in his mind. 'That's what it is.'

'Later, then, Taleb.'

'Yes. Later.'

She rings off and, a second later, the address pings through. Taleb hands the phone back to the Dutchman. 'That's where we're going. It's in Cherchell, on the coast about a hundred and fifty kilometres east of here.'

'We'd better start moving, then.' The Dutchman pockets the phone. 'On the way you can tell me who she is.'

'I never said it was a woman.'

'The way you spoke to her made it obvious. A woman. And not young. You respect her. What's your connection with her?'

'She's the widow of my former superior officer.'

'Leading a peaceful life in her old age?'

'Yes.'

'Which you'd like her to go on leading?'

'Of course.'

'Well, that'll be up to you this evening, Taleb. Get me what the boss wants and there'll be no problem. The widow can go back to her armchair. Otherwise . . . it could be a very different story.'

Algeria is the largest country in Africa following the breakup of Sudan – a vast pentagle at the top of every map of the continent. Hidouchi knows this as a geographical fact. But the emptiness of the country south of the Saharan Atlas mountains means that psychologically, for her as for most Algerians, the country comprises in practice the coastal belt and the immediate interior. Her visits to the desert that stretches beyond that to the remote borders of distant lands in the Sahel have been few and fleeting, all of them dictated by professional necessity. It's an alien place for which she feels no affinity, inhabited by people she's quite certain acknowledge no kinship with the likes of her.

Professional necessity is driving her on this latest journey also. She has no fixed idea about how she'll manage their encounter with Yanik Seghir when it comes, nor what Zoubiri's intentions may be, except that they're unlikely to coincide with hers. He has remained silent throughout the long flight south and the pilot he's hired, Hafsi, has been largely mute as well. There will be time to agree a plan, of course, assuming agreement is possible. But Hidouchi is thinking hard about what may happen in Tamanrasset. There was no need for Bouras to warn her not to trust Zoubiri. She regards him as a snake that will eventually strike at her. A clash is more or less inevitable. When it comes, she must be ready.

They're on the second leg of the flight now, after a refuelling stop in El Golea. Their destination is an obscure landing strip near In Amguel, used, according to Hafsi, by people who need to travel in the Sahara quickly but unnoticed. Smugglers is Hidouchi's guess, though Hafsi refers to them merely as traders. And he has already organized a trade with them: a durable four-wheel-drive vehicle in exchange for a large wad of US dollars. Algerian dinars will not suffice.

The sun is growing ever lower in the sky, corrugating the sea of sand below them with deep shadows and softening the golden crests of the dunes. They are in the heart of the desert, far from anything Hidouchi recognizes as familiar. There is no turning back. They are bound for Tamanrasset – and a collision with their enemies. They are bound for a reckoning.

Hidouchi cannot predict the nature of that reckoning. But she knows it will happen. And she knows it has to.

The car – a big old Mercedes – is heading east along the corniche road, the villages nestled at the feet of the cliffs below them marked by clustered pinpricks of light in the darkness that is mostly sea. Mohamed says nothing, concentrating on the windings of the road ahead. Taleb smokes cigarettes at regular intervals, turning over in his mind how he can best protect

Chahira Meslem when they reach the end of their journey. The Dutchman sleeps. There is nothing to interrupt his rest. For him this is all in a night's work.

Suddenly the headlamps pick out some graffiti scrawled in Arabic on a wall they pass: تعيش فرنسا

Taleb smiles to himself at the meaning, which he imagines is not meant to be taken literally. He murmurs the phrase under his breath, savouring its irony.

'What did you say?' asks the Dutchman, evidently not as deeply asleep as Taleb has supposed.

'I read aloud the slogan scrawled on a wall back there. *Tahya faransa.* Long live France.'

'It amuses you?'

'Not really.'

'Do you think the French had a hand in the Boudiaf assassination?'

'What makes you ask such a question?'

'Well, I'd never even heard of Boudiaf until the boss told me the documents we're after may implicate Yanik Seghir in the plot to kill him. I've read up about it on the Internet since. The subject's awash with conspiracy theories. Several involve French complicity. You're a policeman. What do you think?'

'I'm an *Algerian* policeman. We don't think.'

'But you *do* think, don't you, Taleb? That's your problem, isn't it? You can't stop yourself. So, tell me. This guy they have rotting in prison for killing Boudiaf. Did he act alone?'

'No one acts alone in Algeria.'

'Come on. What's the truth about the assassination – in your opinion? Who was behind it?'

'The truth will never be known. *That* is the truth.'

Taleb is surprised by the all-encompassing validity of the words that have just come out of his mouth. It is as he has said it is.

But it is also as the Dutchman has suggested. Some – including

Taleb – are condemned to go on looking for the truth, even if it can never be found.

The dim lights of the airstrip appeared bright against the inky blackness of the surrounding desert. The descent was smooth, but the landing was bumpy, though Hafsi remained apparently unconcerned throughout the manoeuvre.

Their arrival draws a taciturn individual, most of his face covered by a scarf, out of one of the sheds flanking the strip. He exchanges a minimum of words with Hafsi to confirm all is as agreed, takes delivery of his promised envelope full of dollars and waves in the direction of a Land Cruiser with raised wheelbase parked next to the sheds.

'That's your ride,' says Hafsi to Hidouchi and Zoubiri as they clamber from the plane.

A nearly full moon shines down and a greater abundance of stars than Hidouchi can ever recall seeing seems to bend above her with the curvature of the earth. It is cold and clear and very very still.

'You're in luck,' Hafsi goes on. 'There's no wind. So, you shouldn't run into any sandstorms between here and Tam.' His economy with words extends to abbreviating Tamanrasset to one syllable. 'I'll wait here until noon the day after tomorrow. If you're not back by then . . .'

'We'll be back,' says Zoubiri. 'Well, I will. What about you, Hidouchi?'

She nods. 'You can count on it.'

Shortly after the Mercedes passes a sign showing seventeen kilometres remaining to Cherchell, the Dutchman instructs Mohamed to pull over. 'We're getting out,' he tells Taleb.

They exit into the stillness of the night. Taleb can hear the sea, but it's invisible, a liquid presence somewhere below them. They walk a short distance from the car. The Dutchman lights a cigarette. Taleb does the same.

'We need to agree arrangements for when we arrive at your friend's house,' says the Dutchman in a matter-of-fact tone. 'To avoid . . . misunderstandings.'

'What did you have in mind?'

'What's her name? It's time you told me.'

'Chahira Meslem.'

'And the name of her late husband?'

'Samir Meslem. Retired superintendent.'

'OK. Now, this is how it's going to be. You'll enter the house alone. If everything goes smoothly, Chahira won't meet me at all. It would be best for her if everything *did* go smoothly. You understand?'

'I understand.'

'You'll have your phone with you. The line to my phone will be open, so I'll hear everything that's said. Any interruptions to the line, any indication that you've left the phone in one room and moved to another, any lengthy silence . . . I'll come in. Again, it would be best for Chahira if I didn't have to do that. Get the documents and bring them out to me. Then we'll drive away. Job done. Is that all clear?'

'As a mountain stream.'

'Good. I like plans that work, Taleb. And the simpler a plan is the likelier it is to work. Just so long as those who are party to it stick to what's agreed. You're going to do that, aren't you?'

'Yes. I am.'

By now, Taleb has concluded that doing exactly what he's been told to do is the only rational course open to him. It might be different if his life was the only one on the line. But it's Chahira's life as well. He's put her in danger simply by arranging to visit her. It's up to him to ensure the danger never materializes. What do the documents matter anyway? He's already told the Dutchman that the truth will – can – never be known. So, all he's doing is following the logic of his own assertion.

'Chahira mustn't be harmed.'

'She won't be. Unless . . .'

'There'll be no unlesses. I'll make sure of it.'

'You do that, Taleb.' The Dutchman pats him on the shoulder. 'Let's make this a nice quiet night.'

The Land Cruiser rumbles through the night on the empty road south towards Tamanrasset. Hidouchi is at the wheel, driving carefully, eyes trained ahead. Mountains loom above them to the east, blotting out the starlit sky. Soon they will have to agree how to proceed once they reach the Hotel Oasis. But Zoubiri offers nothing as the journey continues.

Then, quite suddenly, he says, 'The airstrip back there was built by the French to give them access to an underground nuclear test site they constructed in the desert. Did you know that?'

'I've heard about the tests, yes.'

'They conducted one just a couple of months before independence that went horribly wrong. There was a huge release of radioactivity, contaminating soldiers, scientists and local villagers. A couple of French government ministers were among those affected. One of them died of cancer a few years later. I suppose there's some justice in that.'

'Why are you telling me this?'

'It's a warning. The French already knew they were leaving Algeria when they carried out the test. Quite a parting gift.'

'Presumably they didn't expect it to go wrong.'

'It always goes wrong when you let the French in. But we don't seem to have learnt that lesson, do we? If White Leopard goes ahead, they'll be back, ruining our country all over again.'

'The country your generation has run so successfully, you mean?'

'You think you have all the answers, don't you? You think you're better than us.'

'I think we should concentrate on the job in hand. If White Leopard's as rotten a deal as you believe, I'll do everything I can to stop it.'

'Yanik Seghir is a traitor. That's all you need to know.'

'You think I'll treat him too gently?'

'*I* won't. You can take that as certain.'

'We'll deal with him as circumstances dictate.'

'I already know the circumstances.'

'I'm an accredited DSS agent. You're just a private citizen. You're going to have to accept that this will be handled my way.'

'Sure.' Hidouchi senses Zoubiri is smiling as he speaks. 'We'll handle it your way. Of course we will.'

The SatNav has led to a quiet area of small, detached villas in a street running alongside a walled-off area of Roman ruins. They pull up a short distance from Chahira Meslem's house – one of the smallest, sandstone and terracotta, with a gated entrance to a tiny front garden. The porch is overhung by a pair of palms, their fronds filtering the light that gleams from a lantern above the door, lit, Taleb suspects, specifically to welcome him.

'All set?' The Dutchman asks in the silence that follows the dying of the Mercedes' engine.

'Yes,' Taleb replies. 'I'm ready.'

'Remember to speak into your phone when you're at the gate.'

'Will do.'

'Off you go, then.'

Taleb climbs out of the car into the quiet of the evening. The moon is riding high above Cherchell. As he walks along the street, Taleb prays to the god he no longer believes in that all will go well this night.

He reaches the gate of Chahira Meslem's house and raises his phone to his ear. 'Can you hear me?' he says softly.

'I can hear you,' the Dutchman replies. 'Carry on.'

'OK.'

The gate creaks slightly as Taleb opens it. He closes it carefully behind him, pauses for a moment, then heads up the path towards the porch.

And the door opens ahead of him.

FIFTEEN

TALEB REMEMBERS AS SOON AS HE SEES CHAHIRA THAT SHE'S ALWAYS favoured more westernized dress than many Algerian women of her generation, seldom wearing a headscarf, never a veil and generally resembling a sophisticated if conservative Parisian lady. This evening she is in loose trousers and a plain thigh-length top. Her hair is whiter than he recalls, which is no surprise, but her smiling face seems hardly altered by time.

'Come in, Taleb,' she says, holding the front door open for him. 'Did you hear the gate?'

'Yes. Its creak is very distinctive. I was expecting you, of course, so I put in my hearing aid. Without it I'm rather deaf, which is convenient at times, though inconvenient at others. I only know the phone's ringing when I see it flashing.'

Taleb steps into the entrance hall and follows Chahira into a comfortably furnished lounge. Thick rugs cover the tiled floor and a fire is burning to ward off the nocturnal chill. A small dog of no breed Taleb is able to recognize rises from its fireside berth and emits a cautious yap.

'Be quiet, Mimi. Taleb is a friend.' Chahira beams at Taleb.

'The silly little thing's been behaving very oddly this evening. Barking at nothing, running in and out of the room. I don't know what to do with her.'

Taleb attempts to pet Mimi, with mixed results. 'Good company for you, I'm sure.'

'Irritating company, sometimes. Another reason why I sometimes prefer deafness. Now, would you like a cup of hot chocolate? I often make some around now.'

What Taleb would truly like is a glass of the Dutchman's schnapps. But hot chocolate it will have to be. 'That would be lovely.'

'Sit down while I prepare it. And don't worry. Mimi will soon get used to you being here.'

Taleb sits down on the couch as Chahira leaves the room, but almost immediately stands up again and begins walking around. Over by the window there's a table he remembers from visits to the Meslems' apartment in Algiers. Inlaid in the tabletop is a chessboard and to one side of it there's a sliding hatch he'd probably miss if he'd never seen it open. Beneath the hatch is a well for the storage of chess pieces. They're probably there still, he reckons, though never used. He doubts chess has been played at this table since Samir Meslem died.

Taleb goes back to the couch and sits down again. He places his phone on the étagère next to it, where he judges there will be good reception. Beside it stands a silver-framed photograph of the Meslems on their wedding day fifty years or more in the past. Logs crackle in the fireplace. Mimi wanders over and sniffs suspiciously at his trouser legs. Perhaps she can scent the sea he travelled over. He pats her gently on the head and she doesn't object. He seems to have been granted provisional approval. He wonders if Chahira would mind him lighting a cigarette. He decides not to chance it.

Several minutes pass uneventfully. Then Chahira returns,

carrying a tray. She sets it down on the low table in front of the couch and pours the hot chocolate. It looks as if she takes it rich and very dark. Then she sits down in the armchair between the couch and the windows.

'It is good to see you again, Taleb,' she says, smiling warmly. 'Though I sense all is not well with you.'

'The case I'm engaged in is . . . difficult.' He sips his hot chocolate. 'It's reopened a lot of old wounds.'

'Ah. In this country such wounds never really heal, do they?'

'Apparently not.'

'The case arose from your . . . television appearance?'

'In part, yes.'

'And you're here . . .'

'You mentioned some . . . documents Superintendent Meslem retained from an inquiry . . . many years ago.'

'I'm fairly certain I didn't specify documents when we spoke on the telephone.'

'What else could it be? Police work back then was all about paper records.'

'Well, you're right. Documents were what the man who broke in last summer was clearly looking for. Documents he didn't find.'

'But you have them?'

She nods. 'Yes. I have them. I don't know what they actually contain. I've disciplined myself never to study them. Samir more than once told me, "The less you know the safer you are." And he wanted me to be safe, even after his death, perhaps especially then. So, I suppose all I really need to ask you, Taleb, is whether you think it prudent to delve into such matters.'

'Almost certainly not prudent. But . . . necessary.'

'I understand. That is, I don't. But you are driven by the same impulse that so often led Samir into . . . professional difficulties. A quest for the truth, yes?'

'You make my motives sound nobler than they are.'

'I doubt that, I seriously do. But . . . if you want the documents Samir retained . . . you should have them. There's no one else with a better claim to them. No one else, to be honest, with any claim at all. You were his deputy. He trusted you. And his trust remains with you to this day.'

'How was it the man who broke in failed to find them?'

'He didn't know where to look. Perhaps because he didn't know how devoted Samir was to the game of chess.'

'I'm not sure . . .'

Chahira looks over her shoulder. 'The chess table, Taleb. Perhaps you didn't notice it when you came in.'

'Actually, I did. I remember it from your apartment in Algiers. But . . .'

'I'll show you.'

She stands up and moves across to the chess table. Taleb follows her. She slides open the hatch concealing the well in which the pieces are stored and presses down on the partition dividing the black pieces from the white. Taleb hears a click. And the board he thought was inlaid in the tabletop rises slightly from the surrounding surface. Then Chahira edges her fingers beneath the board's outer edges and lifts it free.

There's a well beneath the board, shallower than the one containing the pieces, but deep enough to house several manila files. The topmost one bears the telltale initials *DRS* and has been stamped twice in red. The first stamp reads *DOSSIER CLOS* – closed file; the second *CONTENU NON DIVULGUER* – contents not to be disclosed.

'This is what you've come for, I assume,' says Chahira.

'Yes. It is.' Taleb stretches past her and raises the cover of the first file. Something about the paper on which the documents are printed and the character of the printing itself tells him these aren't photocopies illicitly taken by Youcef Ghezala – they're originals. Then he notices a heading on one page typed in capitals: *PROJET FOUR A BRIQUES* – Operation Brick Kiln. And he remembers that during his long Moroccan exile before returning to Algeria to become president in 1992 Mohamed Boudiaf ran a brickworks.

At that moment Mimi springs up and starts barking. She races towards the half-open door. 'Come back here and be quiet,' Chahira calls after her. 'You're being a nuisance.'

Then Mimi stops. The door is pushed wide open and a man strides into the room. It's not the Dutchman, as Taleb for a split second supposes, though he's similarly dressed, but a tall, muscular man with crewcut hair and a scar on his left cheek. He's Urtan Seghir.

And he's pointing a gun at them.

Tamanrasset by night is largely deserted. Hidouchi and Zoubiri arrive from the north, encountering the streets and buildings of the city as an abrupt transition from the vast emptiness through which they've driven. The SatNav takes them directly to the Hotel Oasis, a medium height tower block of banal design, with a large neon sign on which the middle *s* has failed so that the hotel's name appears to be the *Oa is*.

Hidouchi drives into the car park. There are barely half a dozen vehicles dotted around a space that would accommodate fifty. The hotel's evidently quiet.

She pulls a likeness of Yanik Seghir up on her phone, culled from his Sonatrach personnel file, and shows it to Zoubiri. 'This is the man we're looking for, right?'

Seghir was in his late thirties when the photograph was taken: bearded, long-faced, with a cool, level gaze. Zoubiri nods. 'That's him.'

'I ran this through an ageing program we have to give us an idea of what he'll look like now.'

She scrolls to two computer-generated images of Yanik Seghir in his late fifties, one with the beard, one without. In both his hair is greyer and thinner, his face gaunter, his eyes more hooded. The unyielding gaze remains the same, though. There's no programming that away.

'I'll know him,' says Zoubiri with some conviction. 'You don't need to worry about that.'

'Reassure me that I don't need to worry about what you'll do when we meet him either.'

'What I do depends on what you do.'

'I intend to question him about White Leopard. I want information. That's my priority.'

'Sounds good. As far as it goes.'

'I'll be the judge of how far it goes. The hotel staff will cooperate once they see my DSS ID. I need your cooperation as well.'

'You'll have it, of course.'

'Don't foul this up, Zoubiri. We'll have one chance to take him by surprise and extract the truth.'

'You're in charge, Agent Hidouchi. I'll follow your lead.'

He'll follow it until he decides to stop following it. That's the reality, as Hidouchi is well aware. But, as she's already said, extracting information from Yanik Seghir is what matters now. After they've extracted it . . . is a different situation.

Zoubiri sighs impatiently. 'What are we waiting for?'

'Nothing,' Hidouchi replies briskly, opening the door of the car. 'Let's go.'

'Get this dog to shut up or I'll shoot it,' snaps Urtan Seghir as Mimi stands on her hind legs, yapping at him.

'Come here, Mimi,' Chahira calls.

The urgency of her tone does the trick. Mimi turns and waddles across to her mistress, casting hostile glances back at Seghir as she goes.

Rather like her dog, Chahira appears unintimidated by having a gun trained on her. As she stoops to restrain Mimi, she glares at Seghir. 'How did you get in?'

'I came in the back an hour or so ago. I don't think you hear too well, madame.'

'You tapped her phone?' asks Taleb, who can think of no other explanation for Seghir's arrival on the scene.

'That's right, uncle. I knew you were on your way. Which meant the old lady here would dig out the papers from wherever they were hidden. Under the chessboard? Very clever. But it looks like you've been checkmated now.' Seghir pulls a folded black plastic sack out of his pocket and tosses it across the room towards them. 'Put them in there.'

'These documents implicate your father in the Boudiaf assassination, don't they?'

'Never mind who they implicate in what. Just put them in the bag.' Seghir waggles the gun alarmingly. 'Or I'll shoot you all and do it myself.'

'OK.' Taleb holds up his hands appeasingly, steps slowly forward and picks up the bag, which he unfolds more clumsily than he needs to.

'Get on with it.'

Taleb is wondering how long it will be before the Dutchman intervenes, as he surely will. He flaps the bag open, scoops up the files and drops them in, contriving to snag one on the edge of the bag, scattering several documents across the floor. It is a calculated delaying tactic.

And Seghir doesn't take it well. 'Are you just clumsy or acting smart, Taleb? Put *all* the papers in the bag *now*. Or I swear I'll shoot one of you.'

'All right, all right. Sorry. It might help if you lowered the gun. That would make me less nervous.'

Seghir doesn't lower the gun. '*Do it.*'

Taleb obeys, gathering up the loose documents and dropping them into the bag. He glimpses a chart showing the layout of a building – Maison de la Culture, Annaba, according to the heading: the very building in which Boudiaf was assassinated. It's all there, he has no doubt – the full and dreadful record of what was done, by Yanik Seghir and others, General Mokrani principal among them, thirty years ago.

'You know who this man is?' asks Chahira suddenly.

'Er . . . yes.'

'What is his name?'

'Don't answer that,' snaps Seghir. 'I have no reason to kill you, madame. Don't give me one.'

'You should be ashamed of yourself. Invading my house. Stealing my late husband's property.'

'He had no right to possess such material.'

'He had every right.'

'Just take it and go,' says Taleb, doing his best to defuse the situation. He knots the bag and tosses it across the room. When *is* the Dutchman going to act? Why hasn't he acted already? Is he waiting for Seghir to leave? Taleb is beginning to worry he's decided to let events inside the house take their course.

'My father is trying to serve the best interests of his country,' says Seghir, riled by Chahira's reproaches. 'I can't let him be stopped by mistakes he may or may not have made in the past.'

Mistakes? Taleb is tempted for a second to protest. The assassination of the President, carefully plotted and ruthlessly carried out, can hardly be written off as a mistake. But all he really wants Seghir to do, now he has what he wants, is to go, so he holds his tongue.

'You have something to say, Taleb?' Seghir challenges him, as if he's read his mind.

Taleb shakes his head. 'No.'

'Are you sure about that?' Seghir's grip on the gun in his hand visibly tightens.

Then, just as Taleb has begun to fear it will never happen, there's a loud crash from the direction of the front door. Seghir swings round, but the Dutchman's too quick for him. He lunges into the room, right arm outstretched, and jabs a gun beneath Seghir's jaw before the other man can train his own weapon on the newcomer.

'Drop it,' he says, raising his voice to make himself heard over a renewed bout of barking by Mimi. 'Do it right now or I'll blow your head off.'

Taleb for one has no doubt the Dutchman means what he says. Seghir appears to feel the same. He obeys without a word. The gun clunks heavily to the floor.

'Move the gun away from him and secure his wrists, Taleb,' says the Dutchman, plucking some tie-straps out of his pocket with his free hand and tossing them across the room.

Taleb steps forward, kicks the gun away beneath the low table in front of the couch and picks up the ties. He pinions Seghir's arms behind his back and fastens his wrists tightly together. Then he steps clear. By now, at least for the moment, Mimi has stopped barking. Chahira has picked her up and is holding her in her arms.

'Forgive the intrusion, Madame Meslem,' says the Dutchman, with a bizarre excess of courtesy. 'It wasn't my intention to inflict myself on you. I planned to take charge of the documents only after Taleb had left with them.'

Taleb looks at Chahira. 'I'm sorry. There was . . . no alternative.'

'You can believe him on that,' says the Dutchman. 'My employer can't allow such material to enter the public domain . . . unredacted, shall we say? . . . and therefore . . . it has to go with me.'

Chahira says nothing, though the look of disappointment in her face cuts Taleb to the quick. 'I am sorry,' he repeats.

She nods. 'I know you are.'

'As it turns out,' the Dutchman resumes, jabbing the gun ever harder into the soft flesh beneath Seghir's jaw, 'this evening has delivered me more than I could ever have hoped for. You'll appreciate the irony, Taleb, I'm sure. The Seghirs faked a kidnapping to neutralize General Mokrani. Now I'm going to play them at their own game. Except that this kidnapping won't be a fake. And the ransom won't be anything as cheap as money. You're coming with me, Urtan. Urtan *is* your name, isn't it?'

'Yes,' gasps Seghir, his head pushed back by the thrust of the Dutchman's gun.

'Do you have any parcel tape, madame?'

'What?' Chahira sounds bemused.

'Or Sellotape perhaps?'

'Sellotape? Yes. In there.' She nods towards a bureau in the far corner of the room.

'Fetch it, would you, Taleb?'

Taleb crosses to the bureau and lowers the flap. Amidst an orderly arrangement of stationery and paperwork, he sees no Sellotape.

'It's in the right-hand drawer,' says Chahira.

Taleb opens the drawer and finds the tape. He holds it up.

'OK,' says the Dutchman. 'You have a handkerchief, I think. Stuff it in Urtan's mouth and tape it in place. Then we'll be ready to go.'

Taleb pulls out his handkerchief and steps across to where Seghir and the Dutchman are standing. Urtan's face is sheened with sweat. He's breathing heavily. His eyes radiate enmity as Taleb pushes the handkerchief between his teeth until he gags. Then Taleb tears off a long strip of tape and sticks it across Seghir's mouth and cheeks. He follows this with a second strip, and a third.

'That looks good enough,' pronounces the Dutchman. 'We're leaving now, madame. Taleb, you go first. Take the bag, but leave your phone here. You can collect it later. I'll follow with Urtan. Taleb will be returning later, madame. But he'll travel with us as far as the edge of town. If there's any sign you've called the local police before we let him go ... I'm afraid there'll be a killing as well as a kidnapping for them to investigate. Why don't you sit down and finish your hot chocolate while you wait? Again, my apologies for the intrusion. I hope I haven't upset your dog unduly. Blame Urtan. He has no manners. I may be able to teach him some ... during the time we spend together.'

'I won't phone anyone until Taleb returns,' says Chahira with an emphatic nod.

She's breathing shallowly and there's a tremor in her voice. She's clutching Mimi very tightly. Whether this is for the dog's benefit or her own Taleb doesn't know. But he knows he's responsible for their distress. He brought the Dutchman here – and, unwittingly, Urtan Seghir. He's ultimately to blame for everything that's happened.

'It's all right, Taleb,' says Chahira, apparently intuiting his thoughts. 'No harm's been done.'

No physical harm, it's true, which is a mercy. But the secret documents her late husband went to such lengths to hide are lost now, retrieved by those whose guilt they lay bare. This is the sum of Taleb's achievement. Chahira and Mimi are alive. And so is he. But something has died even so.

'Pick up the bag, Taleb,' says the Dutchman. 'It's time we were on our way.'

The lobby of the Hotel Oasis is a vault of shadows, with the guest-room floors towering above in a progressively dimmer spiral. Canned music of unimpeachable blandness is playing softly. The clerk behind the desk, who looks to have perfected the art of sleeping with his eyes open, stirs himself minimally as Hidouchi and Zoubiri approach.

Sight of Hidouchi's DSS ID swiftly induces full alertness, however. 'Is there a . . . problem?' he asks in the tone of one who already fears he knows the answer.

'Show me your guest list,' Hidouchi replies unsmilingly.

He taps obligingly at the keyboard of his computer and swivels the screen to show them the result. Five names appear, among them Seghir, Yanik. Hidouchi doesn't see Patou, Françoise, which suggests Erica Ménard hasn't yet arrived, or is staying elsewhere. The name Henri Elasse is also absent.

'You have only five guests?'

The clerk shrugs. 'It's a quiet time.'

'Give us Yanik Seghir's room number.'

'Ah . . . three one nine. Two floors up.'

'Is he in?'

'Yes. That is, I think so. He came in a few hours ago and . . . hasn't left since.' He checks the key cabinet behind him. 'His key isn't here, so . . .'

'You have a spare?'

'Yes. But . . .'

'Hand it over.'

'Maybe I should . . . call the manager.'

'Is he on site?'

'Er . . . no.'

'No point, then. This is an official visit. Obstructing us in the execution of our duty would be a serious matter.'

'I . . . I'm not obstructing you.'

'Give us the spare key to his room, then.'

'Right.' He delves in a drawer beneath the desk and produces a key with 319 written on a tag attached to it.

Hidouchi takes it from him. 'Thank you. Tell me, are the doors of the guest rooms fitted with safety chains?'

'Er, yes, they are.'

It seems the bolt-cutters Zoubiri has brought from the car may be needed, though Hidouchi hopes not. 'OK. We'll deal with the situation from here. You don't need to do anything.'

'In fact,' Zoubiri cuts in, leaning over the desk for emphasis, 'you *need* to do absolutely nothing. Understood? A phone call to Seghir's room while we're on our way up, for instance? Bad idea.'

'Why . . . would I do that?'

'Who knows? I can only tell you why you *shouldn't*. Because you'll have me to reckon with if you mess us about in any way.' Zoubiri pats the clerk on his cheek so heavily it's almost a slap. 'Got it?'

The clerk nods energetically, eyes wide in alarm. He's got it.

'Pull over,' says the Dutchman.

Mohamed obeys. The Mercedes comes to a halt a short distance from the entrance to the town's racecourse, although Taleb only knows this because he can see its name – *Hippodrome du Caroubier* – above the gate. The course itself is blanketed in darkness.

The Dutchman turns and looks at him over the back of his seat. 'You can get out, Taleb. Our dealings end here.'

'What are you going to do with your hostage?' Urtan Seghir is confined to the boot of the car and has given up kicking at the lid, to judge by the silence that has fallen behind Taleb.

'I'm going to use him to persuade his father that he should do whatever he needs to do in order to stop White Leopard in its tracks. There's a number for Yanik on Urtan's phone, so contact isn't going to be a problem. I'll be giving him a call in the very near future.'

'And if he does as you ask?'

'Then the boss will tell me what to do with Urtan. But don't worry. My employer isn't an unreasonable man. If he were I wouldn't be letting you go, would I?'

'What about the documents?'

'My understanding is they're likely to contain damaging information about some of the boss's best clients, so obviously it'll be for him to decide what happens to them. But I doubt he'll be making them available to the media.' Taleb senses the Dutchman is smiling, though his face is in shadow. 'Don't look so downcast. You're coming out of this surprisingly well.'

'It doesn't feel like it.'

'No? Well, it will when you've had a chance to reflect on the alternatives. Out you get.'

Taleb clambers out of the car, which accelerates away. He watches its rear lights until a curve in the road carries them out of sight.

He lights a cigarette as he stands in the darkness that stretches between the widely separated street lamps. The night is cold. And there's a long walk ahead of him. With Chahira Meslem and the ghost of his old chief to be faced at the end of it. But he's alive and he's free. As the Dutchman said, it could be worse. Although he is painfully aware it could also be better.

For a few fleeting moments he held the truth about the Boudiaf assassination in his hands. His improvised plan was to return most of the files to their hiding place, surrendering a random few to the Dutchman. But Urtan Seghir's intervention ruined that. And now all Taleb has is the meagre consolation of his personal survival.

He can see a bus stop close to the racecourse entrance and there's another on the other side of the road, which is the direction that leads back into the centre of town. He crosses the road and walks along to the stop.

There's no timetable displayed. And hardly any traffic. He suspects the likelihood of a bus appearing is remote. But he lingers there for a few moments as he finishes his cigarette and wonders if the local public transport system will come to his rescue.

It doesn't. But a beaten-up old Zastava virtually identical to the first car he ever drove comes sputtering along and pulls up beside him. The driver – who looks like a man of Taleb's own age – leans across and winds down the passenger window. 'You've missed the last bus, my friend. Where are you going?'

Taleb names the street Chahira Meslem lives in.

'That's not far out of my way. I'll take you. Jump in.'

Taleb accepts the offer eagerly. 'This is kind of you,' he says as they set off, the car engine emitting the familiar note of an unlubricated sewing machine.

'It's no problem. We're the same generation, I'd guess. There's no one else to help the likes of us . . . except the likes of us. Do you live in Cherchell?'

'No. I'm just . . . visiting.'

'Friends? Relatives?'

'Neither. I came here . . . looking for the truth.'

'Have you found it?'

'Sort of. I found it and then I lost it. Somehow it . . . slipped through my fingers.'

'That sounds careless. Although it could also be fortunate.'

'How could it be that?'

'In this country, my friend, ignorance of the truth is the surest guarantee of a contented old age. Which is what I wish you as well as myself.'

Hidouchi leads the way as she and Zoubiri approach room 319 along a silent, drably decorated, dimly lit corridor at the Hotel Oasis. She hopes Yanik Seghir is already in bed, the better to surprise him. At all events, she's confident of taking him unawares. She signals to Zoubiri to tread softly as she nears the door.

She slides the key gently into the lock and slowly turns it. Then she turns the handle, just as gently, and edges the door open.

The safety chain isn't over. And the room is in darkness. Now is the time for speed. She thrusts the door fully open and, gun clasped in both hands, steps inside. Zoubiri follows, flicking on the light as he enters.

The room is small and minimally furnished. The bed hasn't been slept in. Yanik Seghir isn't there. This she feels sure of at a glance, though she checks the shower room to be certain while Zoubiri pulls open the rickety wardrobe. Seghir isn't hiding in either.

'He knew we were coming,' says Zoubiri disgustedly, tossing the bolt-cutters onto the bed.

'Not necessarily,' says Hidouchi, emerging from the shower room.

'That cockroach down in reception must have warned him.'

'The cowering clerk? I doubt he has the nerve for anything like that.'

'We'll find out what he has the nerve for.'

'Hold on.' Hidouchi picks up a laptop lying on the bedside table. She opens it and the screen comes to life. 'Seghir would surely have taken this with him – or at least turned it off – if he knew we were on our way up.' There are several folders displayed on the screen. One of them, she instantly notices, is entitled *Léopard Blanc*. She clicks on it.

'You can stay here playing with his computer while he makes his escape if you want,' growls Zoubiri. 'I'm going to try and cut him off.'

Hidouchi has her back to the door as Zoubiri opens it. Her attention is fixed on the list of files that has appeared before her on the laptop screen. But the sound of a gunshot, muffled by a silencer, cuts through her concentration. She hears a heavy thump as she whirls round.

Zoubiri is lying on his back on the floor, with a bullet-hole in the dead – literally dead – centre of his forehead. And Yanik Seghir – looking eerily identical to the bearded version of his older self generated by the DSS computer's facial ageing program – is standing in the doorway, holding a gun levelled at Hidouchi.

Her own weapon is at her side. She'll be as dead as Zoubiri before she can aim and fire. She anticipates in that frozen moment that Seghir is about to kill her: that this is the end for her, far from home, in a botched operation, mission unaccomplished.

But no. It's not the end. Not quite, anyway. 'Put your gun on the floor, Agent Hidouchi,' says Seghir. 'Move slowly. Very slowly.'

Hidouchi obeys. There is nothing else she can do. She places her gun carefully on the floor and stands up, keeping her eyes fixed on Seghir throughout.

He pulls a pair of handcuffs out of the pocket of his jacket and tosses them onto the bed. 'Pick those up, walk round to the other side of the bed and cuff yourself to the headrail.'

Hidouchi does as instructed, circling the bed slowly, moving towards Seghir and then further away from him – and from her gun. She has to step over Zoubiri as she goes, trying not to glance down at the hole drilled in his forehead and the sightless gape of his eyes.

The headrail of the bed is solid-looking brass. She closes one of the cuffs round the nearest post and the other round her wrist.

'You're not here on official DSS business, are you? *Officially*, you're on leave. And Zoubiri? He's just Mokrani's gun for hire. *Was*, I should say. So, what we actually have here is two people breaking into a hotel room and the occupant fighting them off.' Seghir kicks the door shut behind him. 'I can talk my way out of this. But you can't. Even if you're alive to try.'

'Why am I alive? What do you want from me?'

'Information. If it's valuable enough, we may be able to come to an agreement.'

'What kind of information?'

'We can start with how much you know about White Leopard. What our . . . exposure is.'

'Right now, I think your exposure is . . . considerable.'

'No. You wouldn't have been desperate enough to go into partnership with Zoubiri if that was the case. I think—' He breaks off. His phone is ringing. He frowns, as if this is the last thing he's expecting, and pulls the phone out of an inner pocket. He looks at the screen, frowns more heavily still, and thumbs a button. 'Urtan?' *Urtan*. His son. 'What—' Something cuts him short. He looks at the screen again. His mouth falls open. He gasps – horrified, it seems, by what he sees. Mouth still open, he moves the phone back to his ear.

The caller speaks to him. Seghir says nothing as he listens. Hidouchi notices the shortness of his breath and the heaving of his chest. There's a skittering look of panic – no, anguish – in his eyes. The monologue continues for what feels like an age.

Then Seghir says quietly, 'Don't harm him.' And at that moment Hidouchi knows it's definitely not Urtan speaking to him, but someone who has Urtan at his mercy. 'I'll do as you ask . . . Yes, without delay . . . It'll be the end of it, I guarantee.'

Seghir is concentrating on the phone call. He's no longer paying Hidouchi any attention. She slips her uncuffed hand into the pocket of her jeans and eases her reserve phone out into her palm.

'I'll make sure it can't go on,' Seghir continues, his voice hoarse with tension. 'Just promise me you'll release him when it's done . . . Yes . . . Yes, I understand . . . What I have to say will definitely finish it . . . But I must—' He breaks off. Then: 'Hello? Hello?'

Hidouchi taps the muting button on her phone, then another button. A second or two from now, Bouras's phone will start ringing at his home in Algiers. She can only hope he's within earshot.

Yanik Seghir leans against the door behind him, then slowly slides down until he's sitting with his back against it, his feet stretched out ahead of him, either side of Zoubiri's. He's looking at Hidouchi in the sense that he's looking in her direction. But he doesn't seem to see her at all.

Hidouchi cancels the muting and raises her phone to her ear. She hears Bouras's voice at the other end. 'Agent Hidouchi?'

Before she can speak, Seghir wrenches his attention back to her, registering the phone in her hand. 'Who have you called?' he asks huskily.

'Someone who can help.'

'Who?' Seghir points the gun towards her. '*Who?*'

'A senior police officer.'

'Hidouchi?' says Bouras. 'What's going on?'

'Police?' Crazily, Seghir laughs. 'It's the police I need.'

'Then—'

'Give me the phone.'

Hidouchi hesitates. But the gun waggling in Seghir's hand tips the balance. She tosses the phone across to him.

He picks it up and holds it to his ear. 'Who is this? . . . How senior are you? . . . I'm Yanik Seghir . . . I thought you might . . . You're in Algiers, right? . . . Can you call the local police here in Tamanrasset? . . . I want them to come here, to the Hotel Oasis, room three one nine, as soon as possible . . . I'm ready to give myself up . . . I've killed a man – Khaled Zoubiri – but that doesn't matter . . . DSS Agent Hidouchi is with me, but she'll come to no harm . . . I want to make a statement – a full statement – about the White Leopard project . . . Don't inform her boss at the DSS or any government ministry . . . When you've heard what I have to say you'll understand why . . . My son's life is at stake, otherwise I wouldn't be doing this, but . . . Yes . . . Yes, I'll wait here. Agent Hidouchi will wait here with me . . . Yes.' He tosses the phone back to Hidouchi.

She bends forward, stretching to retrieve it from where it's fallen. 'Director?'

'Are you all right, Hidouchi?'

'Yes.'

'What's this about his son?'

'Kidnapped, I think. By someone whose orders he's now following.'

'And Zoubiri's dead?'

'Yes. Shot by Seghir. But that was before the kidnappers called him. Now he's . . . going to tell us everything he knows about White Leopard, apparently. On the record.'

'Those are the kidnappers' terms?'

'So it seems.'

'And you're in no danger?'

'Am I in any danger?' she asks, looking at Seghir.

'No.' He throws her the key to the handcuffs. 'Urtan's the one in danger.'

'Do you know where he is?'

'When I last heard from him he was on his way to Cherchell . . . to do something for me.'

'Did you hear that, Director?'

'Yes. Cherchell. Where Chahira Meslem lives. Taleb wanted her address, you'll remember. In connection with documents he thought Urtan Seghir was looking for at HQ. I'll contact her as soon I've spoken to the Tamanrasset police. Just keep the situation in check until they arrive.'

'I don't think that's going to be a problem, Director.' Hidouchi looks at Seghir, who's tipped his head back and is staring into space. 'Yanik Seghir is no longer a threat. Except to the White Leopard project and the people who run it. In fact, I have the feeling he's about to become their worst nightmare.'

Taleb watches the Zastava drive away, then opens the gate of Chahira Meslem's house and hurries up the path to the door. He owes her an apology. And a full explanation. He doesn't know how she's going to react. The loss of the documents she took such care of is bound to have saddened her. And who is there to blame for that but himself? He is the one who brought the Dutchman – and Urtan Seghir – to her door. Her late husband's faith in him hasn't been rewarded.

He presses the bell and waits. A shadow moves behind the blinds in the lounge. Then the door opens.

'Taleb.' She looks relieved to see him. 'Come in. There's someone on the phone who wants to speak to you.'

'But . . . no one knows I'm here.'

'Your chief, Director Bouras, called a few minutes ago. When I heard the doorbell I knew it must be you.' Chahira sets off back to the lounge, with Taleb following. 'Well, I hoped it was, at any rate. I've been worried that terrible man wouldn't let you go, even though he promised he would.'

'He tends to do what he says he will. But why did the director call you?'

'Speak to him yourself.' She points to the landline phone standing on a small bookcase. The receiver is off the hook. 'I've told him what happened earlier. Apparently, he has news for you of his own.'

Mimi looks up as Taleb enters the room. She doesn't bark. It strikes him she's pleased to see him as well, which is a pleasant surprise. He picks up the phone. 'Director?'

'When exactly, Taleb, were you planning to tell me you were alive and back in Algeria?'

'I haven't been able to contact anyone for the past two days. I was held incommunicado.'

'Yet the lady of the house said you called her ahead of your visit this evening.'

'Well, it's a . . . long story.'

'If so, I don't have time to hear it at present. I want you back at HQ right away. I'll send a car to fetch you.'

'Are you in the office, Director?'

'I will be by the time you arrive.'

'Is there an emergency?'

'Very much so. An emergency which, for once, we may be able to come out on the right side of.'

SIXTEEN

'INTERVIEW COMMENCES ZERO FIFTY-NINE HOURS, MONDAY THIRTY-first January, Tamanrasset police station,' says Hidouchi after depressing the switch on the recorder. 'Subject: Yanik Seghir. Interviewer: Agent Souad Hidouchi, *Département des services de securité.* Yanik Seghir will now confirm his identity.'

'I am Yanik Seghir.' His voice is firm but doleful. He looks at Hidouchi directly across the table. The surface is bare but for the recording machine and two cardboard cups of coffee. 'I want to be clear at the outset that I killed Khaled Zoubiri in self-defence, believing he meant to shoot me when I discovered him with you in my hotel room.'

'I'm not here to question you about that. This interview is concerned with what you have yourself described as a pressing matter of national security.'

It is the pressing nature of that matter that has gained Hidouchi the full cooperation of the Tamanrasset police, acting on the instructions of Director Bouras. The issue has not – yet – been referred to DSS HQ. Kadri knows nothing of what she is doing. Her calculation – and Bouras's – is that they will have amassed such critical evidence by the time Kadri and his ministerial superiors realize what is happening that it will be too late for them to close down the investigation.

Yanik Seghir is himself eager to place on the record damaging information about the White Leopard project. Sabotaging it is what he has to do to save his son's life and he appears confident he can achieve that. All Hidouchi has to do is listen while he goes about it in the icy chill of a grimly functional interview room. She has downloaded his computer files about White Leopard, but has not yet had the chance to study them. No matter, Seghir has assured her. His statement will contain everything that is truly significant.

'There's one other point I need to make before we come to White Leopard,' he says, sipping his coffee. 'I will not be saying or admitting anything concerning my activities when I worked as a special contractor for the DRS in the nineteen nineties. Questioning me about them will be a waste of time. And neither you nor I have any time to waste, do we?'

Hidouchi acknowledges the question with a nod of agreement. All she says, though, is: 'Tell me about White Leopard.'

'OK. At its essence it's a scheme to harness solar energy from the Sahara to generate electricity and transmit it by high-voltage cables across the country from a site south-west of here to the north coast, then under the Mediterranean to France, ensuring cheap renewable energy supplies for Europe and an enduring source of income for Algeria as oil and gas drop out of the world economy towards the middle of this century.'

'Sounds great.'

'In principle, yes. But hostile forces hovering on our southern border – Tuareg rebels, Isis, al-Qaeda – pose a serious threat to any Saharan infrastructure. The past twenty years have seen a succession of terrorist incidents, from El Para's kidnapping of tourists to the notorious raid on In Amenas. I probably don't need to tell you that some of the terrorists responsible for such incidents – probably including El Para – were originally recruited by the DRS to carry out false flag actions intended to convince the Bush administration there was a serious threat to US interests in the region. It hardly matters now. The seeds were sown and they have surely sprouted. Mali is falling apart, Chad is unstable, Libya has been in chaos since Gaddafi was overthrown and it's only a matter of time before Niger goes the same way. France and the US have lost influence in the region. No one's in control – except the terrorists. So, the idea behind White Leopard was to reward those hostile forces with whatever they want – money, land, tolerance of drug-smuggling and arms-dealing, other favours – in return for guarantees of non-interference with the construction and operation of the generating array and cabling, enabling White Leopard to go ahead in a secure environment.'

'And that was the purpose of the conference at the Villa des Ormeaux?'

'Yes. Terms were agreed there in conditions of complete secrecy.'

'Overseen by your ex-wife, Lydia Seghir?'

'Lydia handled the negotiations on behalf of our government, with the full knowledge and consent of the French government. The intention is to announce the scheme formally a few days from now, here in Tamanrasset, where the locals can be bought off with promises of employment and investment for decades to come. A new deal for the neglected south. An end to isolation and insurgency.'

'What's your role been?'

'I planted the idea in Lydia's mind and then she planted it in the minds of government ministers.'

'You're saying it was *your* idea?'

'Not exactly. It's a revival in modified form of the Solahara scheme floated by the French and Germans about fifteen years ago. That was eventually abandoned because of political instability in the region – exactly the problem White Leopard was designed to solve. Using my contacts in Sonatrach and exploiting Lydia's government appointment, I was able to get it off the ground again. I also have contacts . . . among those hostile parties I mentioned. Which was a big advantage.'

'Terrorists and insurgents? What are your links with them?'

'We'll come to that. What I need to explain first is that getting this deal over the line required Lydia to make a substantial concession on the government's behalf. The French had no objection to it, but older elements in *le pouvoir* – if they knew about it – would do everything they could to put a stop to the project.'

'Why?'

'Because many in the Islamist groups Lydia was dealing with have long memories. They haven't forgotten – or forgiven – the dirty tricks played by the government to defeat them during *la décennie noire*. Or the betrayals some of their own were tempted into. Their ultimate price for agreeing to allow White Leopard to go ahead turned out to be a far-reaching amendment to the Charter for National Peace and Reconciliation.'

'The amnesty legislation?'

'Yes. This won't be publicly announced, of course, but part of the agreement involves selective removal of amnesty. There'll be a low-key presidential decree amending chapter six of the charter so that a limited number of people thought to be guilty of particularly egregious acts can be held legally liable. After a lot of haggling, a list of names was settled on.'

'I don't suppose you're on it.'

'Naturally not.'

'But General Mokrani?'

'Oh yes. They were most insistent about him. He's number one. If he'd discovered what was afoot, he'd probably still have been able – despite his marginalization since the DRS was wound up – to stop the scheme in its tracks. So, he had to be . . . distracted.'

'By arranging for his son to be kidnapped.'

'We contracted out neutralizing Mokrani to an operative I used to work with in the nineties known as the Major. Karim Mokrani agreed to cooperate once the Major had enlightened him, shall we say, about the full extent of his father's murderous activities in the past.'

'What was Superintendent Taleb's involvement?'

'The policeman? He was just a dupe. A very useful one for the Major, obviously, in sustaining the kidnap fiction.'

'And the ransom money? Who was intended to benefit from that?'

'It was a bonus for the Major as far as we were concerned. We simply left him to get on with that side of things. And he did what we wanted. Mokrani was so distraught after his son was supposedly abducted that he never saw the big picture. I suppose he must have suspected there was one. He just couldn't risk trying to find out what it was while he thought Karim's life was at stake.'

'The government deems Mokrani – and the others on the list – expendable?'

'Yes. A new generation is in power now. They're evidently willing to sacrifice some survivors of the previous generation . . . for the greater good.'

'Is that what you're serving – the greater good?'

'No. I'm sorry to have to tell you that the agenda I'm working to is altogether less . . . patriotic.'

'What does that mean exactly?'

'The Russians, Agent Hidouchi. I've been on the FSB's payroll for some years now, largely because no one else wanted to hire me. I've been assisting them with infiltration of terrorist and rebel groups and the making and unmaking of governments in fragile states to the south of us. Their aim is to fill the vacuum in the region left by the French and the Americans – to create a "coup belt" stretching across the Sahel, using Wagner Group mercenaries to undermine existing regimes and replace them with ones of their choosing who'll be dependent on the Russians for continuing support. That's already happened in Mali, Burkina Faso and the Central African Republic, and they've made big inroads in Chad and Sudan. Niger is holding out, but it'll go the way of the others in the end. Putin's African ambitions are virtually limitless.'

'What does that have to do with White Leopard?'

'The Russians were pulling the terrorists' strings at the Villa des Ormeaux conference. They want White Leopard to go ahead. They haven't actually told me why. But they don't need to. It's obvious. They plan to lure the Europeans into replacing oil and gas – which they're committed to phasing out anyway – with virtually free Saharan energy. Once they've become dependent on that source in the typically soft-headed unquestioning European way, the Russians will be able to blackmail them, threatening to use their terrorist proxies in the region to destroy the generators or just cut the cables. They're looking to the zero carbon future and making sure they'll be able to call the shots when it dawns. With Algeria as their unwitting accomplice.'

'Does your ex-wife know about this?'

'No. She's hopelessly idealistic. Though ruthless with it. Urtan doesn't know either. No one knows. Except my FSB controllers . . . and now you. I can supply you with my bank account details, showing regular and substantial payments made to me by a Russian-registered company that controls several gold and diamond mines in the Central African Republic. It's already on a DGSE blacklist because of its activities in Mali, so linking it through me to Lydia will undoubtedly prompt the French to back out of White Leopard. I'm counting on that happening, of course. And you'll make it happen, won't you? Urtan's life depends on it.'

'If what you say is true, then—'

'It's true. Every word of it. I'm only admitting it because I love my son and I owe the Russians no greater loyalty than the average mercenary.'

'Well, I don't see how White Leopard can continue once the government realizes the extent of Russian manipulation.'

'Neither do I. And that's what Urtan's kidnappers have demanded: the cancellation of White Leopard and the abandonment of the plan to remove amnesty from Mokrani and some of his cronies. There'll be no public acknowledgement of any of this, of course. I understand that. And there'll be no grand announcement of a new era of Franco-Algerian cooperation. There'll be nothing. Except a lot of squabbling behind closed doors and exchanges of huffy messages between Algiers and Paris. Erica Ménard was due here tomorrow – well, later today, that is. But I expect she'll cancel her flight. Bad news travels fast.'

Seghir drinks some coffee. Then he leans forward and switches off the recorder.

'I've said all I have to say . . . for the record. You have my phone?'

'Yes.'

'It's vital for my son's sake that you send a copy of the recording to the man who called me at the Hotel Oasis. Will you do that?'

'Yes.'

'I beg you to move swiftly on this.'

'I won't delay.'

'Thank you. I suppose I'll be taken to Algiers soon and handed over to your DSS colleagues. At which point . . . my fate will be sealed.'

'I think in fact you'll remain in DGSN custody until a judicial decision is made.'

'Judicial? Is that what you'd call it? Don't be naive. What I've revealed makes White Leopard a huge embarrassment for a lot of powerful people. They'll want the story buried. And I'll be buried with it. Just remember when you hear I've committed suicide in my cell that . . . I'm really not the suicidal type.'

Hidouchi would like to be able to tell Seghir that nothing of the kind is likely to happen to him. But she can't. She can't because she knows he knows how these things are managed. He's never going to stand in a court and answer for what he's done. The killing of Zoubiri will be enough for him to be detained until . . . the problem he poses is solved in the way such problems are.

He drains his cup and looks at her, his eyes hooded by the shadows cast from the stark overhead light. 'Enough?' he asks.

Hidouchi nods. 'Enough.' She switches the recorder back on and glances up at the clock on the wall behind Seghir. 'Interview terminated, one forty-four hours, Monday thirty-first January.'

The drab surroundings of Police HQ, Algiers, have never looked more appealing to Taleb, even in their current largely empty state. It's just gone two a.m. when he exits the lift and hurries along the short passage that leads to Bouras's office. The director's secretary is of course absent, so there is no occasion to announce himself. He sees Bouras sitting at his desk in his inner office through the open doorway, the lights of the harbour twinkling through the wide windows behind him. Bouras looks up and actually smiles – which is not how he usually greets Taleb – and waves for him to enter.

'A short-lived period of enforced leave, followed by a hazardous assignment in France and a brush with death in Cherchell.' Bouras spreads his hands. 'You've squeezed a lot into the past two weeks, I must say.'

'Is it only two weeks?'

'Since the occasion of your disastrous appearance on national television? Yes, it is. Though no doubt it seems longer to you. Tell me, when did you last shave?'

'I'm sorry, Director.' Taleb rubs the stubble on his chin. 'The past forty-eight hours have been . . . challenging.'

'Well, I'll soon be able to send you home to attend to such essential matters as personal grooming. I've just finished watching a live feed of Agent Hidouchi's interrogation of Yanik Seghir.'

'How did it go?'

'Illuminatingly. Happily for you, Hidouchi secured amongst the revelations your complete exoneration. I have no doubt the French authorities will soon drop their request for your detention and declare that you are no longer a suspect in Agent Irmouli's murder or Herr Spühler's or indeed any other crime that may have been committed in connection with a kidnapping that does not in fact appear to have taken place. And I strongly suspect the DSS will cease to have any wish to question you. What Seghir had to say leaves them . . . with many more important issues to tackle.'

'So, White Leopard can't go ahead?'

'Not now Seghir has revealed he assisted his ex-wife in setting up the project on the instructions of his secret paymasters in Moscow.'

'Moscow?'

'He's been working for the Russians, Taleb.'

'The *Russians*?'

'Yes. It seems they've been manipulating us all along. It's about gaining a long-term stranglehold on future energy supplies to Europe. Our government has been made a fool of. The French government likewise. You will never hear of White Leopard again. It will be something that officially never existed in any form. I imagine Lydia Seghir will have resigned by the end of the day. Her superiors will be scrambling for cover. And the DSS will have to explain why one of their agents had to disobey orders to uncover the conspiracy. Take a seat and watch the interrogation yourself. Then you'll understand.' Bouras swings the screen of his desktop computer round to face Taleb. 'The threat White

Leopard posed to General Mokrani, by the way, was that he was on a list of people destined to have their immunity from prosecution under the amnesty charter lifted as part of the deal struck at the Villa des Ormeaux.'

Taleb subsides into a chair. 'Le Merz will be pleased,' he murmurs.

'Who?'

'Sorry. I haven't told you about him yet. He's ultimately responsible for the kidnapping that really has happened – of Urtan Seghir. I guess Urtan will be released once the Dutchman – Le Merz's operative – is satisfied his father's lived up to his side of the bargain.'

'I would say he's done that.'

'And the truth about the Boudiaf assassination, which Superintendent Meslem took such pains to preserve, will never be known. Greatly to General Mokrani's relief. He comes out of this a big winner.'

'We are also winners, Taleb, as you'd do well to bear in mind. You cannot have everything in this world. But sometimes – as now – you can have quite a substantial something. I will enjoy speaking to Deputy Director Kadri in a few hours and informing him of what's happened while he's been sleeping – or doing whatever he does during the hours of darkness. The DSS won't be able to look down their noses at us after this.'

'Still . . . I had it, Director – the truth. I had it in my hand.'

'And now you don't. Which in reality is a good thing. Some truths are destined never to be known. Some indeed are better not known. But at least we have Yanik Seghir's truths to work with. And they are quite potent enough.' Bouras clicks the computer mouse. 'Sit back . . . and learn what they are.'

Leaving Yanik Seghir in a cell at Tamanrasset police station, Hidouchi has returned to the Hotel Oasis, where she's booked herself into one of the many rooms available – though on a different floor from 319 – with the intention of trying to sleep for a few hours before Bouras notifies Kadri and the relevant government ministries of what has occurred – and what it means for the White Leopard project.

She needs a shower first, though. She hears her reserve phone ring just as she's stepping out of it. The call turns out to be from Taleb, who won't be having a restful night himself – though surely a less anxious one than for some time past. She calls him straight back.

'I thought it was distinctly possible you were dead.' She's surprised to hear herself laugh as she speaks. The sound is unfamiliar.

'That's what my doctor says whenever I go to see him,' Taleb responds.

'Well, thanks to your activities in Cherchell, I'm alive. And thanks to my activities here you're off the hook. I'm not sure how it's happened, but we've outwitted a lot of people who think they're very smart – and certainly smarter than us.'

'We had a little help from their enemies.'

'Maybe that's the best way to do it.'

'I've watched your interrogation of Yanik Seghir.'

'It wasn't much of an interrogation. He led me where he needed to go to save his son. Will he have done that, do you think?'

'Probably. The man behind Urtan's kidnapping is a gangster. But he's a pragmatic gangster.'

'I'll tell Seghir that when I get the chance. I aim to fly back to Algiers with him and his police escort. You and I can compare war wounds then.'

'Thanks for prompting him to exonerate me, Souad.'

'You're welcome. Meanwhile, I ought to get some sleep.'

And she does sleep – eventually.

*

She breakfasts late the following morning in the deserted hotel restaurant. By now she knows Bouras will have notified Kadri and the Ministry of Justice of Yanik Seghir's revelations. And Kadri will have briefed his boss, DSS chairman General Feradj. The recording of her interrogation of Seghir will have been viewed multiple times by concerned officials – and probably worried politicians as well. The alarm will be spreading through the veins of the system. White Leopard is finished. But the priority of all involved is to ensure they aren't finished as well.

As she sits sipping her coffee, the call comes that she knew had to come sooner or later – from Kadri. She lets him wait a few moments before answering. She'll have the upper hand in the exchanges that are about to follow, though neither of them will acknowledge that. There is a game to be played. And she's going to play it.

'Deputy Director?'

'Souad.' He sounds as self-satisfied as usual. More accurately, to the trained ear, he sounds as if he's trying to sound as self-satisfied as usual. 'I congratulate you. You have . . . performed a remarkable service for the department.'

'There were unanswered questions surrounding White Leopard I felt simply couldn't be ignored.'

'And so you disregarded my instruction to leave the matter alone. But since that resulted in your exposure of a plot to manipulate the state to suit the hostile agenda of a foreign power, we are all undeniably in your debt.'

'I did what I thought I had to – in the interests of national security.'

'Indeed. And no one can dispute that you have served those interests well. For which you will be rewarded. We can talk about the form that may take when you return to Algiers. By then our political masters may have decided how they want to deal with the fallout from the collapse of the White Leopard project. I anticipate I'll be involved in some . . . difficult discussions.'

'If there's any assistance I can give you in those discussions, Deputy Director . . .' She leaves the sentence unfinished, knowing Kadri will want to keep her uninvolved but must realize he won't be able to.

'Thank you, Souad. It's kind of you to offer. And typical. You are one of our most dedicated agents.' His effusions of praise are in danger of becoming excessive. 'Director Bouras has told me the plan is to transfer Seghir to Algiers on a scheduled flight tomorrow morning. On arrival, he will be held and questioned further by the DGSN while the political situation evolves. At this stage we must assist the police in any way we can, although the time will come for us to question Seghir ourselves.' This all sounds suspiciously reasonable. Kadri isn't normally so eager to accommodate the wishes of the DGSN. 'Director Bouras has agreed that you can accompany Seghir during his transfer. We need to know what he knows – *everything* he knows. So, anything further you can get out of him during the journey will be immensely valuable. I can rely on you in this?'

'Certainly.'

'Make sure he boards that plane. I want him securely held in Algiers, not lingering in a cell in a provincial police station.'

'I understand.'

'Good. I'll look forward to seeing you tomorrow.'

Kadri rings off. And Hidouchi runs over in her mind the implications of what he has said. He has no choice but to pay lip service to her ability and commitment, even though he is probably burning with resentment. Promotion of some kind would be the natural reward for what she has done. But Kadri puts himself first, second and third in all matters. And, unlike Hidouchi, he always follows the orders of those above him.

It seems no consensus has yet been arrived at as to how to deal with the implosion of White Leopard. Until it is, he will surely aim to stabilize the situation and wait to be told what is required of him.

On one point at least they can agree. Yanik Seghir has more to reveal – if he can be persuaded to reveal it.

Bouras sits at his desk in Police HQ, Algiers, wondering why his conversation with Kadri has left him feeling uneasy. In reality, he knows the reason, reluctant though he is to admit it to himself. Kadri was more accommodating of the DGSN's priorities than he has ever been before. That is the reason. An enemy is at his most dangerous when he appears to wish to be your friend.

Bouras has sat where he is for half an hour or more, smoking a cigar while his coffee has grown cold in the cup, contemplating his unease and weighing the argument for acting on it. Inaction is the easier course, at least for now. But it may have grim consequences. His instinct is to seize the initiative, for fear that otherwise Kadri will seize it.

A moment passes. The cigar is nearly exhausted. He makes his decision.

Hidouchi answers his call so quickly she might almost have been waiting for it. 'Director?'

'Yes. How is it in Tamanrasset?'

'Hot, despite this being the coolest time of the year. I am walking the streets, which are largely empty. There's a gentle wind – hardly more than a breeze – but it's enough to blow sand into my eyes and nose. And my mouth now I'm talking to you. I think I'll return to the hotel. They claim to have a gym.'

'You have spoken to Kadri?'

'Yes.'

'I am troubled.'

'By what?'

'His excessive cooperativeness. I suspect he may not intend to allow Seghir to remain in police custody once he reaches Algiers. I suspect he plans to remove Seghir to a secure location under DSS control where anything further he has to say can be . . . carefully mediated.'

'Why would he do that?'

'The answer to your question hinges on the extent to which Seghir's evidence may embarrass senior DSS personnel, including Kadri himself – not to mention the politicians whose pockets such people may be in.'

'You don't trust Kadri?'

'Of course not. Do you?'

'He is my immediate superior. And he has instructed me to accompany Seghir back to Algiers – with your agreement, as I understand it.'

'You have disobeyed him before.'

'Once may be forgivable. Twice would be pushing my luck. Tell me what you fear – exactly.'

'I fear Kadri will arrange for Seghir to be removed from DGSN supervision on arrival in Algiers. It lies within DSS competence to request army assistance in its operations. My men would have to give way. And you could hardly interfere with a proceeding authorized by your own department. He may want you there so that you are compromised by what happens.'

'I see.' For the moment, that is all Hidouchi says.

'Had the possibility of something like this occurred to you?'

More silence. Then Hidouchi says, 'Yes. But I hoped I was being . . . overly suspicious.'

'I don't think you were.'

Hidouchi sighs audibly. 'You can only have called me because you have something in mind to frustrate Kadri's intentions – supposing you're right about what they are.'

'You have a plane waiting for you somewhere north of Tamanrasset, don't you? You told me so.'

'Yes.'

'It *is* still waiting for you, isn't it?'

'It should be. The pilot gave us until noon tomorrow to return.'

'Fly back to Zeralda on it. And take Seghir with you. He doesn't need a police escort. He's not going to try to escape with his son's life at stake. Bring him here and consign him to my custody. Then I can ensure he's fully and properly questioned without DSS interference. We can let Kadri go on believing he's aboard that scheduled flight tomorrow morning. I've spoken to the station chief in Tamanrasset. They're holding an embezzler due for transfer to Algiers, but it's a minor case and hasn't been given any priority. We can leave Seghir's name on the passenger list and send the embezzler in his place. By the time Kadri realizes what we've done, Seghir will be in a cell here at Police HQ. I believe we should learn everything we can from him. I believe we should try to persuade him to name *all* the names of those he conspired with. Don't you?'

'Yes,' Hidouchi replies with quiet firmness. 'I do.'

'Then this is how I think we should proceed. I can send Taleb to collect you from Zeralda. No one else will know anything about it. That way there can't be any nasty surprises.'

'There can always be those.'

'What's it to be? Are we going to do this – or not?'

Hidouchi ponders the question. Bouras can hear her footsteps on the Tamanrasset pavement. Then they stop.

'Agent Hidouchi?'

'When do you want me to collect Seghir?'

Taleb has breakfasted late as well, in a café, there being a more or less total lack of provisions in his apartment. *Chakchouka* with extra Merguez sausages, washed down with lots of strong coffee, has cheered as well as revived him. A leisurely haircut and shave in Usma's barbershop has followed and he steps out into the thin January sunshine feeling more like his normal self than he has for far too long. He pauses, takes out his phone and calls Abdou Rezig, thinking it will be nice to report he is back home and out of trouble. Abdou doesn't answer on the workshop phone, so he tries the villa number, reckoning Noussa is likely to pick up.

And she does. 'Mouloud? It is so good to hear your voice. Abdou and I have been worried about you.'

'No need. All is well. I'm back home in Algiers and in the clear with the French authorities.'

'That is wonderful news.'

'Much happening there?'

'No. It is very quiet since the conference ended. Just Abdou and I – and Madame Elasse.'

'Monsieur not back then?'

'No. And Madame will not be here long. She tells me she has to join Monsieur in Geneva to attend to some business.'

'Is that right?' The Elasses are removing themselves from French jurisdiction. Taleb can think of some very good reasons why they might want to do that. But he isn't going to burden Noussa with them. 'I'm very grateful for everything the two of you did for me while I was at the villa, Noussa, I truly am. And I sorely miss your cooking. I dreamt of your *daube de boeuf* last night.'

'I don't believe you.'

'It's true.'

'Well, come here whenever you like and I'll cook it for you again.'

'I'd like that, Nou—' He breaks off. Someone else is trying to call him – Bouras. 'Sorry, Noussa,' he says in a hurried apology. 'I have to ring off.'

'I understand. *Au revoir.*'

'Director?'

'Where are you, Taleb?'

'I've just left Usma's barbershop.'

'I don't know it. But if this means you're looking less like a wanted criminal than you were last night then I approve. Perhaps you'd like to report to HQ now you've smartened yourself up.'

'Of course. I—'

'Shall we say my office in an hour?'

'Yes, Director. I'll be there.'

Hidouchi drives the Land Cruiser into the small courtyard at Tamanrasset police station and pulls up close to the door leading into the building. She climbs out and rings the bell alongside the door. A weary-looking young officer opens it a minute or so later. She gives him her name and he nods, confirming she is expected. 'Wait here,' he says. 'We'll bring him out.'

She waits, gazing up at the utterly cloudless sky. Cloudless, but not as clear as earlier. The wind has strengthened and brought a haze of blown sand to the air of the town. She's eager to start their journey north and would have liked to be under way already, but the local police have taken their sweet time shuffling papers authorizing Seghir's transfer to her custody – although maybe, it occurs to her, they've actually moved quickly by their own standards.

The door opens again. The young officer and a colleague emerge with Seghir, whose wrists are handcuffed in front of him. The young officer passes Hidouchi the key to the cuffs. 'He's yours now,' he announces. 'Sign please.' He holds out a form attached to a clipboard. She signs.

Then she opens the tailgate of the Land Cruiser and tells Seghir to climb in. 'There's a tarpaulin in there. Cover yourself with it. You can join me in the front when we're clear of the town.'

Seghir eyes her sceptically. 'Where are we going, Agent Hidouchi?'

'Algiers. By an unorthodox route.'

'Are you sure you know what you're doing?'

'I'm helping you save your son – amongst other things. Now . . . climb in.'

Bouras has made a rare appearance in the staff canteen at Police HQ. Taleb is sharing a table with him. Fellow lunchers nod respectfully to the director as they pass and cannot fail to notice Taleb's presence.

'I thought this might help restore your status as a valued senior officer, Taleb,' says Bouras, stirring his soup. 'After your unfortunate brush with TV celebrity.'

'That's good of you, Director.'

'Well, never let it be said that I underestimate dedication to duty, which you have always exhibited, albeit not always accompanied by sound judgement.'

'I never want to be in front of a camera again.'

'And I never want you to be in front of one either. Your operational forte is . . . behind the scenes. How is your meal, by the way?'

Taleb is eating a large serving of *al-shetitha*. The privations of recent days have left him with a prodigious appetite. 'Excellent. The lamb is . . . very succulent.'

'It looks it. My wife forbids me to have anything more than soup for lunch when I'm at work.' Bouras pats his stomach. 'She thinks I'm getting fat. Though I swear I've lost weight over the past couple of weeks, thanks to . . . the demands of the current situation.'

'Which will soon be resolved, I think, Director.'

'Let's hope so. I suggest you set off once you hear from Hidouchi that they've left the refuelling stop.'

'I'll do that.'

'If all goes well, we'll have Seghir in custody here by tonight.'

'It'll go well.' Taleb swallows another delicious mouthful of slow-cooked lamb. 'I'm sure of it.'

It's early afternoon, but already, on the long empty road north from Tamanrasset, it's as if night is falling. The light is thinning as the wind strengthens. Sand swirls around the Land Cruiser, rising and falling and turning like the sails of a gybing yacht. The horizon before and behind them is lost in a haze. And the keening of the wind comes to them as the howl of a creature on the hunt.

'This doesn't look good,' says Seghir. 'It's the sandstorm season. And you're a city girl, aren't you? You've no idea what it's like to be caught by a storm out here.'

'It's only another fifteen kilometres to the airstrip.'

'We'll be lucky to make it.'

'Then it's fifty-fifty, isn't it? Either we're lucky – or we're not.'

In the event, they're lucky. Visibility is falling rapidly and the engine of the Land Cruiser is beginning to choke on sand that's finding its way under the bonnet when the sheds and hangars of the airstrip appear as ghostly shapes through the murk.

Hidouchi pulls in by the shed where lights are visible and blares the horn. A scarfed and hooded figure emerges and gestures towards the hangar. He runs ahead and pulls open one of the large doors far enough for Hidouchi to drive in.

Only when the door has closed again and the man has pulled down his hood and scarf does Hidouchi recognize him as Hafsi. The plane behind him is the one he flew her and Zoubiri down from Zeralda in. 'You're crazy driving here in weather like this,' he says neutrally, as if making an observation rather than a criticism.

Hidouchi shrugs. 'I had no choice. We have to get back to Algiers today.'

'Not a chance. This storm will get worse before it gets better. We have to wait for it to pass.'

'How long's that likely to take?'

'No way to tell. But it'll probably blow itself out overnight. Depending on how much sand it dumps on the runway, we should be able to get off then.'

Hidouchi grimaces. Bouras's plan hinges on her delivering Seghir to Police HQ in Algiers before Kadri discovers he isn't on the scheduled flight from Tamanrasset. Setting off at daybreak on a turboprop plane that will travel much more slowly than an *Air Algérie* jet significantly narrows the odds of success.

'Who's this guy?' Hafsi nods towards Seghir. Fortunately, Hidouchi has already released him from his handcuffs, so she doesn't have to explain that technically he's her prisoner.

'Yanik Seghir.'

'You and Zoubiri were talking about him on the way down.'

'That's right. We came here to get him.'

'There's something . . . familiar about his face.'

'I used to work for General Mokrani,' Seghir cuts in. 'We may have crossed paths then.'

Hafsi frowns. 'I suppose that could be it. Where is Zoubiri?'

'He's not coming,' says Hidouchi.

'Why not?'

'We ran into some trouble in Tamanrasset. We . . . had to leave him there.' In the hospital mortuary, to be strictly accurate, which Hidouchi doesn't intend to be.

'What kind of trouble?'

'That doesn't matter. Zoubiri hired you to do a job. And getting the two of us back to Algiers is part of it.'

Hafsi shrugs. 'OK.' His preference, she senses, is to know as little as possible about the reasons behind his discreet ferrying of passengers or cargoes from one place to another on behalf of clients such as Mokrani. 'But I doubt we'll be leaving before dawn tomorrow. And there's nothing I can do about that.'

Taleb's confidence that all would go well hasn't survived long. A terse text message from Hidouchi – *Delayed by sandstorm unlikely to leave until tomorrow morning* – has thrown Bouras's plan into doubt.

Bouras has evidently received the same message himself. He calls Taleb within minutes of the text's arrival. 'This isn't good news,' he says glumly.

'It isn't disastrous news either, Director,' Taleb counters, clinging to some shreds of optimism. 'Kadri won't know where they're flying to. There'll be nothing he can do to stop us. The plan will still work.'

'Why do I have the feeling you're simply telling me what you think I want to hear?'

'That's not—'

'Don't say any more, Taleb. We are both powerless to control a sandstorm. All we can do now . . . is await events.'

SEVENTEEN

ACCOMMODATION AT THE AIRSTRIP IS RUDIMENTARY, BUT AT LEAST they have it to themselves. There are no smugglers in residence. According to Hafsi, they left earlier in the day, knowing a storm was coming. 'You can read the desert,' he gnomically remarks, 'if you take the trouble to learn the language.' He would have left himself, by his own account, if he hadn't promised to wait for Hidouchi and Zoubiri.

They sleep – fitfully, in Hidouchi's case – on mattresses in a cold, high-ceilinged storage room where the howling of the wind and the creaking of the roof trusses form the soundtrack of the night. She senses Seghir is often awake as well, doubtless fretting over his son. She has his phone and has left it on in case the kidnappers call, but they don't, probably because they have nothing to say until they're satisfied White Leopard is a dead letter.

The longest period of sleep she manages is interrupted by a strange sound, or rather the absence of sound. The wind has dropped. Hafsi is aware of it before she is. She looks up and sees him heading out through a door that leads to the front of the building. He walks to the windows facing the runway and peers out.

'What is it?' she calls, sitting up.

'I can see the stars,' he replies, without turning round. Then he moves out of her sight. She hears switches being flicked. The runway lights start to come on.

Seghir stirs and sits up as well. 'Are we leaving?' he asks hopefully.

'No reason not to,' says Hafsi, appearing in the doorway, silhouetted against the glare of the lights. 'The wind was strong enough to blow the sand onto the runway and straight off again. I'll go out and check, but . . . it looks as if we can take off whenever you're ready.'

The message from Hidouchi wakes Taleb from a light sleep. *Storm passed departure imminent.* He knows Bouras will have received the same message. Dawn is still a long way off and his phone tells him it'll be several hours yet before the Tamanrasset police set off for the airport with their pseudo-Seghir. The plan is back on track. All it requires from him – and Bouras – is a little more patience.

Bouras can't get back to sleep after reading Hidouchi's message. He slips out of bed, pads on slippered feet down to the kitchen and prepares a pot of coffee. Then he retires to his study to distract himself as best he can with some of the less pressing matters in his inbox. It doesn't work, of course. Hidouchi and Seghir's earlier than expected take-off means their plan is still intact. But what happens after he's taken Seghir into custody is almost as troubling as what might happen if he fails to. Either outcome will have consequences. And many of them will be unpredictable.

'Why did you change the travel plan, Agent Hidouchi?' Seghir asks suddenly as the plane flies north above the Saharan wastes. The desert remains swallowed in darkness, but on the eastern horizon there's a silvery premonition of dawn. The day has nearly begun.

'I told you when we left Tamanrasset. The fewer people who know how I'm getting you to Algiers the better.'

'You fear treachery?'

'Don't you – as a man who by his own admission knows too much for the comfort of a great many powerful people?'

'Kadri's your boss at the DSS, isn't he?'

'What of it?'

'He's a weathervane. He shifts with each gust of wind.'

'Have you had dealings with him?'

'Not directly.'

'But *in*directly?'

'I've said as much as I need to say to sink White Leopard. Nothing else matters.'

'Not to you, perhaps.'

'What's your idea? To get more out of me? To squeeze out every drop of the conspiracy? It won't work. There are those who'll make sure it doesn't. And Kadri is the kind of man who does their bidding.'

'Better for you to stay clear of him, then.'

'I doubt I'll be able to. And I doubt you'll be able to protect me.'

'We'll see.'

'Yes. Undoubtedly we will.'

Taleb breakfasts on egg *brik*, orange juice and coffee – plus two Nassims to clear his lungs. He's officially on leave for the day – Bouras's idea, to spare him having to put in an appearance at HQ. After breakfast, he goes out to the newspaper stand that somehow remains in business at the end of the street and buys a copy of that morning's *El Watan*. He's on his way back to his apartment when Hidouchi's second message reaches him. *Journey resumed after refuelling.* He checks the time. The scheduled flight from Tamanrasset won't even have taken off yet. Everything's back in their favour. The plan is going to work.

He returns to his apartment for just as long as it takes to collect his car keys, then heads out to the garage where his Renault will be waiting for him.

Also waiting for him is the more loquacious of the two co-proprietors, Akram, who emerges from his cubbyhole to greet him. They have not met since the morning after Taleb's TV appearance.

'A pleasure to see you, Inspector.' (It seems he doesn't intend to start addressing him as Superintendent.) 'I heard you were back.'

'Your brother mentioned it, I suppose. I saw him yesterday.'

'Yes. Did he look disappointed?'

'Why should he?'

'Because he assured me we'd never see you again after your onscreen catastrophe. He reckoned it was a criminal waste of money to connect your car battery to the trickle charger. But I did anyway.'

'You charged the Renault's battery?'

'A car of that age occasionally needs a helping hand. As does a driver of your . . . longevity.'

'That was . . . very kind of you.'

'It's all part of the service.'

'What do I owe you . . . for the electricity?'

'Oh, just . . . do me a favour sometime.'

'I'm a police officer, Akram. What favour could I possibly do for an honest man such as yourself?'

'But there you have it, Inspector.' Akram grins. 'Surely you know that in this country there's nothing more dangerous than being honest.'

*

Taleb doesn't hurry his drive out to Zeralda. He knows he's going to be waiting around when he reaches the airfield. The location of the Zeralda Flying School is in fact closer to Kolea than to the town of Zeralda itself, set in quiet rural country south of the N67.

Very little seems to be happening there. Small planes come and go sporadically. The weather is springlike, still and bright, with the Mediterranean glittering in the distance. No one pays any attention to Taleb's arrival. The car park is virtually empty. He chooses a corner of it remote from the flying school's office and kills time flicking through *El Watan* and trying not to chain-smoke. His phone lies beside him on the passenger seat, but no messages ping through from Hidouchi or Bouras. The morning slips slowly and silently past.

He scans each plane that lands through his binoculars. Hidouchi has given him the model type and serial number of the one she'll be arriving in. It's just a matter of waiting for the right one to fly into view. Taleb isn't worried. He's bored, but not worried. The plan is working. Nothing's wrong. This is actually one of the simplest assignments he's ever been given. All is well.

As if to prove that, just before ten thirty another aerial dot he now knows to be a plane appears in the distance, approaching from the south. It looks very much like the right model. As it circles the field, Taleb focuses his binoculars on the serial number. *Yes.* The waiting is over.

Taleb gets out of his car as the plane touches down. He watches it taxi along the runway. He assumes Hidouchi has already seen him and raises his hand. The plane takes a slow turn off the runway towards the hangar and comes to a halt. Its engine stops and the blur of its propellers becomes a lazy revolution of decelerating blades.

At that moment his phone rings. Bouras is calling him. 'Director?'

'Where are you, Taleb?'

'The airfield. Hidouchi's plane has just landed.'

'Listen to me. Hidouchi's in danger. As is Seghir. And you.'

'What kind of danger?'

'I've just had word from Tamanrasset. The police chief should have told me sooner, but I suppose the whole thing threw him off balance. The decoy car supposedly taking Seghir to the airport was ambushed as it was leaving the town. Riddled with machine-gun fire. All four occupants – the driver, two escort officers and the stand-in prisoner – were killed.'

'Ambushed?' The door of the plane has opened and the steps have been let down by the pilot. Taleb sees Hidouchi appear behind him in the doorway.

'No doubt some terrorist group will claim responsibility – or have it claimed for them – but this can only have been ordered by Kadri. No one else knew what the arrangements were. He ordered Hidouchi to be on the scheduled flight with Seghir. And therefore in the car with him. They were both supposed to die.'

'Kadri's done this?'

'You need to get Hidouchi and Seghir here as quickly as possible. Kadri will be scrambling to find them. He'll have known since shortly after it happened that they got the wrong people. He can't afford to initiate something like this and fail to finish it.'

'I understand, Director.' Hidouchi and a lean, bearded man Taleb assumes is Yanik Seghir are on the tarmac now, walking in his direction. Hidouchi is waving to him. He beckons to her frantically. There's no immediate reaction.

'I'll send a car to meet you at the N1 exit. Kadri won't know where you are or what route you're taking into Algiers, so there's a good chance you'll make it.'

'We'll leave immediately, Director.' Hidouchi and Seghir are moving more quickly in response to his beckoning.

'Call me when you're closer to the city.'

'Will do.' Taleb rings off and shouts to Hidouchi. 'We have to go. *Now.*'

'What?' He sees her frown.

'*We've been rumbled.*'

She breaks into a run, pulling Seghir by the arm. Taleb flings open the rear door and pushes Seghir into the back of the car as they reach him. 'What's happened?' Hidouchi asks.

'I've just heard from Bouras. The decoy car was shot up leaving Tamanrasset. Everybody in it was killed. That would have included you and Seghir if you'd followed the original plan. It has to be—'

'Kadri,' says Hidouchi with swift certainty. 'Let's go.' She runs round to the other side of the car and jumps into the passenger seat while Taleb gets back behind the wheel.

'You're Taleb, aren't you?' Seghir asks. 'Are you saying Hidouchi and I would both be dead if we'd stuck to the original plan?'

'Apparently so.'

'Then our deaths are merely postponed. You realize that, don't you?'

'No. I don't.' Taleb starts up, reverses out of the parking bay, then turns and accelerates towards the gateway leading out onto the road. 'We just need to get to Police HQ.'

But as soon as he sees the two big black SUVs swerving in off the road and heading through the gateway towards them, Taleb knows they aren't going to get any closer to Police HQ than they already are. The rear SUV pulls alongside the front one and they both skid to a halt, blocking the exit. Taleb brakes.

'That's a DSS raid squad,' says Hidouchi as they stop twenty metres or so from the two vehicles. 'We don't stand a chance.'

The doors of the SUVs swing open. Black-clad men in bulletproof vests toting sub-machine guns climb out and begin advancing. Hidouchi's hand moves to the gun holstered at her waist. 'Don't give them an excuse to fire,' says Taleb. 'We'll be dead before you get one shot off.'

'We may be dead anyway.'

'We're DSS officers,' shouts one of the approaching men. 'Get out of the car. All of you.'

'They mean to kill us,' says Seghir.

'If they do, they don't mean to do it here,' says Taleb. 'Another open air hit would be too much for Kadri to explain away.' He presses the call button on his phone. 'Let's make sure Bouras hears this.' Then he opens his door.

'Are you just going to surrender?' asks Seghir.

'We have no choice,' says Hidouchi grimly. 'It's that or die here. They'll shoot to kill if we give them any excuse.' She opens her door as well.

She and Taleb climb out. A moment later, Seghir follows.

'Arms in the air,' the lead officer shouts. They obey. 'One wrong move and we fire.'

'We understand, Djafri.' Hidouchi evidently recognises the man. 'It's OK. I know you're just following orders.'

'That's what we're all supposed to do,' he responds.

'There comes a point when orders must be questioned.'

'You can argue your case back at HQ.'

'You think I'll get the chance?'

Djafri says nothing to that. From the rear of one of the SUVs a figure emerges: Kadri. He walks slowly towards them, then stops about halfway between the vehicles and the cordon of armed officers. 'We're taking all three of you into DSS custody,' he says. 'Any resistance will be met with lethal force.'

'What are the charges against us?' Hidouchi throws the question at him as a challenge.

'Seghir is a traitor to the republic by his own admission. You are also suspected of treason by conspiring with him in what appears to be an attempt to evade justice. And Superintendent Taleb is evidently your co-conspirator.'

'I've ensured Seghir is still alive to face justice. He'd already be dead if your plan to kill us in Tamanrasset had succeeded.'

'The reported terrorist attack on a police car in Tamanrasset earlier this morning is wholly irrelevant.'

'Who were the terrorists – *les souveniristes*, maybe?'

'That's for the police to investigate. You and Taleb need to surrender your weapons right now. Any further discussion will take place at DSS HQ.'

Two officers walk forward. One approaches Taleb, the other Hidouchi. Hidouchi removes her gun slowly from its holster and hands it over. Taleb follows suit.

'And your phones.'

They hand those over as well. The officer taking Taleb's two phones notices that one of them has an open line. He holds it up and looks back at Kadri. 'I think someone's listening in, chief.'

Kadri glares at Taleb. 'Switch it off.' As soon as he's sure the phone's dead, the officer raises his thumb. 'Who was the call to, Superintendent?'

Taleb shrugs. 'Not sure. I often press the wrong button on these things.'

Kadri looks unamused. 'Is that so?'

'How did you know we were here, Deputy Director?' asks Hidouchi.

Kadri allows himself a half-smile. 'General Mokrani told us.'

'Why would he tell you anything?'

'I can be more persuasive than you've ever given me credit for, Souad. As you may come to discover in the days ahead. Now, let's go.' Kadri moves forward. 'Handcuff all three,' he says to Djafri. 'And load them for transport.'

*

Bouras sits at his desk, staring at his phone. The connection has been cut. But he has heard enough to understand what is happening. Whatever initiative he thought he had seized has been seized back by Kadri.

Exactly what he can do to rescue Taleb – let alone Hidouchi and Seghir – is far from clear to Bouras. By specifying treason as the reason for their detention Kadri has cleverly manoeuvred the matter into the DSS's area of jurisdiction. Proving he ordered the attack on the police car in Tamanrasset is next to impossible without access to DSS records. It might be impossible even then, since Kadri will have taken care to obscure his responsibility beneath layers of deniability. As to why he wanted – and must still want – Seghir dead, it's not hard to imagine. DSS agents, acting with the connivance of various ministerial officials and maybe some senior politicians as well, were involved, directly or indirectly, in the fake kidnapping of Karim Mokrani. Their involvement, even unwitting, in a Russian plot would be career-ending if it came to light as a result of further testimony from Seghir. A decision has therefore been taken by them to neutralize the threat Seghir poses. And Kadri has agreed, doubtless motivated by a promise of future advancement and a fear of going down with them, to do whatever is necessary to achieve that objective.

Kadri probably calculates Bouras will accept defeat and abandon Taleb and Hidouchi to their fate. It is, after all, what Kadri would do in his position. It is a natural acceptance of the harsh logic of the system they both exist and thrive in. And there was a time when Bouras would have submitted to such logic.

But that time is past. He isn't going to let Kadri get away with this. He doesn't know how yet, but he's going to stop him.

Hidouchi has been inside a detention cell at DSS HQ on numerous occasions, but never alone. Never as the detainee.

It's a small windowless room, starkly lit, with a narrow bed and the most basic of sanitation. There's a surveillance camera as well, with no blind spots. And a spy-hole in the door. To confinement is added an awareness of potentially constant observation. The mind is penned here as well as the body. Exit is in the control of others. An hour may pass, a day, a night, another day, another night. The detainee has no say in the matter. The detainee has no say in anything.

Hidouchi is angry, but has nothing to vent her anger on. If Kadri stood before her, unarmed and unaccompanied, she thinks she might try to tear his throat out. His treachery has exceeded all bounds. He is her greatest enemy now. It's him or her.

The officers who brought her here said as little as possible and avoided her gaze. They know she's not a traitor. They know she's being treated wrongly on every level. But Kadri calls the shots. The DSS is a hierarchy. Its rules are inflexible. And its most basic rule is never to question the rules.

Hidouchi has always questioned the rules, and has been tolerated only because of the results she has delivered. But now she has delivered a result that cannot be allowed to stand. And tolerance for her is at an end.

She cannot escape from this cell. All she can do is wait – and hope circumstances deliver her an opportunity to outwit Kadri. If they do, however frail that opportunity may be, she has to take it.

On that faint possibility she fixes her mind. And waits.

Taleb lies on the bed in his cell, smoking a cigarette. They took his gun and his phones, but not his Nassims, which is no small comfort. He tries not to wonder what his chances are of getting out of this fix. He won't allow the answer – slim to none – to advance to the centre of his thoughts. He fends it off into the margins. Bouras knows where they are. He will do his best for them. The fact that he has no say in the actions or decisions of the DSS means his best may well not be enough. A treason trial could be held *in camera*, maybe even *in absentia*. Taleb may never walk free again. But all that is beyond his control. Whatever limited power he possessed as a police superintendent has been taken away from him. He can revel in the one liberty bestowed on a prisoner: he does not have to choose what to do. For good or bad – probably bad – it will be chosen for him.

An hour has passed since Bouras placed a call to the Deputy Minister of the Interior with responsibility for policing matters. The deputy minister has not yet called back, despite the assurances of his assistant that the urgency of Bouras's request would be communicated to the minister in unambiguous terms. Bouras knows that phoning the assistant again would be a mistake, tempted though he is to. All he can sensibly do is wait for the call.

He's still waiting when his secretary – who's been told to stall or divert all routine calls – rings through and asks him if he'd be willing to speak to a Foreign Ministry official who claims to be a friend of his: Hammou Chenna. Since Chenna has his mobile number, Bouras is puzzled that he's called on the office line. He tells her to put him through.

'Hammou?'

'I hope I'm not interrupting something crucial, Farid. Your secretary seemed . . . reluctant to connect me.'

'It's a busy time. How can I help you?'

'My minister knows we're friends. He asked me to contact you in the hope that you can provide him with some . . . details . . . concerning . . . the detention of Yanik Seghir.'

'Ah. Seghir.'

'You have him in custody, as I understand it. Is he still in Tamanrasset? We were rather concerned when we heard of the terrorist outrage there this morning.'

'He's no longer in Tamanrasset.'

'Listen, Farid, I'm sorry if I seem to be pressing you on matters that aren't strictly the concern of the Foreign Ministry, but, as I'm sure you can imagine, when Seghir's statement was brought to the minister's attention alarm bells started ringing. The project we discussed over lunch—'

'White Leopard?'

'Yes. White Leopard. It's not going ahead now, obviously. I mean, no decision's officially been taken, but it simply can't happen in light of the doubts raised by Seghir's statement. Lydia Seghir has resigned just in time to avoid being dismissed, but that's hardly the end of the trouble she's in – or the trouble she's caused for others. Diplomatically speaking, this is a complete disaster. A disaster that's bound to have an impact on relations with France. Consequently, the minister regards it as vital to establish just how far-reaching the conspiracy Seghir helped to organize really is. Since he's in DGSN custody—'

'He isn't. Not any more.'

'What do you mean?'

'The DSS have him.'

'How did that happen?'

'He was seized from us this morning. Along with one of my senior officers, as a matter of fact.'

'Seized?'

'Yes.'

'You're saying ... the DSS ... took him ... without your agreement?'

'That's what I'm saying.'

'What do they want with him?'

'I don't think I should answer that question on the phone. What I can tell you is that but for a late change of plan Seghir would have been killed in that terrorist incident in Tamanrasset this morning.'

There's a lengthy silence at the other end of the line. Chenna is finding it difficult to process the information Bouras has given him. And no wonder.

'Are you still there, Hammou?'

'Yes.' Chenna's voice has dropped to a level barely above a whisper. 'In the circumstances, would you be willing . . . to meet the minister . . . at short notice?'

'How short?'

'I was thinking . . . right away.'

Hidouchi doesn't wear a watch and without her phone has no reliable way of keeping track of time. She's been served a meagre lunch of couscous in a plastic bowl with a cardboard spatula, delivered through a flap at the foot of the door, and estimates – which is all she can do – that a couple of hours have passed since then . . . when she hears the key being turned in the lock.

The door opens. Lieutenant Djafri, who's so tall he has to stoop slightly to see into the cell, stands outside. There's a junior officer behind him. No machine guns are on display, but both men are carrying side arms. 'Come with us, please,' Djafri says, in a surprisingly gentle tone.

'Where are you taking me?'

'You'll find out soon enough. Come on.' He beckons for her to leave the cell.

'Where's Taleb?' she asks as she steps out into the corridor.

'Three cells along. He's fine.'

'And Seghir?'

'Next corridor across. No harm's come to him.'

'I have your word on that?'

Djafri glances over his shoulder at her as they start walking. 'You do, Hidouchi, yes. Last time I checked, Taleb was lying on his bed, smoking. And Seghir was pacing up and down, muttering to himself.'

'I'll hold you personally responsible for their safety.'

'Fine. Like I told you at the airfield, I just follow orders. That's how this department functions. Except for you, apparently.'

They reach the end of the corridor, where there's access to the stairs and lift. The junior officer presses the button to open the lift doors.

'Get in,' says Djafri.

Hidouchi enters the lift, which is longer than it's wide, the better to accommodate a stretcher to move a detainee who may no longer be able to walk – for whatever reason. Djafri enters behind her and presses the button for the top floor of the building. The lift doors close. Hidouchi is surprised the junior officer isn't coming with them. She's also surprised by their destination.

'Why are we going to the top floor?' she asks.

Djafri smiles. 'Well, it must be for one of two reasons, don't you think? Either we're going to throw you off the roof in a suicide-while-trying-to-escape scenario ... or the chairman wants to see you.'

'He's here?'

'As a matter of fact, he is.'

General Feradj has been an almost wholly absentee chairman in Hidouchi's experience. His penthouse office is more often used for retirement parties than actual business. If he's come in, it's probably with a good deal of reluctance and because there's no way round it. She can't decide whether that's good news or bad.

Evidently, Djafri can't decide either. 'Remember, it's nothing personal. I'll do whatever I'm told to do.'

General Feradj has put on weight since Hidouchi last saw him. The buttons of his army uniform are straining and a surgical collar's worth of fat has accumulated under his chin. His hair, meanwhile, has apparently darkened with age. He is seated at the head of the large conference table, across the polished surface of which the afternoon sun has cast a rhombus of golden light. To his left, scowling at Hidouchi as she enters the room, sits Kadri. No one else is present. This, clearly, is to be the encounter that decides her fate.

'Sit down, Agent Hidouchi,' says Feradj, waving a hand towards the chairs on the side of the table opposite Kadri.

She sits, throwing a cold glance at Kadri. Djafri closes the double doors behind her. Feradj nods to him, a silent instruction to stand and observe what happens.

'I have been taken to task by the Foreign Minister *and* the Defence Minister today,' says Feradj. 'They weren't enjoyable conversations. The Interior Ministry has also been in touch, complaining about our detention of a DGSN officer without their agreement. Now, I don't need to spell out to either of you the scale of the disaster that the collapse of White Leopard represents. It's laid to waste months of planning and negotiation and exposed this department to censure for its failure to detect the hand of the Russians in the scheme. It's also set back relations with France, probably by several years. Heads will have to roll. That is inevitable – and appropriate. I am accountable for the work of this department, of course, but as chairman I play no active part. So, let's begin with the obvious question. Where did it go wrong? How did we – you – miss what was really going on?'

'That's why I took steps to take Yanik Seghir into custody, General,' Kadri jumps in. 'We need to be the ones extracting information from him and deciding the best use to make of it in the apportionment of responsibility for such a failure.' His words are carefully chosen. *Apportionment of responsibility.* Yes. That is the crucial consideration for both of these men. How can they escape unscathed?

'But you virtually abducted him, Kadri. From the DGSN. Director Bouras has complained at the highest level.'

'I considered the urgency of the situation justified extreme measures. Besides, it's questionable whether he was really in the hands of the DGSN at the time. I believe Superintendent Taleb was planning to let him make a run for it.'

'You have no evidence to back that up,' says Hidouchi.

'Don't I? There was no proper escort for Seghir when we tracked him down. You and Taleb had departed from all normal protocols in extracting him from Tamanrasset.'

'It's just as well we did in view of the ambush *someone* set up for him there.'

'What's the latest intelligence on that incident?' asks Feradj.

'Responsibility hasn't yet been claimed by any one group,' Kadri replies with a glib lack of irony. 'We suspect either al-Qaeda or, more likely, Tuareg dissidents. There has been tension between smugglers and the police in the area for some time. It's simply a coincidence that the police vehicle they hit was the one in which it was originally planned to transport Seghir to the airport.'

Feradj doesn't react to this bare-faced lie. He simply looks down at a sheet of notes in front of him and taps the paper thoughtfully. Then he strokes his moustache and looks at Hidouchi. 'Why did you travel to Tamanrasset with General Mokrani's assistant – Zoubiri – in defiance of the deputy director's orders, Agent Hidouchi?'

Kadri cuts in before she can answer. 'She went there to get her police friend, Taleb, out of trouble.'

'I went to Tamanrasset,' Hidouchi says with quiet emphasis, 'to find out what Seghir was doing there. I advised the deputy director that it was dangerous to disregard the evidence of sinister intent behind the White Leopard project. When he rejected that advice, I decided that the situation was so potentially perilous – on a national level – that I had to investigate.'

'And your investigation led to the Seghir revelations as a result of . . . Seghir's son being kidnapped by some . . . French criminal group . . . for reasons of their own?'

'Exactly, General,' says Kadri. 'The breakthrough was nothing to do with her. She just happened to be on the scene at the time.'

'But that was valuable for us.' Feradj nods to himself. '*In*valuable, in fact.'

'She tried to ensure Seghir wouldn't fall into our hands. She's been working against our best interests all along.'

'Yet thanks to her Seghir wasn't killed by . . . Tuareg dissidents. If she hadn't altered the travel plan – with, as I understand it, the full agreement of Director Bouras – we wouldn't have Seghir sitting downstairs in a cell awaiting questioning.'

'He's here because I intercepted their journey, the true destination of which I intend to establish during her interrogation.'

'The destination was Police HQ,' says Hidouchi. 'I calculated he'd be safer in their custody than in ours. And the attack on the police car in Tamanrasset proved I was right.'

Feradj frowns at her. 'You don't believe the attack was carried out by Tuareg dissidents?'

'No, General. I don't.'

'Who do you think was responsible, then?'

She looks across at Kadri as she replies. 'I feel certain that responsibility rests much closer to this department.'

'That is a very serious allegation.'

She's still looking at Kadri. 'Indeed it is.'

'Agent Hidouchi is treacherous and disloyal, General,' says Kadri, jabbing his finger at her. 'I'd like your permission to carry out a thorough investigation of where her allegiances truly lie – and everything she may have done to our detriment in the service of those allegiances.'

'The true purpose of such an investigation would be to cover—'

'*Enough!*' Feradj slams the palm of his hand down on the table. 'I have heard more than enough. From both of you.' He sits back in his chair. 'I am a soldier. I live and die by the chain of command. In the army we call disobedience mutiny, which is punishable by death. I realize nothing is quite so clearcut in the world of espionage, but disobeying the direct order of a superior can only be justified in the most extreme circumstances.'

Hidouchi is tempted to point out that the circumstances *were* extreme, but she senses Feradj won't tolerate being interrupted. Nor will he be deflected from the decision he has now taken – whatever that might be.

'There is only one way to proceed in the best interests of the department,' Feradj continues. 'I confirm my confidence in the Deputy Director for Intelligence Operations.' He has used Kadri's full job title. His meaning seems clear. Kadri has won. And the price of defeat will be severe.

'Thank you, General.' Kadri treats Hidouchi to a tight little smile. 'Djafri, take Hidouchi back to her cell.'

'Stay where you are, Lieutenant,' says Feradj. 'You've misunderstood me, Kadri.'

'But you just said—'

'What I *said* was that I confirm my confidence in the Deputy Director for Intelligence Operations. And I do. But you no longer hold that office. In the end, I have to recognize that trust is more important than obedience. You've lost my trust. It's as fundamental as that. I'm therefore suspending you with immediate effect. And I'm offering the position of acting deputy director . . . to Agent Hidouchi.'

EIGHTEEN

WHEN THE DOOR OF HIS CELL OPENS, JUST ABOUT THE LAST PERSON Taleb expects to see standing outside is Souad Hidouchi. But there she nevertheless is. And she's smiling.

'It smells like an unemptied ashtray in there,' she says brightly. 'Are you coming out?'

He steps cautiously into the corridor and is bemused to see she's alone. 'We've been released?'

'We have.'

'How? Why?'

'Orders of the new deputy director – acting deputy director, I should say.'

'What happened to Kadri?'

'A long overdue reckoning.'

'He's out?'

'In the cold.'

'Who's the new man?'

'Not a man, Taleb. A woman. Me.'

He gapes at her in astonishment. '*You?*'

'It's always surprising when merit is rewarded, isn't it? Now, let's get moving.' She heads off along the corridor, Taleb trailing behind her. 'Your gun, phone and car keys are waiting for you at the processing desk. Your car was brought here following our detention. I was wondering if you could drive me to General Mokrani's villa.'

'Why do you want to to go there?'

'I feel I ought to tell him in person what happened in Tamanrasset. Besides, I need to collect my motorbike. I left it there before heading to the airfield with Zoubiri. I do my best thinking when I'm riding my bike. And I'm going to have to do some serious thinking in my new post.'

'This is all . . . a lot to take in.'

'For me too.'

'What about . . . Seghir?'

'Still in his cell. Don't worry. He's under my supervision now. He can wait.'

Ten minutes or so later, they're in Taleb's Renault, exiting the underground car park beneath DSS HQ. Hidouchi takes out her phone and calls Bouras as soon as they clear the basement's mobile dead zone.

Taleb smiles to himself as he hears Hidouchi relate the unexpected turn of events. She assures Bouras Seghir will be transferred to police custody shortly and requests unrestricted DSS access to the prisoner so she can continue to question him. Naturally, Bouras has no objection. At this moment, Taleb reckons, DSS/DGSN relations are at their most harmonious ever. How long this happy state of affairs will last is another matter. Hidouchi is only *acting* deputy director, after all. Nothing is permanent. But he doesn't intend to think about the long term or even the medium term today. A triumph such as this deserves to be savoured.

'He said you should take it easy,' Hidouchi announces after ending the call. 'After all, you're supposed to have the day off. He suggests the three of us meet tomorrow to discuss . . . next steps. Of which there'll be plenty after everything that's happened.'

'How did you get the better of Kadri, Souad?'

'I didn't. He got the better of himself. And the chairman discovered the power of trust. Or so he said. Actually, I think he concluded he had to be seen to be doing something decisive in response to the White Leopard débâcle and Kadri was a convenient sacrifice. I'm under no illusions. I'll be walking a tightrope from now on.'

'But you have a good head for heights.'

'Which is no guarantee I won't fall off. Plenty of people will be watching in the hope I do.'

'My advice? Don't look down. Then you won't see them.'

Hidouchi laughs. 'Thanks, Taleb. That's a great help.'

All is quiet at the Mokrani villa. Taleb speaks to the housekeeper on the entryphone and the gates swing open to admit them.

She's waiting for them at the rear entrance to the building. Taleb didn't encounter her during his one previous visit, but she evidently knows Hidouchi. 'The general isn't here,' she announces. 'He is in the hospital.'

'What's wrong with him?' asks Hidouchi.

'His heart. It only gets worse, not better. He collapsed after your people came here this morning.'

'*Our* people?'

'DRS.'

The housekeeper doesn't seem to have kept up to date with the DRS's change of identity. And Hidouchi doesn't bother to correct her. 'We don't need to come in if General Mokrani's not here. I'll collect my motorbike and go.'

'It's where you left it.'

'We won't keep you any longer, then.'
'Before you go . . .'
'Yes?'
'It is true Zoubiri is dead?'
Hidouchi nods. 'Yes.'
'How did he die?'
'He was shot.'

The housekeeper nods inscrutably and says nothing as she closes the door. The manner of Zoubiri's death does not appear to surprise her.

Taleb starts back towards the car. 'My bike's by the garage, screened by those bushes,' says Hidouchi, pointing towards a row of shrubs further along the drive. She heads in that direction. 'Wait here.'

Taleb gets into the car. As he does so, a stout, elderly woman wearing an *abaya* and headscarf appears from inside the villa and hurries across to speak to him. He recognizes her as General Mokrani's wife – and Karim Mokrani's mother. He wonders if she wants to retrieve the photograph of her son she gave him and begins checking his pockets for it.

'*Salam alaykum*,' she says to him breathlessly through the open driver's window.

'*Salam alaykum*,' he responds.

'You have come back.'

'Er . . . yes.'

'I want to thank you, Superintendent, for saving my son. As you promised you would try your utmost to.'

'You've heard from him?'

'*I* have, yes. Two days ago. My husband does not know. But I know. Karim is safe.'

'Where is he?'

'It does not matter. He will come here soon, I think.'

Perhaps she means for General Mokrani's funeral. Taleb

doesn't press the point. His search of his pockets has located the photograph, now somewhat creased. He pulls it out and hands it back to her.

'Thank you.' She briefly clasps and presses his hand. 'You are a good man.'

'Not as good as I'd like to be.'

'Who can be that? Perfection is not possible in an imperfect world.' She smiles and hurries back into the villa.

Taleb falls into the briefest of reveries, from which he is roused by the throaty rumble of Hidouchi's motorbike. She rides into view and pulls up beside him. 'Ready to go?' she asks.

'Ready as I'll ever be.'

'I'm heading for the coast. Pointe Pescade. I need to breathe some sea air. Watch the sun go down over the Mediterranean. Reflect . . . on everything that's happened.'

'Good idea.'

'You want to come?'

'I'd like that.' He can give her the news of Karim Mokrani then.

'I'll see you there.'

Taleb starts up, turns the car round and follows the drive out to the gate, where he finds Hidouchi waiting in range of the sensor to hold it open for him. She looks back at him and gives him the thumbs up, then flicks down her visor and takes off.

Taleb follows, in time to see her accelerate ferociously away, the roar of the motorbike engine piercing the somnolence of the residential neighbourhood.

'Come on,' he says, addressing the Renault as if it will understand him. 'We'll have to move faster if we're to keep up with her now.'

GLOSSARY

Acronyms, foreign phrases and personalities from Algerian history featured in the text:

Bendjedid – Chadli Bendjedid (1929–2012), president of Algeria from 1979 until he was forced out of office by the military, January 1992

Bensalah – Abdelkader Bensalah (1941–2021), acting president of Algeria between Bouteflika's resignation in April 2019 and the election of his successor in December 2019

Boudiaf – Mohamed Boudiaf (1919–1992), recalled from exile to become Algerian head of state, assassinated 29 June 1992 during a televised speech

Boumaarafi – Lambarek Boumaarafi (b. 1966), junior army officer convicted of assassinating President Boudiaf, imprisoned for life

Bouteflika – Abdelaziz Bouteflika (1937–2021), president of Algeria from 1999 until he was forced to resign following prolonged streets protests, April 2019

DGSE – *Direction générale du renseignement et de la sécurité extérieure*: France's external intelligence agency, equivalent to MI6 or the CIA

DGSN – *Direction générale de la sûreté nationale*: Algeria's national police force

DRS – *Département du renseignement et de la sécurité*: Algeria's intelligence and security agency, reconstituted in 2016 as the DSS

DSS – *Département des services de sécurité*: successor body to the DRS

La décennie noire – the 'dark decade' of terrorist violence that claimed tens of thousands of lives in Algeria during the 1990s

Les décideurs – the decision-makers said to wield ultimate authority within *le pouvoir*

Les disparus – the thousands of people killed, kidnapped and 'disappeared' during *la décennie noire* whose bodies were never found

FIS – *Front islamique du salut*: the Islamic Salvation Front, whose likely victory in Algerian elections in January 1992 was blocked by the military, sparking *la décennie noire*

FLN – *Front de la libération nationale*: Algeria's nationalist political party, founded in 1954 at the outset of the Algerian War of Independence and the dominant party of government since independence from France was achieved in 1962

FSB – Federal Security Service of the Russian Federation

De Gaulle – Charles de Gaulle (1890–1970), president of France from 1958 to 1969, who brought the Algerian War of Independence to an end in 1962

GIA – *Groupe islamique armé*: Islamist insurgent organization blamed for much of the violence in Algeria during the 1990s

Harkis – Muslims who fought for the French in the Algerian War of Independence, many repatriated to France after independence, many who stayed in Algeria massacred by the FLN

Hirak – Protest movement that began in major Algerian cities in February 2019 campaigning for Bouteflika's removal from office and general liberalization of the state

Hizb fransa – Literally the 'party of France', a malign secret network dedicated to undermining Algeria, believed by some to have been seeded within their society by de Gaulle at independence to ensure their country could never prosper

Merbah – Kasdi Merbah (1938–1993), head of the SM (*Sécurité militaire*, the Algerian intelligence service, later reconstituted as the DRS) from 1965 to 1978, prime minister 1988–89, assassinated while trying to broker negotiations between the government and the FIS, 21 August 1993

Pieds noirs – The term generally applied to colonial settlers in Algeria of European descent, the derivation of which is variously attributed to the polished black shoes worn by the French military or the patronizing view of the metropolitan French that the colonists spent too long barefoot in the North African sun

Le pouvoir – The description applied by Algerians to the secret power structure believed to dictate political events in the country

Rimitti – Cheikha Rimitti (1923–2006), popular Algerian singer of *raï* music, a blend of traditional, modern and protest elements

Sonatrach – *Société nationale pour le recherche, la production, le transport, la transformation et la commercialisation des hydrocarbons*: Algeria's national oil and gas company, established in 1963, later hit by a massive corruption scandal

Robert Goddard's first novel, *Past Caring*, was an instant bestseller. Since then, his books have captivated readers worldwide with their edge-of-the-seat pace and their labyrinthine plotting. He has won awards in the UK, the US and across Europe and his books have been translated into over thirty languages.

In 2019, he won the Crime Writers' Association's highest accolade, the Diamond Dagger, for a lifetime achievement in crime writing.

THIS IS THE NIGHT THEY COME FOR YOU

Robert Goddard

On a stifling afternoon at Police HQ in Algiers, Superintendent Taleb, with not even an air-conditioned office to show for his long years of service, is handed a ticking time bomb of a case which will take him deep into Algeria's troubled past and its fraught relationship with France.

To his dismay, he is assigned to work with Agent Hidouchi, an intimidating representative of the country's feared secret service, who makes it clear she intends to call the shots. They are instructed to pursue a runaway former agent, but their search will lead them towards a greater mystery, surrounding a murder that took place in Paris more than fifty years before.

Soon, Taleb will face a choice he has long sought to avoid, between self-preservation and doing the right thing. And, ultimately, the choice may not even be his to make.

'A delightful double act, crunchy dialogue, strong action scenes'
SUNDAY TIMES

THE FINE ART OF UNCANNY PREDICTION

Robert Goddard

Umiko Wada never set out to be a private detective, let alone become the one-woman operation behind the Kodaka Detective Agency. But so it has turned out, thanks to the death of her former boss, Kazuto Kodaka, in mysterious circumstances.

Keen to avoid a similar fate, Wada chooses the cases she takes very carefully. A businessman who wants her to track down his estranged son offers what appears to be a straightforward assignment. But she should have known that the simplest cases are never really simple at all. Soon she finds herself pulled into a labyrinthine conspiracy with links to a twenty-seven-year-old investigation by her late employer and to the chaos and trauma of the dying days of the Second World War.

As Wada uncovers a dizzying web of connections between then and now, it becomes clear that someone has gone to extraordinary lengths to keep the past buried. And the deeper Wada digs, the more danger she finds herself in. Soon those she loves most will be sucked into the orbit of one of the most powerful men in Tokyo. And he will do whatever it takes to hold on to his power . . .

The Fine Art of Uncanny Prediction is another tour de force from the cunning mind of master storyteller Robert Goddard. Spanning seventy years, it takes the reader on a head-spinning journey of twist and counter-twist which keeps you guessing until the final pages.

'The world's greatest storyteller'
GUARDIAN